NO MERCY

LG880

Tweed—once top Yard detective, now SIS Deputy
Di... ...pect
Mi... ...ent
Bu... ...s in
Wl... ..., 'I
wit...

A... ...our
bru... ...o on
Da... ...ian,
Ar... ...in—
an... ...his
ass... ...with
the... ...d in
de...

W... ...ows
an...

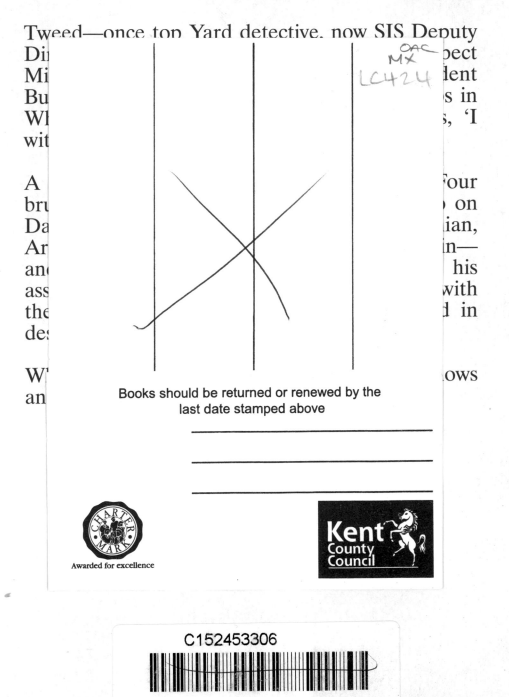

NO MERCY

Colin Forbes

WINDSOR
PARAGON

First published 2004
by
Simon & Schuster
This Large Print edition published 2004
by
BBC Audiobooks Ltd
by arrangement with
Simon & Schuster UK Ltd

ISBN 1 4056 1027 1   (Windsor Hardcover)
ISBN 1 4056 2020 X   (Paragon Softcover)

British Library Cataloguing in Publication Data available

Printed and bound in Great Britain by
Antony Rowe Ltd., Chippenham, Wiltshire

Author's Note

All the characters portrayed are creatures of the author's imagination and bear no relationship to any living person.

The author has taken certain liberties with the geography of the West Country, and no village or residence named exists. The same principle applies to companies, streets and apartments, which are also purely imaginary.

Prologue

If Tweed had not been at a loose end—a rare event—it is likely he would never have got involved in what became known as the notorious Volkanian Case—and the horrific developments that followed.

Seated behind his desk in his office on the first floor of Park Crescent, with tall windows overlooking Regent's Park in the distance, he doodled on a pad. Leaning against a wall, Marler, a key member of his SIS team, stared out of a window. Close to him Paula Grey, the right hand of the Deputy Director, sat behind her desk as she watched Tweed. He is so bored, she thought, now he's solved that espionage case. Someone knocked urgently on the door.

'Come in,' Tweed called out, turning over the pad. He was a man of uncertain age, sturdily built, wearing horn-rimmed glasses. His eyes were penetrating, his reflexes swift.

His old friend, Chief Superintendent Roy Buchanan of Scotland Yard, appeared quickly, smiled at Paula, stood in front of Tweed's desk. A tall lanky man exuding energy, the Yard chief was in his forties with dark hair, a trim moustache, wearing a smart blue business suit.

'Welcome. Sit down, Roy,' Tweed invited.

'No time. Bumped into your colleague Bob Newman when I was running for my car in Victoria Street. He told me you were taking a rest. You owe me one.'

'What's this leading up to?'

'I've got a weird problem. Like you to take it over. You may have heard I've temporarily been put in charge of the Anti-Terrorist Squad. Up to my neck. Now I've—'

'What is the problem?' Tweed interjected.

'Found this strange chap sitting on a step in Whitehall a while ago. All he said was, "I've witnessed murder." Nothing else. He's suffering from amnesia. Memory completely gone. Never said one more word. Took him back to the Yard for interrogation. No good. Never repeated that worrying statement. I took him to Bella Ashton, the top psychiatrist, left him with her for testing—'

'Roy,' Tweed interjected again, 'where is all this leading to?'

'I want you to take over this fellow Michael, see what you make of him.'

'Have you forgotten,' Tweed protested, 'that I'm Deputy Director of the SIS?'

'Last year, on that grim case involving the Vice-President of the States, you acted as a detective. Proved you hadn't lost your flair, hadn't forgotten your days at the old Scotland Yard before you took up this job.'

'And,' Paula called out, 'you were their star turn, solving three major murder mysteries while there.'

'Paula,' Tweed snapped, 'you have so many talents. One of them is *not* keeping quiet at the right moment.'

'Leave Michael in your hands, then,' Buchanan said. He took an envelope and a printed card from his pocket, dropped both on Tweed's desk. 'That's all you need.'

'How do you know his name is Michael if he never said another word?'

2

'I don't. We had to call him something and he looks like a Michael to me. Oh, no means of identification on him. No wallet, no nothing. Labels cut out of his expensive clothes. Must go.'

'I'll be damned,' said Tweed, his clenched fist hitting his desk as the door closed.

'Dumped that one on you skilfully,' said Monica, seated by the door behind her computer. She was in her fifties and had been with Tweed for ever. She wore her brown hair tied back in a bun.

Tweed had opened the unsealed envelope Buchanan had dropped on his desk. Inside was a brief letter introducing him to Mrs Arabella Ashton. Her card giving the Harley Street address was gold-rimmed. Tweed sighed and the door opened briefly. Buchanan reappeared.

'Should have told you. Michael's face is unusual. Just so you're prepared . . .'

'Thanks a lot,' said Tweed, but Buchanan had gone again. He showed the letter and card to Paula, who had walked briskly to his desk. She read out the Harley Street address.

'I suppose we'd better phone this Arabella Ashton before we go round and see her,' she said.

'No, we'll just turn up,' Tweed replied. 'A perfect day for a trip out.'

He was looking out of the window. Mid-February was living up to its reputation. A heavy grey sky shrouded London and it was bitterly cold. Paula was dressed for the weather, clad in ankle boots, a warm fur-lined overcoat and jeans. As Tweed struggled into a heavy topcoat, Paula gave Monica details of their destination, found she'd already written them down when she'd spoken aloud.

Paula, Tweed's long-time assistant, was in her

thirties, slim and five foot six tall. Attractive, she had jet-black hair falling to her shoulders, alert blue eyes, well-shaped features with a determined chin. Round the organization her vitality was a legend.

She ran over to a cupboard, hauled out two small cases containing night clothes, a change of underwear and toiletries for herself and her chief. Tweed frowned.

'We don't need those.'

'Who knows where we'll end up?'

1

Tweed parked the car near the far end of Harley Street. Their destination was one of many old terrace houses which cost a fortune these days. Built of stone, it was four storeys high with a short flight of steps up to the heavy front door. Harley Street was deserted as Tweed and Paula left the car. Before driving off from Park Crescent, Paula had dumped their suitcases in the boot.

'Waste of time,' Tweed had commented.

'Maybe . . .'

At the top of the steps Tweed paused and looked at the polished chrome plate attached to the wall by the front door. He grunted.

ARABELLA ASHTON, then an incredible string of letters denoting her qualifications. Paula peered at the plate.

'Buchanan once said she was at the top of her field.'

Tweed pressed the highly polished bell-push. A young woman clad in a maid's outfit opened the door. 'Can I help you?'

'Mrs Ashton is expecting us,' Tweed bluffed.

He showed her his SIS folder, which obviously meant nothing to the maid but impressed her. She invited them in and they followed her down a long narrow hall fitted with a white wall-to-wall carpet. A narrow antique table was perched against one wall, supporting a large Swedish glass vase full of artificial roses, which looked real. Paula smelled money.

They were ushered into a small kitchen full of the latest equipment. A tall blonde-haired woman,

5

early forties, was chopping carrots with great speed. The knife she held had a razor-sharp blade on one side, a serrated edge on the other side.

'These visitors say you are expecting them,' the maid explained in a shaky voice.

'I damned well am not. Who the hell are you?'

Arabella Ashton finished chopping another carrot at the same dizzying speed, turned to face them, the large knife held by her side. She was clad in an apron patterned with roses. Her blonde hair was trimmed short and her dark penetrating eyes, which gazed at Tweed and ignored Paula, were her most striking feature. Her cheekbones were prominent, her nose Roman and below it the lips were sensuous. Not at all what Tweed had expected. He handed her the letter from Buchanan, showed her his SIS folder.

'I see. Like Roy, another of these government officials.'

'He is the Deputy Director,' Paula told her.

'I can read, dear.'

'This is Paula Grey,' Tweed snapped, 'my most trusted assistant.'

'So why are you here?' Mrs Ashton snapped back.

'I want to ask you a few questions about Michael.'

'Then we'd better repair to my consulting room.'

She turned sideways to take off the apron. Underneath she was wearing a dress revealing her slim figure. As if for Tweed's benefit, thought Paula. We have a case and a half here. Mrs Ashton led the way into the hall, walking very upright towards the back of the house. Opening a door, she ushered them inside.

6

Paula took in the consulting room with swift glances. At the rear were windows heavily masked with net curtains, presumably so patients were not distracted by the view. Their hostess pointed towards a long leather couch with a sloping end. The patients' couch?

'Perch yourselves there. Fancy a drink? Anything you like.'

Her voice was now soft and soothing, attractive. Tweed refused her offer and Paula also declined as they sat down.

'I need a Scotch,' she said. 'Up at five a.m.' Opening a cupboard fixed to the wall, the shelves stacked with every kind of drink, she poured herself a stiff tot, drank it down in two quick gulps. 'That's better.' She sat down in an armchair facing them, and crossed her legs.

The white close-fitting dress ended at her knees and she had very shapely legs. She leaned forward, staring at Tweed with an engaging smile.

'My friends call me Bella. Can't stand Arabella. Never stopped shouting at my mother when she used that version. Tamed her in the end. She's dead now, so is my father. Now, Tweed, what do you want to know?'

'I'd first like your impression of Michael. Then I would much appreciate seeing him.'

'I'll give you my impression, but you can't see him. He's not here any more. Explain that later.' She leaned back in her chair, glanced at Paula, then fixed her gaze on Tweed. 'Michael is suffering from complete, total amnesia. Can't recall anything. Who he really is, where he comes from. How he came to be sitting on that doorstep in Whitehall when Roy spotted him. Mind a blank. Did Roy tell

7

you about the bump on the right-hand side of his head?'

'No, he didn't.'

'His dark hair hides it. The police doctor at the Yard said that it could be the result of someone hitting him or he may just have fallen down on something hard. I've little doubt that caused the amnesia.'

'What about physical movements? Getting himself dressed when he gets up? Eating a meal? Everyday things like that?'

'He can do all those. You probably find that strange but a habit is often not damaged by amnesia. I've known other cases like that.'

'Like Michael?'

Her thick eyebrows compressed. Paula had the feeling she was anxious to give a precise answer.

'No, not exactly like Michael. He's very odd.'

'Could Michael be faking amnesia?'

'Faking it?' She threw back her head and laughed. 'I couldn't get one damned word out of him while he was here. It was eerie.'

'So where is he now? Do you know?'

'Just round the corner. With the Yerevan Clinic. Seventy-two Eadley Street. Gregor Saxon, another psychiatrist, is looking after him. You drive up Harley Street and take the first on the left. It's hardly more than an alley.'

'Why is he there and not here? If I may enquire.'

'You just did. After two weeks here I felt it was time he was moved on. I was going nowhere with him.'

'Money,' Tweed said and paused. Mrs Ashton stiffened. 'I am sure it costs a lot to keep someone here,' Tweed suggested quietly.

'Two thousand a day.'

'That's pretty expensive. I appreciate, Mrs Ashton . . .' Tweed began.

'It's Bella to my friends.' She leaned forward with another engaging smile. 'You're impressing me, Tweed. Maybe we could meet again, say one evening.'

'Let me think about it . . . Bella. So I do need to know who was paying for Michael to stay here.'

'I don't know. It was rather peculiar. I had a phone call. Funny voice. I thought they were speaking through a silk handkerchief. Could have been a man or a woman. When I told them how much they said they would deliver the fee weekly by courier. In cash. Which they did. After two weeks they phoned again. Same person, I suspect. Asked me for somewhere less expensive. I suggested Saxon, who charges rather less. Fifteen minutes later the same person calls back, instructs me to have Michael ready when a cab calls to take him to Dr Saxon. That is the last I see of Michael.'

'You said he was in your care for two weeks. How long has he been with Dr Saxon?'

'Nine weeks. I phone occasionally to see how Michael is progressing. He isn't.'

'In your experience, Bella, how long before he recovers his memory?'

She lit a cigarette, waved a hand. '*If* he ever recovers it may be a week, a month, six months,' she rapped back. 'Quite impossible to predict.' She checked a diamond encrusted wristwatch.

'I would like to thank you for giving us your time and for what you have said. I think it's time we called on Dr Saxon.'

Tweed stood up with Paula. Bella fished in the

9

drawer of a small table. She brought out a visiting card. 'I've got a pile of these things. I shan't warn Saxon you're coming. No pleasure in talking to the man, but he's competent and useful for taking patients I don't want to deal with.'

Tweed took the card. It was printed on cheaper material than Bella's cards. Bella leaned forward, tucked one of her own cards into Tweed's top suit pocket as he donned his overcoat. Paula noticed handwriting on the back.

'I'll show you out. I hope we can meet again. How would I reach you?' The engaging smile was glowing.

Tweed extracted a card from his wallet. It was printed with General & Cumbria Assurance Co., the cover name for the SIS. Bella tucked it down the top of her dress, led them back into the hall. She chatted as she strolled alongside Tweed while Paula brought up the rear.

'A word of warning before you meet Michael. His face and head may startle you. He looks very strange. As to Dr Saxon, I don't think that's his real name. Armenian, I'd guess, or one of those mysterious little states east of Turkey.' She opened the door and ice-cold air entered the hall. 'Mind the steps,' Bella called out cheerfully before closing the door quickly.

Tweed flashed open the car doors, ran round to the driver's seat as Paula dived into the passenger seat. Starting the engine, he turned up the heater, then sat without moving.

Paula pulled up the bottom of her jeans, exposing the small holster strapped to her right leg. Inside nestled her Beretta automatic. She took out a Walther automatic and two spare magazines, and

10

handed them to Tweed. He thrust them into his coat pocket and stared at her.

'We're just calling on Saxon, then returning to Park Crescent. You think we're going to a war?'

'We were followed here all the way from Park Crescent.'

'I know. A big blue Volvo with amber tinted windows. When I parked here it cruised past us. Several men inside, I thought. It's gone now.'

'I know. I don't think this Michael case is going to be straightforward. Don't laugh. My sixth sense. Nothing seems normal. Almost sinister.'

'Have it your way . . .'

Eadley Street, hemmed in by old buildings on both sides, was just wide enough for two cars to pass. Paula thought it would always be gloomy even on a sunny day. On the grimy wall outside the door where Tweed had stopped a large board proclaimed in elaborate curving letters YEREVAN CLINIC. Paula pursed her lips.

'Bella was right. Yerevan is the capital of Armenia.'

Below the large letters were the words DR GREGORY SAXON. DIRECTOR. Paula pointed, loath to leave the warmth of the car.

'Gregory. Bella called him Gregor, so I was expecting a German.'

'She doesn't like him. She twisted the name out of malice.'

Paula peered past Tweed out of the window. 'The house next to his place has bars over all the windows. Ground floor and upwards. Part of the clinic?'

'I doubt it. The occupants are probably guarding against the burglars infesting London these days.

11

We'd better go inside now.'

'And have the same boring experience we had at Bella's.' She nudged Tweed. 'Not that you were bored. Are you going to have dinner with the attractive lady?' She was grinning.

'There are some more questions I wish I'd asked her. Why are we so reluctant to interrogate Saxon? Must be the atmosphere of this street. On your feet.'

Paula could not have been more wrong when she had foreseen another boring experience.

2

Tweed's finger had hardly pressed the bell-push when the door swung inward. Framed in the opening was a grotesque figure. He would be almost six feet tall if he wasn't hunched forward, a very large man with a protruding stomach, clad in a dark business suit, overcoat slung over his left arm. His unblinking eyes had pouches under them, his nose was wide and plump. His shoulders were broad. On his head was crammed, at a tilted angle, a wide-brimmed trilby hat, as though he didn't care how he looked.

'We have come to see Dr Saxon,' Tweed said, holding his folder open.

After a pause: 'You are looking at him.'

'Since we wish to talk about a patient perhaps we had better come inside,' Tweed suggested.

'Perhaps you had . . .' After another pause.

Saxon then gazed straight at Paula. His lips twisted into a lascivious smile which she disliked.

She stared straight back at him with a blank expression. He ushered them inside what appeared to be a waiting room. Piles of pamphlets lay on tables; wooden chairs stood against the walls. Tweed glanced at several pamphlets.

As he did so Saxon closed the door with his foot, laid one outsize clammy hand on Paula's shoulder, touching her bare neck, which she disliked even more. 'This way, my dear,' he whispered, guiding her into a larger room, kicking its door shut.

She gathered she was in his consulting room. It was very different from Bella Ashton's. A large leather chair stood in the middle with spotlights beaming down when Saxon switched on illumination. Before she realized what was happening, he had lifted her, perched her on the chair. His movements were surprisingly swift for a large man. Automatically she had rested her arms along the arms of the chair.

'You've got this wrong,' she snapped.

Only then did she realize he had fastened handcuff-like straps over her wrists. She couldn't move. Taking a deep breath she yelled at him. 'Take these bloody things off my wrists. You're out of your mind.'

'Hysteria,' he whispered. He was by a sink, pouring liquid from a bottle into a plastic cup. 'This will quieten you down while I check your eyes—'

The door into the consulting room was flung open, banged back against the wall. Tweed stormed in. He ran forward, turned the leather straps round, found the chain lock, his fingers fiddling with each strap, and Paula was free. She jumped out of the chair, glared at Saxon.

'What is the matter with you, you fat pig?'

13

'I'll take that for analysis,' Tweed growled, grabbing the plastic cup out of Saxon's hand. 'This should do.' He took an empty beaker off a shelf, poured the cup's contents into it and snapped the beaker lid shut.

'I do not understand this commotion.' Saxon stood as though bewildered. 'That cup contained a mild dose of Valium to quieten her down.'

'I'm not the bloody patient,' Paula shouted at him.

'Then who is?'

'You have a patient here called Michael,' Tweed rasped at him. 'That is why we are here. Mrs Ashton passed him to you.'

'A thousand apologies.' Saxon spread his hands. 'Surely you understand . . .'

'Shut up!' snapped Tweed. As Saxon approached him he took hold of the psychiatrist, shoved him into the chair that Paula had occupied. 'Where is Michael?' he demanded.

'In his room. I have just returned from taking him for a walk. Such a patient needs exercise.'

'What is your diagnosis of him?' Tweed continued in the same demanding voice. 'You saw my SIS folder. You could help us.'

'Anything concerning one of my patients is confidential.'

'Then we'll call the Yard and you'll be charged with obstruction—for withholding vital information. Paula, you have the mobile?'

'Yes, you want Chief Superintendent Buchanan?'

'*Please.*' Saxon, on his feet now, was at his most oily, smirking as he gestured to the couch. 'Ask your questions,' he pressed, settling his huge bulk into a large leather chair, which groaned under the

14

pressure. 'I really am at your service, sir.'

'I've already asked,' Tweed said coldly. 'Your diagnosis of Michael.'

'An exceptional case of extreme amnesia.' He clasped his hands and twiddled fat fingers. 'Michael doesn't know where he is, how he got into London, where he lives. He has a bump on the right side of the head, probably due to a blow from a heavy object. That, I believe, brought on the amnesia.'

'He has, perhaps, uttered a sentence or two?'

'Nothing, no things at all. No words. He can dress and get himself ready for bed.' He smirked at Paula. 'Excuse me, but he is also capable of using facilities and eating. That is it. You wish to see him?'

'Yes. Now.'

'Prepare yourselves . . .'

Paula glanced at Tweed. A similar warning to Bella's final remark when they'd left her. What horror was about to appear?

*   *   *

Saxon opened a door at the back, gestured to a tall slim figure, in his thirties, Paula guessed. What gave her a shock was the way he held his long head stiffly erect, even more the bloodless pallor of his face and the pale eyes which passed over her as though she didn't exist.

Michael wore an expensive grey suit jacket and well-ironed trousers. His shirt was pale grey with a matching tie. All grey, she thought. Like the man. She looked at his well-shaped hands—she always checked hands.

Michael's hair was dark, thick, neatly trimmed.

15

Presumably Saxon brought in a hairdresser. Maybe he wasn't completely the ogre she had thought. The psychiatrist took Michael by the arm, guided him into the treatment chair, swivelled it round so it faced Tweed and Paula.

Michael had walked stiff-legged, almost martial. In the chair he sat erect, stared into the distance. This is eerie, Paula thought, like watching a robot. Saxon opened a hand and gestured.

'So now you have seen Michael.'

'A personal question,' Tweed said, waving Saxon well away from the chair. 'Money. He's been here nine weeks, so who pays his fee?'

'I do not know.' Saxon's lips tightened as he observed Tweed's expression. 'When he arrived from Mrs Ashton's someone phoned me, asked how much each week. I told them and they said the fee would be delivered by courier. It has arrived each week. The courier delivers a thick envelope. Inside, well wrapped in thick blank notepaper around a cellophane envelope, is the fee. In banknotes.'

'Which firm does the courier work for?'

'I have no idea. One of those motorcyclists. Different man each time.'

'Was the person making the calls a man or a woman?'

'I couldn't tell. Sounded as though they talk through the tissue paper.' He stared at Paula, who had joined them. 'No need to be secret. Michael does not understand anything he hears.'

'You're probably right,' Tweed agreed. 'But it is still an assumption. I don't take chances. We'll be going now, Dr Saxon.' He walked past the front of the treatment chair to fetch the overcoat, which

16

he'd dropped on another chair. He began to put it on in full view of Saxon's patient. Michael climbed out of the chair, walked stiffly to his room, closing the door.

'He can at least move,' Paula commented.

Almost at once the door opened again and Michael walked out. He was wearing a grey overcoat with an astrakhan collar. He then headed towards the exit door leading to the outside world. Tweed looked quizzically at Paula.

'He wants to leave with us.'

'*No!*' thundered Saxon. 'He cannot do this. You cannot take him with you. You hear me?'

'I can hardly avoid doing that when you start bellowing like a bull elephant.'

Tweed was thinking rapidly. Saxon was advancing on him, shaking a clenched fist as he ranted on.

'It is illegal. I am responsible for him.'

'You have a letter from a close relative authorizing you? Plus a letter from a doctor?' Tweed enquired genially.

'I do not need such a thing.'

'Which means you haven't. Also, you know little about the law. He's here at his own wish. Now he's clearly sick to death of you and your clinic. He can do what he likes.'

Pushing past Saxon, he headed for the door, which Michael had already opened. 'Excuse me,' Paula said as she gave the psychiatrist her most wintry smile.

When Tweed got to the outer door he saw Michael standing on the pavement by the car. Tweed used his remote to unlock the doors. As soon as Michael saw the flash of the lights, indicating the car was unlocked, he pulled open the

17

front passenger door, got inside and pulled the door shut.

'What's Michael up to?' Paula asked.

'We'll find out, won't we?' Tweed opened the rear door, Paula climbed inside, sat behind Michael. Tweed walked round the back, stared at the rear bumper. Only his sharp eyes would have detected the small silver disc attached to the end of the bumper. He had to pull hard because it was attached magnetically. He went back to Paula, who lowered her window. He showed her the disc.

'That's how we came to be followed. It's an electronic disc, which will show our location on a screen somewhere. Special Branch were stupid enough to use a design I recognize as one of theirs.'

He walked a few feet up the street, dropped the disc, used the heel of his boot to crush it, then swept the debris down a nearby drain.

He returned to the car, got behind the wheel, next to Michael. He switched on, turned up the heater. At the top of the steps Saxon was waving his arms, shouting. Paula lowered her window again.

'You've still got your hat on.'

Saxon raised a hand, felt the crumpled trilby, snatched it off. His greasy black hair was streaked down the sides of his head. Tweed completed a five-point turn and headed back towards Harley Street.

Neither Tweed nor Paula realized they were beginning quite the strangest drive either had ever experienced.

3

'Where is Tweed now?' the rough-voiced man growled.

Abel Gallagher was sitting in a hard-backed chair on the first floor of his office in an obscure street leading off Whitehall. The front door into the building was made of reinforced steel, supposedly bombproof. This was the headquarters of Special Branch, the government organization concerned with security.

Gallagher was the newly appointed chief. A heavily built man with a brutal face, he was held in fear by his numerous staff. His cold blue eyes stared across the desk at Jed Harper, his subordinate, a cruel-faced man, nervous now as Gallagher waited for his reply and then lost patience.

'I presume you did attach the advanced location disc to the rear of Tweed's car parked outside his HQ?'

'Attached it myself, Abel,' Harper assured his chief.

'Then why the hell isn't it on the screen?'

On a side wall two electronically controlled maps were hanging. One of Britain and the other, in greater detail, of London. The electronic disc Gallagher had referred to should have shown up as a red dot, indicating exactly where Tweed's car was, whether stationary or in motion. Harper wet his lips, took a deep breath.

'You said it was on the screen when Tweed parked in Harley Street. In addition we followed him in the Volvo. When he stopped we cruised past—'

'Anyone except an idiot like yourself would have parked further up damned Harley Street.'

'That street is very quiet.'

'I know the street is quiet. Don't you realize Tweed is the one man in the SIS standing in the way of my increasing the influence of Special Branch? Well, you know now. You have to locate Tweed. Use the camera checkpoints on all the motorway exits from London. The camera will pick him up if he's left town. Jed, you didn't think of that, did you?'

'No . . .'

'And when you address me you will never again use the name Abel. "Sir" is how you address me. We may have to think of a way of stabilizing Tweed,' he remarked, lighting a cigar.

'Stabilizing? He's the Deputy Director of the SIS.' Harper sounded appalled.

'He's also on good terms with the Prime Minister, who may well consult him about the plan for closer cooperation between the Special Branch and the SIS. Tweed will persuade him to veto the idea. Can't have that, can we?' Gallagher's tone became amiable. He even smiled.

'I'd better call on the checkpoints.' Harper couldn't wait to get out of the room.

'When you locate him, drive like hell to the checkpoint in an unmarked car, then follow him wherever he's heading for. Don't fall down the stairs on your way out. Follow the bastard.'

The moment Harper had left the room Gallagher reached under his desk, operated a lever. A tread halfway down the wooden stairs would slide forward when Harper stepped on it. He waited, heard a yell, the sound of a body crashing down the staircase. He chuckled, got up, opened the door.

Harper was picking himself up painfully from the bottom of the stairs. His right shoulder was hurt. Gallagher stood at the head of the staircase, puffing his cigar. The tread that had swivelled through ninety degrees when Harper's foot pressed on it had automatically returned to its level position. A fat man in a boiler suit stood near Harper, grinning.

'Jed,' Gallagher bawled, 'you're wasting time.'

'Slipped on the staircase . . .'

'Warned you, didn't I? Get cracking, for God's sake.'

He waited until Harper, nursing his injured shoulder, had left the building. Then he called down to the man in the boiler suit.

'Carson, change the mechanism to three treads higher up.'

'A long way down then, sir. Harper could break his neck.'

'So we replace him.'

4

When Tweed drove the car to the end of Eadley Street and prepared to turn down Harley Street, Michael gestured vigorously with his right hand. Turn right. Which was what Tweed was going to do. Paula stared, then decided Dr Saxon probably had brought him this way for his exercise walk.

She was startled when they came to Oxford

21

Street. Normally Tweed would turn left here to head back to Park Crescent. Michael gestured furiously. Turn *right*. Tweed changed his signal and swung right. Paula was really startled now—startled by their passenger's gesturing, by Tweed's obedient turn away from Park Crescent. What was going on?

They were on the M4, the M25, driving on and on. At junctions and roundabouts Michael would navigate with positive hand gestures. Paula shifted her position so she could catch Tweed's eyes in the rear-view mirror. What on earth are we doing? He raised his eyebrows, as if to say, Let's see where this leads us.

Next on to the M3. Well out of London with snow-flecked fields on either side. Paula saw the enormous Gantia plant and Tweed had to pause. Police were directing traffic round a stranded juggernaut. The plant was almost beautiful, built in a circle, painted a pale shade of green. Columns of firs masked the building. There were even firs on the roof laid out like a garden. While the car was stationary she took out a camera, photographed the plant.

'Gantia is huge and so well designed,' she remarked.

'He has supermarkets all over the country,' Tweed replied.

'He?'

'Drago Volkanian, the owner. From Armenia originally, I've heard. A billionaire. He also produces armaments somewhere else. Location secret. The City would love him to go public so they could handle his shares, say they'd go up through the roof. Volkanian is having none of that. Keeps the huge company under his personal

22

control. He's a very remarkable character.'

'You've met him, then?'

The police had waved Tweed on. He was speeding down the M3, just within the limit, making swift progress. Paula leaned forward, repeated her question.

'No, I haven't met him,' Tweed told her. 'But I've heard of him from people who *have* met him. An overwhelming personality.'

'Overwhelming? In what way?'

'Excuse me . . .'

They were close to Junction 8. Michael was gesturing madly for Tweed to turn off. At the junction he turned to the right on to the A303. They were now heading southwest for the distant West Country. Just before they turned off the M3 Paula noticed a car parked with red triangles warning it was not moving. From now on there were plenty of dual carriageways and Tweed really moved. They bypassed Andover and kept moving.

*　　　*　　　*

Gallagher grabbed the phone as soon as it rang. It was Jed Harper.

'Chief, I found Tweed. Last camera on the M3 caught him. It was his number plate,' he said, pleased with himself.

'So you're following him?'

'Well . . . not any more. My car broke down in the middle of nowhere. So . . .'

'You tracked him, you idiot. Then you lost him. Repair the car quickly.'

'I'm no mechanic . . .'

'You're no nothing,' Gallagher roared. 'So you've

23

no idea where he is now?'

'Yes, I can tell you that. I saw the car turn off on to the A303 . . .'

'A303! Christ! How many people in the car?'

'Couldn't tell. Went past in a blur and it turned off on to the A303 . . .'

Gallagher slammed down the phone. The A303 led to the West Country. What could be going on in that part of the world?

＊　　　＊　　　＊

Just before the little town of Wylye Michael had gestured again, directing Tweed at a roundabout to continue along the A303. Paula had shifted in her seat to catch sight of Michael's expression as he navigated. She saw the same strange white face, the blank eyes fixed immovably on the road ahead. A bloodless drawn face. More like a ghost. Inwardly she nicknamed him the Ghost.

Paula was normally calm and cool, especially in a crisis, when she went cold, intensely alert. She was fuming now. What on earth did Tweed think he was doing accepting instructions from a man who'd lost his memory completely? Driving on and on, into the wild blue yonder.

'That light aircraft is still following us,' she burst out eventually. 'I first saw it some distance beyond the Gantia plant. It's still with us—over to your right.'

'I know,' Tweed responded dismissively. 'Lots of light aircraft about. The countryside is bespattered with private airfields. All those planes look alike.'

'If you say so.'

She gave up until they paused near Honiton to

get a quick meal at a rather awful chain café. Paula made herself eat a floppy poached egg on toast. For Michael Tweed had ordered two fried eggs, bacon and tomatoes, together with a generous supply of toast. Michael devoured everything on his plate, drank three mugs of tea, then got up to disappear behind the door marked TOILETS. Paula seized her chance.

'Tweed, what do you think we're doing? This is crazy.'

'You remember what Buchanan said? The only sentence Michael had uttered was "I witnessed murder."' He stressed the words. 'Now Buchanan is very clever. He'd be looking at Michael when he uttered that single sentence. Sufficiently impressed to take him to a psychiatrist, a good one. Buchanan had obviously believed what Michael said.'

'I've been thinking about that. Maybe Michael said instead, "I witnessed *a* murder."'

'I think you're wrong. You know Buchanan well. He is very precise when he reports anything. And we're driving to find out where Michael takes us to. We need a link.'

'But if he's a complete amnesiac how come he can remember the route we're following? I'm suspicious.'

'It's not beyond the realm of possibility that in the past he has driven over this very route so many times it's the one thing still imprinted on his mind. Quiet now, he's coming back.'

'Good job we left when we did,' she whispered. 'It will start to get dark soon.'

*   *   *

25

For much of their journey they had driven with dull green fields on both sides. Here and there a stretch of brown soil where ploughs had been at work preparing for spring.

'We've left the snow behind,' Paula called out as they approached Exeter.

Overhead a sea of grey cloud seemed in places almost to touch the landscape. More complex navigation by Michael took them on to the A38, bypassing the city of Exeter. It was not quite dark and to the north Paula gazed at the massive endless hulk that was Dartmoor. Covered with snow, it was white, appeared to dominate everything.

'I should have kept my big mouth shut,' Paula commented. 'I think that looks like a heavy fall.'

'Can be deceptive,' Tweed replied. 'When I was a detective and took a holiday with my wife we used to walk over Dartmoor. Away from the hell of London I could *think*.'

Tweed continued driving along the A38 until, to his surprise, Michael gestured again to their right. Tweed turned off the busy highway north heading directly for Dartmoor. He had turned into a wide lane hemmed in on both sides by gorse hedges. He looked at Paula in the rear-view mirror.

'This leads to only one place. Post Lacey. A small village on the edge of Dartmoor. I doubt if it's changed much since I was last here.'

'What's beyond it?'

'Dartmoor.'

To Paula it sounded like the knell of doom.

Post Lacey was a small village with cottages built of granite on either side of the main street. The *only* street, so far as Paula could see. The clouds had vanished and illumination came from the moon as dusk fell. They had passed the ancient cottages, which had lights in their windows, when they saw a pub, the Little Tor. Michael tapped the wheel for Tweed to stop.

A short man with a bald head and a warm smile came out of the pub. He reached out a gnarled hand to Tweed, then stared at Michael, who had alighted, standing while he stretched his arms, flexed his hands.

'Alf Garner at yer service,' the publican greeted Tweed. 'I bet you didn't expect a Cockney to walk out of 'ere. The wife and me came down 'ere ten years back. To get away from the mess Lunnon has become. Called the pub the Brown Owl but the locals didn't like that. Not one bit. So I changed the sign to THE LITTLE TOR. A name they could live with.'

Tweed was now watching Michael, who had started to walk further up the street to a point where it ended as a wide track.

'Where does that lead to?' he asked.

'On to the moor,' Garner replied.

'So to nowhere in particular?'

'Dunna say that, did I? Years ago, centuries back, there was tin, lead and copper mines on the moor. The rich lot used to bring that stuff down on horse-drawn wagons. Track's still there.'

'So it doesn't lead anywhere really?'

'Yes, it does. At the top of the moor, end of the track, a very rich man lives in his marvellous house. Used to be a monastery going to ruin. He turned it into a great mansion. Called Abbey Grange.'

'The rich man has a name?'

'Difficult. Can never get that one right. "Volcano" is the nearest I can come to.'

'Drago Volkanian?'

'Yes.' Garner slapped the side of his leather jerkin. 'You got it. I've seen that chap before a while back.'

He was looking at Michael, who was now striding, stiff-legged, up the track. Paula pulled at Tweed's sleeve. 'We're going to lose him.'

'Mr Garner, we have to go. Don't want him to vanish.'

'And 'e could do that. You going after him? Keep to the track. Move away from it and you're up to your neck in a lake of green slime. Treacherous marshes on the moor. Walk into one and you'll not be seen again. Ever.'

'I think we'd better hurry,' Paula said impatiently.

'Do excuse us, Mr Garner,' Tweed said, shaking his hand again.

'Molly—that's my better half standin' in the door—would 'ave given you something hot to drink, to eat . . .'

'Give her our thanks. That chap is inclined to lose his way.'

'Keep on the track. Watch out for marshes. Green slime, they are. Here, take this . . .'

He handed Tweed a walking stick. Tweed thanked him and followed Paula who was following Michael. Garner ran after Tweed, caught him by

28

the sleeve.

'One more thing. It's rained buckets for days before the snow fell. The ground could shake under your feet. Moor sinks and you'll think it's a small earthquake.'

'Thanks again,' Tweed called back.

It was bitterly cold, Siberian. Tweed saw Paula clapping her gloved hands together. She was thanking heaven she was wearing leather boots and her fur-lined overcoat. Michael was a silhouette ahead of her, striding out like a soldier, keeping to the wide track.

Soon they had left Post Lacey behind. The loneliness of the moor was sinister as the track climbed and climbed.

Paula looked all round as she strode briskly to keep up with Michael. He never once looked back and she had the impression he no longer cared whether they were with him or not. By the light of the moon she saw that the track they were following mounted steadily. Dartmoor seemed to incline from south to north. The wilderness on both sides was covered with gorse and clumps of heather, partially draped in snow. Tweed caught up with her.

'I think the snow is melting,' she remarked. 'It doesn't seem so Arctic now. I think the temperature went up.'

'My impression, too. No sign of Volkanian's Abbey Grange yet.'

'You think that's where Michael's making for?'

'Old Garner said it was at the end of this track.'

'You said Drago Volkanian was an Armenian. So, according to Mrs Ashton, is that wretch Dr Saxon. Could there be a connection?'

'No idea. We're nearly coming to the end of the part of Dartmoor I used to walk over with my wife when I was with the Yard. I told you she'd run off with a millionaire, a Greek shipping magnate. Time goes by.'

'Haven't you ever thought of divorcing her?' Paula asked gently.

'Too much fuss. No idea where she is now. Haven't heard of her for years. Originally they sailed off in one of the Greek's motor yachts to Buenos Aires. End of story.'

They crested a high ridge. Beyond, the track sloped down before climbing again in the distance. Tweed pointed to their right.

'There's a valley down there. Valleys are called combes, old Devonian word.'

'Look, there's a snowman by the side of the track. And Michael walked past it without a glance. I wouldn't have thought children came as far as this.'

As they reached the large snowman Tweed flicked at the head with the walking stick. A large slab of snow fell from the head, exposing a skull.

'Oh, my Lord!' Paula gasped, horrified.

The skull was attached to the neck. The ground trembled under their feet. The skull appeared to sit up higher, grinning at them. What increased its hideousness was that on the right side sodden brown hair was clinging to it. Tweed took a torch from his pocket, beamed it on the macabre sight.

Tweed tapped again at the figure, dislodging more snow to reveal the torso. Frozen flesh clung to one side of the breast, which struck Tweed as very odd. He leaned forward, pursed his lips, then stood up.

'What is it?' asked Paula.

30

'Some instrument has been used to hack halfway through to the spine. That's why the skull remained attached. It needs a pathologist to confirm my impression. That means it's . . .'

'Murder,' whispered Paula.

'I need to use your mobile phone urgently.'

'Here you are,' she said impatiently.

'We need a bright marker that can be seen from the air.'

Paula unwrapped her long red scarf, almost the size of a flag. Tweed tucked the mobile in his pocket, spread the scarf across the track, anchoring it with rocks he collected from the track's edge. He looked at Paula before pressing numbers.

'I'm calling Buchanan. Getting him to fly down with a team. You keep after Michael, otherwise we'll lose him. Are you armed?' he asked suddenly. 'Yes. Of course you are.'

She withdrew her right hand from her shoulder bag. It was gripping her .32 Browning she kept in a special pocket for easy access. Returning the automatic to its pocket, she took out a camera.

'One more thing to do. This horror may have collapsed by the time Buchanan makes it here.'

She clicked the special non-flash camera invented by the boffins in the basement of Park Crescent. Clicking it ten times, not liking what she saw through the viewfinder, she returned the camera to her shoulder bag as Tweed started making the call. She hurried after Michael, now no more than a tiny figure climbing a slope.

Before she caught up with him she checked the photos, her pocket torch clenched between her teeth. One print made her feel sick. She had placed a hand over one side so she saw only the side of the

31

head. The side where frozen flesh fell over the skull with a glimpse of grinning teeth. She slipped them back into an evidence envelope, took a deep breath and began running after Michael.

The atmosphere of the moor seemed unnerving as snow melted rapidly, revealing its menacing sweeps, which she felt were closing in round her. Rocks appeared, jutting up like dragons' teeth. It was almost a relief to have company when she slowed to a swift walk ten yards or so behind Michael. She knew he must have heard the thud of her approaching feet. He never looked round once, continuing his erect march like a soldier.

She looked back, saw Tweed approaching, running at quite a pace. Separately and recently, both of them had travelled down to the training mansion in remote Surrey. A younger head of training called Nick had taken over from the older Sarge, who had gone on holiday.

'I'm going to kill you,' he had yelled at her as his first greeting.

He hadn't been joking. She'd been hauled out of bed at seven, hustled along to the showers, allowed five minutes to get dressed and permitted ten minutes for breakfast. With a fresh training outfit he'd led her out to the acres of training area.

'You have one hour to complete the course with me on your heels all the way,' Nick had announced. 'Now run a mile and then keep moving on the obstacle course.'

It had been a diabolical experience but she'd returned to Park Crescent feeling much fitter. The extraordinary sequel to this event was Tweed, travelling down a week later, completing the same.

No wonder he was hurtling up behind her. She

looked down a steep slope, saw a wide stream at the bottom crossed by a three-span bridge built of large stone slabs perched on granite pillars. She paused as Tweed stood beside her.

'What they call a clapper bridge,' he said. 'Constructed ages ago of enormous granite blocks.'

Michael had walked swiftly across the bridge despite the fact that the slabs looked slippery in the moonlight. It did not fill her with confidence. She glanced to her right, pointed.

'There's that aircraft again. It's still following us.'

'I told you this part of the world is full of that type of plane.'

'Tweed!' she snapped. 'I'm sure I saw the same plane cruising in the distance well before Exeter—and after we'd left that place behind.' She gripped Tweed's arm. 'My God! It's going to hit the huge rock perched on that ridge.'

They paused, standing very still.

'He's going to crash,' Paula whispered.

'Looks rather dicey,' Tweed agreed. 'I hope the pilot isn't . . .'

The plane flew on, disappeared behind the massive rock. He had obviously seen it from his height. Paula walked on, gazing at the clapper bridge. Don't like that, she was thinking. Gritting her teeth, she walked on to the first slab. She crossed the bridge, turned to watch Tweed, her heart in her mouth. He crossed it calmly. He talked as they followed Michael, who had slowed down.

'Buchanan's flying down in a chopper with a technical team. He's bringing the pathologist Professor Saafeld with him. Said there's something he forgot to give me, so he's bringing that too.'

'He's talking as though you're in charge of this

case. And now it's murder.'

'I'm becoming intrigued. And I suspect that's Abbey Grange.'

He pointed into the near distance, where a final ridge was silhouetted in the moonlight. Perched on top of it, Paula could vaguely make out a large, long, two-storey house which was very old and had a mansard roof. Volkanian's retreat. Tweed pointed to their right.

'Hook-Nose Tor. Eighteen hundred feet high. The view from the summit must be magnificent.'

Well, *you* can climb that, Paula said to herself. She didn't like it. Glancing round across the endless sweeps of moorland, rolling, dipping, then rising again, she shivered inwardly.

The further they went, the more Dartmoor seemed to close round them. Nor could she get out of her mind the skeleton, the photo of the poor man at the edge of the track. She was pretty sure it was a man.

Abbey Grange was built of granite, probably using some of the original monastery walls. Lights shone behind the leaded panes. A wide flight of steps led up to a terrace, which ran the length of the Grange. From what she could see, the mansion was well maintained and above them, at the top of the steps, tubs stood on either side, each containing a trim evergreen shrub shaped like an exclamation mark.

Michael had run up the steps and was hammering an iron ring on the massive front door. Tweed hurried after him, Paula by his side. From below she had seen to the left of the mansion the silhouette of a tall church bell tower. The massive door opened inwards.

34

Framed against a blaze of lights from ancient wall lamps inside stood the figure of a tall young man. He had neatly brushed dark hair and was smiling. Paula liked the look of him at first sight. The smile vanished and was replaced by a look of astonishment.

'Michael,' he said, 'what the devil happened to you? Been away over three months this time.'

6

Tweed stood stock still. He gazed intently into the spacious hall with an oak-beamed ceiling and wall-to-wall fitted carpet. Michael walked straight past the man who had opened the door and headed for a wide straight staircase with wooden steps which climbed up to a landing.

At the foot of the stairs Michael paused. He placed his right hand on the top of a wooden upright carved with a man's head. After standing still for a short time he marched up the stairs, reached the top, turned right and vanished. They heard the sound of a key turning in a lock, the creak of a door opening, closing, being relocked. The younger man—younger-looking than Michael —shrugged, smiled.

'He's gone straight up to his bedroom, locked himself in. He always locks himself inside. Never said one damned word to me.' He looked at Paula. 'Excuse me. Come inside, both of you. This is a surprise. Let me take your coat.'

As Paula started to remove her coat he came behind her and took hold of it. She waited for his hands to touch her, a trick of so many men. The hands never touched her. Then he was taking Tweed's coat, putting them away in a deep cupboard.

'I fear we're intruding . . .' Tweed began.

'Not at all. I'm Larry Voles. Maybe you can tell me something about Michael, that is if you want to.'

'Is there somewhere more private we could talk?'

'In my study. Are you hungry? I'm sure you are. The lady is, I suspect.' Another welcoming smile. 'You're just in time for a late supper.'

A door to the right of the hall swung open. A short, heavily built woman with a hard expression appeared. She was almost fat but Paula detected strength in the bare arms exposed beneath her apron. She glared.

'I'm preparing supper,' she growled. 'Is that three more I should provide meals for?'

'Yes, it is, Mrs Brogan,' Larry said cheerfully. 'Timing must be perfect for you.'

'Some might call it that,' she growled again.

Her expression was hostile. Probably always would be, Paula was thinking. Her hair was grey, long and thick, tied back with a black ribbon. Her eyes were small and penetrating above a pugnacious nose. The mouth was thin-lipped and revealed small sharp teeth. Her hands were large and below the apron she wore a black skirt over large strong legs clad in black stockings. She left, closing the door with a bang.

'This way,' Larry invited, opening a door on the left into a comfortable study with a roaring log fire.

'We should have introduced ourselves,' said Tweed. He showed Larry his folder. 'I'm Tweed.

This is Paula Grey, my highly trusted assistant.'

'I would have guessed that. She radiates competence. Now, what are you going to have to drink? It must have been beastly on the moor. I'm joining you.'

'Thank you Mr Voles . . .' Paula began.

'Larry, please. Now what is your tipple?'

'A gin and tonic for me.'

'Think I could do with a neat brandy,' Tweed decided.

Larry had perched Paula in a comfortable armchair next to the fire with Tweed facing her. Paula studied Larry as he fixed drinks from a cocktail cabinet placed against a wall. He must be in his thirties, she decided. Well built but slim, about six feet tall. His movements were nimble, his face of a good colour. He had a high forehead, startling blue eyes and a prominent well-shaped nose. His mouth and jaw were strong without suggesting aggression. He handed round the drinks, giving himself a strong neat Scotch, hauled a chair and sat between them.

'I'd better tell you about Michael,' Tweed began.

He described how a police officer had found him seated on a Whitehall step. No mention of what he had said at the Yard. Larry lit a cigarette, listened without interruption as Tweed continued explaining why Michael had been transferred to the care of a top-flight psychiatrist. He provided Mrs Ashton's diagnosis, said after two weeks she'd moved him to a clinic nearby after deciding she couldn't help any more. He passed quickly over Michael's sudden departure, how he'd, of his own volition, sat in Tweed's car, guided him to Post Lacey, then led the way to Abbey Grange. He also left out the discovery of the skeleton masked by a covering of snow.

'That's about it,' Tweed concluded, sipping more brandy.

'This amnesia, total amnesia he's suffering from. Explain it to me again, please,' Larry requested quietly.

'It means that for the present he's forgotten everything. His name, who he is, which, I presume, is why he never speaks.'

'You said the police at the Yard nicknamed him Michael, his real name. I find that very odd.'

'The world is full of odd coincidences. They must have thought he looked like a Michael,' Tweed suggested offhandedly.

'Something else I don't understand. If he's totally lost his memory, how was he able to guide you all the way here from London? It's a complex route.'

'It is. Has he travelled that same route before?'

'Countless times. To get to the Gantia plant outside Basingstoke, or to the admin. His office is in the City.'

'That's probably the explanation,' Tweed replied amiably. 'The one thing that's familiar to him, which he recalled, was a route he'd used so often. Including his walking up the track from Post Lacey to here. How did he make his way to work?'

'He liked to walk down that track to get some exercise before he started his day's work, which was high-pressure. He left his car with the old boy who owns the Little Tor, the pub.'

'Sounds plausible, explaining his actions despite the amnesia.'

'I'm still stunned. Maybe after supper we could come back here so I can ask more questions.'

'Certainly. You said Michael had a high-pressure job. May I ask what it is?'

'One of three international sales directors for Gantia. He's far and away the most brilliant and successful. He travels abroad a lot for quite lengthy periods. We don't hear anything from him until he arrives back with a load of fresh orders. He likes to surprise us, to keep things to himself. Even from me. I'm Gantia's managing director.'

There was a loud hammering on the door. They clearly heard Mrs Brogan's voice growling. 'Supper's ready. I'm calling Michael down.'

'Be interesting to see whether he comes,' Paula said, speaking for the first time.

Larry drank the rest of his Scotch at one gulp. 'I needed that. Uncle is going to be shocked when he gets back.'

'Uncle?' Tweed queried.

'Drago Volkanian. I changed my name by deed poll to Voles. Doing business in Britain it doesn't help to have a name like Volkanian. In any case, although Drago's brother was Armenian, my mother was English.' He smiled. 'I think I take after her. Michael is my younger brother. Doesn't look like it at the moment. That awful white face.'

'I believe Mrs Ashton, his first psychiatrist, had him checked by a doctor,' Tweed said glibly, making it up. He felt sure she would have taken this precaution.

'Not *Bella* Ashton, the psychiatrist?'

'Yes. You know her, then?'

'Vaguely. I meet so many people.' He stood up. 'If you don't mind, I think we should go to the dining room before Mrs Brogan breaks that door down.'

39

*   *   *

They entered a long, large, panelled dining room. Again, light came from ancient lanterns suspended from the walls, casting a warm glow. Against the rear wall inside a huge arched cave was a roaring log fire. Mrs Brogan stood with arms akimbo checking them in. Larry escorted his guests to their places, then skipped over to the housekeeper. Paula was close enough to hear their conversation.

'Brogan, Michael has lost his memory. He won't say a word to anyone.'

'I know,' Mrs Brogan sneered. 'Left it behind at the office.'

'Listen to me.' Larry's voice hardened, he gripped an arm with one hand. 'I mean it. You don't speak to him now, you understand me?'

'If you say so,' she rasped. She used her other hand to grasp his, prised it loose. 'You knows I 'ates being touched so you keeps your 'ands to yourself.' She looked at Paula and winked. 'Michael's sulking. Silly boy.' She pushed open the kitchen door and disappeared.

Paula was startled. The woman's expression when she had closed one eye was venomous, verging on evil. The thought flashed across her mind that the housekeeper didn't like men.

They had all sat down when Mrs Brogan appeared again. She darted at surprising speed to the one empty place. Michael's, Paula assumed. She switched cutlery from left to right, from right to left. Again she winked at Paula, who lowered her eyes. Would Michael notice everything was on the wrong side? He walked in at that moment,

40

wearing his smart suit. She almost held her breath as Mrs Brogan reappeared, carrying an enormous tray with soup plates.

Michael stared at his placing. Without a pause he changed the cutlery back to the correct sides of his place mat.

'Mushroom soup,' Mrs Brogan announced as she served a plate to everyone. 'Anyone who doesn't like it can do without. Wait for the main course. Don't stand on ceremony 'ere.'

Michael waited until everyone had been served, and Paula lifted her spoon, then he got to work, scooping up spoonfuls of soup in rapid succession. In between he took two chunks of home-made bread from a basket, broke pieces and quickly ate them, reaching for two more chunks. He finished his soup before anyone else. That pig, Dr Saxon, can't have fed him very well, Paula mused.

Mrs Brogan appeared with a larger container of more soup. She stood behind Michael and waited. Her patience was short-lived. 'Want a second 'elping?' Michael remained still and silent. 'Oh, well,' Mrs Brogan began. 'No manners . . .'

'Yes!' Larry snapped. 'He would like more. Have you forgotten what I told you already?' There was steel in his voice.

The housekeeper refilled Michael's bowl. She looked across at Paula, her mouth twisted in a sneer. Some people have no manners, her look conveyed. Paula looked away. Larry was going to have to give her a good talking to. Again, Michael devoured the soup between helpings of more bread.

'Shepherd's pie comin' up,' Mrs Brogan called from the open kitchen door. 'With greens. Anyone who don't like it can wait for the sweet.'

'You said you were both brothers,' Tweed remarked to Larry. 'But you referred to Uncle. Are your parents living in the vicinity?'

'Unfortunately not. They're no longer on this planet. They had the idea of travelling to Armenia to see where the earlier Volkanians had come from. My uncle did everything possible to stop them going, ended up by roaring at them that it was too dangerous. They'd have to pass through Turkey. They wouldn't listen and outside Istanbul they were attacked by Turks and slaughtered. About five years ago.' He smiled grimly. 'Which is why we're not all that fond of Turks.'

Paula looked at Michael to see if that had penetrated. She decided it hadn't. He was staring at her with the same glazed blank look in his eyes. She had the uncomfortable feeling he was staring through her at the wall behind her.

At the end of the meal Paula stood up and started to clear the plates to take them into the kitchen. Maybe Mrs Brogan would respond to a little help.

'Not a good idea,' Larry warned. 'Kitchen is the holy of holies.'

'We'll see . . .'

She had collected a tray from a sideboard and piled it with the dishes. She used her shoulder to push open the swing door into the kitchen. Once she was inside, it closed behind her and she was alone with the housekeeper. Placing the tray on a metal drainer, she stood with her back to it, arms folded, feeling more secure with her back to something.

'My, oh my.' Mrs Brogan stared in amazement at

her. 'You is the first visitor who's ever given me an 'and.'

'I'm surprised.'

'This be a good time to warn you.' The large woman moved closer. 'About the cult.'

'Cult?' Paula's flesh began to crawl.

'Goes back 'undreds of years, they say. A secret lot, they is. They 'old rituals in middle of night. Horrible, they is. Make sacrifices to some god they calls Wrangel. Use the church, they do, sacrifice someone, then eat them.'

'Cannibalism, you mean?' Paula asked in a low voice.

A vision flashed into her mind. The skeleton with frozen remnants of flesh below the shoulder. Immediately she got a grip on herself, imagination running wild. Mrs Brogan nodded in reply to her question. She moved closer, whispering in her throaty voice.

'Reverend Stenhouse Darkfield, vicar, turns nasty if you mention cult to 'im. Mixed up in it, is my suspicion.'

'How long has he been vicar?'

'Ages. He was 'ere when I came—two years back. Folk in this part of the world gets told about the cult at their mothers' knees. That's 'ow it's passed down the centuries, is my belief. Other folk lives round 'ere and 'as no idea what's goin' on. Thought you should know.'

Her lips were moist now, her piercing eyes half closed. She struck Paula as a deceptive curmudgeon, that in her eyes really was a streak of evil. Mrs Brogan turned away and swept a glance over the large pile of dirty dishes. She grunted.

'Plenty more in the dining room. No, you've done

43

enough. Time for Tarvin to come.' As she spoke a closed door on the far side of the kitchen began to swing inward very slowly. A man appeared.

'Here he is,' Mrs Brogan said. 'Tarvin, time to clear up the dishes. Fetch them from the dining room. Not the dishwasher for this mess. Clean by hand.'

Paula stared. She couldn't help it. Tarvin was of medium height; plump beneath the white coat he wore. He had a large head, heavy eyelids half closed over froglike eyes, a pug nose, a round deep jaw. He moved slowly, almost like a robot. Paula found him disturbing, had an instinct to get out of the kitchen quickly, which was unlike her.

'I'll go now . . .'

She felt relieved to get out of the atmosphere. What was it about Tarvin that bothered her? The only person left in the dining room was Larry, who stood up with a warm smile.

'The others have gone into my study. I thought I'd wait for you. I get the impression something has bothered you. Mrs Brogan?'

'No. Tarvin,' she said impulsively, immediately regretting what she'd said.

'He's peculiar.'

He put his arm round her shoulders as they walked into the hall, halted her. He lit a cigarette extracted from a silver case. He offered her one. She shook her head.

'We have a problem here,' he explained. 'Staff. Difficult to impossible to find people who'll stay. That's why Mrs Brogan is so important. She's capable, runs the whole place and is a good cook.'

'She's first-rate. I should have told her so but something cropped up and I got diverted,' Paula

44

remarked.

'She brings in a couple of local girls, often from Post Lacey. They last a few months, then rush off to Exeter. En route to London, I suspect.'

'They feel isolated,' Paula suggested.

'Exactly. That's why I let Mrs B bring in Tarvin. I find him peculiar; don't like him. Bit like something out of a horror film. But I can't risk upsetting Mrs Brogan. She likes Tarvin, gets on with him, anyway. Which is more than I do. Then there are a couple more local girls. This is their evening off. They won't last. Enough of domestic chitchat. Let's join the others.'

*   *   *

Paula had a shock. Tweed was perched in a secluded nook beyond the fireplace. Larry whispered to Paula that Tweed wanted to talk to him privately. Michael had gone back up to his room. The shock was a glamorous blonde, the colour not out of a bottle, who came running up to Paula after jumping out of her seat by the fire.

'I'd better introduce myself. Larry wouldn't. I'm Lucinda, his sister. I've been chatting to your boss. Now he is one of the most remarkable men I've ever met. Come and sit with me by the fire. There, now we're comfortable. I prefer older men—the young ones these days have only one idea when meeting a woman, and no intellect. May I call you Paula? Mr Tweed has been talking about you. Oh God! Here comes that awful man with the coffee.'

Tarvin was approaching them with cups and a silver pot. He moved slowly in his white coat, a spotless cloth folded over his arm. He padded

45

towards them, eyes down, with a deliberate tread. Paula found his way of moving disturbing, more like an animal prowling.

'Black for me, please,' Paula said before he could speak.

'Me too,' chimed in Lucinda in her clear musical voice.

As he poured the coffee Tarvin's eyes suddenly gazed straight down at Paula. He gave her a cold searching look as though he were staring at a brick wall, the eyes weighing her up for some future purpose. Lucinda produced a gold cigarette case, inserted a cigarette in a long black holder, lit it with a jewelled lighter, avoiding giving Tarvin a glance.

'I find that man creepy,' she said when they were alone again. 'In fact I find the whole staff here strange. I've asked Larry to change them but he simply waves a hand, says the servant problem is not one he's involving himself in.'

As she sipped her coffee Paula was studying Lucinda. In her early thirties, she had a good figure, emphasized by the close-fitting gold evening dress, the wide belt round her slim waist. Her eyes were almost lapis-lazuli, which made her even more striking. But it was her vitality that intrigued Paula most.

'I don't like Tarvin either,' Paula commented. 'Do you live here, then?'

'Heavens no. I have a flat near Baker Street.' She sat back and her personality changed dramatically. She held her neck high, her expression became serious. 'I have a job with Gantia's plant near Basingstoke. I'm the security director. This is just a flying visit.'

46

Paula realized she had misjudged Lucinda. Thinking she was talking to a socialite whose main interest was probably an endless programme of night-time parties, she was instead facing a formidable woman who wouldn't stand any nonsense.

'I'm impressed,' Paula said.

'No, you're surprised. You thought I was a playgirl. Well, I like to enjoy myself now and again, but my job comes first. Drago, Uncle that is, laughed aloud when I applied to him for the post which had become vacant. So I told him for a year I'd worked my back off training at Medford's. As I'm sure you know, Paula, Medford's is the top security outfit in London. I produced a glowing reference from their director, shoved it into Drago's hand and said, "Read that, then—and I'm not the sort of person who appreciates ridicule." To cut a long story short, he hired me on six months' probation. That was two years ago.'

'Good for you. I've had the impression Drago is rather an overwhelming sort of person.'

'He is. If you let him be. I don't.'

Tweed, who had been talking to Larry in the secluded nook, appeared. He laid a hand on Lucinda's bare shoulder. She looked up, smiled.

'Yes?'

'We've exchanged cards so we know how to get in touch. As soon as I can after returning to London.'

'Do that thing,' Lucinda replied crisply.

'I think it might be as well if Paula got to bed. She's had a rather unusual day. See you, Lucinda.'

Larry came over to say goodnight. 'You each have a room at the front overlooking the moor. Mr Tweed has the numbers. Sleep well.'

'Does Larry accept that Michael has amnesia?' Paula asked as they walked together into a deserted hall. 'And does Lucinda know?'

'Wait until we get upstairs. Larry's insisted we stay here for the night.'

'And what are you up to—with Lucinda? Or shouldn't I ask?'

'Wait until we get to our rooms. I'm very worried about this whole Dartmoor business.'

7

At the top of the stairs they turned right, as Larry had told Tweed. The wide hall was long, ill-lit by a few lanterns attached to the walls. A gloomy atmosphere. Tweed gave Paula a large key, holding another in the other hand.

'We're rooms 16 and 17. Next to each other. I'm glad both rooms overlook the moor. We can see what's going on.'

'Chilly up here.'

As they arrived at the door to Paula's room, a stout wooden affair with iron studs, it opened, Mrs Brogan walked out. Her expression was blank as she addressed them.

'Just put 'ot water bottles in both rooms. He won't 'ave central 'eating up 'ere. Wants to keep the feeling of the old monastery. Lord knows why.'

She padded away down the hall, turned a corner to her left and disappeared. Tweed gestured with his hand to the left.

'There's another wing projecting out—as it was hundreds of years ago. Servants' quarters.'

'You realize,' Paula said as they walked inside, 'we'll have to sleep in what we've got on. We left the cases in the car. No. Look. My case is at the foot of that enormous bed. How did that get here?'

Tweed closed the door. 'When I had my private chat in the nook with Larry he said we could stay here for a night—or longer if we wanted to. I mentioned we'd left our cases in the car at Post Lacey. He said he'd send Tarvin on his motorcycle to get them so I loaned him the car key. They're only light so he was easily able to carry them.'

'That means Tarvin would see the skeleton.'

'Not necessarily. He'd be concentrating on keeping his machine on the difficult track. And I told Larry about that skeleton, that a police team would be arriving from London by chopper sometime in the night. At my suggestion he's promised not to mention it to a soul. No point in letting it get into the local grapevine until Buchanan and Saafeld have removed the remains.'

'How did Larry react to the news?' she asked quietly.

'Shock. He recovered quickly. He's got a lot of self-control. Asked me if it was a man or a woman. I told him I'd no idea. Decomposition had gone too far.'

'I'm going to switch off the light. There should be quite a view of the moor from the strange windows.'

Strange was the word. The windows were curved inwards like the original monastery arches. He stood beside her as she pulled back a curtain. By the light of the moon the view was breathtaking. A great sweep of dark moor rolling like the waves of a frozen sea. She took out a monocular glass from

49

her shoulder bag and focused it.

'The skeleton has fallen backwards. I can see the skull.'

She handed the glass to him. 'Follow the track.'

'I've got it. More earth movement, I imagine. Fortunately your scarf shows up clearly. The chopper will bring a searchlight.'

He reached out to another switch on the wall, turned on the dim lanterns as she pulled the curtain closed. She sat down on a tapestry-covered chair. She was tired and had to force herself to speak clearly. She told him about her encounter with Mrs Brogan in the kitchen. The housekeeper's tale about the cult operating on the moor. The reference to cannabalism.

Tweed smiled. 'I'd forget about that if I were you. Both Devon and Cornwall have old families who've lived here for generations. They pass on age-old legends. Plus there are some cases of intermarriages. I think you'd better get some sleep. But when I get to my room I'm going to try an experiment.' He took the walking stick that Alf Garner had given him and hooked it over his arm. On the panelled wall he tapped a tattoo. 'I'll repeat that when I get inside my room on the connecting wall. If you can hear it, repeat it back to me. Just something so you know you can contact me.'

'I've also brought two rubber wedges,' said Paula. 'I'll jam them under the door . . .'

When Tweed had left Paula hauled off her boots. When they arrived she had followed Tweed's example, cleaning them carefully on an old iron bar on the terrace. She walked to the adjoining wall, heard the agreed tattoo clearly. Thankfully, she repeated the tattoo with the heel of one boot.

There was one tap from the other side. Tweed had heard her.

Sagging with fatigue, she rammed the wedges underneath the door to the hall. She then forced herself to explore, opening another door. She was taken aback to find a large modern bathroom with a loo. Opening a heavy glass door, she peered into a shower room. She'd have given anything to have a shower but she was dropping.

She washed at the marble basin and cleaned her teeth. Going back into the bedroom, she stared at the huge high bed. 'Need a bloody ladder to get into it,' she said to herself.

Hauling herself aboard, she pulled back the eiderdown and sheets. A large rubber hot-water bottle radiated heat. She tested it with a finger. Boiling hot. She eased it down to the bottom of the bed, took off her clothes, folded them and draped them on a chair beside the bed. Exhausted, she reached up to a dangling switch cord and pulled it. The room was pitch black. Her head flopped on the soft pillow. She fell into a deep sleep.

*   *   *

She was standing on the ice-cold moor near where the skull had been found. A strange figure was stooped over the skull, its head hooded.

The nightmare deepened. The hooded figure was wielding the serrated edge of a large blade, scraping flesh from the side of the skull. She opened her mouth to scream as a hand from behind her grasped her shoulder. The hand was skeletal.

She tried to back away. Her feet wouldn't move.

51

As though glued to the moor. Trails of white mist floated across her face. The hooded figure had ceased its foul work on the skull. Now it was turning slowly towards her, the knife in its gloved hand turned so the blade with the serrated edge was held towards her. She vaguely recalled something about the skeleton's throat being cut to the spine. She still couldn't see the figure's face.

She heard what sounded like some monstrous bird hovering above her, slapping its wings. The figure behind her was peering round to see her. It was Mrs Brogan's face, also hooded. She was smiling evilly, her small sharp teeth exposed. Paula tried to lift her arm to strike at Brogan, found she couldn't move her arm. She opened her mouth to scream. No sound emerged. She remembered Mrs Brogan telling her about the cult. Were the hoods their bestial 'uniform'? She was terrified by her powerlessness. Heard a thump.

She jerked herself upwards, found she was in bed. Then she heard several stealthy creaks. The hall outside. The floor had creaked when she and Tweed had approached the bedrooms earlier.

She reached up, desperately trying to locate the hanging cord which switched on the lights. Her hand closed round it. She was alert enough now not to jerk it, to break it. She pulled the cord and the lights came on. No one in the room.

She rolled carefully out of bed. Grabbing the Beretta she had placed on the bedside table, she tiptoed across to the door. She saw immediately the door was open an inch. Someone had tried to enter, had been defeated even after pushing hard at the wedges. She heard more creaks on the floorboards outside. She kicked away the wedges and opened the door with the hand not holding the automatic.

Tweed, fully dressed, stood outside, gazing at her with concern. She beckoned him inside. He closed the door quietly.

'What's the matter, Paula? You've lost your usual colour.'

'Had a nightmare. Doesn't matter. What are you doing?'

'The police arrived a while ago. I heard the chopper landing. I'm going down to see Buchanan—I'm sure he'll be there. So get back to bed.'

'Not in a million years. I'm coming with you.'

*   *   *

In the deserted hall where lights were still on Tweed scooped up the door key from under the carpet. He explained he'd warned Larry he might go out when the team arrived. Larry had shown him where the key was hidden, reminded him of the combination to the numbered keypad.

Despite the fact that they'd put on their overcoats, which they had taken from the cupboard near the door, the cold hit them as soon as they reached the terrace. Tweed handed her a torch like the one he held.

'Be very careful to keep to that track.'

'Looks like a lot of activity down there,' she said as they made their way down the moor.

Over the area where the skeleton had been found a large canvas was slung. Beyond were police tapes. A Sikorsky helicopter was perched on the track nearer to Post Lacey. A lot of policemen were

53

moving round, visible by the torches they held.

'Buchanan has brought a big team,' Tweed commented.

They were close enough to see details when Paula saw Warden, Buchanan's assistant. He had a large bandage round his left arm. Buchanan, with Professor Saafeld, the pathologist, behind him, ran to meet them.

'Grim news. There's a second corpse, a second murder.'

8

'Where is it? Tweed asked quietly.

'First of all,' explained Buchanan, who wore a police cape, 'the near skeleton you found has been taken by ambulance up to Professor Saafeld's place in Holland Park so he can perform an autopsy.'

'The ambulance was able to get here from London quickly.'

'I phoned Exeter police HQ and asked for two ambulances to be sent here at once. Exeter wasn't very pleased. Thought *they* ought to handle the case. I told them the Yard had been called in. That settled it.'

Saafeld, clad in a sports jacket, hands covered by latex gloves, appeared behind Buchanan. In his fifties, he had an unruly mop of thick white hair. He was a well-built man of medium height. His weathered face had sharp features, observant eyes. He smiled at Paula.

'When I heard Tweed was down here I guessed you'd be with him. Must have been a shock when

54

you discovered the corpse.'

'It goes with the job,' she said, returning his smile. She liked him and felt confident the feeling was mutual.

'The second corpse?' Tweed prodded Buchanan.

'Warden discovered it by accident. He was cordoning off the area with tape. I'd warned him to watch his footing. Then he treads on wooden planks, which give way. He finds himself hanging by his hands over a deep hole. It's an old mine shaft. Hence his injury to his arm—he grazed it badly on a piece of sharp wood. Saafeld disinfected it after I'd hauled him up. At the bottom of the shaft was another skeleton.'

'Near-skeleton,' Saafeld corrected him. 'It still has chunks of frozen flesh attached. Want to see? You place your footsteps where I place mine.'

They left the track, walking slowly along a narrow path, their torches beamed downwards. Tweed followed Paula only a short distance behind. Saafeld's powerful torch beamed down the shaft. At the bottom they could clearly see a skeleton stretched out, as though asleep. Except the eye sockets of the skull were staring straight up at Paula. She suppressed a shudder. It was macabre.

A telescopic ladder was perched against one side of the shaft. On the far side, near the edge of the shaft, was a long fold-up cradle wrapped in clean white sheets. A rope coiled round a central wheel dangled down into the makeshift grave. Saafeld pointed to it.

'I always travel with everything I might need. Folded, the cradle easily fitted into the chopper, as did the ladder. I went down there, using the ladder. Took photos, then made a careful preliminary examination. We'll use the cradle to bring up the corpse. Under my supervision.'

'What are your conclusions so far?' asked Tweed.

'There we go again.' Saafeld smiled at Paula. 'Normally, as you both well know, I never comment until I complete the postmortem.'

'I need something,' Tweed persisted. 'I'm investigating this case. That poor devil down there. Man or woman?'

'This one is a woman. The one you discovered was a man. At a wild guess they both died about four or five months ago.' He took off his latex gloves and Paula noticed traces of what looked like dried blood. 'I have several pairs,' he remarked, stuffing them inside a transparent evidence container, which he shoved inside a pocket.

'What I can tell you is they were both murdered. Brutally. The killer used a knife with a serrated blade to slash through their throats to the spine, without completely severing it. Could have been a double-edged blade. Razor-sharp on one side. He jerks his victim's head back from behind, cuts the throat, then reverses the knife and uses the serrated edge to saw halfway through the spine. So the skull remains attached to the body.'

'Someone with anatomical knowledge?' Tweed enquired.

'Don't think so. After he completed the killing process he used the knife to savage the flesh, randomly removing chunks.' He shone his torch down inside the shaft. Piled up in a corner were small transparent bags. 'See those?'

'What's inside them?' Paula asked without much enthusiasm.

'Bits of decomposing flesh. If the bodies had

been dumped anywhere else there wouldn't be a shred of flesh surviving.'

'Why here then?' Paula prodded.

'Because this is Dartmoor.' Saafeld swept a hand round over the landscape. 'It's like a refrigerator in winter—and the recent winter has been exceptionally cold. I've put ice in those bags you were looking down at—to preserve the remains until I get back to Holland Park.'

Paula had been aware that Buchanan had been standing close to them. He hadn't moved or said a word, but had simply listened. Now he placed a hand on Tweed's arm, nodded for him to come with him. Paula stayed with Saafeld, sensing Buchanan had something to say to Tweed he didn't want anyone else to hear.

'When I dumped the Michael amnesia business on you,' the chief superintendent began quietly, 'I had no idea it was going to turn into this. A search which may never end. For a maniac.'

'A psychotic, possibly,' replied Tweed.

'What's the difference?'

'You know as well as I do, Roy. A psychotic can appear to be quite normal for long periods. Then the mood and the opportunity come together. He starts a killing spree.'

'What I'm saying, Tweed, is I can root round the Yard and hand the case over to someone else.'

'I don't think so,' Tweed said quietly. 'This case has got a hold on me. Besides which, I have information, know people up in that house perched on the ridge. Any idea who owns it? Thought not. Drago Volkanian.'

'The armaments and supermarket king?'

'Yes. Which reminds me, I must try and locate

57

their plant where the arms are produced. It will probably be hidden away.'

'So you're determined to carry on with this case?'

'Yes, I am. I'm ahead of anyone else who might take it over—knowing some of the family. A new man might not be accepted by them.'

'In that case,' Buchanan sighed, 'I'll give you the one item we found on Michael when we searched him to try to identify who he was.' He took out an envelope and extracted from it a folded sheet of paper, which he handed to Tweed.

'It's just a list of four typed names and, presumably, all first names. I suspect it could be the devil of a job tracing them. I wonder what it means,' Tweed mused.

'I agree.' Buchanan grinned. 'You've taken the case on so that will be your problem. Incidentally, that's your car parked down the track in Post Lacey. You don't want to have to slog it back to that house. I'll get Warden to drive you.'

'Would be a help,' Tweed agreed.

*　　　*　　　*

Warden, obviously glad of the chance to leave the moor and the horrors found there, assured Tweed his injured arm had not affected his ability to drive. Tweed and Paula sat in the back and relaxed.

Beyond the southern outskirts of Post Lacey, Warden turned to the right, away from the route that had brought them to Dartmoor. Warden looked at Tweed in his rear-view mirror.

'I know the quickest route back to where you want to get.'

'Fair enough.' Tweed closed his eyes and

appeared to fall asleep. Paula also felt drowsy, but later sat up as Warden turned the car right on to a country lane. She opened her mouth to say something, then desisted as Tweed placed his finger over her lips. They soon started to climb and she realized they were recrossing the moor. Arriving at a main road Warden drove across it into another wide gorse-lined lane. She gripped Tweed's arm, whispered.

'He's just crossed the B3212. Isn't Abbey Grange somewhere close to that? It's perched on the side of it. The rear wall at the back of the mansion is just beyond it I'd have thought.'

'You're right,' he whispered back. 'Say nothing.'

He was sitting upright, staring fixedly through the windscreen beyond Warden. In the full-beam headlights he stared at black pools on the lane, frowned, called out to Warden asking him to pull up.

'We could do with stretching our legs,' he said.

Paula followed Tweed as he walked up the lane in the blaze of the headlights. He felt in his pocket, tore out a sheet of paper, bent down over the largest black pool, wiped the sheet forcefully over the mark, sniffed it. Paula couldn't grasp what had caught his attention. He straightened up.

'Diesel oil. Now look over here.'

Beyond the pools of black he bent down again, Paula switched on her pocket torch. By its light, beyond the car's headlight beams, she could see the impression of a very wide tyre. She took out her camera, pressed the button several times. Tweed then walked to the far side of the lane, near the ditch which bordered it. Another impression of a wide tyre. Paula photographed that as Tweed

59

looked up.

'Got a tape measure?'

'You're lucky. I carry a sewing kit in my bag.'

'I want to measure the width between the tyre marks.'

They completed the measurement between them, Paula holding one end, Tweed the other. He stood up and made a note in his small book.

'A very large vehicle has driven up this lane to nowhere,' he explained. 'Some wheelbase. I'm curious. Let's see where this route takes us to.'

Returning to the car, he asked Warden to continue along this route at a medium speed. Characteristically Warden didn't ask any questions. They drove on through countryside with no habitations anywhere. Tweed was now sitting very erect, leaning forward as he gazed at the road ahead.

At intervals he spotted more wheel tracks, more patches of oil. At a junction where the lane divided he asked Warden to pause, to swing a few feet towards the left-hand lane. In the headlights he saw another set of wheel tracks.

'Turn left here, please.'

Paula was puzzled as they drove mile after mile through open country. A signpost pointed to Bideford to the right. As they passed it she whispered to Tweed.

'We're one hell of a long way from Abbey Grange. Soon we'll hit the Bristol Channel.'

'I know. And still we see the wheel tracks now and again. A huge truck of some sort travelled this way,' he said, keeping his voice down.

'I'm sorry,' Warden said eventually as they descended a steep lane with a view of the sea, a rough sea glowing in the moonlight. 'I missed a turning somewhere. We're miles off course.'

'Don't worry,' Tweed assured him cheerfully. 'After our experience on Dartmoor this is a relief, it's waking me up.'

He continued to guide Warden, following the trail of oil stains and wheel tracks. Then they were driving east along the coast, the road so close to the sea that they could see huge waves crashing against the wall, threatening to flood the highway. They had left the world of lanes and moved along a made-up road. Soon the view above them to their right was dramatic.

'I know this area from walking years ago,' Tweed remarked.

The massive cliff climbed sheer from the road, then sloped back. Paula pressed her face against the window, gazed up. Perched on the slope was a huge boulder, which appeared to move slightly. It had to be her imagination. Tweed pointed to it.

'Toppling Rock, they call it.'

'Well let's hope it doesn't topple now,' she said as Tweed asked Warden to stop the car. He did so and put on his hazard lights.

'It won't,' Tweed assured her. 'It's been like that for over a hundred years. Above it you can see Harmer's Head. It is thought that time has made that mountain unstable. Again, I imagine they've been saying that for a hundred years. Inside that monster at the top is a cave. I've sat inside it.'

'Rather you than me,' she commented.

'Drive on slowly,' Tweed ordered.

Warden crawled. The road had dropped and sea water was receding from sections of it. They were

61

passing a deep gully vanishing into the mountain when Tweed called out to stop. He was sounding more cheerful all the time. Paula wondered why. She followed him out and he walked back and entered the dark gully, waving his torch about. He stopped suddenly.

'What on earth have we here?'

The beam of his torch was illuminating a strange contraption. Paula had her .32 Browning in her right hand. She found the atmosphere claustrophobic, had a vision of their being buried for ever inside the gully. Tweed was examining what he'd found.

It was like a long gangway, the floor built of sturdy planks. Wooden railings lined either side and it was mounted on thick rubber wheels. Several pairs were attached at different sections of the gangway, if that was what it was. Tweed bent over it, shining his torch closely. He grunted.

'And of recent construction. I didn't see a jetty. Did you?'

'No.' She thrust her automatic back into the special pocket in her shoulder bag. Then she took out her camera and took photos of the contraption from different angles quickly. 'Now, if it's all the same to you, I think we ought to get back to the car.'

'Let's do that. Nothing more here I can see.'

'No point in looking, then.'

They got back into the car and Warden drove off again. He speeded up, but not recklessly. They drove through a sector where the sea had recently covered the road. Warden made one of his rare remarks.

'Good job the road climbs again. The sea

62

swamped that area of road while you were away.'

During the journey to the coast Paula had felt all round her side of the car for her map without success. Dropping her torch, she reached down and her hand located the map. She began studying it with the aid of her torch.

'Harmer's Head is marked,' she said. 'To get back we take the first right pointing to Bideford, then keep all the way on the A386, which eventually gets us almost home.'

'Spoke just in time, miss,' Warden replied. 'There's the signpost. So sorry I made such a pig of it. Buchanan will give me stick. I'll be lucky to stay sergeant.'

'Then,' Tweed said amiably, 'you tell him you followed a route into the wilds on my specific instructions. Don't mention any details of our getting out of the car.'

'Thank you, sir. I do appreciate that.'

*　　　*　　　*

They parked alongside the high wall at the back of Abbey Grange. Paula showed Warden on her map how to circumnavigate Dartmoor until he arrived back in Post Lacey. He smiled—the first time she'd ever known he could do that. Tweed guided Paula to the entrance in the wall, saw the gate was open and took her by the arm so they both walked along the side of the mansion on the grass verge. He pointed at the slab path he was avoiding.

'Knowing the place is well protected, they've probably laid pressure pads under those slabs. We'll enter by climbing up the steps on to the terrace. Officially we've just returned up the track

63

over the moor.'

When they reached the foot of the steps they saw that the whole ground floor was a blaze of lights. Paula checked her watch: 6 a.m. As they approached the heavy door it opened and Larry stood in a thick colourful dressing gown, smiling.

'Dirty stop-outs,' he greeted them with a grin. 'There's some hot coffee in the pot. In my study.'

'I could do with a cup.' Paula agreed.

They stood up to drink it, despite Larry's urging them to sit and be comfortable. When he spoke his expression was serious.

'They've dealt with the skeleton?' he enquired.

'With the first one,' replied Tweed.

'The *first*!' Larry jumped up from his chair. 'What does that mean?'

'They found another one. Tell you about it later.'

'I'm off to the works early.'

'When we next meet, then.'

'You can stay here as long as you wish. Eat here. Up to you.'

'We'll see.' Tweed waved a hand. 'Maybe the whole of Dartmoor has become one vast burial ground.'

'Don't!' said Paula. 'I'm off to bed now before I fall over.'

9

Ken
Lee
Christine
John

Seated at the breakfast table in Abbey Grange, Paula studied the list of names Tweed had given her. She scooped up the rest of the boiled egg Mrs Brogan had prepared. It had been 11 a.m. when she had descended the staircase from her room. Warily, she had slipped into the kitchen, apologizing for being so late. Mrs Brogan had immediately suggested an egg when she'd asked only for toast. Returning with her breakfast to the dining room, she'd found Tweed, fully dressed, seated at the table. He had handed her the sheet containing the names.

'What do you make of that? Buchanan gave it to me. The only item found on Michael when they thoroughly searched him at the Yard.'

'It's typed badly. The typewriter is an old portable, maybe an Olivetti Lettera. The "e" jumps out of line every time. So if we ever found it—doubtful, I know—it would be evidence. Of what, I'm not sure. It's typed on good paper.'

'Good paper you can buy at any decent stationer's. No way of tracing where it came from. Not even a watermark. It's going to be the devil of a job identifying those names but we'll have to try.'

'Not even any surnames to help us.'

'Which should make the search more interesting,' he said ironically. 'Let's hope it's not a list of victims.'

'Four. I think that's unlikely. Where is Michael?'

'He came down from his room earlier, walked straight out on to the terrace, wearing a blue business suit. Then he marched down the track to Post Lacey, gazing ahead all the way. I watched him from my room through the monocular. He reached Post Lacey, paused, turned round, came back. His posture was the same—stiff-backed as a martinet—the face bloodless as ever, gaunt.'

'The Ghost Man,' Paula said quietly. 'Did he look at those tapes the police must have left round the area of the graves?'

'No. Didn't even seem to notice them. When he arrived back he came upstairs to his room, went inside, locked the door.'

'What on earth was he doing?' she wondered aloud.

'My guess is his old habit of going to the plant at Gantia reasserted itself. Hence the suit. He arrives in Post Lacey and his car isn't there. He forgets what he was going to do, comes back.'

'Everything about this part of the world is strange.'

'I've had a walk while you were in the land of Nod,' Tweed told her. 'I walked along the A382 beyond the wall towards Moretonhampstead. Now I'd like to go the other way. Want to come?'

'Fresh air is what I need. I'll grab my overcoat from the hall.'

'I would. Since Michael came back mist has blotted out just about everything. Dartmoor weather!'

Opening the gate in the wall, Tweed turned left. He warned Paula to keep on the grass verge. The mist was dense and a car coming might not see them in time. At that moment a loud church bell started clanging, its chimes pealing through the mist, which crawled over Paula's face. Combined with the pealing bell, it made the atmosphere unsettling.

'We can visit the church on the way back,' Tweed suggested as they passed the ancient granite-walled edifice. The bell tower reared up apart from the church like a sentinel. Further along the deserted road they passed a long row of thatched cottages, their walls of new stone. Shutters were drawn over every window and each cottage joined its neighbour. Paula pointed.

'It's a solid block of cottages. Is that a Devon tradition?'

'If it is I've never come across it before. That bell is deafening.'

Again the atmosphere was peculiar. Despite the mist muffling the clanging to some extent, it was still a blasting sound. Paula was staring at the cottages, which showed no sign of life, when Tweed began shifting his feet among the gritting which covered this part of the road. He cleared a small area and below was another oil mark.

'We'll start back,' he decided. 'Might as well explore the bell tower first. Pity we haven't brought cottonwool to save our eardrums.'

They opened an old door at the base of the tower, went inside. Paula stiffened. Another 'character'. The man hauling on the rope which activated the large bell high above them wore a thick pullover rolled up to his elbows. Muscular, he was about six feet tall and wore corduroy trousers covering his legs.

His white hair was thick and untidy. His long lean face was bony and Paula guessed his age as sixty. The nose was hooked, the eyes pouched. His mouth was a rat trap, the jaw heavy and aggressive. She took an instant dislike to him. He glanced at them, continued his arduous hauling of the rope.

'The Reverend Stenhouse Darkfield?' Tweed shouted.

'That's me. Need the exercise. Reminds the flock that the church is here for them,' he shouted back.

They stood while he continued his labours. Paula noticed that at intervals he checked his watch. Timing himself? Tweed gazed up at the swinging bell, which seemed enormous.

'They must have heard it now,' he shouted.

'The Lord expects,' Darkfield bellowed back.

'Thought we'd just say good morning.'

'*Goodbye!*' Darkfield shouted.

They left the tower, made their way to the ancient church. It was a relief to get inside. The walls seemed to muffle the clanging effectively. They strolled down the central aisle towards the altar. Paula started shouting, then lowered her voice.

'Didn't like the look of the vicar a bit. Something sinister about him.'

They had almost reached the altar when she stood stock-still. Her face lost its normal colour and she grasped Tweed by the arm. He also halted, following her gaze. They were looking at the altar.

On the top of it was a horrific sight. A calf's severed head was perched on the altar. A recent execution. The head faced them; blood was spilling down on to the altar, dripping over its edge.

'The cult,' Paula whispered.

'Let's get out of here, collect our things and walk down the track to the car,' Tweed said decisively.

*   *   *

Paula had never packed her things more quickly, cramming her small case without care in a way she'd never packed before. Descending the staircase, she found Tweed, carrying his own case in the hall.

'Should we say goodbye to Mrs Brogan?' Paula suggested.

'No. You've had enough. We'll head down the track now. Get out of this weird place fast.'

'The bell's stopped clanging,' she remarked as they moved quickly through the mist down the track, guided by Tweed's powerful torch. 'That must have been an obscene sacrifice.'

'That cult business is nothing but simple people occupying their time,' he replied.

'I was wondering whether the Reverend Darkfield had been inside the church. Could it be he was the one who beheaded the calf? He looks capable of it.'

'We must concentrate on a double murder case,' Tweed told her abruptly, anxious to get her mind on something else.

'It is possible,' she insisted, 'that someone who could do that to a calf could murder people and strip off flesh from their bodies.'

Tweed paused. 'Stop it, Paula. I've had enough of the subject. So have you. How did you sleep? Any more nightmares?'

'I slept like a babe.' The mist had dispersed and

they had paused where the police had ringed the fatal areas with their tape. 'I can't see how Michael passed by this without seeing it.'

'I can,' he snapped. 'I saw his eyes when he was coming back. The same blank stare, the same gaze straight ahead. Now we'll get back to the car and head for London. If that's all right by you.'

They resumed their walk. Paula realized she had irritated Tweed, a rare event in their lives. She focused her mind to try to think of a less controversial subject. Their car was parked where they had left it outside the pub. She kept quiet until they were well past Exeter, then glanced at Tweed, whose expression was placid.

'I gather you were quite impressed with the glamorous Lucinda. She's very intelligent.'

'It's not her glamour I'm interested in. But she could be the key to my learning a lot more about the Voles family and their servants.' Lord, she thought, I've messed up again. But then he went on, 'I'm at the stage of nosing out every bit of information I can, hoping I hit on something significant.'

'As an opening gambit,' she suggested, 'you could call in at the Gantia plant where she works. We pass it on our way back to town. And make your dinner date with her at the same time,' she added tactfully.

'Actually, I was thinking of that.'

He had just spoken when they saw ahead a juggernaut parked on their side of the road. A red triangle in the road warned that the vehicle was disabled. Tweed stopped, waiting to ease his way safely round the huge vehicle.

A sound of breaking glass. In the window

70

alongside Tweed was a small hole.

'A bullet,' said Tweed quickly.

He eased his way round the stationary juggernaut, saw the road was clear, rammed his foot down. He kept up the speed for some distance, slowed, then pulled in close to the cover of a wayside café, sat back.

'You're all right?' he asked.

'Not a scratch. You OK, I hope.'

'Yes.'

'That same light aircraft which followed us down to Dartmoor reappeared before we bypassed Exeter.'

'I know. What makes you think it's the same aircraft?'

'It has a peculiar blue flash on its tail.'

'Then I agree. It was the same pilot. We were stationary when the bullet hit. I suspect the gunman aimed to miss, a warning shot. Someone doesn't want us investigating those two murders. The question is, who?'

10

Inside a little-used phone box down a side street in Hammersmith, London, Charmian checked the list of phone numbers he had been supplied with by his mysterious employer.

Charmian, French, was the top assassin in Europe. His unknown employer, M, had located him by making discreet enquiries on the exclusive grapevine in Soho. The first half of his large fee had been transmitted to his secret bank account in

Zürich. He checked his watch. All calls to M were timed.

He put his pilot's helmet, concealed in a carrier bag, on the floor. He checked his watch again, dialled the number. At the other end, wherever that might be, the receiver was lifted immediately.

'Is that M?' he enquired in his near-perfect English.

'M for mosque.'

The agreed code, which had been suggested to him, confirmed he was speaking to his unknown employer. He took a deep breath. The news he had to report was not good.

'Just got back,' he reported. 'Landed at City Airport.'

'Continue with your story.'

Charmian could never tell whether the strange voice was that of a man or a woman. Must be speaking through a handkerchief.

'I hijacked the juggernaut as planned. Flagged it down, then used chloroform as you suggested, concealed the driver inside a hedge by the side of A303. Took over vehicle, parked it at the selected point on the road. All right so far.'

'I do not like the sound of this.'

'Meantime,' Charmian continued in a rush, 'I returned to the plane, which I'd left on a nearby airfield. I spotted Tweed and his woman on their way back from Abbey Grange, close to the ambush point. Am I speaking clear?'

'Just go on,' M ordered.

'Tweed's car arrives at juggernaut roadblock. It stops, as we knew it would. I fired once. Missed target by millimetres. Tweed drives on very fast.'

'You botched the job.'

Botched? Charmian did not know the word. But he could guess its meaning. He decided it was best to say nothing.

'You will kill Tweed as quickly as possible. Only then,' warned M, 'will the balance of the fee be transmitted.'

The connection was broken. Charmian swore foully to himself in choice French. M had not sounded pleased. He had no way of knowing M was now worried. So early in the investigation Tweed was getting too warm. The reference to Abbey Grange proved that. Dangerously too close.

11

Tweed had decided it would be wise to linger at the wayside café. Inside, the well-furnished establishment was empty of other customers. He chose a table at the rear so they sat with their backs to the wall.

A spotlessly clad waitress took their order when Paula pointed to a confection oozing cream inside a refrigerated container on the counter. Not normally her choice, but she needed sugar. They both said they'd like black coffee.

'We'll wait here awhile,' Tweed explained after a few minutes. 'Just in case whoever is responsible organized a back-up ambush for us nearer London. They'll think we've turned off to Guildford or somewhere else.' He paused to taste the coffee. 'This is very good.'

'So is this,' said Paula, who had sampled her cake. 'The cream's very fresh. Where are we now with this horrific case? It's good to get away from Dartmoor. At Abbey Grange I wondered where Drago Volkanian was.'

'One of the things I hope to discover from Lucinda. You've had a rough ride, so take your time.'

Eventually they left the café and the sun came out, casting a cheerful light over fields where sheep grazed. Arriving at the giant Gantia food plant, they found that the high iron gates were closed. Tweed got out to use the intercom. When he came back he was smiling as the gates swung inward.

'Guess what,' he said as they drove inside. 'When I gave my name the guard said Miss Voles had warned him I might be coming.'

'Perceptive lady.'

Paula was gazing at the Hampton Court-like gardens in front of the artistically shaped building. Evergreen shrubs, some trimmed into birdshapes, others perfect spheres, lined the drive. Volkanian was obviously a perfectionist when it came to presentation.

After parking their car, they climbed white stone steps to the main entrance. The door opened before they reached it and a smart uniformed guard greeted them, after removing his peaked cap.

'Welcome to Gantia. Miss Voles is expected back any moment. Oh, here she comes.'

They heard the approaching roar of a high-powered car. At speed, a red Porsche appeared. Brakes were jammed on as the golden-headed driver swung her car round through the still-open gates. The guard, a man in his late fifties, chuckled.

'She does step on it. She seems to have an instinct

for all the speed traps. She'll be here the moment she's parked in the garage.'

An automatic door had swung upwards, the Porsche slid inside, the door slowly closed down. Tweed decided there had to be another exit leading directly into the building. As the guard led them into a large hall decorated with expensive vases full of flowers, Lucinda appeared, smiling warmly, hugging Tweed, then Paula.

'I think you've broken a record, Miss Voles,' the guard said.

'Come a long way?' Paula asked.

'Never let on whom I've been to meet. Security,' Lucinda replied with another smile.

'I have to check you before you enter,' the guard said as he pressed a button.

'It's procedure,' Lucinda explained.

You look terrific, Paula was thinking. Lucinda was clad in a leather jacket, which was tight round her figure, and a pair of leather trousers. At her throat she wore a scarf Paula thought was Chanel. As the guard came to pat Tweed down he produced the Walther from his holster to hand over.

'Let him keep that, Ken,' Lucinda told him. 'This gentleman is higher security than I'll ever be.'

A uniformed woman guard appeared. In response to Ken's pressing the button, Paula assumed. She produced from her shoulder bag her Browning; again Lucinda said she could keep the weapon. The guards were backing away when Lucinda spoke abruptly, her tone hard, her expression grim.

'Ken! Haven't I told you before that everyone must be checked before they enter the building? Including myself. I could have gone mad and be

75

smuggling in a bomb.'

The woman guard, looking appalled, went over to Lucinda and patted her down carefully. Ken looked equally appalled that he had fallen down on the job. Lucinda fired one more verbal shot before she led Tweed and Paula towards an elevator.

'Don't ever slip up again. Now, incident closed.'

Paula hesitated as Tweed followed Lucinda inside the elevator. Then she spoke.

'Miss Voles . . .'

'Lucinda, please.' She smiled.

'Is there somewhere I can wait down here? I think Mr Tweed wants to talk to you very confidentially.'

'All right. I wouldn't have minded but that's considerate of you. Ken can show you to our staff restaurant. Have a full meal by all means. It will be on the house.'

*   *   *

The elevator glided smoothly to the first floor. Lucinda stepped out briskly, escorted Tweed to her office. The room overlooking the front was tastefully furnished but still had the atmosphere of a working office. On the walls were colour prints of paintings by Gauguin, Matisse and other French artists. She gestured to a large couch, suggested coffee, which he refused.

'I'm a caffeine addict,' she remarked as she filled a cup from a pot, adding milk. The chinaware was Wedgwood. She settled down beside him, put the cup and saucer on a table, turned to him and smiled warmly.

'Fire away. I presume this is an interrogation.'

76

'I prefer the word "conversation". First, could you tell me the present location of Drago Volkanian? I had hoped to meet him at Abbey Grange.'

'New Orleans. At least he was. When he gets back he's going to want to see you. He pounces on any new development—if that isn't too callous considering someone's skeleton was found on the moor. Oh, I went up to see Michael in his room. A disturbing experience. He didn't recognize me. Also never said a word. His eyes look strange, so does his face. How long will this amnesia last?'

She spoke at speed, her mind embracing several topics. Her articulation was perfect and Tweed again liked her soft voice. She had turned on the couch so she faced him, her knee almost touching his thigh.

'As regards the amnesia, two psychiatrists have had him under their care. The first—and best—one is a Bella Ashton.' He reached into his top pocket, took out Ashton's card, gave it to her. 'You can mention my name. It might help.'

Lucinda reached for a notepad and Mont Blanc pen on the table. She wrote down the details swiftly in an elegant script, gave him back the card and thanked him.

'As regards how long his condition will last, Ashton will confirm it's impossible to say. Incidentally, under his hair on the right side of his head there's an old wound. It's been suggested he was either struck a heavy blow or even fell down in London. Which might just be the cause of his complete loss of memory.'

'A doctor,' she said briskly. 'Even a specialist. Should we contact one?'

'Up to you. I suspect it will be a waste of time. He was checked by a doctor in London. Time —duration unknown—will be the healer.'

'My uncle, Drago, will want to hear all this from you.'

'You could tell him what I've explained.'

'No way.' She tucked back a blonde curl from her face. 'Drago will want it straight from the horse's mouth.' She grinned. 'If you'll excuse the phrase. Drago won't accept second-hand data. Even from me.' She removed her scarf, revealing a string of coloured beads which she took off, dropped them on the table. 'My worry beads.'

'So you do worry? Even though you never show signs of it?'

'Only occasionally. When under very heavy pressure. You will find Drago,' she went on, 'a very formidable personality.' She laid a hand on his and squeezed it. 'But you'll cope.'

'Well, this is the food depot. Where is the armaments factory located?'

'Ah!' She smiled again. 'That's a secret I can't tell you. If I did I'd be sacked overnight by Drago. Really.'

'I gather it's Larry who runs this outfit.'

'Managing director. Since two years ago. It was a toss-up between him and Michael. But Michael said he didn't want the job. He likes being sales director, travelling abroad.'

'How long is he away on these sales trips?'

'Anything up to three months, even longer. Drago complains at times because Michael won't send any reports back. He waits until he has at least two big deals sewn up tightly. Often more. He insists that's the only way he can work.'

'So,' Tweed said slowly, 'when you didn't hear from him for just about three months you assumed he was abroad. Is that right?'

'Absolutely.' Her hand pressed his again. 'You know I'm getting the impression this is a subtle interrogation. You're very good at it, Mr Tweed. I hope we can meet for dinner in town.'

'What about Santorini's tomorrow night?' Tweed suggested. 'Say eight p.m.? Do you know the place?'

'It is a wonderful restaurant projecting out over the Thames. You are going to town on me. I'll be there. Eight p.m. will give me time to get myself togged up to be a credit to you.' Her tone was ironic.

'I'll look forward to your company in relaxed surroundings.' He paused. 'Just before I go, have you had any unusual visitors here during the past three or four months? A visitor you've never seen before or since?'

'Let me think, we get so many people calling. Oh, I meant to ask you earlier. A grisly subject. How is your investigation going into that skeleton you found on the moor? Who on earth was it?'

'Too early to say. May be a long time before I break it. If I do.'

'You will,' said Lucinda confidently. Tweed had stood up and she also did so. 'I have remembered an odd case of a one-time visitor. She called on the phone, turned up late one afternoon. She had a letter from Drago, signed by him personally. It gave her permission to examine the company accounts. Give her every cooperation, the letter demanded. "Every" was underlined heavily. So I did. Left her alone and thought I'd be here all night, but she was amazingly quick. She left at seven just after the plant closed.' Lucinda grabbed her notebook, went to her desk and whisked through a Rolodex. 'Here she is.' She scribbled data down. 'Funny thing was I had a phone call from her sister, Anne. I remember the name because it was the same as my late mother's. Anne wanted to know if her sister had been here, when she left. She'd expected her back and was getting worried. Gave me her address and phone number. I'm writing that down too.'

She gave him a folded sheet of paper and tucked her arm under his as she led him to the door and out to the elevator. She kissed him on the cheek and excused herself. Waiting for the elevator, Tweed glanced at the names on the sheet and stiffened.

The visitor was a *Christine* Barton. Her sister was Anne Barton. Both addresses in London.

The third name on the list found inside Michael's pocket?

*   *   *

He waited until he was settled behind the wheel of the car with Paula by his side before he told her. Paula studied the sheet of paper Lucinda had given to Tweed. He began driving through the gates that Ken, the guard, had opened for him, and then back along the motorway towards London.

'The trouble is,' Paula commented, 'Barton is a common name.'

'The intriguing fact is, according to her sister, Anne, the lady was never seen again.'

'Christine lives at Yelland Street. That's off the

80

Fulham Road. Anne is in Champton Place. I'm sure that's near Victoria Station.'

'So we'll try Yelland Street first, then move on to Champton Place.'

'It's a long shot.'

'When I was at the Yard years ago it was the long shots that turned up trumps.'

12

They turned into Yelland Street off Fulham Road. It was an area of prosperous terrace houses, all well painted, and was probably built before the First World War. Unlike the traffic-choked streets they had passed through to get there, it was quiet. A Rolls-Royce was parked outside one house. No one seemed to be about until they reached No. 158, Christine Barton's dwelling. Just beyond the flight of steps leading up to the front door a blue Ford was parked, a man smoking behind the wheel.

Tweed pulled in to the kerb, got out with Paula. He had just mounted the steps when the man in the parked car got out and ran up to them as Paula followed Tweed. In his forties, he wore a dark suit, a rather grubby white shirt and a blazing yellow tie.

'Identification,' he shouted up.

Paula took an instant dislike to him. He had a bony face, a broken nose and aggressive lips, which matched the tone he'd used to shout up. Tweed descended swiftly to the pavement with Paula at his heels.

'Who the hell are you?' Tweed barked.

Paula was intrigued. Tweed's personality since his

training trip down to the mansion in Surrey had become more ferocious. He glared at the intruder.

'You show some identification now without more jabbering,' the man demanded in a coarse voice.

'No, you show me,' Tweed barked again.

Broken Nose produced a folder, shoved it in Tweed's face. Tweed grabbed it to check it more closely. The photo was poor but close enough to be Harper.

'And who,' sneered the man, 'is the bit with you? Charge a lot for her services, does she?'

Tweed's elbow jerked forward, hit Broken Nose in the ribs. Then he scraped his shoe down the shin bone. Broken Nose screamed, staggered back, almost fell over. Tweed went after him, shoved the identity folder inside his jacket. He pointed to the parked Ford.

'Get into that and drive away. People high up are going to hear about how Gallagher's staff behave. Including how you accused a senior member of my staff of being a prostitute.'

'I'm reporting . . .' Harper began as he stumbled, bent over, back to the vehicle.

They waited until he managed to open the driver's door and ease himself inside. He sat very still. Tweed waved his hand, indicating he should leave immediately. The engine was started and the Ford moved slowly past them towards Fulham Road. Paula sighed.

'What trash Special Branch employs these days. I imagine that's the type Gallagher feels comfortable with.'

'Forget it.'

They mounted the steps again. A chromium plate on the wall carried the words CHRISTINE BARTON,

82

FCA. Paula stared at it.

'Hmm. Fellow of Chartered Accountants,' mused Tweed. 'She was very well qualified for her work. So well paid. Hence living in this street.'

'You just used the past tense,' Paula said quietly. ' "Was".'

'A slip. I hope. The plate's been polished quite recently. Let's see what happens.'

He pressed the bell. No reaction. When he pressed it again Paula bent down to peer through the letterbox. Her expression was serious as she stood up.

'You can hear the bell throughout the house, I'd have thought. And there are cobwebs in the hall. Don't like this too much.'

'Neither do I. We'll move on to Champton Place. I hope her sister Anne's at home.'

*   *   *

'Did you tell Lucinda about the truck left stationary on the road?' Paula asked as they threaded their way amid one traffic jam after another.

'No, I didn't. And she didn't say anything about a vehicle being missing.'

'That's odd. What about the strange statement Michael made only once—"I witnessed murder"?'

'I'm not mentioning that to anyone until Michael's amnesia clears up. If it ever does.'

Champton Place was well down the property ladder compared with Yelland Street: blocks of small four-storey terrace houses, the walls shabby, the curtains old, scraps of paper floating down the street in the breeze that had blown up.

'Here we are,' Tweed said, parking outside No.

187. The next curtains on the ground floor were clean; the few steps leading up to the front door had been washed; the metal bell push had been polished recently. Tweed looked up and down the street to make sure they had not been followed, then rang the bell. The freshly painted green door was opened swiftly. A pleasant-looking woman in her thirties with red hair neatly brushed peered out, keeping the door on a heavy chain.

Tweed introduced himself and Paula, held his folder close so the occupant could read it easily. The response was instantaneous: the door closed, they heard the chain being removed, the door reopened.

'You have news about Christine? I'm Anne, her sister. Do come in.'

All spoken in a rush. As they entered a narrow hall Paula noticed that the cheap wall-to-wall carpet had been hoovered recently. A mirror on the wall carried not a speck of dust. Anne Barton showed them into a small sitting room, invited them to sit down, then pulled a chair close to them and sat down. Her expression was hopeful, tinged with doubt.

'I'm sorry to say we have no positive news,' Tweed said quickly. 'We're endeavouring to find out where she might have disappeared to. And have you any idea when she was last seen—maybe by you?'

'Four months ago today. She worked from home in Yelland Street. She bought me that beautiful Swedish glass vase on the window ledge over there. Must have cost a packet but she was always so generous. I haven't seen her since.'

Anne Barton was about five foot eight tall, slimly

84

built with grey eyes and a pleasant face with good features. She wore a print dress and smart high-heeled shoes. Paula suspected she had little money but splashed out on shoes. The room's furniture, tasteful but inexpensive, bore out her theory. Anne started talking.

'I'm so glad to see you, to know that someone is doing something. She was supposed to be back the same day after going to see an important client . . .'

'Excuse me,' Tweed intervened, 'do you know the name of the client?'

'No idea. Christine was always so discreet about her work. She told me a lot of it was confidential. She was always smarter than me. Not that this affected our close friendship. She was a forensic accountant. Top-of-the-tree stuff. A firm would be worried about the state of its accounts, had gone to one of the big outfits who said everything was OK. The firm wasn't satisfied so they'd call in Christine. If anything was cleverly hidden, she'd find it.'

'Did you report she was missing to anyone?'

'Yes, I did.' Anne sat up straight and Paula sensed indignation. 'I went to the police, was guided to a particular department and saw a real thick-headed chap. He opened a ledger, started asking questions. Had she a boyfriend? No, I said. What about her parents? Maybe she had run off to them. I told him our parents were dead. I could tell he wasn't interested. He gave me a lecture about the number of people who disappear for various reasons and are never seen again. He said he'd taken down the details and they'd go on file. I was furious. By the time I got back here I was in despair.'

'So what did you do next?' Tweed asked gently.

'You're very perceptive. I did what I should have done in the first place. Christine left me a key so when she had to go off on a trip I could keep an eye on her place. It looked OK when I walked in. I went straight to her wardrobe, checked her clothes. Nothing missing. Her two travelling cases were there. In the bathroom I found her toilet bag. If she'd gone for more than a day she'd never have left that. I wished I'd done this before I visited the police. Then I realized it wouldn't have made any difference to Thickhead.'

'We called at Yelland Street before we came here,' explained Tweed. 'The name plate on the wall has been polished.'

'That was me,' Anne replied. 'I couldn't stand it when it started to get mouldy.'

'You said you had a key to her place,' Tweed recalled. 'If you'd be willing to loan it to us we'll go back to search. We might just find something.'

'Oh, would you?' Relief flooded her pale face. Reaching into the handbag she had perched on the back of her chair, she produced a Chubb key, then a Banham, and handed them to him.

'When you've finished you can drop both keys back through my letterbox in this envelope. Save you time. If you could phone me briefly with news, I'd be so grateful.' She handed him a card. 'There's the phone number.'

'We'll phone,' Tweed promised. He gave her his own card. 'If something occurs to you, don't hesitate for a minute to call me at this number. However trivial. A stranger calling, say. Note his description.'

'I can't tell you both how grateful I am,' she repeated.

86

They had left Champton Place, were getting into their car, when the front door flew open and Anne came running down the steps, clutching a small frame. Paula was back again on the pavement when she arrived. She smiled as she caught her breath.

'Sorry to hold you up. Here's a photo of Christine. Should have thought of it while we were talking.'

'No,' Tweed called out, '*I* should have thought to ask you—I must be losing my grip.'

'I doubt that very much, Mr Tweed,' Anne replied, giving him a glowing smile. 'I've got another. Keep it as long as you like.'

'Return it to you as soon as we can.'

Although both were experts at searching, after two hours checking the ground floor and the basement, which contained the sleeping area and a bathroom, they had found nothing. Tweed had used a pick-lock to open a batch of steel filing cabinets in a small room obviously used as a study.

It was crammed with files of papers, and each file had the name of a firm he'd never heard of. Taking out his notebook he wrote all the names down. He didn't feel they were going to lead him anywhere. Just evidence that Christine was a furious worker.

When they had arrived Paula had, for the third time, used her mobile to tell Monica at Park Crescent where they were. The team became nervous if either of them was away a long time without being in touch. She went to find Tweed.

'Any luck?'

'Zero.'

'Me too. Oh, the kitchen. I should have started there. It's the place where a woman might just hide something.'

Wearing latex gloves still, she tried to haul open the huge door of the massive American fridge. No good: it was stuck. The equipment was modern and expensive. She opened drawers, one jammed halfway. She started on the cupboards, then found a slim corner cupboard which had two Banham locks. There was evidence that someone had tried to force it open. She called out for Tweed to come, and showed him.

'They didn't try very hard,' he commented. 'It's a very thin cupboard so there can't be much inside. I'll call for Harry Butler to come over. He can open anything with the minimum of damage.'

He stopped speaking as Paula's mobile began buzzing. It was Monica. She listened, asked Monica to hold on and handed it to Tweed.

'Think you should hear this.'

'Tweed here.'

'It's Monica. I think you should know we've been invaded. By Abel Gallagher. He shoved George aside downstairs and went up to your office and barged in. He is now having the mother and father of arguments with Bob Newman.'

'I'm coming. Be there in fifteen minutes—or less.'

'This drawer just won't open,' Paula said aloud while Tweed was talking.

She tackled it once more. Again it stuck halfway. She pushed her fingers under it, pushed the drawer in a short distance. Her fingers touched a manilla envelope, which she eased out. The flap was not sealed. She pulled out a sheaf of papers, all neatly typed with a maze of figures. Several were circled in red ink. Including a figure '400 mil'.

'We've got to get back now,' Tweed said impatiently.

'Look at this. It was well hidden. Can't make head or tail of it. It's hieroglyphics to me. What do you make of it?'

He took the sheaf from her, just before he'd taken off his gloves. Frowning, he studied the mass of figures. They meant nothing to him. Paula took back the documents and slipped them back inside the envelope. She then turned over the envelope where Christine had started to write something and had then changed her mind: 'Dr'.

She waited until they were in the car and Tweed was driving back towards Park Crescent through the side streets. When they were stopped by a light suddenly turning red, she showed him the front of the envelope.

'Could be Drago Volkanian she was going to write.'

'Could be anything. Abel Gallagher has barged into my office after shoving the guard aside. Newman is confronting him. I can't wait to confront him myself.'

*   *   *

While on their way back, Tweed asked Paula to phone Keith Kent, his friend and brilliant accountant, for an urgent favour. He was to come over to Park Crescent immediately, then wait in the downstairs visitors' room. He would be down to see him very quickly.

'He laughed,' she said after she'd made the call.

'Said if ever you didn't want something yesterday he'd know it wasn't important. He's coming straight over. Now I must call Anne Barton.'

At Champton Place the phone was picked up at once. I must be careful how I word this, Paula thought.

'Anne, Paula here. We've checked your sister's place. We did find a hidden document which might tell us something when we've had it checked by an expert. Sorry not to have more.'

'The main thing is I don't feel so alone any more. Thank you so much for calling. For all you've done so far.'

'We'll keep in touch,' Paula promised.

'Two things I think we need Harry Butler's help on,' she reminded Tweed. 'Couldn't open the fridge or the thin cupboard with two Banham locks.'

'Those giant fridges from the States,' Tweed grumbled. 'Do the Americans really eat more than we do? Here we are. There's Gallagher's big brown Volvo.'

Paula glanced at Tweed as he pulled in to the kerb. His lips were tight, his eyes seemed larger. He was livid. But when George opened the door Tweed's tone was quiet as he gazed at him.

'I'm really sorry about this, George. How are you?'

'I'll survive. Gallagher elbowed me in the ribs before he charged upstairs. I'm feeling much better.'

'Get a doctor to check you now. Call Westholme to come *now*. That's an order.'

He took the stairs two at a time. They could hear voices through the almost-closed door to his office

90

on the first floor. Bob Newman's first, calm, controlled, deadly.

'I really am going to have to throw you out.'

'Like to try it?'

Gallagher's sneering tones. Tweed walked in slowly with Paula behind him. The whole team was in the office. Just inside the door to the left Monica sat at her desk, glaring. Marler was leaning against the far wall, smoking a cigarette, his expression amused. Harry Butler was close to Newman, his expression not amused. Their unwanted visitor, over six feet tall, broad shoulders straining under his dark suit, had his back to them, pointing at cool-tempered Pete Nield perched on Tweed's desk.

'Mr Gallagher,' Tweed said slowly, quietly, 'I want you to leave my office immediately, please.'

The Special Branch chief turned round. Paula had her first good look at his face. An ignorant vicious brute was her verdict. Untidy dark hair, eyes that radiated aggression, a boxer's nose and a hard jaw. He seemed taken aback by Tweed's tone, then recovered his voice, the tone lower.

'I'm here to find out what you're doing messing about down at Abbey Grange.'

Newman slipped past him, handed Tweed a copy of the day's *Daily Nation*. It was folded so the headline jumped up at him. TWO SKELETON MURDERS ON DARTMOOR. Tweed handed the paper to Paula, addressed Gallagher again in the same quiet tone.

'I suggest when you've left, which I advise you do now, that you buy a copy of today's newspaper. You don't seem to keep up with the latest developments.'

'What the hell does that mean?'

'Another thing,' Tweed went on as he walked and sat behind his desk. Pete Nield immediately slid off it, stood very erect alongside Newman. 'I may feel obliged to report what happened to my guard to the Home Secretary. You could, of course, apologize to him on your way out. Bob, please open the door for Mr Gallagher.'

Gallagher, a man used to a verbal brawl, was stunned. While Newman held the door open he walked out quickly, hurried down the stairs. The phone rang. Monica answered and reported to Tweed that Keith Kent had just arrived.

'Splendid!' Tweed smiled. 'Ask him to come up at once.' He stood up to greet Kent and shake his hand. 'You must have come by Concorde. I appreciate it.'

'Buttering me up will get you nowhere,' Kent replied with a grin.

In his forties, Keith Kent wore a smart blue bird's-eye suit, his neat dark hair trim, his young-looking face exuding intelligence without vanity. He sat down in the chair Tweed indicated and looked around.

'Hello, all of you. Don't know how you have the energy to keep up with this chap—especially after his recent bout of training. So what is it this time?' He took the envelope Paula handed to him, glanced up at her. 'We must have dinner sometime. Just you and me.'

'Name the day.'

'Tonight. The Ivy. Seven p.m. any good?'

'Perfect.' She laid a hand on his shoulder. 'Make it tomorrow. Tweed will be having dinner with his blonde bombshell.'

'Don't think Lucinda would like that description,' protested Tweed, smiling.

'Well, she is blonde and has the energy of a bombshell.'

Kent had been examining the shcaf of papers covered with the maze of figures. He raised his dark eyebrows while he looked at Tweed.

'If you're expecting a report tomorrow, forget it. This is sophisticated accounting. Someone really good who has his own method of working. Or is it her?'

'Her.'

'Not a forensic accountant?'

'Yes, indeed.'

'Thought so. "400 mil". Four hundred million. This firm's turnover is much bigger than even that. More than that I can't tell you. I'd better get started.' He looked across at Paula, now seated at her far corner desk. 'Seven p.m., the Ivy?'

'Nothing wrong with my memory, Keith. I may be a bit late.'

'Women always are.' He grinned again. 'Clever women like yourself.'

When he had left, Harry Butler, short and burly, wearing, as always, an old windcheater and denims, darted across the office to near Paula's corner, picked up a Gladstone-like bag, which carried his tools.

'Paula whispered when she passed me that you have an urgent job for me. Have bag, ready to travel.'

'A monster American fridge we can't open. A thin cupboard with two Banhams. I'll drive you there. Bob,' Tweed said to Newman, 'take over while I'm gone.'

'I'm coming with you,' Paula said in a tone that brooked no contradiction.

*   *   *

Yelland Street was as quiet as when they had last visited it. As Tweed was pulling in to the kerb, Paula produced a camera.

'I'm going to photo that pic of Christine, then we can give it back to Anne on the way back. I know she said she had another but I'm sure she treasures it.'

Once inside, Tweed led Butler to the kitchen at the back of the house. Paula nipped into the living room. Tweed had perched the framed picture on top of the piano. With her hi-tech, non-flash camera she quickly took three shots, tucked the framed original under her arm and went to join the other two.

'Banham's are good at making locks,' Butler commented as he operated a small machine, inserted a key he had brought with him, opened both locks. He then stood back and gestured to Paula to open the cupboard.

She opened the door slowly, peered inside, then she froze. Piled on top of one another were racks she recognized as trays from the fridge. Rows of neatly piled packs of food were stacked on the floor. She took a step back. The smell was distinctly unpleasant.

'This fridge isn't stuck,' Butler called out. 'The handle has to be pushed down, then lifted.'

He stood back again. She wiped her clammy hands on her jeans and approached the handle. Tweed had been double-checking cupboards. She

94

forced herself to follow Butler's instructions. She pressed the handle down, then paused. She took a deep breath, then she lifted the handle, grasped it with the latex gloves she'd put on. She heaved the huge door open. The unique smell drifted immediately into the kitchen.

'Oh, God!' she gasped. 'Oh, no!'

She was staring at the face of Christine Barton, throat cut from ear to ear, the head supported by a fridge bar. Another bar held the rest of the naked body against the back of the fridge, the body brutally slashed, chunks of flesh stored in plastic bags on the fridge's floor.

'Jesus!' exclaimed Butler.

Tweed, already sampling the horrible odour of decomposition, pushed Paula aside, closed the fridge door. The hideous odour was polluting the kitchen. Tweed grasped Paula by her arm.

'Back into the living room. Harry, close the door into the hall.'

Inside the living room Paula sank into a chair and took deep breaths of the fresh air. Tweed was holding out his hand and she was unsure why.

'Your mobile, please,' he demanded. 'I'm phoning Buchanan. Let's hope he can bring Professor Saafeld. He likes to see a body before it's moved.'

'I'd . . . better . . .' Paula shuddered. 'Call Anne.'

'Not yet. I'm hoping Saafeld can cover the throat once he gets her to the morgue. It's awful that Anne will have to identify her.'

13

An hour later Tweed was driving back to Park Crescent alone. Buchanan had arrived before he left, together with a team of technical experts. Fortunately, by some miracle, Professor Saafeld had arrived a few minutes before. He was insistent that he should see the corpse before 'the clodhoppers mess up the evidence,' as he impolitely put it.

Paula was with Anne at Champton Place. Tweed had called Pete Nield and told him to get over fast. He had decided Peter, a calm, sympathetic man, would be the best company to stay with Anne when she came back from the morgue, after being driven there by Saafeld.

He crawled back, his car edging forward by inches. He had run into rush hour. Reaching the peace and quiet of Park Crescent, he parked and studied George, who unlocked the door. He was standing quite upright, seemed to be moving normally.

'You saw the doctor?'

'Yes. He was in the area. Apparently I have an open cut near a rib. When Gallagher threw me back I hit the sharp edge of a cupboard. He treated it with antiseptic, then put on a large bandage. He left a report about it. Here it is.'

'I'll keep that. Gallagher will already be wondering whether he went too far, whether I'll be reporting the incident. Let him wonder. You feel OK?'

'Ready for Gallagher to come back. He won't

catch me off guard next time.'

Tweed ran up the stairs to his office. Some of his staff were present. Monica was at work at her computer. Newman was seated, reading a newspaper. In his forties, he was well built with fair hair and a strong face, which women stared at when he walked into a restaurant. Thugs in the street took one look at Newman and gave him a wide berth.

Marler, reputed to be the best marksman in Western Europe, occupied his normal position, standing up, leaning against a wall, smoking a long cigarette. In his late thirties, five foot eight tall and slim, he wore a smart blue suit, a pristine white shirt, a Hermès tie. His movements were deceptively slow, deliberate, his face good-looking, his expression sardonic.

Tweed took off his overcoat, slung it on a hanger and slipped behind his desk. Tersely, he brought his staff up to date, starting with the strange case of Michael's amnesia, continuing with the drive to Post Lacey, the skeletons on Dartmoor, Abbey Grange and the mixture of characters there, including the servants. As he continued, Monica was watching him.

Of medium height, with a strong build, Tweed was ageless, with alert eyes behind his horn-rimmed glasses. He had been the sort of man you passed in the street without noticing him, a feature he'd found useful in his work. Now, since returning from the murderous training course at the Surrey mansion, he seemed more dynamic, his tone of voice more commanding. He definitely seemed younger, she thought.

'So that's it, up to date,' Tweed concluded.

'You're missing bits out,' Marler drawled in his upper-crust voice. 'The bullet fired when you and Paula were west of the Gantia plant. Someone doesn't like you investigating this case.'

'Well, there was that too,' Tweed admitted.

Marler brought an Ordnance Survey map to his desk, unfolded it, gestured.

'Could you mark the location of that ambush?'

'Yes, why?'

'Just locate it for me, please.'

Tweed bent over, pen poised. 'This is a good map. I'd say it was about here.' He made a cross. 'A very good map,' he repeated. 'I noticed an isolated hill to our left about a hundred yards back in the field. Has a single fir tree on the top.'

'That should do me. I'm off now. See you gremlins.'

'Hold on.' Newman had risen to his feet. 'You might tell us where you're going.'

'Curious, old chap? You may have been a famous newspaper correspondent, but you don't need to know everything.'

Tweed sat back, amused. Although great friends these two were often mocking each other. It was part of their relationship.

'Righty-ho,' Marler replied. 'I'm going to check out where we nearly lost our Deputy Director of the SIS. Takes one marksman to identify another.'

'You won't find a damned thing,' Newman joshed him.

'I won't standing around here.'

Marler was gone, closing the door quietly. Newman shrugged, picked up the newspaper to show Tweed something. The phone rang. Monica looked at Tweed and said it was Paula.

'I'm listening,' Tweed said.

'First, Pete has arrived. I think Anne likes him. I'm down in the master bedroom in the basement. He brought Butler, who's busy securing all the windows and doors. I was going to suggest to Anne I cook a meal. She shuddered, said not after her trip to the morgue in Holland Park. As you know, Saafeld has already supervised removal of Christine's body to the morgue.'

'Then I think that's it.'

'I had a thought,' Paula went on. 'Michael stayed at Bella Ashton's place for two weeks, and was then moved to Dr Saxon's charming clinic. He charges far less. This suggests to me the mysterious caller to Bella Ashton—man or woman—is short of money in substantial amounts.'

'That really does narrow the field,' Tweed said ironically. 'How many hundreds of thousands are short of money?'

'I said substantial amounts,' Paula persisted obstinately.

'I'm leaving now. To pay a brief call on Saafeld at Holland Park. He's so quick he'll have conclusions he's drawn now from the three corpses. Then back here. Bob has something he wants to show me in the paper.'

'Then I'll also go to Holland Park. Pete's coping wonderfully here.'

'This item in the paper could be important,' protested Newman.

'I won't be long. When you can, find out everything you can about our friend Abel Gallagher.'

*   *   *

Paula was waiting for Tweed when he arrived in Holland Park. She stood outside the large mansion screened by evergreen trees from the road. It was drizzling and she sheltered under an umbrella.

'Came here by taxi,' she explained as Tweed said he hadn't expected to see her here so quickly.

At one time they could have opened the gate and walked up to the front door along the winding drive. Now, Saafeld had top security. Tall wrought-iron gates were closed with an intercom in a pillar. Tweed pressed the button and announced himself and Paula. The gruff voice of Saafeld said he supposed he'd have to let them in.

The gates swung inward, and closed soon after they had walked inside. Paula had always found the drive bordered with massive clumps of rhododendrons depressing. With the heavy overcast, the drizzle and the drip-drip of rain off the rhododendrons, the atmosphere seemed even more depressing. Not because she had previously visited the best-equipped autopsy suite in the basement. It seemed as though Saafeld felt more comfortable with his grisly work shut away from the world.

He met them in the large entrance hall furnished with small, beautiful antiques. Their footsteps clacked on the polished woodblock floor as he led them into a sitting room. They were seated in comfortable armchairs when Saafeld's wife entered, carrying a silver tray with tea and cakes. She placed it on a table near to Paula. A tall white-haired woman, she had a pleasant smile. She studied both her visitors.

'You two look younger.'

'Nothing but outrageous flattery,' Saafeld

growled amiably as his wife served the tea.

'Now,' he began, 'your three-time killer, possibly middle-aged, no older, is strong and fit. Has to be to wield the knife in the way it was used.'

'*Three*-time killer?' Tweed interposed.

'Yes. I have no doubt. The two skeletons on Dartmoor, Christine's body in that fridge, all were accomplished with the same modus operandi, as I told you before. Victims attacked from behind, heads jerked back, sharp edge of the blade used to cut the throat, blade reversed to serrated edge, used to slash halfway through to the spine. Heads still left attached. Chunks of flesh savaged off with fine edge of blade. Time of deaths, probably three to four months ago. Get the picture?'

It was a typical Saafeld diagnosis. Not a wasted word. He conjured up a vivid picture without a trace of the dramatic. The fiercest defence counsel, cross-examining him in the witness box, trod warily. One had confessed to Tweed he'd sooner have any other pathologist to confront than Saafeld.

'Yes,' Tweed said. 'Just an opinion. A psychotic at work?'

'Meet one in the street, man or woman, and you'd think they were perfectly normal. I suspect there has to be a psychotic streak in this killer. Why carve out chunks of flesh?'

'Any signs of a struggle put up by the victims?' Paula enquired.

'Can't say with those two on Dartmoor. As regards Christine Barton, I don't think so. Fingernails were intact. Not a trace of someone's skin under them.'

'Suggests she knew the killer,' Tweed mused.

'That's your job.'

'The fact,' Tweed continued musing aloud, 'that two were found on Dartmoor, one in London, wipes out certain vague theories I was developing. Anything special about the knife used?'

'Not really.' Saafeld drank more tea, shrugged. 'You can find that kind of knife in any kitchen, maybe one of the tools in a carpenter's kit. Who knows?'

'I appreciate the data you've given us.'

'Not much to go on.' Saafeld ate a cake swiftly. He gave one of his rare smiles. 'Expect you'd hoped I'd be able to say look for a man six feet tall, dark hair and with bony wrists. Can't oblige you.'

'Then we'd better go. Thank Mrs Saafeld for the tea. The cakes were home-made, I'm sure.'

'Sit down. I did find something that might help.' From his pocket he produced a transparent evidence envelope. Tweed and Paula could see inside a gold ring embedded with a large diamond. Saafeld held up the envelope tantalizingly. It was a typical manoeuvre of the pathologist. He enjoyed surprising people. 'When you get it back to your office look at the interior under a glass. There's an inscription.'

'Can I ask you where you found it?'

'It was just before I decided I'd done all I could. The ambulances had taken away the two skeletons; the police, including Buchanan, had flown off in their chopper. One local uniformed bobby was left to keep watch on the tape surrounding the key areas. Not too bright. He started to smoke a pipe. Had to tell him to put it out. If he dropped ash it might be confusing evidence. He marched off towards Post Lacey. I still had the telescopic ladder—could easily take that away in my car. Something made me go down inside the mine shaft where the woman's body was discovered. It was broad daylight. I used a stick to poke among the debris, found that ring.'

'You think then that it was originally on a finger of the skeletal woman?'

'Seems likely. The killer missed it. So did the police.'

'And the inscription reads?'

' "From Lee to Lucinda".'

*　　　*　　　*

'It's weird,' Paula commented as Tweed drove them back to his office. 'Lee could be the name of a man or a woman.'

'Could be.'

Tweed had the evidence envelope containing the ring inside his pocket. He also had two sheets, headed 'Your skeleton' and 'Mine shaft skeleton'. The first contained Saafeld's estimate of the height, *possible* weight and age of the skeleton they had discovered while walking behind Michael up the track. The other sheet contained the same data about the woman in the mine shaft. *Possible* age ranges were also given.

'Don't forget your date with Lucinda tomorrow,' Paula teased him. 'You'll have to wear something suitable. For Lucinda you need that smart grey suit.'

'Bossy. And don't you forget your date with Keith Kent. And turn up on time. He's a stickler for punctuality.'

'I asked for that. Poor Christine must be some

103

accountant. I never heard Keith say before it may take some time to sort out.'

'Another thing,' Tweed told her as they approached Park Crescent, 'I've asked Newman to dig up a complete biography on Abel Gallagher. I was alarmed when he let slip he knew we'd been to Abbey Grange. How on earth could he know that?'

'Suggests he has a contact down there. Wonder who it is.'

*   *   *

Newman reached for his folded newspaper the moment they entered the office. He waited until Tweed was behind his desk, then spread out the paper.

'You know Drew Franklin, the top political correspondent on the *Daily Nation*?'

'Of course we do,' said Paula. 'He's almost as smart as you are,' she joked.

'This is serious,' Newman snapped. 'You've both heard vague references to Angora, the new rebel state in the Mediterranean. Washington's really worried since a fundamentalist government took over. Extreme Islamic. Our government, of course, plays down any idea of a menace. Read that.'

ANGORA ROCKETS FOR LONDON?
Reliable informants report Angora has received from North Korea 100 rockets with a range of 2,500 miles. This means the missiles could easily reach Paris, Berlin or London. The rockets are waiting now for the expected delivery of missiles which are on their way from North Korea. Our government complacent.

Tweed read the article twice. Then he got up, walked over to the windows, which had a distant view of Regent's Park. He wasn't seeing the view. In his mind he was running through all the events they had witnessed since first visiting Michael with his amnesia. Vivid pictures came back. The strange trip with Michael to Dartmoor. The skeletons. The people he had met. Snatches of conversation. The bullet aimed at him on the way back. Gantia. Lucinda. Anne Barton. Fourth name on the list in Michael's pocket. He turned round.

'My instinct tells me this murder case is far more sinister, more dangerous than we realized. Powerful invisible forces are at work. The momentum is building up at frantic pace. We must solve the case, a case of unimaginable magnitude.'

14

It was dark outside when Marler walked into the office. Harry Butler arrived back as Marler dropped something on Tweed's desk. Newman stood up and alongside Paula hc stared at the metallic object. A large cartridge case neither recognized.

'I now know who tried to kill you on the A303,' Marler said in his offhand way.

'What is it?' Tweed asked.

'A specially moulded cartridge for a deadly French assassin called Charmian. No one's been able to identify this killer for hire. At a price. A high one.'

'You're sure?' Tweed persisted.

'Of course I am. I also know the gun maker in Paris. He was drunk when I last called on him, let slip Charmian's name when he swept some of these cartridges into a drawer. This is off the record. If Charmian finds out, the gun maker is dead.'

'So where did you find it?'

'Inside that fir tree on the isolated hill from where he aimed at you. It's all getting very French.' He went over to the wall, leaned against it, lit a cigarette.

'You are going to tell me what that means?'

'Why not? On my way down there I kept a meeting with Marin, my best informant in Europe.'

'That's his name?' asked Tweed.

'Such naïveté,' Marler mocked good-humouredly. 'Of course not. That's his code name. You know how carefully I protect my informants.'

'I suppose we're going to hear what he told you before we get to midnight,' Tweed rapped back.

'He says a ship's picking up crew from the Ile des Oiseaux close to the famous Château d'If island off Marseilles. Then it's on its way to collect long-range missiles from somewhere in Europe. Angora is becoming very aggressive. It has long-range rockets obtained from North Korea. Kim, the mad dictator of North Korea, was cunning. Too cunning. So the rockets travelled to Angora some time ago. Then Kim sent the missiles later on a different ship—which collides with an American destroyer in the Sea of Japan. Ship with the load of missiles sinks to bottom of the sea. Kim demanded Angora paid for the lost missiles and the ship. Angora has refused and has found another source.'

'Where?' asked Tweed grimly.

'Source unknown. Marin's sending me a coded signal when you should visit the island. Heavily guarded.'

'I once visited Marseilles a long time ago.' Tweed stood up, wandered over to the windows, hands inside his trouser pockets. Paula knew the stance. Tweed was concentrating furiously. He stopped, looked down at Newman.

'You see. My instinct was right. This murder case is the tip of a huge iceberg, a major conspiracy, I sense. I have a lot of loose links I have to join up to form a chain. I want to locate Gantia's armaments factory.'

'Ask Lucinda over dinner tomorrow night,' Paula suggested. 'Late in the meal. And Keith Kent has again confirmed my dinner with him tomorrow night. He's wrestling with that sheaf of accounts I found in Christine's flat.'

'I'm going home,' Tweed decided. 'I want to think hard.'

'I'll drive you to your flat,' Newman said firmly. 'No walk for you tonight. Not after Charmian's bullet missed by inches.'

'I love babysitters,' Tweed grumbled.

'You have no option,' Newman told him.

*　　　*　　　*

Tweed, unusually, arrived at his office the following day in the early evening. He had spent the late afternoon with Anne in Champton Place. She had seemed more settled, greeting him with a smile.

'I do appreciate your sending two of your team,' she began. 'Pete—that is, Mr Nield—is clearing

107

up in the kitchen after cooking me a meal. And Harry Butler's turned this place into a fortress, which makes me feel much safer.'

They were seated in her living room as she spoke rapidly, her manner almost relaxed. Tweed avoided any reference to her visit to Saafeld's morgue to identify Christine. Nield appeared with a tray of tea, then left them alone.

'I feel rather a fool,' Anne went on. 'There's something I should have told you about earlier. It completely slipped my mind because of ... yesterday.'

'Better late than never,' Tweed assured her cheerfully. 'I'm all ears.'

'This goes back over three months ago, when I started to worry about Christine's absence. I called an ex-boyfriend who was a policeman and asked him if he could recommend a good private investigator. He immediately gave me details of a John Jackson. Said he'd been an inspector, a clever one. Jackson had resigned because he couldn't stand the politics, then established his own agency.'

'You did say *John* Jackson?' Tweed queried.

John was the fourth name on the typed list found inside Michael's pocket.

'Yes, that's right. He gave me his address and phone number. His office is in Parson Street, Shadwell. Down in the docks area, I gathered. I called him, told him what it was about. I suppose my voice was a bit shaky. When he arrived here he brought me a small bunch of lovely flowers. I was quite touched. I answered all his questions, gave him fifty pounds as a deposit. He gave me a receipt. His details are on this card.'

Tweed took the card, a modest affair but well printed.

John Jackson Agency, Private Investigator. 159 Parson Street, Shadwell, East London. Marital problems not accepted.

'May I keep this?' Tweed asked.

'By all means. He sent me a brief confirmation that he was acting on my behalf. That's the last I ever heard from him. He struck me as very intelligent and honest. I don't think he'd pocket my fifty pounds and then disappear. I hope he hasn't had an accident.'

'Did you phone his office to try and contact him?'

'Twice. Both times I got an answerphone. I hate those things. I didn't say a word each time. Then I gave up.' Anne smiled wanly. 'Sometimes I think I give up too easily.'

'You did try twice. So Nield is looking after you?'

'Oh, yes. He's so helpful. I'll miss him, but I do understand you need him.'

'He can stay for a day or two longer, unless I run into an emergency. I'll just have a word with him before I go.'

'Oh, how much do I owe you for all of Mr Butler's work? I'll give you a cheque now.'

'No you won't.' Tweed stood up. 'We have a large fund at my disposal for just such situations,' he lied. 'Don't hesitate to call me if something develops—or worries you in any way.'

* * *

When Tweed arrived back at Park Crescent,

wearing his grey suit, most of his team were there as he took off his overcoat. It was 6 p.m. Paula eyed him up and down.

'Lucinda will swoon when she sees you.'

'That I doubt very much.' He looked at Paula closely. She was wearing an electric-blue two-piece with a striking petal-shaped jewelled brooch—a birthday present he'd given her. 'It's Keith Kent who won't be able to take his eyes off you.'

'When you two have finished admiring each other,' Marler began in a lordly tone, 'maybe I could report on developments.'

'Fire away,' said Tweed from behind his desk.

'Marin, my informant, has now left for the Continent.'

'Nice and vague,' Tweed commented.

'I hadn't finished. His guess is he'll want you to travel to Marseilles in about a week to ten days from now. We go by train. Marin insists on that. The French Secret Service are photographing all passengers alighting from aircraft—and they'd recognize you. Might even follow us.'

'Not exactly a holiday.' Tweed checked his watch. 'I'm off to Santorini's in a minute. Traffic's terrible and I want to be there on time.'

'Mustn't keep the luscious Lucinda waiting,' Paula chaffed him. 'That's rather a good description. Luscious Lucinda.'

'I'm getting out of here,' responded Tweed, putting on his camel-hair overcoat.

'Hang on a sec,' said Newman, who had been quiet as he sat in his armchair. 'I've been busy today. Went down to the East End to meet a chap who runs a chain of barges—and is a race-goer during the season. He knows everything that's going on. I asked him about Abel Gallagher. He threw his hands into the air, said there was a mate in deep water. Gallagher haunts the races during the season. Did last year. My informant knows his bookie. Gallagher's twenty thousand quid in debt to him. Always picks losers. Bookie's getting restless.'

'His name?'

'Torture wouldn't make him reveal that. Gallagher? Chief of Special Branch. He could set up anyone who talks for a drug bust.'

'I'm going down to have a word with George.' Tweed had the door half open. 'I'll be back.'

'Good,' said Newman. 'Because I'm driving you to the restaurant. You don't have to be on the A303 to get a bullet through your window.'

Paula drifted over to the window. Mist was invading London's streets. She was still able to see below her. She waited, then turned to Newman.

'You won't be driving Tweed. He's just disappeared in his car.'

*   *   *

Tweed arrived at Santorini's five minutes early. A doorman came out to park his car. The head waiter greeted him effusively.

'I have your table waiting, the best in the house.'

'I'm expecting a lady guest. Blonde hair.'

'You'll find her in the bar, sir.'

Held up several times in the traffic on his way, Tweed had pondered what he'd been told. Marseilles. Did that link up with anywhere—or anyone—he'd seen or met? He felt he was missing

111

something. Then there was Abel Gallagher. Twenty thousand in debt to a bookie. What bookie would let anyone pile up such a huge sum? The answer was clear. The bookie knew he might need Gallagher's protection one day if he found himself in a dangerous situation.

'We're looking for someone in need of substantial funds,' Paula had said. Something like that.

In the bar, almost empty at that early hour, Tweed found Lucinda perched on a stool, drinking champagne. She looked stunning. She wore a green dress, slashed up the side of her right leg, and the colour was just right for her long blonde hair. On the counter was a second glass of champagne, untouched.

She had seen him come in from his reflection in the mirror behind the bar. He headed for the stool to her left. She swung round to face him.

'Tweed, you're late. I've been here ages. Cheers!'

She pushed the full glass towards him. He picked it up after perching on the stool. They clinked glasses. She swallowed half the contents of her drink, which the barman had filled up. Tweed sipped.

'I'm not late,' he told her. 'I'm exactly on time. So what are we drinking to?'

'To us! May our relationship be long and fruitful.'

'I'll drink to that.'

Tweed drank only occasionally and then moderately. But he had the capacity to drink a lot—and still remain alert and sober. He turned to face her, smiled.

'May I say you are looking terrific?'

'Thank you.' Her left hand reached out, plucked gently at the sleeve of his suit. 'This suit is having

112

an effect on me. So smart.'

'The waiter said our table's waiting. We could take our drinks with us.'

As they walked into the spacious and tastefully decorated restaurant, the barman followed, carrying a silver tray with a bottle of Krug. The wine waiter appeared as they settled themselves at a corner table, placed two new champagne glasses on the table, uncorked the Krug, poured a little into one glass. Tweed sampled it, gave a nod of approval. Menus were presented, they studied them, then ordered. Lucinda leaned forward, her voice low, although there was only one other couple in the room so far.

'The morning you came to see me at the plant one of our trucks was hijacked early in the morning. The driver was waved down, a masked man chloroformed him and shoved him into a hedge. Truck was found on the M3. The police soon lost interest. The driver recovered quickly. No aftereffects. Strange.'

'Mysterious,' said Tweed.

They had finished their starters and main courses when they decided they needed a pause. Lucinda lit a cigarette. The Krug bottle was now half empty, the greater part of its contents swallowed by Lucinda.

'Tell me about Larry,' Tweed suggested. 'What sort of chap is he?'

'Brilliant. A quick brain. Decisive. Won't suffer fools gladly. Can be tough. Loves travelling abroad. Is often away for longish periods, meeting big customers. Half the time we don't know where he is. Very independent.'

'What was Michael like before amnesia hit him?'

'Here we go!' She shook her cigarette holder at him. 'I just knew you'd veer into an interrogation.'

'I'm interested in people.'

'OK,' she sighed and grinned at him. 'Michael is even cleverer than Larry. A superb sales director. We have two more and they're keeping things afloat. They lack Michael's initiative. We survive, Mr Detective. Now, have you identified those two poor skeletons on Dartmoor?'

Tweed took a silk handkerchief out of his pocket. He gave her the ring found inside the mining shaft. Told her to read the inscription inside: 'From Lee to Lucinda'. Her reaction was electric.

'Oh, my God! Lee tried to give this to me. See the size of the rock? I declined it. It was too much. So she wears it herself. Where did you find it?'

'Who is Lee? What's her surname?'

'Never stop, do you? Interrogating. She calls herself by her maiden name, Lee Charlton. She's married to one of our directors, Aubrey Greystoke.'

'What kind of director is he?'

'God!' She drank more champagne. 'He's the finance director. Their marriage is breaking up. Which doesn't surprise me ...' She paused, staring at the entrance to the restaurant. 'Talk of the devil, Greystoke's coming in here with his latest girlfriend.'

Tweed turned in his chair. Greystoke was a tall, well-built man wearing a black tie. In his early fifties, he exuded self-satisfaction, scanning the restaurant with an imperious expression. His thick brown hair was carefully coiffeured, a pair of gold-rimmed spectacles were perched on his Roman nose, his lips were sensuous, his chin

114

pointed. Lucinda had lowered her eyes but he had spotted her, began to walk over.

On his arm was a short slim girl with jet-black hair falling to her shoulders. Not yet thirty, Tweed judged. Greystoke's voice was lofty.

'Well, well, gathering of the clans, Lucinda. This is Martina Martello.'

'Any news of Lee?' asked Lucinda with deliberate lack of tact, her expression cold.

'Not a dickey-bird. Didn't expect any. You know how she is, my dear.'

'No. *How* is she?' Lucinda shot back.

'Chasing her chances somewhere in the world, I expect.'

'I'm still here in case anyone's not noticed,' Martina snapped.

Tweed stood up, introduced himself, shook her hand. She gave him a thankful smile. Greystoke stiffened.

'Tweed? The gentleman who's investigating the unfortunate occurrences down at Dartmoor?'

'Yes.' Tweed's tone was grim. 'If you can call two exceptionally brutal murders unfortunate occurrences.'

'Nice to meet you both.' Greystoke waved a well-manicured hand. 'Martina, time we grabbed our table before someone poaches it.'

They were an odd couple. As they strolled to a table at the far side of the room Tweed noticed Greystoke's large wiry hands, the careful and slow way he walked.

'When did Lee dump him?' he asked.

'Must be over three months ago. Left him a note. "To hell with you, Aubrey".'

'Handwritten?'

'No. On his computer.'

'And Lee hasn't been seen since? Why did she try to give the ring to you? Must have cost a packet.'

'If you must know, I was in a bad temper—Aubrey was late in giving me some accounts. Lee was in the waiting room. She'd been there an hour. Her husband was taking her to lunch. I said maybe he was calling one of his dolly birds. Which was a bad mistake on my part. Lee, who was a close friend of mine, pinned me to the wall, demanded details. I gave them to her. I felt it was time Aubrey was pulled up sharp.'

'How did Lee react?'

'Surprisingly calmly. Thanked me, said she was going to the loo. If Aubrey came down would I tell him she'd left. Which I did a minute later.'

'So how did he react to that?'

'You'd get information out of a mute. Oh Lord! I'd forgotten about Michael. That was tactless. Aubrey said, "Good. Saves me the most boring lunch." I was going to give him hell but he walked out. End of story. Maybe we could have a fun conversation now. Just for a change, Tweed.'

'Bear with me. Just two more items. How do I contact Larry here in town? I need to have a chat with him.'

'A bloody interrogation, you mean.' She smiled, spread a spare paper napkin on the table, took out a pen, wrote swiftly in capital letters, folded the napkin and handed it to him. 'That gives the address of the London offices in the Tower and his private phone number.' She leaned towards him. 'Now, Mr Detective, what was the other thing?'

'I need to talk to Drago Volkanian very urgently.

116

How do I reach him?'

'You don't. I'm not sure which country he's in.' She paused. 'But I can tell you he wants to contact you.'

'He knows about Michael and the amnesia?'

'No idea. Tweed, thank you for a marvellous dinner. I stay up late. Come back to my place and we'll have a nightcap.'

'Let me think about it, please.'

He paid the bill. As they walked towards the exit he glanced over towards Greystoke's table. His girlfriend, Martina, was stroking his cheek. Greystoke looked at Tweed, looked away without any sign of recognition. The head waiter brought their coats.

'Your car will be waiting outside, sir, in just a minute,' he told Tweed. 'Your Porsche,' he informed Lucinda, 'is parked on the other side of the road. A waiter's kept an eye on it. He's been feeding the meter.'

'Thank you,' she replied with a smile, handing him a large tip.

They walked out into a bitterly cold night. Tweed's car had not yet arrived. Lucinda told Tweed to follow her and skipped across the wide street. A large BMW with tinted windows pulled up in front of her. It all happened so quickly. The driver's door was thrown open and a big man dressed for dinner jumped out and accosted her.

'Hello, dearie. Just what I need. On my way to Scargo's, a super nightclub. Hop in.'

'Get lost!' she snapped.

He grabbed hold of her arm to drag her into the BMW.

'Come on,' he demanded. 'You all play hard

to get.'

Tweed was halfway across the road, his right hand clenched in a fist, when he witnessed an extraordinary spectacle. Lucinda's movement was too swift for him to see exactly what she did. She had hold of the big man, spun him round, shoved him backwards. His head hit the top of the open car doorway and he sagged. She lifted him bodily, pushed him face down inside, checked his pulse as he lay inert, reached in, pulled out the ignition key and threw it along the gutter. It dropped down a drain.

'He'll live,' she told Tweed calmly. 'Pulse ticking over nicely. Now, are you seeing me safely home?'

'Of course I am.'

He had been going to tell her he had to get back to Park Crescent. Now he had no option. He got behind the wheel of his car, now waiting outside Santorini's. He heard the purr of Lucinda's engine starting, was driving behind her when she got moving. No police about, he hoped.

Along the empty streets they soon moved up Park Lane and turned off into Mayfair. Lucinda turned down a side street, used her remote to open the door into an underground garage and waved for him to hurry up before the door closed. She swung into an empty space, and Tweed pulled up alongside her.

'You handled that big ape brilliantly,' he said when he joined her.

'Jujitsu.' She grinned. 'No problem handling the ape.'

He followed her across to a bank of elevators. She summoned the lift and the doors opened, she jumped inside, pressed the 'hold' button and stood inside, facing him, her arms folded.

'I'm gasping for that nightcap. Come on. Move your feet.'

Tweed was tempted. Every limb in his body urged him to get into the elevator. He took a deep breath.

'I'd love to,' he said. 'I'd really love to. You're a truly magnetic woman. But I have to get back to Park Crescent. I'm expecting vital information about my murder case.'

'You and your bloody murder case.'

She ran out of the elevator, threw her arms round him, kissed him, lingering. He responded, clasping his hands round her waist, and edged her gently back inside the elevator. As he did so she produced a card from somewhere and tucked it inside his coat pocket.

'Now you'll know where to find me. Thanks for a terrific evening.'

He was about to take a step forward when she pressed two buttons. As the doors closed she threw him a kiss with her hand. He walked swiftly back to his car, wishing he had joined her. But among other things she was a suspect in a hideous murder case. He couldn't get out of his mind the efficient and speedy way she'd handled the ape.

15

Tweed had found his office empty when he returned—except for Monica, who never seemed to leave the place. She had been producing the long report Tweed had dictated to her for Buchanan. It was an account of everything that had happened so far, starting with his first visit to Arabella Ashton, his first encounter with Michael. It concluded with the finding of the ghastly contents of the monster fridge at Christine Barton's flat. Certain events he conveniently omitted.

Monica showed him the note left for him by Paula.

Hope you had a wonderful evening. I had a good time with Keith at the Ivy. Left at 10 p.m. Keith is still struggling to unlock the key to Christine Barton's sheet of figures. Love, Paula.

He checked his watch: 1 a.m. Time to go home. Monica warned him to take a taxi, said she was phoning for one. Walking the four miles to his flat was not a good idea. He agreed.

The taxi took him to Drayford Street, well beyond Holland Park. He forced himself to take a shower, which woke him up. He didn't sleep well. He kept seeing people he'd met at distant Abbey Grange, then at Santorini's. Lucinda's face kept coming back to him. He again wondered whether he'd made a mistake not stepping into the elevator with her in the underground garage. She was a fascinating woman. Should he ...? He then fell into a deep sleep.

*   *   *

'Have you eaten?' Paula asked the moment Tweed walked in the following morning.

'Well, no . . .'

She walked out, came back half an hour later

from the nearby deli. Removing the metal cover, she revealed a dish of fried bacon and two eggs with grilled tomatoes.

His team watched him as he devoured the meal and drank the coffee Monica had made. He felt a new man as he wiped his mouth with the paper napkin. He looked round the room.

Newman was seated while he absorbed the morning's *Daily Nation*. Marler was standing against a wall while he smoked. Next to him Paula was compiling a list, lost in her concentration. Harry Butler was checking the mechanism of a Walther automatic. Pete Nield was reading sheets as Paula handed them to him.

Tweed stood up, put on his overcoat.

'Going somewhere?' asked Paula.

'You and I are doing just that. You remember a private detective, John Jackson, whom Anne Barton hired? We're going to pay his office a visit. One five nine Parson Street, Shadwell.'

'Shadwell?' Butler slid the automatic into a hip holster. 'In that case a lot of us are coming with you. You travel with Paula in your car. We follow close behind—Pete, myself and Bob Newman.'

'Is that really necessary?'

'It's Shadwell. It's ruddy well vital.'

They left Marler with Monica to look after the office. It was still February, dark clouds shrouding the sky, and there was a miserable drizzle. As they drove off with Tweed behind the wheel, Paula checked her .32 Browning, made sure she could haul it out of the pocket in her shoulder bag.

'I think Harry's overdoing it,' Tweed grumbled.

'I don't. Harry knows the area.'

They soon passed out of the West End and the

atmosphere changed. There were blocks of grimy terrace houses with, here and there, a modern office building. They edged their way through a street market, stalls covered with canvas to protect the varied goods for sale. Paula's mobile buzzed. She listened.

'That was Harry. This is Shadwell. He says watch our backs.'

'They're still close behind us. Newman's car, Bob at the wheel, Harry beside him and Nield in the back. Makes us look like a convoy of gangsters heading in to take out a rival gang.' Tweed spoke with a note of amusement.

'Harry usually knows what he's doing,' Paula rebuked him. 'Slow down, turn left in a sec, I can see the entrance to Parson Street.'

'Miserable-looking place,' Tweed remarked as he swung the wheel round. 'Still, running a small detective agency, I imagine John Jackson had to watch his overheads.'

He parked in the narrow street by a crumbling kerb. One hundred and fifty-nine was a shabby terrace building. A plate screwed to the wall announced JOHN JACKSON AGENCY, PRIVATE INVESTIGATIONS. The stained glass in the upper half of the front door was surprisingly clean. As Tweed alighted with Paula the door opened. Tweed glanced back down the street, was relieved to see no sign of his escort.

A tall burly individual wearing an ancient overcoat, cap pulled well down, appeared at Tweed's side. His rough voice was a snarl.

'Mister, there's a fifty-pound charge for coming in this street. Protection is what they call—'

He stopped speaking as the metal muzzle of

122

Harry's Walther pressed into the back of his thick neck. He dropped the knife from his right hand.

'Mate!' Harry's voice growled. 'Wrong place, wrong street. Scarper back to the river. Now!'

The burly man began running fast to the end of the street, vanished round a corner. Harry kicked the knife off the kerb into a drain and slid his automatic back into his hip holster.

Tweed turned to the door, which was now closed. He pressed the bell, pressed it again when no one appeared. The door was opened less than a foot on a heavy chain. Behind it a frizzy-haired girl with intelligent eyes peered out. She looked frightened.

'Saw a man with a knife . . .' she stuttered.

'He's gone,' Paula told her firmly. 'Mr Tweed has a bodyguard.'

'Mr Tweed?'

'That's me.' Tweed was holding up his folder. 'We need to have a word with Mr Jackson, please.'

'You're police?'

'Something like that. If you were leaving for lunch it will only take a few minutes.'

'I'm leavin' for good. I suppose you'd better come in. Both of you,' she said, looking at Paula.

They entered a narrow hall with a desk in one corner on which sat an old typewriter. The girl, in her twenties, took them into another larger office. Paula shivered. The place was freezing.

'I need to see Mr Jackson,' Tweed repeated.

'He's gone. For good is my guess. I've stayed on since he paid me a month's salary. Electricity's been turned off, so has water. Unpaid bills are stacked in the clip. He was a nice man, Mr Jackson. Didn't want to let 'im down, so I stayed longer than he'd paid me for. Can't understand it. He's

123

just gone.'

'Disappeared, you mean?' Tweed said quietly. 'How long ago since he was here?'

'Over twelve weeks ago. I stayed as long as I could but I've run out of money. I managed to get another post yesterday. I've left a note for him, giving details of the two clients who wanted him.' She pointed to an envelope on the desk. 'He's a nice man,' she repeated. 'Worked for 'im for a year.'

'Could I look at that message to see the names of the clients?' Tweed suggested.

'They'll have gone off elsewhere now.'

She handed him the unsealed envelope. He read the typed note full of errors. The names meant nothing to him. He showed the sheet to Paula.

'Dead end,' she whispered.

'Is this the only place Mr Jackson has?' Tweed asked.

'No. He 'as the 'ouseboat down at Wensford. Often went down there for a day or two studying details of a case.'

'Where is Wensford?'

'Somewhere down the M3. The 'ouseboat's on the River Ley, he told me. Joins the Wey River . . .'

'Excuse me,' Paula said. 'Back in a minute.' She darted off after taking Tweed's key. She was back quickly after shuffling through her collection of Ordnance Survey maps. Selecting the map for Surrey and Sussex, she spread it out on the desk.

'Any idea where Wensford is?' she asked the girl. 'I don't know your name,' she said with a smile.

'Jenny Oxton.' She bent over the map. 'John once showed me where he went. It's down the M3, then you turns off 'ere to Wensford. The 'ouseboat is

124

near a bridge over the Ley River.'

'Are there any records here of Mr Jackson's dealings with clients?' Tweed asked.

'Always took them with 'im in 'is briefcase. Nothing else 'ere. Could I leave with you?'

'Certainly. We can drop you wherever you live.'

'Would 'elp. My boyfriend, Jeff, will be waiting for me at the caff on the corner at the end of Parson Street.'

Tweed had given her envelope back to her. Opening a drawer, she took out another envelope, then picked up a well-worn briefcase. She looked at Paula.

'My stuff. On our way out I'll lock the door, put the key inside this envelope, push it through the letterbox in the door. Best I can do. I 'ope John's all right.'

Outside they saw Harry leaning against the opposite wall, pretending to read a newspaper. Newman appeared, driving his car down from the other end of the street with Nield next to him. Harry dived into the back. Tweed drove to the end of Parson Street, dropped Jenny Oxton off at the door to the café. He had given her a ten-pound note just before she alighted, and had brushed aside her astonished thanks. She rushed into the café, sat at a table by the window opposite a rough-looking young man. She was leaning over to kiss him when they left.

'Some people have a tough life,' Paula remarked.

'She'll survive. I like the Cockneys. Worth a hundred of the Aubrey Greystokes. Now we've got to find Wensford and the houseboat.'

* * *

125

Pausing outside Park Crescent Tweed had a fierce argument with Newman and told him not to follow them down to Wensford. He had to issue a direct order that under no circumstances was anyone to follow him and Paula.

It was lunchtime when Tweed drove at top speed down the M3 with Paula by his side. They reached the turn-off very quickly, driving along a country lane. Earlier Paula had insisted he stop briefly outside the Gantia plant. She quickly took several photos. For the first time since he had reached his office earlier, Tweed found himself thinking again of Lucinda, recalling the scene in the underground garage when she had tried to coax him into the elevator. He should have joined her, he told himself wistfully. No, he'd made the right decision. Or had he?

'A penny for those deep thoughts,' Paula suggested as she put the camera back inside her bag.

'I was just thinking I should have warned Jenny Oxton not ever to go back to Jackson's place.'

'How can she? She dropped the key through the letterbox.'

'Of course she did. I'd forgotten that.'

'Really?'

She gave him an old-fashioned look.

*   *   *

A short distance along the lane they drove slowly through Wensford, a village with council houses lining both sides. No shops. Tweed slowed to a crawl as they approached an old hump-backed

126

bridge. Inscribed in a brick pillar were the words LEY BRIDGE. He parked outside a dreary inn on the other side.

'I think we get out here and stroll around,' he said.

They crossed the empty road, clambered down to the towpath. Berthed to the bank was a brightly painted houseboat, a rope from its deck attached to a heavy rock on the bank. *Mary Lou*, its name, was painted on the bows. A wide heavy plank led from the bank to the deck. It was very quiet, no sound of traffic, only the desolate caw of rooks perched in a nearby tree. Paula didn't like the sound.

'I'll go and check the boat out,' said Tweed. 'You stay on guard here.'

'Excuse me,' Paula rapped, hands on her hips, her tone angry. 'I was under the illusion I was a member of the team. If you fall off the bloody plank I won't be rescuing you, *Mr Tweed*.'

'All right. We'll go aboard together,' he said after seeing her expression.

He crossed the plank and it hardly wobbled. Paula followed. He stood on the deck, studying it for footprints. He had put on his latex gloves and when Paula joined him he saw she already had hers on.

'I suppose we get inside through that door,' she said.

He walked up to the closed door at the front of the interior. When he pulled at the handle he couldn't shift it. Looking down he saw a thick wooden wedge jammed underneath it. He looked round the deck, saw a sturdy marlinspike shoved down inside a leather holder attached to the port side. Clasping it, he withdrew it, noticed immediately brownish stains. He said nothing as he carried it over to the wedge. It took five hard blows to dislodge the wedge.

'I'd like you to stay on deck,' he told Paula.

'Don't start that again,' she snapped.

Gritting his teeth, he hauled on the door handle. It came open easily. Immediately a noxious aroma he knew meant only one thing seeped out. He took out a handkerchief, wrapped it round his nose, pulled the rest of it lower. When he looked at Paula she had already masked her face. She was holding her powerful torch, extracted from her shoulder bag.

It was dark inside but he had the impression he was entering the main cabin. The smell was overpowering. Paula's torch illuminated an empty old leather couch located against the starboard side. She held the torch tightly, swivelled the beam to the other side. Another leather couch, this one occupied. A skeletal figure was stretched out, and on the deck beside it were small transparent bags containing discoloured blobs. Flesh. Scraped from the skeleton. Tweed was nearly choking with the odour. Paula pulled at his arm.

'Let's get out of here,' she said, voice muffled behind the handkerchief.

The cabin had been ransacked. Drawers had been pulled out, their contents scattered on the deck. Tweed swayed. Paula hauled at his arm. They headed for the outside deck.

On deck, Tweed slammed the door shut. He took a deep breath. Paula was walking quickly to the starboard side. He felt sure she was going to throw up. Then she stiffened, took off her gloves, threw them on the deck, grabbed a bottle of mineral water from her bag, tore off the cap and drank deeply. Then she handed the bottle to Tweed, who was beginning to feel queasy. He swallowed several large gulps and felt his stomach settling.

'We'll get back on the towpath,' Tweed said hoarsely.

'Watch your step on that plank.'

He walked backwards and forwards on the deck, stiffening his legs, then walked swiftly across the plank. She followed him as he watched her anxiously. They both sank into sitting positions on the towpath.

'Give me your mobile,' Tweed said. 'I'm calling Buchanan.'

She walked back and forth along the towpath while he made his detailed call, concluding by saying they'd wait at the inn opposite the houseboat side of the bridge. He gave her back the phone.

'He's coming. I warned him no screaming sirens or flashing lights in Wensford. We don't want an audience.'

'Shouldn't we go back and search? I think I saw something floating in the river on the other side.'

'No, we shouldn't. That's Buchanan's job.'

*   *   *

A woman with rosy cheeks and a pleasant smile opened the door of the inn. Tweed explained they hadn't eaten for hours. The woman told them lunch was finished, but tea started in an hour's time. Then she looked at them again.

'You do look hungry. What about bacon

sandwiches?'

'That will do fine,' Tweed said. 'We're grateful. Any chance of a pot of coffee and a jug of water?'

'That won't take long. I'll show you into the tearoom.'

It was at the back of the inn, a small room with tables laid for tea, toby jugs perched on a mantelpiece, net curtains masking the back garden. No one else was there.

'I'm not sure I can face bacon sandwiches,' Paula said.

'Then don't eat them. Drink water if you're in shock.'

'I am not in shock,' she protested. 'I've seen enough of these murders to feel they're almost a part of the landscape.'

The food appeared, and the woman left them alone, closing the door. Tweed picked up a bacon sandwich. As he'd hoped, Paula devoured hers. They were substantial and she felt much better.

'That has to be Jackson, poor soul,' she said.

'Subject to positive identification.'

'Where are we now?' she asked.

'In Wensford.'

'For God's sake, you know what I mean. That list in Michael's pocket. Are they all victims of this hideous murderer?'

'The woman's corpse found in the mine shaft on Dartmoor may be Lee Greystoke, wife of the finance director of Gantia. I found out last night during my dinner with Lucinda that she'd left him, supposedly, over three months ago. Marriage was breaking up. Lucinda identified that expensive ring with a diamond as a present Lee tried to give her. She refused to take it. Tell you why later.'

130

'And "Christine",' Paula reflected, 'we know is Christine Barton, forensic accountant. What about the male skeleton on Dartmoor?'

'No idea who he was. We'll have to find out.'

'And John Jackson,' she continued, 'is just across the road, I'm sure. That just leaves "Ken".'

'Looks like it,' Tweed agreed.

'And both Christine and Jackson are closely linked with Anne Barton,' she mused. 'Can't possibly be her. Not strong enough.'

'You can't assume that,' Tweed warned. 'While we were in her flat I watched her lifting a very heavy hard-backed chair to sit in. She whisked it up as though it weighed nothing.'

He stopped speaking as their hostess returned. He asked her the question as he paid the modest bill, leaving a generous tip.

'We came to see the chap who owns the houseboat on the river on the far side of the bridge. Did you ever see him?'

'No, we didn't. That's me and my husband. He used to leave his car in the car park in the village, then must have walked here. My husband saw lights on in the boat late at night. Haven't seen them for quite a long time.'

'Any idea how long since you last saw the lights?'

'Must be about three to four months ago ... Excuse me, there's the doorbell.'

'I think the police have arrived,' Paula commented.

'I think you're right. I heard vehicles pulling up.'

He stopped talking as the door opened and their hostess ushered Chief Superintendent Buchanan into the room. Hauling up a chair, he sat with them.

131

'I've brought a complete technical team. And an ambulance. We've had orders not to touch the body. Professor Saafeld's on his way here. You know what a stickler he is.'

'Someone should sweep the river on the starboard side,' Paula suggested. 'I saw something floating in the water, could be half an identification card.'

'The skeletal corpse may be a John Jackson, private investigator,' said Tweed.

'Jackson!' Buchanan looked appalled. 'He was a brilliant inspector at the Yard. I liked him. He would have gone far. He resigned against all protests from me. Fed up with the paperwork the government has showered us with. Said he'd sooner work on his own, helping people. I'd better get over there now.'

'We're just leaving. I've sent you a report on most of what we've discovered so far.'

'Thanks. I must go now.'

*   *   *

Tweed had driven Paula back only a short distance along the M3 back to London when a Rolls-Royce passed them going the other way. Saafeld tooted them twice.

'Buchanan and his team got there quickly,' Paula commented.

'Probably came down the motorway with sirens blaring and lights flashing at ninety miles an hour. Good job it wasn't rush hour.'

'Where to now?'

'Straight back to Park Crescent. Could be news, but I very much doubt that.'

132

In this assumption Tweed was wrong.

*   *   *

'I've checked up on Abel Gallagher's tough history,' Newman greeted him.

'Tough?'

Monica sat at her computer, burning the keyboard. Butler was on the floor playing with a hand grenade. Paula pulled a face. 'I hope that thing isn't live?'

'Of course it is,' he chaffed her.

Nield sat in the other chair, studying a map of London. He looked up as Tweed asked the question.

'I see you're back from Champton Place, Pete. How is Anne?'

'She's recovered surprisingly quickly. I got the impression she wasn't all that close to her sister, even felt she'd been a dominating influence. That slipped out while we were chatting, and she covered it up quickly.'

'I didn't get that impression myself.' Tweed sat behind his desk looking thoughtful. 'You were there much longer and she was probably glad of your company, so less guarded.'

'We did seem to get on well together,' Nield remarked.

'According to Pete,' mocked Butler, 'he only has to look at a woman and she swoons.'

'Remind me to punch your silly face,' Nield rapped back.

'If you've all finished,' Newman protested, 'I was going to tell you what I found out about Abel Gallagher. Not a nice person. At school he led a

133

gang which beat up other pupils. Later he joined the worst section of the army—he applied to become a military policeman, they accepted him. He had a very tough reputation when he became a quartermaster sergeant. Any squaddie he didn't like he'd find an excuse to put him in the stockade.'

'What's the stockade?' Paula asked.

'A fenced-off guarded area where the bad boys are sent. The training's tough, very. They're made to run back and forth for ages with heavy packs on their backs. Gallagher made his special choices keep running until they dropped. Some had to be put into hospital.'

'A sadist,' Paula commented.

'A notorious one. When he left the army he applied for a job at Medford's, the big security agency. He can grovel when it suits him. He joined Medford's, worked his way up by stabbing colleagues in the back. He can be cunning and play the gentleman when it suits him. Result? He gets the top job when his predecessor retires. Rumour has it he had political influence. That's our Abel. Oh, when he plays darts he uses knives to aim at the board instead of darts. I thought that said a lot about him.'

'A real charmer,' remarked Paula.

'He's also reputed to be dangerous to the ladies,' Newman concluded.

'Sounds as though he could be capable of anything,' Tweed decided. 'And he'd revel in cruelty.'

'So a suspect in our murder investigation,' Paula suggested. 'But what could be the motive?'

'Whether it's him or someone else,' Tweed reflected, 'I have an idea money is the motive.'

134

'There you go,' said Butler. 'We all know now he's up to his neck in a huge debt to a racing bookie.'

'The real problem,' Tweed warned, 'is to link up all the victims. Buchanan insists they're random killings by a psychotic. I think there's more to it. Maybe something very dangerous indeed.'

He looked at Monica, who had answered the phone and was waving madly. Tweed asked who it was without enthusiasm.

'A PA who says Drago Volkanian wants to speak to you now.'

*　　　*　　　*

The voice responding to Tweed's was booming without being domineering. A voice with a lot of character.

'Mr Tweed, we must meet urgently. At your convenience—would tomorrow afternoon suit you? In Jermyn Street.'

'I'd like a hint as to the subject.'

'Aha!' A rumbling laugh. 'I regard you, sir, as a man of rare and exceptional intelligence and insight. Also I never employ flattery, which I regard as hypocrisy. Heaven knows I have been subjected to a flood of that nonsense.' Another of his rumbling laughs. 'I heard your assistant call out my name. Could you please correct that, sir? I do not wish anyone to know I have called, that you are coming to see me.'

'I can deal with that easily,' Tweed said quickly.

'I am sure you can, sir. With your usual finesse. I would greatly appreciate it if you ensured that no one knows you are coming to visit me. The address

135

is 490 Jermyn Street, well past Floris, the ancient perfumier. So, would four p.m. tomorrow be convenient to you? If not we can—'

'That will be quite convenient,' Tweed interjected.

'My dear sir, your instant cooperation is a response which puts me in your debt. One more point—you can bring the rare Paula Grey with you. Indeed, you are fortunate to have the services of such a remarkable lady.' Another bellowing laugh. 'So, four p.m. tomorrow. I wish you my warmest regards. Guard your back, sir. We live in a dangerous world.'

The phone went dead before Tweed could reply. He sat gazing into space. It was a long time since he had heard a voice that radiated such power and courtesy.

*   *   *

Tweed had been pacing slowly round his office for over ten minutes by Paula's reckoning. Sometimes he paused to stare through the windows towards Regent's Park. Night had fallen, a gloomy evening with drizzle gleaming on the pavements. Commuters were hurrying, crouched under umbrellas as they prepared to face the ordeal of the journey home with few trains running, the street a solid mass of stationary buses and cars. Misery. Only Paula realized what was happening. Tweed was coming to a major decision.

The door opened and Marler strolled in, wearing a smart beige suit Paula had never seen before. 'Ummm,' she said aloud as he came and stood

136

close to her.

'For that,' he told her, 'I'll be taking you for dinner to the Savoy Grill.'

'Not yet you won't,' barked Tweed. 'You're the fifth interrogator I need.'

He walked swiftly to the front of his desk, leaned against it, surveyed his team. This is it, Paula thought. Tweed's voice was brisk, commanding.

'We are running out of time. As you know, the likelihood of locating this vicious killer fades with each day that passes. And Saafeld has confirmed the bodies discovered so far were murdered three to four months ago. Action this day is the order. Each of you will be given a key character to visit, to interrogate harshly. Use your SIS folders to gain entrance if anyone tries to keep you out. No pussyfooting this time. Newman, your target is Larry Voles, managing director of Gantia.'

'Have you already questioned him?' Newman wanted to know.

'No. You can be tough—whatever it takes. Monica's given each of you a copy of my report to Buchanan. You're well armed with data.'

'Can't wait to hear who I'm paying a visit to,' Paula said.

'You'll have to wait. I'm taking the targets in a certain sequence. Nield, you visit Lucinda Voles, put her under a lot of pressure.'

'If you don't mind,' Nield said quietly, 'I'll handle her in my own way when I meet her.'

'Anything, but get results,' Tweed snapped. 'Butler, you take on Anne Barton. I know you've met her but only briefly. Don't let her apparently demure temperament fool you.'

'I'll catch her out on some detail, you'll see.'

137

'Marler, your target is Abel Gallagher. He'll try to fend you off with his Special Branch position.'

'I'm rather afraid that won't impress me,' Marler drawled.

'Paula,' Tweed snapped, annoyed at her earlier interruption, 'you'll come with me tomorrow morning while I interrogate Aubrey Greystoke, finance director of Gantia,' he added for the benefit of everyone. 'And one discovery you don't reveal to anyone. I'm sure the woman's body found in the Dartmoor mine shaft is that of Lee, Greystoke's missing wife.'

'I'd sooner have my own target . . .' Paula began.

'There's one more aid for you all,' Tweed drove on, ignoring Paula's second attempt to intervene. 'As I said earlier, you all have a photocopy of my detailed report to Buchanan. But the amazing Professor Saafeld has provided me with a description of the probable age, height and weight of the skeletons he's examined. Monica will give you a photocopy of that report before you leave.'

Newman opened his mouth to ask 'when?' but Tweed guessed he was going to say that. He was behind his desk in a whirl, remained standing up.

'Why are you all still here? You've got an urgent job to do.'

*   *   *

After the scurry of people leaving, collecting from Monica a photocopy of Saafeld's report, Paula made up her mind to say what she thought. Tweed's whole posture and mood had changed. The swift movements, the tension, the grimness of his expression were transformed as he relaxed in his chair behind the desk.

'Permission to speak?' Paula asked sharply.

'Don't be silly. Come and talk to me. I always find your company soothing.'

She lifted the hard-backed chair opposite Tweed's side of the desk, carried it round, turned it at an angle and sat down facing him.

'Can I assume the targets chosen for interrogation include all the suspects?'

'Not necessarily. It's information I'm after. Quickly, too.'

'I'm not sure you've always chosen the right person to go out and meet these people. Is Harry right for Anne Barton?'

'Perfect. First, she's apparently reserved. Also I gathered she hasn't got much money. If that's true, Harry also comes from a poor background, plus the fact he's already met her. I think she might open out to him.'

'You know what,' she said ruefully, 'I think I'd better enrol in some psychology class.'

'You're the shrewdest woman I've ever known. So forget any classes, unless you want to lecture at them.'

'I'll keep quiet when we meet Greystoke tomorrow.'

'Not if you want to ask him a question, challenge him. He has a weakness for attractive women. Since his wife, Lee, disappeared—again, three to four months ago—he's been playing the field.'

'Could be a motive.'

'For murdering Lee, but what about all the others?'

'Sending Marler to roast Gallagher was smart. That brute's going to get the surprise of his life if

139

he tries it on with Marler. And Newman was a good choice for Larry, from what I've seen of him. On second thoughts I think you got it right. Sorry if I was aggressive.'

'Don't ever lose your aggression.'

An hour later the phone rang. It was Nield.

'How did you get on?' Tweed asked. 'You've been quick.'

'Because I didn't get on. Lucinda wouldn't let me in her flat. Said if you needed more information you'd better damn well come yourself. I couldn't shift her.'

'Don't worry. Where's your car parked?'

'In the underground garage below Lucinda's place. It's left open during the day. I'm there now.'

'Does she know your car? Have you any way of disguising yourself in case she comes down if you stay where you are?'

'A ridiculous pork-pie hat, pair of glasses with plain lenses, a yellow scarf. Why?'

'I'm coming over to see her myself. If she leaves I want you to follow her. You know Paula's number? Good. Stay there unless she comes out. That's it.'

He turned to Paula, who was holding out her phone for him. 'I'm going over to Lucinda's,' he said.

'Time you got your own phone,' she told him.

'Thanks. I'll see you later. You and Monica hold the fort.'

*   *   *

When Tweed drove down inside the underground garage most of the slots were empty. Didn't anyone else live here? Probably most were away at their

140

workplaces. He found Pete's blue Ford, checked the number plate to be sure. No sign of Pete. What had happened?

He parked, got out, approached the Ford cautiously. Pete had pushed back his driving seat. He was sprawled in it out of sight. The pork-pie hat *did* look ridiculous but, combined with the glasses and the scarf, he was hardly recognizable even to Tweed. He sat up, lowered the window.

'She hasn't come down so must still be up there. Alone, I'd imagine.'

'Hold tight. I'm going up.'

He entered the open elevator, pressed the button for the third floor, where it had stopped the time she had left him after the dinner at Santorini's. No, where *he* had left *her*.

The third-floor hall he stepped into was luxuriously furnished. Wall-to-wall carpet, mirrored walls, a Regency half-table against the wall outside her door. He caught sight of himself in a mirror, looked away. Never had liked seeing his reflection. He pressed the bell, the heavy door swung inward immediately, so swiftly he was startled. She stood in the doorway, waved him inside.

He immediately thought he'd made a mistake coming. Lucinda wore a white sweater and white trousers, a gold belt round her slim waist, a pair of gold slippers on her feet. She closed the door once he was inside and locked it.

'I'll take your coat,' she said in her soft voice, which Tweed found so appealing. 'And don't send a boy over again. You come yourself, whatever you want,' she went on with a slow smile. 'How about a brandy?'

'A glass of Chardonnay would be acceptable.'

'Coming up. That's your chair by the couch.'

Chair? He saw she had prepared the furniture for his visit. The seat of the chair was very long with a sloping back. It had been placed close to the wide couch. More like a bed. She was bringing the drinks when he tried to sit on the chair with his feet on the floor. Impossible. Placing the drinks on a table by his side, she slid on to the couch, her back alongside his, sloping against a large cushion. He handed her the brandy. They clinked glasses.

'Here's to us,' she said with a ravishing smile. 'We should do this more often.'

'Lucinda,' he began firmly, 'I've come to ask you questions concerning my murder investigation.'

'Time you relaxed. Good for that fertile brain of yours.'

'You knew Lee Greystoke quite well, I gather. Can you describe her? Height, weight, that sort of thing. Hair colour.'

'Don't like the sound of this. Well, here goes. Height five feet six, I'd say. Weight about eight stone. Hair a lovely brown.'

Tweed almost gulped on his Chardonnay. The statistics she'd given matched those suggested by Saafeld for the skeleton of the woman found down the mine shaft on Dartmoor. She pushed a lock of her blonde hair from her face, laid the hand on his lap.

'Why?' she asked.

'It's an exercise we're conducting about everyone concerned in any way in the case. For our records.'

'I hope Lee's OK,' she said slowly.

'Well, Aubrey should know about that. When did she do a moonlight flit on him?'

'Thought I'd told you that. Three to four months

142

ago. At a guess. She could have gone to the States. She had a woman friend in Richmond, Virginia.'

'What was her connection with Gantia?' he persisted.

'You're a beaver. You know that?' She used her index finger to stroke down the side of his face. 'Nice clean shave. For me? Lee's connection with Gantia? She was close to Drago. For some reason he liked and trusted her implicitly.'

'In what way?' Tweed asked.

'Apart from the main directors—myself, Michael, Larry and her not loved husband, Aubrey—Lee was the only other person who had a master key to the plant. She'd arrive in the middle of the night, tell the guard to stay at his post, then check the executive offices to make sure they were locked.'

'She'd hardly come at that hour just to do that.'

'I know. She'd stay awhile. Maybe she was searching her husband's office—looking for evidence of his numerous infidelities. That's a guess.'

'But what was she like? Her personality?'

'Lively. Highly intelligent. Maybe a bit nosy, but I liked her. Full of life.'

Not now, if I'm right, Tweed thought grimly. His expression must have changed briefly. Lucinda laid her hand on his sleeve. He waited.

'You look worried. You're here to enjoy yourself. I'm sure you don't get enough fun out of life.'

'I've never really thought about it.' He jumped up, checked his watch. 'You'll excuse me but I have to be going.'

Now, the look on her face was not pleasant. He wanted to get out of the room. He wanted to stay. But he had no intention of becoming involved with

143

someone, however attractive, who was on his list of suspects. He walked quickly towards the door, grabbed his overcoat, put it on swiftly, opened the door and walked into the hall, closing the door behind him.

*   *   *

He'd pressed the button and the elevator seemed to take forever to arrive. He was half expecting to hear the apartment door behind him open. Lucinda was a determined woman. The elevator doors opened and he stepped inside, jamming his finger on the button. With a sense of relief he felt it descending.

The doors opened and he was stepping into the underground garage. Pete was sitting in his parked car, staring at the elevator. He waved.

'Get what you wanted?' Nield asked him.

Tweed nodded, told Pete he was driving back to Park Crescent. Pete followed him out. Tweed was driving along Park Lane when a large brown Volvo with tinted windows cut straight in front of him. He swung out of its way but found he was heading for a pavement full of pedestrians.

Pure horror. A woman pushing a pushchair with a baby inside. Three teenage girls, transfixed. An elderly couple, gazing at him in terror. Tweed had a vision of bodies sprawled on the pavement. Blood everywhere. He swung his wheel way over to his right, signalling. He'd slam into the Volvo. He hoped.

The road ahead was clear. No Volvo. Honking of horns behind him. He proceeded at a sedate pace up Park Lane, searching for the Volvo. It had gone, lost inside another traffic crawl. He took a deep breath, glanced in his rear-view mirror. Pete Nield's vehicle was behind him. He headed back for Park Crescent.

*   *   *

'That was deliberate,' Nield growled as they walked to the entrance of the SIS building. 'Imagine the trial, the headlines. Your career would have been ruined. Someone doesn't like you.'

'Someone wants me out of the way,' Tweed mused calmly. 'I've triggered someone's worst fears. By what I've said or seen. The devil of it is I don't know what the trigger was.

'I must phone Lucinda,' Tweed continued as he entered the office.

'And you've just been with her for ages!' exclaimed Paula.

'One vital question I forgot to ask,' he told her as he picked up the phone.

'Tweed here, Lucinda.'

'Can't keep away from me?'

'I forgot to ask you where Lee Greystoke lives.' He just stopped himself saying 'lived'.

'She has a retreat of her own out in the country. Ready with a pen and pad? Address: Ivy Cottage, Boxton, Heel Lane. You take the A355 from Beaconsfield to Amersham. About halfway along on your right Heel Lane turns off. The cottage is very much on its own, very isolated. It's what Lee liked. Ivy Cottage is on the right.'

'Thank you. Incidentally, how's Michael?'

'According to Larry he's just the same. At eight in the morning, after breakfast, he walks down the

145

track to the village, turns round, comes back to the house, then straight up to his bedroom. He's reading a lot.'

'What sort of books?'

'No idea. I haven't been down to Abbey Grange recently. The whole business is weird. Don't understand it.'

'Amnesia's weird. I must go now.'

The phone rang the moment he'd ended the call. Monica said it was Newman on the line.

'How did you get on, Bob?'

'I didn't. First time I've been rebuffed. Larry has a grim assistant. Attractive but, after contacting Larry, she came back and said under no circumstances was he available. When I persisted she shut the door in my face.'

'Right. What's Larry's address?'

'Five Marlow Street. That's off Pall Mall. St James's Square side of the Mall.'

Tweed repeated the address, told Newman to come back. When he stood up swiftly Paula was fetching his overcoat, helping him on with it, then grabbing her own. Tweed looked at her.

'Five Marlow Street,' she said. 'Larry's address? Then I'm coming with you. He likes women.'

'How do you know that?' he asked as they hurried downstairs.

'Saw the look he gave me at Abbey Grange. Not the leering type, but he noticed me.'

As they drove to their destination it was getting dark again. Not because of the time of day, but because of a threatening overcast that was descending on London. Tweed found a space, parked, then walked swiftly back to Marlow Street. Larry's personal HQ had a heavy black door, a spy camera perched above it. Tweed pressed his thumb on the bell and kept it there.

A slim girl with an aggressive expression, smartly dressed in a black two-piece suit, opened the door and stood with her arms crossed, glaring.

'Do you have to keep pressing the bell? Once is—'

'I'm here to see Mr Larry Voles.' Tweed held his folder under her nose. 'We have an urgent appointment.'

'I don't think so.'

'Can't you read?' he growled. 'Left your glasses on your desk? When I arrive I have an appointment. Get moving—go and tell him. I've met him, for heaven's sake.'

'That doesn't mean—'

'Stop wasting my time or I'll arrest you for obstruction of the security services. We'll wait inside.'

'You can't—'

'Excuse me.' Gently but firmly he sidled past her with Paula in his wake. He closed the door, checked his watch openly. 'I said tell him we're here. I haven't got all day!'

She opened her mouth to say something, then closed it without uttering a word. By now she was worried, almost intimidated, as she scuttled off.

'You don't have to scare the girl stiff,' Paula said quietly.

'I'm in no mood to be road-blocked. I feel time is not on our side.'

The girl had knocked on a door, disappeared inside. It was Larry who came out, smiling at them. He wore a smart blue suit with a chalk stripe.

'Do come in,' he invited. 'And good to see you again, Paula.' He held out his hand, clasped hers,

147

but did not hang on the way some men did. His large office was well furnished without flaunting wealth. He hauled three leather chairs in front of his cedarwood desk, waved a hand for them to join him. He offered drinks. They both refused. Tweed also kept on his overcoat when Larry offered to take it. Paula was studying him as he sat in the circle of chairs, facing both of them.

His blue eyes looked at her briefly, conveyed interest without embarrassing her. His manner suggested a managing director who dealt with his staff politely but didn't hesitate to show a tougher side with inefficiency.

'How can I help you, Mr Tweed?' he asked with a smile.

'I gather you gave my senior assistant, Robert Newman, rather a rough ride. Hence my coming over myself.'

'That was my mistake, not Cherry's, my assistant. When I heard he was here I immediately thought a journalist, the press. Newman *is* famous as a reporter. When he'd gone I thought, Lord, that was someone on Tweed's staff. Do give him my apologies.' He smiled again. Paula noticed he smiled a lot. 'Now, how can I help you?'

'I'm a bit muddled about the relationship of the Voles family.'

No, you're not. It's a ploy, Paula thought.

'Well, Michael is my younger brother, as you know. Only a couple of years between us. He's still in the same worrying state. I whisk down there when I can to see how he is. Not a word so far. I find it unnerving. If I can't get down to Dartmoor I phone Mrs Brogan. Not that she's a lot of help, as you might imagine, having met her.' He smiled

148

again. 'Lucinda is my sister.'

'And do you know where Drago is now?'

'No idea. He could be in America, France, Sweden. You name it. I'm sending reports in code to a postal address in New Orleans. Doesn't mean he's there. Simply that he *has* been there. Then he turns up out of the blue without warning. He's a character.'

'What does that mean?'

Larry laughed. He waved both hands in a circular motion.

'He's everything we'd all like to be. I can't describe such a fabulous character. You'd have to meet him to understand—that is if you ever do.'

'A personal question, Mr Voles . . .'

'Larry, please.'

'Here goes, then. A personal question. Are you married?'

'Wonderfully so. That was my lucky day when I met Evelyn ten years ago. She's very much a member of the family but doesn't mix with them a lot. We also have a penthouse flat in the same building as Lucinda. One floor above her.'

'Really. So Evelyn maybe has Lucinda as a friend? Living in such close proximity.'

'I suppose you could say that.' Larry rubbed a hand over his chin as though deciding how much more to say. 'On the rare occasions when they meet they are ultra-polite to each other.'

'Which means,' Paula suggested quietly, 'they tolerate each other when they do meet but are not on the same wavelength.'

Larry leaned forward, patted Paula's hand perched on an arm of her chair, withdrew his hand quickly. 'It takes a woman to detect female relationships. I couldn't have put it so well. These things happen in the best—and the worst—of families. Lucinda is a very independent lady. Goes to a gym regularly. Among other delights she boxes with the instructor. Once knocked him out. A fiercely efficient lady, our Lucinda.'

'Fierce?'

'She's a tigress. I wouldn't like to take her on—physically, I mean.'

'Larry,' said Tweed, standing up, 'I appreciate the time you've given us. You've been more useful than you perhaps realize.'

As they crawled through the West End towards the City, Paula locked her shoulder bag with the special device invented by the boffins in the basement at Park Crescent. Tweed had told her the final interview for that day was with Greystoke, finance director at Gantia. He used Paula's mobile to check Aubrey was in the building known as the Tower. She guessed the security would be strict.

Tweed kept glancing in his rear-view mirror to see if they were being followed. Paula asked him why he was worried.

'Just a precaution.'

He hadn't told her about the brown Volvo incident in Park Lane. He didn't want to recall an incident that had terrified him. The traffic was a solid wedge at times. They weren't crawling; they were stationary. It was in such a situation that a Jaguar was stopped behind them. The driver jumped out. Marler. He ran along to Tweed's open window, kept his voice down.

'Crisis. Marin wants us to travel to Marseilles tomorrow. We go Eurostar, transfer to the TGV.

I'll need a couple of hours in Paris on my own. Weapons. In late afternoon we're at Waterloo.'

Then he was gone.

'Marseilles, here we come,' Paula said enthusiastically.

'You may change your mood,' said Tweed. 'Marseilles is the most dangerous city in Europe.'

16

Eventually they reached the Tower. Paula stared out, pressing her face close to the window. The Tower was so tall, shaped like a torpedo, the cone at its summit. As Tweed parked the car at the foot of the escalator leading up to the monster's entrance, a warden appeared.

'Can't park that here.'

'Can't you read, man?' Tweed demanded, holding up his identification folder.

'Oh, well, I suppose you have the authority, sir.'

'I damned well *know* I have.'

Tweed hated the pompous manner adopted by certain lowly officials. At the top of the escalator his folder took them past a guard armed with an automatic weapon. Inside, a severe-looking girl behind a counter stared unpleasantly at Paula.

'You can't take that bag into this building.'

'So why don't you keep it for me?' Paula said, perching her bag on the counter.

'It's locked,' the girl in uniform snapped. 'I have to see inside. It could be a bomb.'

'I've been holding my folder for you to look at. Look at it and tell us where we'll find Aubrey

151

Greystoke.'

'You might have shown me that before,' the girl griped after looking carefully at the folder.

'I've been holding it up for you to look at ever since we walked into this architectural monstrosity. I want my bag locked away in one of those steel cupboards behind you. I will also need a receipt.'

'Mr Greystoke is in Room 750. Seventh floor. Take that second elevator over there. Welcome to the Tower. It's had an architectural award.'

It took them only five minutes to wait for the elevator in the much-vaunted twenty-first-century Tower. Room 750 was opposite the doors when the elevator reached the seventh. Impatiently, Tweed pressed the bell. The door opened and a smartly dressed girl with a nice smile stood there.

'What can I do for you? My appointments book doesn't register visitors.' Another smile. 'Maybe my system is breaking down.'

'My name is Tweed.' He showed her the folder. 'Nothing's wrong with your system but I urgently need to see Mr Greystoke. We have met.'

'Oh, Lord,' she said, staring at his folder. 'Mr Greystoke has left the building ten minutes ago for a business dinner. I'll tell him you called.'

'I wouldn't bother,' Tweed replied, smiling. 'When I can I'll phone him. May not be for a while.'

As they drove back, creeping through the gridlock, Paula asked her question as they sat, going nowhere.

'What did you think of Larry?'

'Apart from Greystoke, I think I now have a picture of the Voles family.'

'And that's important?'

'I'm convinced that, eventually, we'll find the solution to these dreadful murders near Abbey Grange. Which is why every scrap of information I can obtain about them—and their relationships—is the key to the massacre.'

'Well, we do have the interview with Drago Volkanian. It should be interesting.'

'Except from all accounts he's a past master at revealing only what he wishes to. The vital question I'm going to ask is the location of his armaments works.'

'You think that's really important?'

'It is probably the real key to what's going on. We'd best spend the rest of the day preparing for the trip to Marseilles.'

'I can't wait.'

'You may well wish you had done when we get there.'

*　　　*　　　*

Marler was waiting for them when they arrived back at Park Crescent. So was everyone else. Marler lit a cigarette.

'I've been educating the team as to what faces us. And we must all go. We'll need every man, according to Marin.'

'What did he say?' Tweed asked calmly.

'I'll start again,' Marler said quietly. 'The freighter we want to check out—coming from Angora—arrives at the Ile des Oiseaux in two days' time.'

'Can't we fly there?' asked Paula.

'Do you mind?' Marler snapped. 'We don't fly because the French Secret Service is photographing

153

all arrivals at both Charles de Gaulle and Orly airports. The top man would certainly spot Tweed when he checked the photos. So it has to be Eurostar. I need two hours in Paris to purchase weapons—for everyone. Then we board the TGV for Marseilles. I've booked rooms for us at a hotel overlooking the Vieux Port.'

'I stayed there once,' Tweed interjected. 'There used to be a good one along the promenade.'

'Marin told me the Vieux Port place,' Marler said firmly. 'That's where he hires a boat to take us out to the Ile. A boat with a powerful engine which can really move.'

'Sounds delightful,' said Tweed, who hated the sea.

'Marin says the Ile may be quiet, but he doubts it. We have to identify the freighter they're using, then race back to the Vieux Port and from there to the station. We catch the TGV back to Paris, then Eurostar to home.' He paused. 'It was emphasized by Marin that on the Ile we may well run into the worst thugs in the world. Algerians and Moroccans. If so, we take no prisoners. They won't.'

'Just my cup of tea,' Harry said.

Tweed turned to Newman. 'Bob, you'll stay here to look after the shop. I need someone with strong character and authority. We may find Gallagher comes crashing in again. You've sorted him out before.' He saw Newman's expression. 'Bob, what I've just said is an order.'

'They said Gallagher was out when I called,' Marler remarked. He looked at Paula. Before he could open his mouth she jumped up, grasped him round the neck with both hands, her face close to his.

'Whatever you were going to say, don't. Unless you want me to throttle you. I'm going to Marseilles.'

17

The interview that afternoon with Drago Volkanian was one of the most unusual Tweed had ever experienced. With Paula he arrived at 490 Jermyn Street and rang the strange square-shaped bell.

'I've wanted to meet Volkanian ever since I heard he existed,' he told Paula as they waited. 'His invisible presence hangs over this case like a giant cloud.'

The door opened and Paula gazed at one of the most imposing men she had ever encountered. Over six feet tall, he had very broad shoulders, a large regal head and white hair. His face had a dominant cast, his nose long and beaked, the eyes above green, darting swiftly. Clean-shaven, he had a wide mouth, the jaw below expressing willpower.

'Welcome to both of you. Please do come inside. You are so punctual. I do, sir, approve of punctuality.' Volkanian held out an outsize hand. 'Miss Grey, so kind of you to come. Mr Tweed, sir, you are someone I have looked forward so much to meeting.' His hand clasp was a strong grip. 'We will repair to my study.' He had closed the door, turning two wall switches.

As they entered his study off the hall, its walls furnished with hanging Persian rugs, they were in a different world. The spacious study was furnished with English antiques, carefully placed against the walls. It was the finest collection Paula had ever seen.

'May I make a comment on security?' Tweed enquired as an attractive girl with Eastern features took their coats with a glowing smile.

'Of course you may, sir,' Volkanian rumbled in his deep voice. He chuckled. 'After all, you are the expert on such matters.'

'You kindly came to the door yourself. London is these days a dangerous place. I could have been anyone.'

'Aha!' Another chuckle. 'I appreciate your concern for my safety but you omitted to look up. There is a mirror above the front door with a hundred and eighty degree sweep. It allows me to see who is calling—and whether someone hostile lurks in the vicinity. Now, what can I provide you with in the way of a stimulant? I shall be sipping an excellent Scotch whisky. Or would you prefer coffee or something else? Sasha,' he said, gesturing towards the girl with the glowing smile, 'will bring you anything you fancy.'

'I think,' Tweed said to Paula's surprise, 'I could also do with a Scotch.'

'So will I,' Paula decided as their host turned to her with an open hand.

Volkanian escorted them to a circle of comfortable chairs, waited until they were seated, then lowered his bulk into a large chair he could just fit into. When the drinks arrived Volkanian raised his glass, smiling.

'Devastation to our enemies.'

'I'll drink to that,' said Tweed.

'Miss Grey, you live in a pleasant first-floor flat in

a cul-de-sac off the Fulham Road,' Volkanian remarked. 'But maybe it would be safer to send it to Park Crescent? Yes, I think so.'

He seems to know everything about us, Paula thought.

Paula resisted the temptation to ask what 'it' might be. She was curious, but it would be bad manners to enquire. Tweed was speaking.

'Mr Volkanian . . .' he began.

'I would be honoured if you would both call me Drago. Miss Grey, may I be so bold as to call you Paula?'

'Please do.'

Paula was thrown off balance. She had never been in the presence of a man with such a powerful personality. His aura seemed to fill the room with warmth but without any hint of aggression. He wore a grey two-piece suit, the jacket unbuttoned over his ample stomach. A regimental tie splayed down over a crisp-collared blue shirt. She felt sure at some time he'd had an association with a regiment. He was not a man to wear such a tie unless entitled to do so.

'Drago,' Tweed had begun, 'it would be helpful to me if I knew the location of your armaments plant.'

Drago roared with laughter, his whole body wobbling. He took out a handkerchief to wipe his eyes. He chuckled again.

'You are a man after my own heart, sir. You go straight for the jugular. That is a secret I cannot reveal to you, sir. Only five people—apart from myself—know its location.'

'Michael, Larry and Lucinda,' Tweed said quickly. 'Also Aubrey Greystoke. The fifth I don't know. I'm guessing.'

157

Drago let out another burst of laughter, looked at Paula. 'Your chief is a very shrewd man.' His expression became serious. 'At the moment I understand we must forget Michael. His amnesia distresses me. I will tell you one thing about the armaments plant, Tweed. At one time it produced both missiles and shells for artillery pieces, for the MoD. The design was my own. I was once an engineer. So you simply turn a lever and the machinery switches from making artillery shells to missiles. Then I saw a film of the impact made by missiles. Supposedly totally accurate. They are not. In this film a missile aimed at a military HQ missed and hit a schoolhouse full of children instead. I banned the production of missiles immediately. At least artillery is aimed at the enemy's own guns. That I can live with. I assume everything at this so entertaining meeting is off the record.'

'Completely,' Tweed said emphatically. 'And you can trust Paula as much as you can trust me.'

'I know that.' Drago chuckled again, sipped his whisky. 'I would not have her here otherwise.'

'You seem to know a great deal,' Paula ventured.

'My dear.' He leaned towards her. 'Information is more valuable than gold.'

'Something I have always remembered.'

'Tweed,' Drago said suddenly, his eyes still. 'Have you yet a suspect for these four frightful murders?'

'Four?'

'Oh come, sir, do not underestimate me. I refer to the late Christine Barton, brilliant forensic accountant; poor Lee Greystoke, her skeleton found by yourself in the mine shaft on Dartmoor; John Jackson, the detective Christine's sister,

Anne, employed. The fourth victim is the male skeleton on Dartmoor—so far as I know still to be identified.'

'If you find the suspect yourself you might let me know,' Tweed joked to lighten the atmosphere. 'And now I think the fifth person who knew the location of the armaments plant was Lee Greystoke.'

A rumbling burst of laughter, Drago's body shaking with amusement. 'Glory, sir, no wonder you have such a reputation as a detective. Yes, the fifth was Lee. I miss her dreadfully. So who is your suspect?'

'If I had one I'd tell you.' Tweed swallowed the rest of his drink. 'I feel we have taken up enough of your time. That time you've given us is appreciated.'

'Please wait a little longer. Give me your opinion of Larry.'

'Very competent, likable, excellent with staff.'

'And now Lucinda.' Drago was leaning forward again.

'Extremely competent. Just the person for her job. Tough with staff if someone doesn't do their job properly.'

'Michael?'

'He has never said a word. How can I tell?'

'*I witnessed murder.*' Why, Paula mused again, was Tweed keeping these three vital words to himself? He had quoted them to no one after hearing them from Buchanan. Tweed was walking towards the door into the hall when he asked Drago the question.

'It makes sense to me that the five people who know—or knew—the location of the armaments plant would have keys to enter the plant. Including Lee.'

'Your clever deduction is correct. There is one more element which might help you. They all have Armenian blood in their veins. Armenians have survived down the centuries by their instinctive deviousness. You cannot always trust someone who has Armenian blood to tell the truth.'

'With the exception of yourself,' Tweed said politely, 'I think everyone has been lying to me over one thing or another.'

'You are on your guard, then. You are a wise man, my friend. I am sure we will meet again.' Drago gave Tweed a card. 'If you wish to communicate with me call that number, give your name. There will be a delay, then you will be transferred to another line.'

They were in the hall. Paula noticed Sasha was near the front door. She slapped shut a lid against the wall. Drago took hold of Paula's arm. 'I saw you admiring the wall rugs. Which most caught your attention?'

'This one. The design is so brilliant. Quite unique.'

Sasha lifted the lid when they reached the closed front door. On a screen was a clear view of Jermyn Street, probably fifty yards in each direction. She turned to Drago.

'I have been watching Mr Tweed's car. No one has been anywhere near it. The car is safe.'

'That was very thoughtful of you,' Tweed told her. 'I'm most grateful.'

Drago operated the two switches to unlock the door, opened it, shook their hands and closed the door as they stepped into the street.

160

18

The following afternoon they were in France, aboard the TGV as it thundered south like a Concorde flying on land. Their first-class coach was empty except for the two of them—Tweed seated next to Paula.

It was now March and a brilliantly sunny day. Paula gazed out of the window at a distant straight line of poplar trees, like a cavalcade of giant bristle brooms. Too early for any leaves. She guessed they bordered an autoroute—she had caught an occasional glimpse of cars moving at breakneck speed. By her side Tweed sat very still, taking no notice of the view. Outside the entrance to their coach Marler stood on guard. At the far end Nield was performing the same duty, also out of sight.

'You're brooding,' Paula said to Tweed eventually.

'Churning over all we've seen, all the people we've met. I know I'm missing something. Had a weird dream. Church bells clanging in my head. The vicar, the Reverend Stenhouse Darkfield, was advancing on me, holding a large knife, sharp edge on one side of the blade, serrated edge on the other. Then I woke up, couldn't sleep again. One of those things.'

'Dreams can be significant—recalling something you didn't observe at the time. You think he's a suspect? There is the cult business.'

'Forget it. You think a cult would extend from Dartmoor to Champton Place?'

'That's where Anne Barton lives. You're thinking

161

of Christine, her sister.'

'Of course. I must be tired. You think a cult would extend to Wensford, where Jackson, the detective, was cut to ribbons? Pretty unlikely.'

'We still haven't identified the skeleton we found on the moor—covered in snow. I think that's important.'

'I agree,' said Tweed. 'Could be the key we're looking for. Don't ask me how we're going to identify him. But it's a priority when we get back. And Keith Kent is taking a devil of a long time checking those sheets of figures you found Christine had hidden under that drawer. Her coding of the data must be complex. Understood only by whoever hired her.'

'Any idea who that could be?'

'None at all.' The racing express was now going so fast that the view from the window was a blur. It heeled to the right as it swayed round a long curve. 'This thing is going to end up off the line,' Tweed grumbled.

'Don't say things like that. Makes me nervous. You had a good lunch in the restaurant car. Try to get some sleep.'

She had just spoken when a uniformed official appeared. He had a large leather satchel slung over his shoulder. Dipping his hand inside the satchel he grunted the word.

'*Billets* . . .'

The hand came out of the satchel holding a large knife. He aimed it at Tweed's chest. A pistol butt descended with force on the man's head. The gun was held by Marler, who had arrived silently. The fake ticket collector began to sag. At the other end of the coach Nield appeared. Marler used his head to gesture for Nield to hurry. His two hands had grabbed the slumping body by the armpits.

Nield, wearing a latex glove, picked up the knife. Marler was hauling the body backwards towards the rear entrance. Nield shoved the knife inside his belt, crouched to lift up the legs. They disappeared rapidly.

Paula was in a state of shock. Her right hand gripped the .32 Browning inside her shoulder bag. She released her grip, her hand shaking. She stiffened it. She felt she should have seen what was happening, should have protected Tweed.

'I really f— that up. I'm so sorry. It was so quick. No excuse for me. And I'm wide awake . . .'

Tweed realized she was in shock—she hardly ever used that expletive. He grasped her arm, squeezed it.

'Don't talk rubbish,' he reassured her. 'I was in the aisle seat, you were by the window. I should have seen him. You're too far back. So don't give me any more twaddle. Relax.'

He looked up as Marler reappeared. Butler was alongside him. Marler drifted into the middle of the coach, took a seat facing them. Butler was carrying a violin case.

'What happened to the assassin?' Tweed asked quietly. 'Did you kill him?'

'Of course not. He's in the loo next to the exit door. Nield used a tool to turn the slide to *occupé*. I checked his pulse. Ticking over nicely. He's soused with cognac.'

'Really?'

'When we get to the next stop,' Marler explained, 'two of us will be standing by the doors, holding up the drunk. Just before the automatic doors close we'll heave him down on to the platform. A cognac-soaked drunk will be found after the train's gone.'

'Neat.'

'The bad news is they know we're on this train.'

'So?'

'We can expect a reception committee soon after leaving the *gare* at Marseilles.'

'And Harry is going to make them swoon by playing on his violin?' suggested Paula, who had completely recovered.

Harry lifted the case, held it past Tweed so Paula could see inside. He lifted the lid. She stared in disbelief at the violin resting on a velvet cloth, then looked at him.

'I'm not at my best this morning, but I can't see that's going to help if we have hostiles meeting us outside the station.'

'Lift the velvet cloth.'

She peeled it back slowly. Underneath rested a Sten gun and a number of spare magazines. She glanced at Marler, who was standing holding a golf bag. She wondered what that contained. At the two-hour switch in Paris from Gare du Nord, after leaving Eurostar, Tweed had taken her in a cab to the Gare de Lyon. They had spent their time waiting for the rest of the team drinking café crème in the station buffet. Plenty of time, she now realized, for Marler to have visited his contact. Which was why he'd handed her a .32 Browning now tucked inside the shoulder bag, and a Beretta, concealed inside the holster strapped to her lower right leg.

'That false ticket inspector,' Tweed enquired. 'Any ideas?'

'My guess,' said Marler, 'is he caught the real collector back at the *gare*. Knifed him probably —for silence. Stripped him of his clothes, gear, including the satchel and ticket machine. Got rid of his identity papers. Having seen you board the TGV, gets on board himself at the last moment. I was waiting for something like that.'

'Why?' asked Paula.

'Because someone on a motorbike followed us from Park Crescent to Waterloo.' His expression became serious. 'Marin warned me how to handle our arrival in Marseilles. There's a second-class coach a little way behind us. Arriving at Marseilles, we hurry back into that.'

'Why?' asked Paula, again.

'So we mingle with other passengers when we get off. Tweed, with Paula you get into the back seat of a yellow Citroën waiting outside. The first one. There'll be a second vehicle, same make, same colour, a little way back. I'll get into that one with Pete and Harry. Marin will be driving your cab. Both vehicles have been fitted with very tough rams.'

'What are they for?' Paula persisted.

'If there's trouble driving us to the hotel, you'll see why.'

Marler left them, followed by Harry. Nield moved back to his earlier position beyond the entrance to the coach. All this tension, she was thinking, on such a glorious day. Gazing out of the window, she saw endless grids of vineyards spreading up the sloping fields. She thought they were already beginning to sprout under the blinding rays of the glowing sun.

Her mind wandered. Why had Tweed had that dream of the clanging bells they'd heard in the

165

Dartmoor tower near the church? Then the vicar, Stenhouse Darkfield, advancing on him with a knife. She'd thought the vicar a sinister man from the moment she'd clapped eyes on him. She glanced at Tweed, who appeared to be enjoying a doze. The TGV began slowing down.

White-walled houses and factory plants appeared, hemming in the rail track on both sides. Poor properties with grubby walls. The usual approach to any major terminus. Tweed was awake as Marler appeared, and waved to Pete.

'Time to get moving.'

He hauled their luggage down from the rack, including a large flat case of his own. Paula wondered what was inside that. She decided she'd asked too many questions already.

'I'll lead the way,' Marler instructed. 'Shuffle along—no hurrying.'

They were approaching the coach with quite a few passengers when the platform began to slide past. Tweed grunted.

'Here we are,' he said. 'Marseilles. Cesspit of Europe.'

*　　　*　　　*

The express stopped smoothly. Paula stretched her legs, stiff from sitting so long. The automatic doors opened. Passengers began alighting. A mix of businessmen, poorly dressed women with scarves over their heads. It was a different atmosphere from bustling Paris, a hint of brutality. She forgot the steep step down and nearly fell. Marler steadied her. He smiled. 'On the Continent they built the train steps for giants.'

166

He kept hold of her, guiding her away from the passenger exit as Tweed followed with Harry and Pete bringing up the rear. Paula glanced along the platform in both directions. It seemed to go on for ever. Marler had reached a pair of double doors. They were closed. He lifted the handle on one of them, pushed it open.

'You can't go out that way,' a small portly uniformed official screamed at them in French. 'That's for luggage.'

'Police,' Marler snarled back at him in French. 'Keep your voice down. This is a police operation. Shut your stupid trap or I'll have you demoted.'

Paula's French was good enough to understand every word. The rail official opened his mouth, then closed it like a fish. He had been thoroughly intimidated by Marler's outburst. Paula walked quickly out on to a pavement and saw a yellow Citroën parked opposite. The driver, an Arab, waved to her to hurry. Carrying her small suitcase—she had foreseen they were unlikely to be dining in a top restaurant—she crossed the street into the blinding sun.

'Is this right?' she whispered to Marler, carrying the strange flat case in one hand, another case in the other, golf bag slung over his shoulder.

'Yes, get in the back.'

She caught a glimpse of massive rams attached to the front and rear of the car. The heat beat down on her. Settling herself inside, she rested her case on her lap and looked through the rear window as Tweed joined her. Marler had jumped into the second Citroën behind the wheel of the car with Harry beside him and Pete clambered into the back.

167

'Get ready for a rough ride, Paula,' the driver told her with a smile and in perfect English.

'I thought you were an Arab,' Paula said, astonished.

'That's the idea.' The driver smiled again as he started the engine. 'I've been out here long enough to get brown as the genuine article. That, plus the clothes, helps me to merge into the scenery. I also speak fluent Arabic.'

'This,' Tweed said, 'is Philip Cardon. I knew all along that he and Marin were one and the same. Used to work for me. And he was good at his work. Second to none. Then he experienced a grim tragedy.'

'My dear wife died,' Cardon explained as he watched through his rear-view mirror to check that the second Citroën crew were ready. 'Long time ago,' he said casually. 'I still have bad days. Her birthday, our wedding anniversary, the day she died.' His voice changed, became urgent. 'Got your seat belts fastened? I may be going at speed and then stop very abruptly.'

He drove off at a moderate pace. Paula peered out of the window. So far she wasn't impressed with Marseilles: a lot of shops on ground floors of shabby two-storey white buildings. Kids ripping off tyres from parked cars, already little more than battered wrecks.

'Main street coming up,' Cardon informed them. 'Hardly the Champs-Élysées.'

It wasn't, Paula thought. Litter was scattered everywhere. The shops were cluttered with junk. Cardon nodded his head to both sides.

'See that travel agent on the left, the currency-exchange outfit opposite? An American tourist

168

wanted to change a load of dollars for euros and went to the travel agent. Owner said he never kept cash on the premises—too dangerous. Pointed out the exchange just yards opposite. Warned him to be damn careful. The American starts to walk to the exchange, is knifed in the back, wallet taken, rushed to hospital. DOA. Marseilles.'

'Charming,' Paula commented.

'We're near your hotel. A quarter of a mile. To hell with kilometres. Hold tight! Here we go.'

Paula looked back. A black Renault with tinted windows was on their tail. No sign of the other Citroën. Cardon rammed his foot down. They shot forward like a racing car at Le Mans. Paula braced herself, gripping the door handle, but couldn't resist looking back. The Renault was also moving at high speed. She caught a glimpse of the second Citroën coming up behind it.

'*Now!*' Cardon shouted.

He braked suddenly. The Renault rushed into the ram at the rear of Cardon's car. Behind it the second Citroën slammed its ram into the rear of the now stationary Renault, which concertinaed between the two Citroëns. Hurled forward, Paula was saved by the seat belt, as was Tweed. She looked back again. Compressed by the two rams at top speed, the Renault was hardly recognizable, looked much smaller. Its windscreen was shattered. No sign of movement. Marler reversed a few feet, jumped out, peered inside the squashed vehicle, ran to Tweed, who had lowered his window. Marler talked across him to Philip Cardon.

'They're all dead. Automatic weapons scattered over the inside. We move on?'

'We do.'

Cardon revved up. Paula heard the crunch of the Citroën's ram, tearing itself from the Renault's radiator, then they turned a corner and Tweed saw the Vieux Port for the second time in his life.

*　　　*　　　*

The ancient oyster-shaped port was crammed with pleasure craft—small powerboats, big jobs, yachts and smaller craft. Tweed stared in disbelief.

'Where are the fishing vessels? From my hotel window I used to watch them sailing out at all hours to catch the fish.'

'Not here any more,' Cardon explained. 'They have to use another harbour these days. Vieux Port is strictly for rich men's pleasure craft. Some expensive stuff down there.'

A short distance further on he swung the car up a curving drive, stopped at the entrance to the hotel above the harbour.

'Won't that smashed-up Renault cause the police to come looking for us?' Tweed wondered.

'No way.' Cardon grinned. 'They find four Arabs inside the wreck, assume it was the result of gang warfare. They'll just want to haul it out of the once famous Canebière.'

'Once famous?' Paula asked.

'Years ago the Canebière was a street of expensive shops. Parisian women with money went there to buy the best. Like Marseilles, it's deteriorated into a filthy slum.'

Tweed managed to get the same room he had once occupied on his earlier visit years before. He was staring down out of the window when Paula tapped on his door and he called out for her to come in. She joined him.

'This place isn't the Ritz but I guess it will do. You look nostalgic,' she remarked.

'I should have foreseen this. Everything changes, not always for the better. When I was last here I used to love watching the fishing craft coming in, moving out—often in the late evening. It was beautiful. Now they've ruined it. Look at those boring horrors. They weren't here then.'

He pointed across the harbour to the mainland, where large ugly office and apartment blocks stood shoulder to shoulder. It could have been anywhere. 'Progress' had advanced with leaps and bounds.

'I wonder why Cardon chose this place,' Paula mused.

'Marler said he was insistent we should stay here.'

He paused as someone knocked on the door, which Paula had locked when she came in. Holding his Walther automatic by his side, Tweed went to the door, asked who it was, then unlocked the door and Philip Cardon walked in. Paula stared in surprise. Cardon was now clad in a smart cream suit with open-necked shirt.

'What happened to your Arab outfit?' Paula asked. 'You really look something.'

'After I'd dropped you here I drove to a quiet nearby alley, stripped off the clothes I was wearing, put on this gear. Not the thing to walk into this place like an Arab. Asked the nosy girl on reception for your room numbers. She was stubborn until I showed her my fake DST card —French counterespionage—then told her France hoped to conclude profitable commercial deals with you. I hauled the register round, found where

171

you all are. I noticed Marler is in the adjoining room on that side, with Nield adjoining you on the other side. Good strategy.'

'Why do we need to be in this hotel?' Paula asked.

'I remember you always asked the key question.' He grinned at her. 'See that second landing stage from here? Now count three boats from the shore.'

'Got it.'

'That's a pretty powerful motor launch,' Tweed observed.

'The suspect freighter calls at the Ile des Oiseaux tomorrow. We'll be there to see what it's up to.'

'Why suspect?' Tweed asked.

'Sailed from Algiers named the *Bougie*. Somewhere at sea the name changed to *Oran*. Plus it's carrying too large a crew for a fifteen-thousand-ton freighter. A very rough crew—some without sailing experience.'

'So in the morning we sail in that boat down there to the island?' Tweed asked.

'In a word, yes. Now, if it's OK, I can drive you to somewhere from which you get a clear view of the island.'

*   *   *

They drove in a different Citroën from the version with the rams. As Cardon moved carefully out of the entrance a young Arab jumped in front of the car, waving a dirty squeegee on the end of a stick. Cardon leaned out of the window.

'*Yallah!*' he shouted, throwing a crumpled piece of paper a long distance.

'What does that mean?' Paula wanted to know.

172

'Shove off—not so politely. I threw a crumpled euro note. That got him away from us—so he couldn't smear our rear window with that filthy squeegee.'

'Well, I suppose the poor little devil got something,' Paula replied.

'Listen,' Cardon told her, 'these days never go east or south of Suez. To Asia or Africa. Unless it's *South* Africa.'

'I agree,' Marler called out. 'Cut your throat for tuppence—and steal your clothes.'

'Terrorists?' asked Paula.

'Not necessarily,' called out Butler, seated with Marler. 'A white face means loot.'

They were driving away from Marseilles along a wide promenade, calm glittering blue sea on their right, a white rocky wall on their left. Cardon pointed upwards above the rock wall.

'That's where we're going. See that church? Notre-Dame de la Garde. Tremendous view from a platform in front of it.'

Peering up, Paula saw, perched very high, an ancient edifice which looked large enough to be a cathedral. Cardon swung the wheel, began driving up a steep winding road, which caused the vehicle to bump about as he kept his foot down.

Suddenly they were at the summit. Paula changed her mind about Marseilles as she climbed out. Inland, a bare few miles away, an immense limestone ridge curved round for ever. Awe-inspiring, it was like the world's greatest amphitheatre. She let out her breath. Cardon waited while she gazed at it, then led the way past the ancient Notre-Dame on to the vast flat platform stretching out in the direction of the sea.

Arriving at the thigh-high wall, she gazed down the drop to the promenade road far below. Then she stared at the vast sweep of the Mediterranean—a turquoise blue sheet with, at intervals, a white streak of surf. The colour, the immensity of the sea, fascinated her. She stood still, taking in its vastness so she'd be able to recall it later. Cardon, next to Tweed, was pointing as he held binoculars.

'There are the islands. See that one with the sun reflecting off something? That's the well-known Château d'If, the core of Alexandre Dumas's famous novel *The Count of Monte Cristo*.' He had given the binoculars to Tweed, who was focusing on the island, a great chunk of limestone rock rising out of the sea.

'Got it? Good,' Cardon said. 'Hold the lenses on it. Now move slowly to the right, a bit further out. You're looking for a triangular-shaped island with steep limestone cliffs.'

'I'm there.'

'Well, that's where we're going today when I get a signal to tell me the *Oran* has docked.'

'Docked?'

'There's a small harbour on the far side of the island you can't see from here. But we land on this side. At one point only there's a narrow gulch leading up to the summit.'

'Think I've got it. Doesn't look more than a crevice in the rock.'

'That's where we climb up to the top, get a good view of the harbour—the top of the island slopes down to it. I should warn you we may walk into a firefight. They have tough Arab guards and automatic weapons. Let's hope the arrival of the

174

Oran attracts them all to the west side.'

Paula was thrilled when Tweed handed her the binoculars. It took her no time at all to view Ile des Oiseaux in her lenses. She studied the gulch carefully. Steep, but here and there were massive chunks of limestone by the side of the gulch. Possible hiding places.

Then she swept the binoculars out to sea, and froze. A long way out she caught sight of smoke, the vague silhouette below it of a distant ship heading for the islands. She handed the binoculars to Cardon.

'There's a vessel coming in, still a long way out. Could it be the *Oran*?'

'Yes, it will be,' Cardon told her. 'No other vessel is going to be heading for the islands from so far out. I estimate it should reach Oiseaux in a couple of hours. We'll get back to Vieux Port now.'

Turning round, she saw Marler posted a long way back by the church. His golf bag, unzipped, rested against the wall. At the other end of the platform Butler was standing with his large satchel open at his feet. They were guarding the rear of Tweed and his companions. This was Marseilles.

19

They drove straight to Cardon's boat in the harbour. It was a larger craft than Paula had realized. On the bridge a flat sheet of steel was securely attached to the deck. It was about the height of Paula's neck and she could just see over the top.

'What's that for?' she asked.

'Protection.' Cardon grinned. 'Against a hail of machine-gun bullets.'

'This could be exciting, then.'

'Doubt if we'll need it.' As he talked he was checking parts of the vessel that meant nothing to her. She became aware of the craft swaying at anchorage, the hull moving up and down. Large waves were sweeping in through the harbour entrance, but the sun still blazed down, bathing her neck and arms.

'Change in the weather?' she wondered.

'The heat at this time of the year happens about once in a decade. It's often accompanied by a strong breeze. It'll be more bumpy once we've left harbour.'

'Excuse me, I want to find Tweed. He's gone below.'

'First cabin on your right at the bottom of the steps.'

She found Tweed leaning back on a bunk, looking unhappy and grim. He managed a smile as she closed the door.

'Even in harbour this thing dances about all over the place,' he commented sourly.

'It'll be worse when we get on to the open sea.'

'Thanks a lot.'

Tweed had never been happy afloat, complaining once that he didn't like the sea at all. It wouldn't keep still. She took a small bottle from her shoulder bag, emptied a pill into her hand, handed it to him, her expression stern.

'Dramamine.' She picked up an opened bottle of mineral water. 'Don't argue with me. Just swallow it.'

'Seems silly that I suffer from seasickness in this gentle swell.'

'Lots of people do. The swell won't be so gentle out on the Med. *Take it!*' she commanded. 'I think we'll soon be leaving.'

With a grimace he swallowed it, washed down with plenty of water. She sat beside him on the bunk, smiling cheerfully. 'If you're worried about Marin—Cardon, that is—knowing, I shan't say a word. Now relax. I'm exploring the rest of this vessel.'

She found her fellow team members, except Cardon, in the spacious main cabin. They were very occupied. Marler was examining his Armalite rifle, then loading it. The golf bag in which he'd concealed it was lying on a couch. Butler was testing his Sten gun, aiming and firing without ammo. Nield had a Glock pistol, which he was tucking inside his belt under his windcheater. Butler dived inside his holdall, brought out something he handed to Paula.

'An egg. Might come in useful.'

The 'egg' was a hand grenade. She checked it carefully, then tucked it firmly inside her bag. During her recent retraining trip, the new instructor had made her throw three live ones over a wall, had not been satisfied and had handed her more. Altogether he'd made her throw thirty live grenades. 'You'll do' had been his final comment. Later she'd heard from Sarge, the normal trainer who had returned before she left: 'That's the highest compliment he ever pays.'

'Where were you, Pete?' she asked Nield. 'You didn't come with us.'

'Tweed told me to stay behind to keep an eye on

177

all our rooms. I kept up a walking patrol.'

'I didn't realize he was so nervous.'

'Not nervous.' Pete squeezed her shoulder. 'Typically careful. Someone could have planted a bomb in your absence.'

'Doesn't miss a trick.'

'Which is why we survive.'

The engine suddenly started up, making the vessel vibrate. Paula decided she'd visit Tweed, see how he was. When she entered his cabin he was standing up, walking about, slapping his arms round his body. He winked at her.

'You're OK?'

'I'm going up on to the bridge. The *Capulet* is about to leave harbour.'

'Is that what it's called?'

'Yes, I noticed when we came aboard. Cardon has a soft spot for *Romeo and Juliet*. Want to join me?'

Arriving on the bridge, they saw Harry on the landing stage, releasing the ropes, bow first, then stern. He leaped aboard agilely as the vessel edged its way into mid-harbour. Paula was always surprised at how agile Harry was with his stout figure.

'Port master has radioed permission, confirmed the exit passage is clear,' Cardon told them, both hands on the wheel. He took off one hand, grabbed two yellow oilskins and threw them to Tweed. 'If both of you are staying up here you'd better put those on. Sea's a bit choppy out there.'

As they emerged into the open, Paula saw larger waves than she had expected. Tweed was gripping a handrail, peering over the steel sheet. He seemed to be in his element despite the swaying movements of the *Capulet*. He grabbed a

178

sou'wester hat from a deep shelf, clapped it on his head. Spray was now spattering them on the bridge as the vessel plunged down the far side of a wave. Tweed took off his horn-rimmed glasses, tucked them in his suit pocket under the oilskin. As on earlier occasions he found he could see just as well without them. Sometimes he wondered why he bothered with them. Fumbling in a pocket, he found his monocular. Cardon had increased speed and they were racing away from the mainland.

Looking back, Paula was enthralled by the view. Now she could clearly see that vast limestone amphitheatre enclosing the city from a distance. The sun's glare was reflecting off the limestone so strongly she blinked. A panoramic sight she would never forget.

'I'm picking up speed,' Cardon explained, 'because it occurred to me the *Oran* may arrive at Oiseaux earlier—to get under cover of the island.'

'We must expect trouble when we're close to the gulch on this side,' Marler warned. 'They're bound to guard the only other landing place. If possible, we should avoid the sound of shooting,' he told Butler and Nield, who had joined them. 'Leave it to me if you can.'

'So they won't hear you,' Harry said sarcastically.

Marler showed him the Armalite. Paula had noticed that the barrel seemed longer than she remembered it. Marler tapped the tip of the weapon.

'This is an advanced silencer invented by the boffins down in Park Crescent's basement. I brought it with me through the Waterloo checkpoint. As I'd hoped, wrapped in a special material it wasn't picked up by a metal detector.

179

So, if it works, leave the killing to me.'

Paula was gazing at the Ile du Château d'If as they passed a good way to its north. A brutal-looking rock—just the place to keep Alexandre Dumas's captive hidden for years. Beyond it the Ile des Oiseaux came into view, its triangular shape now clearly visible. Tweed was staring through his monocular at the approaching gulch.

Cardon had slowed down, to make less noise. They were close in now and the savage narrow gulch was clearly visible with the naked eye. Tweed studied it with his monocular from the flat base projecting into the sea up its twisting climb.

'No sign of life,' he reported. 'Some convenient limestone chunks at intervals which could be used as firing platforms.'

'I saw them from when we were at the Notre-Dame viewing point,' Paula recalled. 'Let's hope the brigands aren't waiting for us behind them.'

Tension was rising aboard the vessel. No one showed it outwardly but Paula could sense it. Cardon had explained the vessel would have to be moored to the rock platform with huge hooks he'd had attached to another set of mooring lines.

Harry leaped ashore with one rope while Marler, at the prow, took another hooked rope. Rusty rings sunk into the platform were used to secure the *Capulet*.

'Proceed with great caution,' Tweed warned before jumping on to the platform, gripping his Walther.

It seemed strangely still and silent on the little-used platform, an atmosphere Tweed didn't like. Crouching low, he darted into the entrance to the gulch with Marler, looking up. He kept moving

180

with the others at his heels. The surface of the gulch was an ankle-breaker. Small rocks scattered everywhere as the walls closed round them. Still no sound, no sign of life.

Marler was in front now while Tweed followed with Paula by his side. Arriving at a massive chunk of limestone as big as a small house, Marler peered round it. All he saw was the steep incline of the gulch climbing above him. He began to move faster, Armalite held at the ready.

They negotiated a stretch of path no wider than passage for one person at a time, past another massive limestone chunk. Marler paused frequently to listen, to stare up. The only sound was the lap of the waves against the platform way below them now.

They reached the summit suddenly—so unexpectedly that Marler dipped his head. Tweed and Paula peered over the edge. They were stunned by what they saw below beyond the edge of the summit sloping steeply downwards.

*   *   *

'It's been and gone!' exclaimed Paula.

'They came in more quickly than I'd thought possible,' said Cardon, who had followed them up, risking leaving the *Capulet* unattended. 'And they've dumped their cargo. Why?'

They had a clear view of the landing platform at the edge of the sea. It was littered with large bales, some burst open, spilling their contents. Tweed was using his monocular to scan the *Oran*. The large freighter was broadside on as it headed out to the open sea.

181

'That ship has a large square dent near the prow on the port side,' he observed. 'Must at some time have slammed into a harbour wall. It also has a lot of Arabs on deck—far more than I would have thought were needed to crew the vessel.'

'But why dump their cargo?' Cardon persisted. 'It looks like fibrous materials used in Muslim food mixed with other ingredients.'

'Taken aboard at Algiers to give it a legitimate reason for sailing,' Tweed told him. 'I suspect its real purpose is to collect something else from another destination. Paula, see the large wheeled landing stage shoved off the edge. Visible because the water is so clear.'

A strong breeze was increasing in strength. Waves washed over the platform, sweeping the bales back into the sea. Tweed pocketed his monocular, turned to Cardon.

'I want us to get back to your launch fast. We need to shadow the *Oran* for a distance. I want to know which course she takes when she gets out into the main channel.'

'I suggest we get back very fast,' Paula warned. 'They've left guards behind on this island.'

All eyes turned to where she was staring. Six Arabs armed with automatic weapons had appeared a distance away to their left. They were hurrying towards Tweed's team. Cardon rapped out an order. 'Run like hell for the gulch. We've got to get down to my launch and away from here pretty damned quick.'

Harry, carrying his Sten, led the way, his short legs working like pistons as he disappeared down the gulch. Tweed followed him with the others at his heels. Scrambling down the large crevice was

182

harder than climbing it. Their feet slithered on small limestone chips. Marler stayed behind as Paula passed him. Nield was ahead of her and they'd both lost sight of Cardon, who was darting down the gulch like a fox running after hounds. Marler was now lying full length on the ground behind a small rock.

The six Arabs had divided up into two sections with three men in each. They were moving faster than anyone had expected. Marler aimed his Armalite at the right-hand, near section. He fired three times rapidly. Three shots, and three Arabs sagged to the ground. The second section had located him. Machine-gun bullets spat up alarmingly close to him.

He jumped up, ran, disappeared down inside the gulch. He was moving so fast he failed to notice Paula had slipped, turning an ankle behind a massive limestone rock. She was on her own now.

*   *   *

Paula peered round the side of the limestone block, which gave her a view of the lower gulch. The team was spread out in a line at a point where the narrow path ran straight. She heard the crunch of boots coming down from above.

Three huge Arabs hugging machine pistols were moving fast down the gulch. They only had to pass her rock, continue a short distance, then they could stand and aim a lethal fusillade, killing every member of her team.

She reached inside her shoulder bag and extracted the 'egg' given to her by Harry. A grenade of great explosive power, she felt sure. Her crawl behind the rock had covered her from head to foot in limestone dust. She realized she merged with the ground she was lying on. Her ankle was half-killing her. She gritted her teeth, gripping the grenade.

The tallest of the three Arabs gave an order in Arabic. She didn't understand a word. But she understood the act of the three levelling their weapons, barrels aimed downwards. It was going to be a slaughter.

She pressed the red button, as instructed by Harry. With an agonizing effort, she eased herself round the rock, saw the three Arabs standing still, machine pistols aimed at their target. The whole team. She lobbed the grenade, saw it land at the heels of the tall Arab. She jerked her head back.

The explosion, penned inside the gulch walls, was deafening. A round ball-like object, covered in blood, shot up the gulch past her rock. It was the head of the tallest Arab. Peering round again, she saw a horrible mess of shattered bodies. Easing herself back behind the rock, she extracted a water bottle and her scarf from the shoulder bag. After soaking the cloth in water, she stuffed it down inside her boot. The relief was indescribable. Hauling herself upright, she found she could walk. She hobbled down the gulch, past the shattered Arab bodies, continued on down until she reached the platform where the launch was tethered.

'Where's Paula, for God's sake?' Tweed was shouting.

'Bloody Paula is here,' she yelled back. 'What is this—women and children last?'

'I thought you were ahead of us,' Tweed replied, rushing over to her.

184

'Didn't damned well think at all, did you?' she blazed.

'What was that explosion?' Harry asked.

'Your flaming egg detonating. Killing three Arabs seconds before they blasted you all to kingdom come.'

'Oh, heavens! I'm so sorry,' Tweed said, grasping her by the arm to help her hobble aboard the launch.

'Won't forgive any of you for one hell of a long time,' she shouted. 'Cardon, hadn't you better get this old tub moving? Tweed wants to check the *Oran*'s course.'

Marler ran forward to where she sat on the bridge. He had the sense to say nothing. With a first-aid kit tucked under his arm he carefully removed her boot, checked her ankle after gently taking off the scarf. He examined it, squeezed ointment from a tube over it. Paula sighed with the pleasure of the coolness, bent down and kissed Marler. He looked up, winked. Then he slowly wrapped a bandage round her ankle and told her to hit him if it hurt. He used only one layer of bandage, told her she might be able to get her boot back on and this would give support. She didn't look at Tweed, who was checking the route the launch was taking.

By now Cardon had revved up, steered the launch away from the platform and was guiding it round the end of the island and into the open sea. Marler slowly slid Paula's foot inside the boot and then waved his hand. He thought it best for her to see how it fitted. She leaned down, pulled it up inch by inch. No pain. Gripping a handrail, she stood up, maintaining her balance. Tweed kept turning round to look at her but never once did she return his glances. Marler shook his head and Tweed sensibly said nothing. Give her time for her fury to fade.

The island was now behind them and the *Capulet* was racing towards the distant *Oran*. The sea was now calm, a sapphire plate. The gap between the two vessels was closing as the *Oran* changed course. Tweed was leaning over the protective plate, staring intensely.

'It's well out now,' he shouted above the engine sound, 'and it's changed course to southwest. That means it's heading for the Straits of Gibraltar and the Atlantic beyond. It will turn north. Europe is its objective. So, now I know.'

'We're in trouble,' Cardon warned. 'They've seen us and they're winching a big power launch over the side.' He was studying the vessel through binoculars. 'A lot of men on board with guns. They're coming for us.'

'Pancake time,' Marler called out, lifting his flat case.

'Pancakes?' Paula said incredulously.

'Latest development in sea mines.'

Marler grinned. Opening his case, he produced a slim metal object, circular in shape. He took out another, put it on the deck between his feet, gazed at what was coming at them. A big power launch, its prow was reinforced steel. If it hit them broadside on it would cut them in two. Its speed was alarming, slicing through the sea like a torpedo. Arabs aboard it were already firing automatic weapons. A hail of bullets hammered against the protective metal plate. Crouched down behind it, Tweed put a hand on Paula's shoulder,

186

firmly pressed her lower. The hostile power launch was moving like the TGV.

'Don't fire back whatever you do!' Marler shouted. 'I want it to stay on its present course.'

'It's going to ram us head on,' Cardon shouted back, peering through a small hole covered with armour-plated glass.

Paula couldn't resist peering over Tweed's neck. Marler, during a pause in the bombardment, was standing up. In one hand he held a pancake mine, another in reserve in his other hand. He skimmed the circular mine across the water like a boy skimming a pebble over a pond. Then he skimmed the second mine.

The steel prow of the attacking power launch was so high up that whoever was steering it would never see Marler's action. Cardon crawled swiftly to Paula, grabbed her by the arm and hauled her across the deck to his original position.

'Look through that spy-hole. Don't worry—it has armoured glass . . .'

Paula wasn't worried. She had her eye glued to the spyhole. The power launch was further away than she'd expected, but coming at them fast. She caught a brief sight of a mine as it floated over a small wave. The prow of the enemy's vessel hit it square on. The explosion was fantastic. The steel prow rocketed into the sky, the hull was split into two pieces, one section upended and plunging out of sight deep into the sea. The other section was in flames. The crew, on fire from head to foot, dived into the sea in a desperate, futile attempt to save their lives. Then the launch was gone, leaving behind a spreading patch of oil on the sapphire blue.

'Home, James,' Tweed ordered Cardon.

* * *

They returned to Vieux Port, climbed on to the landing stage, hurried to their hotel. Tweed, who had the train times in his head, said they'd just catch a TGV back to Paris if they moved.

He had paid the bill and collected his case, when Paula rushed down, followed by the others. When Tweed, who had calculated the amount, had pushed a sheaf of euro notes on the counter, the temporary girl had counted quickly, slipping out ten, which she hid in her pocket. When she had told Tweed he hadn't paid enough he told her to add the tip she had stolen.

Outside, in the blazing sun, Tweed led the way to a battered old cab waiting with an Arab at the wheel. She paused, tugged at his sleeve.

'That cab might not be safe.'

'With Cardon in his Arab gear as driver?'

At the station they dived out. Paula left last and whispered to Cardon, 'You stay here, Philip?'

'Not on your life,' he whispered back. 'Heading East—to slit a few throats.'

They boarded the waiting TGV scarcely a minute before it glided out of St Charles, building up speed once the suburbs were left behind. The team had found an empty first-class coach. As Tweed settled in a seat Paula joined him. Marler and Nield again took up their sentry posts at each end of the coach.

Paula's mind was still full of blue sea, the great limestone amphitheatre circling the city, the warmth of the sun, their first sight of the Île des

188

Oiseaux, a limestone triangle perched in the sapphire blue. She squeezed Tweed's arm.

'I want to apologize. For the awful things I said when I arrived back at the bottom of the gulch. I feel terrible—I can recall every dreadful thing I said.'

He put his arm round her waist, hugged her, looked straight into her eyes.

'I'm the one to say sorry—and a feeble thank-you for saving our lives. I looked back a millisecond before your grenade detonated. I saw three huge Arabs about to spray us with bullets. We'd all have gone down. My mistake was thinking you'd gone down ahead of us. When I realized you weren't with us I was appalled, overcome with emotion. On this grim trip there were three top players —yourself, Marler and Cardon.' He gave her a clean handkerchief. 'No need to cry. Or maybe it'll make you feel better . . .'

When she had recovered, she asked the question. 'Did you find out what you wanted to?'

'Yes. That freighter, the *Oran*, is headed for the Straits of Gibraltar. Once in the Atlantic it can head for Europe, to collect something I'm sure is pretty diabolical.'

20

The team had spent the night at a hotel in Paris, then caught an early Eurostar to Waterloo. Approaching Waterloo, Tweed turned to Paula, keeping his voice down.

'You'll come with me.' His voice was vigorous.

'It's time I grilled all the suspects, got the hunt for the killer moving. My first target is Aubrey Greystoke, finance director at Gantia.'

'So he's on your list of suspects?'

'All of them are.'

At Waterloo they divided their luggage between Marler and Nield and caught a taxi for the Tower in the city. As it crawled along, Paula found her visions of the Mediterranean fading, overlain by earlier experiences.

The strange drive with Michael to Dartmoor, the two skeletons, Abbey Grange, its peculiar servants—Mrs Brogan and Tarvin—the hideous discovery of Christine Barton's skeleton in the kitchen fridge, the trip to Wensford and the equally hideous locating of private detective John Jackson's deteriorating body on the houseboat, it had become a panorama of horror.

It was a cold morning with a low cloud bank. Looking up to the conical summit of the Tower, Paula saw it shrouded in mist. The same receptionist stood behind her counter. She had the same severe expression. Paula beat her to it.

'I know I can't take this shoulder bag with me. So lock it away in one of those boxes.'

'The bag is locked. I want to see inside it.'

'Because it might contain a bomb?'

'Can't you read?' Tweed was holding his identity folder under her nose. 'Stop fooling about. We're here to see Aubrey Greystoke.'

'He's—'

'In Room 750. Seventh floor,' Tweed said. 'We take the second elevator. Welcome to the Tower. It has an architectural award,' Tweed went on, mimicking the receptionist's patter on their previous visit when they had found Greystoke was out.

The girl stared at him, speechless, as they walked to the bank of elevators. When the doors opened at the seventh floor the hall was empty. They walked across to 750, opposite the elevator. Tweed was about to press the bell when the door opened. A slim blonde woman walked out, pulling the door shut, her coat over her arm.

Tweed turned to watch her walk to the elevator, noticed that the zip at the back of her dress was halfway down her shapely back. He walked over before she could call the lift.

'Excuse me, but it's cold outside and your zip isn't done up properly. Allow me.' With a quick motion he pulled the zip up to the top. 'May I help you on with your coat? You'll need it outside.'

She wasn't in the least disconcerted. As he helped her on with the coat her green eyes studied him. He pressed the button for the ground floor, walked back to Paula as the woman stepped inside the elevator. The doors closed.

'His latest bit on the side,' Paula remarked. 'A bit early in the day I'd have thought.'

'I'm looking for someone with stamina and strength,' he remarked as he pressed the bell.

They had to wait. Then the door opened and Greystoke was blinking as he gazed at them. Tieless, his shirt was open at the neck. He wore a waistcoat and suit trousers. He eased his right foot inside a slip-on shoe. A smell of whisky drifted out.

'Might ... have made an appointment,' he grumbled.

'We're investigating a case of four murders.'

'*Four?*' He peered at Paula. 'You're Petula Grey.'

191

'Paula,' she corrected him. 'We're coming in.'

'If you say so.'

He backed away, they walked in, he shut the door, led them into a spacious living room-cum-office. A large desk stood against the far wall, with all the technological 'junk' so disliked by Tweed: a fax machine, an advanced computer connected to the Internet. There was also a swivel chair, leather-bound and a screen on the wall above the desk.

In the living area was a long leather couch—Paula noticed the cushions had been hastily piled untidily. She peered through an open door. It was the kitchen and on a counter, waiting to be washed, was a glass rimmed with lipstick. On a low mahogany table by the couch was the twin glass, half full of Scotch. The bottle of the finest Scotch, half empty, stood beside the glass.

'Now you've barged in you might as well sit down,' Greystoke suggested.

He staggered a little as he arranged three armchairs in a circle, one close to the Scotch bottle and glass. He waved a hand, glared at Paula.

'That was the kitchen. Do you normally poke around in other people's places?'

'I wanted to be sure we were alone,' she said politely.

'I've just finished one of those brainstorming business sessions. The businessmen needed liquor to oil their so-called brains.'

A one-blonde business meeting, Paula would have liked to say, but she kept quiet.

'OK,' Greystoke began as they sat down and he chose the chair nearest the bottle. 'What is this in aid of?'

'I am investigating four especially hideous

murders,' Tweed told him, 'where all the bodies were horribly savaged with a knife. Chunks of flesh cut off, preserved in bags.'

Greystoke reached for a carafe of water, filled a glass, drank it all down, refilled the glass, repeated the process. Deciding he'd better sober up, Paula thought.

'Sounds like a friggin' maniac,' Greystoke said.

'When he's doing his foul work. But I do believe that it is someone who most of the time appears perfectly normal. Could be a business executive.' Tweed leaned forward. 'I understand your wife, Lee, disappeared three to four months ago.'

'She has her way of life, I have mine. So eventually she has the idea she wants to live her own life—without me. I'm not bothered.'

'Mr Greystoke,' Tweed began in a grim voice, leaning closer to him again, 'one of the skeletons discovered on Dartmoor is that of Lee.'

Paula was taken aback. She had never known Tweed conduct an interrogation in such a brutal manner.

'Lee? Can't be. Are you sure?'

'I have a witness who positively identified the corpse. She was wearing a certain piece of jewellery the witness associates with Lee. No doubt. Lee is dead as a dodo.'

'Who is the witness?' Greystoke poured Scotch into the glass. 'Hair of the dog,' he explained after swallowing the contents.

'I cannot reveal the identity of the witness,' Tweed snapped.

Tweed was studying the suspect, recalling how he had looked at Santorini's when he had dined there with Lucinda. Tall, a man in his fifties with gold-rimmed glasses perched on his Roman nose, his brown hair now awry—due no doubt to his recent visitor. Attractive to a certain kind of woman, Aubrey knew this. So what was different? As at Santorini's he had an air of self-satisfaction when they arrived. Now, though, he looked uncertain, his sensuous lips compressed. Like a man holding himself together with an effort.

'This is a shock,' he said suddenly.

A rather belated reaction, Paula thought to herself.

'Did Lee have any enemies? Had she a woman friend in the States, say in Richmond, Virginia?'

'First,' Greystoke said, his replies now prompt, 'she did not have any enemies that I know of. Second, ten years ago I took her to the States and she disliked it intensely. We never went anywhere near Virginia.'

'I think that will be all—for the moment,' Tweed decided, standing up. 'I expect to be back as I learn more.'

Paula accompanied Tweed striding towards the exit door. Greystoke followed them. Before he opened the door Greystoke said in an emotional voice, 'I did love Lee . . .'

Tweed spun round. 'In that case why did you never inform the police she was missing?'

'Well . . .' He was almost stuttering. 'I didn't want the news to get round the staff at Gantia. It's a gossip shop. I was so sure that she—'

'Thank you for your time,' Tweed said harshly.

He opened the door himself. They didn't hear the door close but Tweed never glanced back as he pressed the button for the elevator. Once inside, doors closed, they were able to talk.

'What do you think?' Paula asked.

'They're all lying,' he growled. 'I think even Greystoke has been infected by the devious Armenian element. He was hiding something, at the best.'

'I thought his reactions were all wrong. And you'd have expected him to ask what he should do about arrangements for his wife's body.'

'Yes, you would.'

*   *   *

'Where are we going now?' Paula asked as they drove away in a taxi from the Tower. 'Who's next on your hit list?'

'Lucinda.'

'All the way down the M3 again to the Gantia plant?'

'No,' stated Tweed. 'Her London apartment. If we're lucky that's where we'll find her. I think she starts work late to avoid rush hour, then stays late after the staff have gone home.'

'Which would give her free run of the plant?'

'I'd already thought of that.'

'Do you think *Aubrey*'—she pronounced the name with a posh accent—'is capable of these ghastly murders?'

'I am looking for someone who strikes me as being capable of grabbing a man—or a woman—from behind, jerking them back by clutching their hair, then cutting their throat with a sharp blade. Next, switching their grip on the knife so the serrated edge is used to saw through the neck and half the spine, plus later using the same knife to mutilate the dead body.'

195

'You make it sound so horrible.'

'It *is* horrible.'

He was silent until they arrived at Park Crescent, transferring to his own car. He drove to Mayfair and into the underground garage below Lucinda's apartment. Parking in one of the many empty spaces, he got out, hurried over to the elevators while Paula ran to catch him up.

'Is it a good idea that I come with you?' she wondered. 'Or do you need me for protection?' she teased.

'You come with me. She'll know it's serious then.'

As they stepped out of the elevator the door to Lucinda's apartment opened and she was coming out, clad in a leather driving jacket and trousers. Paula had her overcoat on but was still feeling the damp cold of London—the sudden contrast to the heat of Marseilles.

'I was just on my way down to the plant,' Lucinda snapped and pushed back a lock of hair from her face.

'You can go down later,' Tweed said grimly. 'I'm investigating a case of mass murder. That comes first.'

'If you say so. March in.'

This is going to be interesting, Paula thought. She's in a bad mood. Slamming the door shut when they were inside, Lucinda took off her jacket, threw it on a chair. Without being asked, Tweed took off his overcoat as Paula took off hers. Tweed hung his coat on one of a row of wall hooks and did the same with Paula's.

Lucinda sat behind a desk, took out a cigarette, inserted it into her long holder, lit it. Tweed hauled three armchairs in a circle, rather as Greystoke had done.

'I want you closer,' he told Lucinda.

'You do? With Paula here?' she said with a malicious smile.

She stood up, came over and sat in one of the armchairs. Leaning back, she blew smoke rings into the air.

'I'm rather glad you've come,' she said suddenly in her soft appealing voice.

'Why?' demanded Tweed.

'I had another visitor, not exactly a friend—or friendly. Mr Abel Gallagher, head of Special Branch. He was aggressive, rude, helped himself to the bottle of Scotch from the drinks cupboard, poured himself a glass, swallowed the lot. I'll have to have the glass screen over the drinks cupboard replaced by solid wood panels. That is, if I'm going to have thugs like that calling on me.'

'When was this?' Tweed asked.

'Earlier this morning.'

'So what did he want to know?' Tweed asked, his tone gentler.

'How much progress you had made with your investigation. I told him damn-all. Said I wasn't on your staff. Told him to go and ask you. He didn't like that. He threatened me.'

'How?'

'Said I was involved in the murder cases up to my neck, that if I didn't cooperate he'd send a car to take me to his HQ. He said I must know where Lee Greystoke had vanished to, that I was very close to her according to information received, close in any way I might like to interpret that. I nearly picked up the bottle of Scotch and threw it at him, but I kept my cool.'

'Did he say anything else?'

'Wanted to know where Michael was. I said I hadn't a clue. I'd had enough. I erupted. I stood up and told him to get the hell out of my apartment or I'd throw him out. He's a big man and that made him sneer.'

'What happened next?'

'Oh,' she said calmly. 'I got up, used my jujitsu on him. Pushed him to the door, opened it, flung him out so he landed flat on his face, closed the door, locked it. End of story.'

Tweed was in a quandary. He'd intended to put Lucinda through the wringer with his interrogation. Not a good tactic after what she'd just described.

'I was disturbed,' he began quietly, 'when I realized you had lied to me.'

'*Lied?*' Lucinda was taken aback. 'What are you talking about?'

'You gave as a possible reason for Lee's disappearance that she had a woman friend in Richmond, Virginia. That she might have gone there. I've recently talked to Greystoke. He says his wife disliked the States when he took her there ten years ago. Also, they never went anywhere near Virginia. I'm afraid you won't look back on this as one of your best mornings. Lee is dead,' he said gently. 'Her body was found in a mine shaft on Dartmoor.'

'Oh, my God!' Lucinda sat very still before reacting. 'That is simply ghastly.' She stood up. 'I need a good stiff Scotch.' She brought a glass back, sat down.

'Might be best to drink water first,' Paula advised.

Lucinda poured water from a carafe into the glass, swallowed the contents, refilled the glass,

198

swallowed again. She took deep breaths, then poured herself a stiff Scotch into the same glass. She sipped it.

'Aubrey's lying about Lee and America,' she said.

'*Someone* is lying,' Tweed responded.

'Then you'll have to decide which one of us is. Is he handling funeral arrangements?'

'I don't think so.'

'Then I'll take care of them. Where is poor Lee now?'

Tweed took one of Professor Saafeld's cards from his breast pocket, handed it to her. 'Quote my name. That gentleman should know. Does Aubrey travel much? I'm thinking about, say, three to four months ago.'

'Yes, on any excuse. And during the period you mention he was in the States, apparently checking costs with suppliers.'

'And you were away during that time?'

'I think so. Yes, I was—also in the States. I like to keep up with any new security developments. The Americans can be very good—and very bad—with new ideas. Can I go soon? I should be at the plant.'

'Yes. I'm sorry to have to tell you about Lee. Thank you for your patience,' Tweed said, standing up.

'Drink some more water before you drive,' Paula advised. 'In case you're stopped by the police.'

*   *   *

'What do you think?' Paula asked as they descended in the elevator.

'The most significant item was how she so easily handled Gallagher, a very large and tough

199

individual.'

'And just before we arrived at Lucinda's apartment you said you're looking for someone capable of grabbing a man—or a woman—from behind and murdering them. Makes me wonder,' Paula mused.

Her mobile rang as they approached the underground garage. Tweed unlocked the car and settled himself behind the wheel and waited for Paula to join him.

'Next on my programme of interrogation is Larry Voles,' said Tweed. 'I know we've only recently interviewed him, but I know a lot more now.'

'Wait . . .' Paula laid a hand on his as he reached for the gear lever. 'That call was from Monica. Keith Kent has arrived at Park Crescent and wants to see you urgently.'

'Then we'd better first head back to the office.'

*   *   *

Kent was seated when they walked in, a slim leather folder in his lap with a blue folder on top of it. Smartly dressed in a business suit, he started to stand up when he saw Paula. She put a hand on his shoulder, pressed him back into the chair.

'Don't stand on ceremony for me, Keith. You're always so polite.'

'Have you got anywhere with those balance-sheet figures?' demanded Tweed. 'I'm convinced now that the motive for these ghastly murders is money and power. Christine Barton may have found something vital.'

Kent stood up as Tweed sat behind his desk, and spread out in front of him several sheets. Most

200

contained figures but two sheets were Kent's typed report. He smiled.

'Funny you should say that. I've cracked Christine's code. According to Christine's calculations Gantia is worth two to three billion —and Drago owns it outright. But four hundred million has gone missing.'

'Four hundred million!' Paula gasped. 'You do mean four hundred million pounds?'

'Exactly. A huge amount by any millionaire's standard.'

'How was it done?' Tweed asked, his eyes gleaming. 'Can you tell me that? Where did it come from?'

'Gantia's enormous reserves of money. I do know this huge sum was transmitted to a shell company called Livingston, Antilles, Cockcroft and Keyforf —LACK for short. Somebody secretly bought LACK—which was worth nothing, then sent the money to it. Shortly after the money was in LACK it was withdrawn by electronic transmission and vanished. You have to use a reference and it was AB200017 X. I can't identify whose is that reference number.'

'When did all this happen?' Tweed asked quickly.

'The dates are a bit muddled, but it was quite some time ago.'

'And the murders of four people took place about three to four months ago, according to Saafeld.' Tweed had jumped up, was pacing restlessly. 'And who was murdered? Christine Barton, forensic accountant who produced the figures you've just deciphered, Keith. She was hired by someone suspicious that something was terribly wrong . . .'

'Drago Volkanian, who was abroad?' Paula

201

suggested.

'Very likely. Then the detective, John Jackson, is hired by her sister, Anne Barton, to find her. The detective is murdered. And then Lee Greystoke, whom I think Drago trusted, starts ferreting around late at night at the Gantia plant. She is also foully murdered. It's beginning to form a pattern.'

'What's a shell company?' Paula asked.

'It's a company,' Kent explained, 'which has gone bust or out of business. You can buy one cheaply. Financiers do it to start up a new enterprise. Incidentally, those sheets—' he pointed to them on Tweed's desk '—that Paula found hidden in Christine's flat are original. I don't think they were ever sent to whoever hired her.'

'Drago,' Paula repeated.

'I think you might be right,' Tweed agreed.

'So what do we do now?' she asked.

'I'm recalling that abandoned landing stage we saw deep in the clear water off the Ile des Oiseaux.'

'Now I'm confused,' Paula protested.

'That makes one of us.'

'Thanks a lot,' she snapped.

'We have to narrow it down to certain suspects.' Tweed was still pacing like a caged tiger. 'We need to locate anyone with accountancy knowledge who could have worked this trick.'

'Unless two people were working together,' Paula told him. 'The killer and the accountancy person. Once the scheme is pulled off the killer then murders his collaborator.'

'That is a remote possibility. We *have* to identify who *needed* four hundred million pounds urgently. For a while now I've sensed the killer was in a desperate state—someone who had to eliminate

202

anyone who might expose the motive.'

Kent checked his watch, stood up. 'I've done all I can and concentrating on this has put me behind work from regular clients. I'll send you my bill.'

'Do that,' said Tweed.

'It'll be a hefty bill. I've worked through nights on it.'

'Congratulations on pulling it off, Keith. It will be worth every penny.'

'Pennies won't come into my fee,' Kent said. He went over to Paula, kissed and hugged her. 'You have my sympathy—I can tell Tweed is in a relentless hunting mood.'

'So,' an exasperated Paula said once more, 'what do we do now?'

'Drive down to Gantia. I need more information from Larry.'

'If I could get a word in now,' Monica said, 'before you rush off I had a phone call from Professor Saafeld. He wants to give some data to you personally. He said it could be important. You ought to phone him *now*.'

'All right.' Tweed, his overcoat already on, sighed impatiently. 'Get him on the line.'

'Tweed here, Saafeld,' he said, sitting on the edge of his desk. 'I gather you called.'

'I owe you an apology. I fear I'm not infallible. When you rang me from your flat you said you wished we could identify the fourth corpse, the one of a man found in the snow on Dartmoor.'

'Yes, I did.'

'I decided to check the corpse again myself,' Saafeld went on. 'Most of the work on this one was done by an assistant. He had overlooked the right ankle. At some stage the victim had broken it.

203

Someone had done the best they could to fix him up but I have no doubt he walked with a limp.'

'I see. That is valuable. No apology is necessary. I must go now.'

'Wait, I haven't finished. I started from scratch. I found a tiny screwed-up ball of paper caught under the right big toe. It was wet. Working with a chap who is good at this sort of thing, we dried it carefully, then managed to straighten it out and, under a microscope, read certain lettering. Jacko Kenwood, broker, Haldon Street.'

'You're a genius. I'll buy you dinner at the best place in town. I'll call you when I'm less rushed.' He stood up. 'Locate Haldon Street for me,' he told Monica as he opened the door. 'Place where brokers work. Stocks and shares and so forth.'

'I do know what a stockbroker is,' she told him sarcastically.

'Where are you going?' called out the only other occupant of the office, Harry Butler.

'Can't I go anywhere without reporting in?' Tweed snapped.

Monica stood up, blazing. 'I know you're the boss but here we work as a team. Just in case you'd forgotten.'

'We're driving down the M3,' Tweed told them, 'to see Larry Voles so I can interrogate him. And anyone else who catches my eye while we're there.'

*   *   *

Paula waited until they were driving well down the M3 before she spoke. They were close to the Gantia plant.

'You really should remember every member of

204

the team knows about the bullet which missed you by inches further down this route. They're concerned for your safety.'

'I know. You're right. But I'm building up a head of steam to track down this hideous killer. What he—or she—did showed no mercy. I want to get my hands on them.'

The gates were closed at the entrance to Gantia. Tweed grunted. 'I'm not wasting time on their blasted speakphone.'

He began honking his horn nonstop. Paula pursed her lips. As she looked towards the front of the building she saw someone peering out of a first-floor window. She put a hand on Tweed's arm.

'I think Lucinda's seen us. She'll open the gates.'

She had hardly spoken when both gates automatically swung inward. Tweed pressed his foot down, scuffing up pebbles from the drive, braked suddenly at the platform below the entrance door. Paula was jerked forward against her seatbelt. She raised her eyes to heaven.

The door opened and Lucinda greeted them with a smile. 'I'm beginning to get used to you both appearing without any warning. Welcome to Gantia.'

'I've come to see Larry,' Tweed said. 'It's urgent.'

'It's getting more urgent all the time,' she chided him. 'I'll take you up. Larry's in his office. I'll leave you alone with him.'

'Thank you,' Tweed said as they entered the elevator. He took off his overcoat. It was warm inside the building. Lucinda took it off him, looked at Paula, who shook her head. They walked down a long corridor. The walls were decorated with a selection of Van Gogh prints.

205

'I like Van Gogh,' Tweed remarked. 'Who chose the prints?'

'Larry, of course.' Pausing before a closed door, she rapped on it. Larry's distinctive voice called out 'Come in.'

Not just 'Come', thought Tweed, who disliked the single-word invitation. It betrayed arrogance, someone who thought he was the cat's whiskers. Lucinda inserted a card in a slot, turned the handle, opened the door and ushered them inside.

Larry was already walking to meet them, after jumping up athletically from his large desk facing the windows overlooking the front. Dressed in a polo-necked white pullover and white trousers, he was the image of informality. He is good-looking, Paula thought, had such a nice smile, and yet there was a commanding air about him. The perfect managing director.

'Saw you coming,' he said, kissing Paula on both cheeks. 'Hoped you were here to visit me. Do sit down. What are you drinking? Coffee, something stronger? The sun's going down.'

They both asked for coffee and Lucinda disappeared to get their beverages. Larry escorted them to a large couch, pulled up a chair to face them. A very easy manner, Paula was thinking.

'How can I help you?' Larry enquired as Lucinda appeared with the coffee on a tray, placed it on a small table, then left.

'This has become a very serious murder investigation,' Tweed began grimly. 'So I have to ask some personal questions. For example, where were you three to four months ago?'

'Which means I'm a suspect,' Larry replied with a smile.

206

'We do have a number of suspects,' Paula assured him.

'I don't even have to refer to my diary to answer your question,' Larry said with another smile. 'I was touring the States. Visiting some of our more important customers. I felt it important to keep up contact when our top salesman, Michael, went missing. We have two other sales executives, but not up to his calibre. Half the people I wanted to see were away—golf tournaments. Would you believe it? But I'd left a note so they knew we were trying to look after them.'

'So no alibi?'

'I agree. I could give you a list.'

'Not necessary,' Tweed said abruptly. 'Another question. Who has keys to get into any office at night?'

'Myself, Lucinda and Michael had one—but I gather all his belongings had been taken by whoever left him sitting on some steps in Whitehall. Superintendent Buchanan's been to see me.'

'Anyone else?' Tweed whipped back.

'Yes. Aubrey Greystoke needs one. And . . .' He paused. 'This is sad. Lee Greystoke had a key, which I assume she'd obtained from Drago. No one else. Lucinda's very hot on security.'

'Who among the executives has a knowledge of accountancy?'

Larry leaned back in his chair, frowned. 'That's an odd question. I'm not going to enquire why you've asked it. First, I have a broad knowledge of balance sheets. I need to because of my position. But no qualification. Aubrey, of course, is a qualified chartered accountant. A finance director

207

must have that. Lucinda doesn't like figures but she is qualified. Oh, and Michael also is a chartered accountant. Disliked the subject but qualified in half the normal time. Typical of his astute brain. Didn't like the subject so he wolfed it down.'

Tweed sipped some coffee, then spoke more quietly. 'How is Michael now?'

'No change so far, I regret to report. Never says a word. I find it perplexing, distressing.'

'So how does he spend his days? He's still at Abbey Grange, I presume?'

'All the time, so far as I know. Promptly at eight every morning he walks down the track to Post Lacey as he used to do when he was working for us. Then walks back to the Grange. Spends a lot of his time in his room reading odd books.'

'Odd?'

'Strange. *Gray's Anatomy* seems to be his favourite.'

'What did you think of Lee Greystoke?'

Paula smiled to herself. She'd experienced this before when Tweed was in full flood. The unexpected switching to some quite different topic.

'Lee? I liked her.' He stood up. 'I think I need a Scotch. Would you join me?'

'No, thank you,' both of them said.

Larry returned with a large glass of Scotch. He drank half of it, put down the glass. 'I liked Lee,' he repeated. 'I didn't know her all that well, but I once had a long conversation with her. I was struck by her exceptional intelligence. You do know, of course, that Aubrey can't keep his hands off an attractive, willing woman. Tragic. For Lee. So when she disappeared we all thought she'd at long last walked. A ghastly business.'

'Indeed.' Tweed stood up. 'I don't think there's anything else. For the moment. Thank you for your time.'

'Anything else you want to know, just contact me.'

*　　*　　*

Earlier, Charmian, the expert French assassin, had got off his motorcycle, hiding it behind a hedge. Then, after checking this isolated spot to make sure no one was about, he walked into a public phone box.

He attached a small metal device to the phone before he made the timed call to M. The device ensured that, if the call was hacked into, the number that would come up would be that of a Mrs Wilson. This innocent lady lived in Hammersmith, a long way from the phone box. Charmian had obtained the number by the simple method of tracking through the London phone book.

The phone rang at the agreed time. Impossible to tell whether the voice that now spoke was that of a man or a woman.

'M here.'

'M?' Charmian queried.

'M for mosque. Have you tracked Tweed?'

'Driving down the M3 with that woman of his. They are heading for the Gantia plant, I suspect.'

'Kill Tweed. Do it immediately. He is getting too close.'

'Depends where he parks his car. It will be dark soon so I do not see any problem.'

'You want the other half of your fee, you had better succeed this time.'

'I always succeed.'

It was getting dark as Tweed and Paula left Larry, walked into the corridor and bumped into Aubrey Greystoke, standing suspiciously close to the door of Larry's office.

'Good evening, Aubrey,' Tweed said politely. 'Listening in?'

'Don't know . . . what you are meaning. Come to my office. Just along the corridor.'

Greystoke led the way, walking slowly, placing one foot carefully in front of the other. Tweed recalled this peculiar habit from when he'd seen Greystoke walking away from them at Santorini's when he'd had dinner in town with Lucinda.

'He's drunk,' Paula whispered. 'I smelled whisky the moment we met him.'

'Shh!' Tweed whispered back.

He was not convinced that Aubrey was drunk. He suspected it was a pose, to fool people. The slow-march way of walking was a little too deliberate. When they entered Aubrey's office located at the front of the building with a view towards the main entrance, he was not surprised to see a bottle of Scotch, a half-filled glass beside it, on his desk. More camouflage?

'Do sit down, you nice people.'

He sank into one armchair, wiped his high forehead with a handkerchief and smiled foolishly.

'Saw you arrive through the window ages ago. Getting dark.'

Clambering laboriously to his large feet, he padded over, pressed a switch. Automatic blinds closed just before Tweed had been going to peer out to see his car. Returning, he placed two glasses on a square glass block, which Paula assumed passed for a table, and sagged down again.

'Drinks all round. To celebrate.'

'Celebrate what?' asked Paula.

'Any excuse will do.' The silly smile again. He filled his own glass up, raised it, sipped. Paula noticed that the front of his open-necked shirt had a damp patch. Where he had spilled Scotch to create an alcoholic odour?

'Ever travel to the States?' Tweed asked suddenly.

'All the time. If I don't check the costs those Americans are charging, no one does.' He sat up straight. 'I am the finance director.'

'What about three to four months ago?' Tweed demanded.

'I'd be in the States then.'

'So you could give me a list of the firms you called on?'

'Won't do you any good. I'm so well known the receptionists never bother to record my arrival.'

'I think that's all. For the moment,' declared Tweed, standing up. He looked back as they reached the door. 'Lucinda is dealing with funeral arrangements for Lee.'

'A job I could do without.'

Callous bastard, Paula said to herself.

*   *   *

Charmian had completed his mission. Under the cover of night he had inserted the powerful bomb inside Tweed's car. The moment Tweed switched on it would detonate.

211

As he made his way to the rear of the building the glaring lights illuminating the building's front were switched on. For a moment his shadow was cast against the front wall below the windows, then he was gone.

For Charmian the security had been easy to evade. Arriving on his motorcycle, parked nearby, close to the M3, he had taken out the folded telescopic ladder from his pannier. The electric wire running along the top of the fence was no obstacle. His ladder was covered with rubber.

Working his way round to the rear, he found the blind spot. He always found a blind spot, this one facing a section of rear wall without windows. Arriving at the top of the fence, he had pressed a button. A fresh section of ladder had extended upwards. He turned a lever, and the extension dropped on the far side of the fence at an angle, giving him access to the plant.

After planting the bomb he returned to the ladder. A bony-faced man, he sported a thin black moustache curving down round the ends of his cruel mouth. His eyes were like ice. Reaching the top of the ladder, he climbed over, turned the lever again and waited as the extension slid back inside the section he stood on. He swiftly arrived on the ground.

Pressing another button, he watched the first section telescope into a compact square. He slipped it inside the leather satchel slung over his shoulder. It was this satchel that had originally transported the bomb. He checked the illuminated hands of his watch. Fifteen minutes. The time he'd allowed for this assignment.

To arrive back at his parked motorcycle he made

a detour away from the fence across grassy fields. He wore rubber-soled shoes with no identifiable pattern on their surface. Arriving at the edge of the M3 he stopped, listened. No sound of traffic.

He walked swiftly across and entered the fields on the far side. He then hurried back to the motorcycle. A professional to his fingertips, he never waited for a bomb to detonate. His policy was to be as far away as possible from the devastation.

* * *

Walking down the corridor to the elevator, ready to leave the building, Tweed and Paula were intercepted by Lucinda. She appeared out of her office, stood in their way.

'Not leaving without talking to me? And I thought you both liked me.'

She ushered them inside her office. The blinds were drawn over her windows with a glow of light behind them. She poured water from a carafe into three glasses, then coffee from a cafetière into three Wedgwood cups.

'Make yourselves at home,' she invited, perching herself on a swivel stool and crossing her long legs. 'Sit,' she said. They sat close to her in armchairs with a small table near them. Tweed reached for his coffee, took a long drink. He felt more lively. Paula drank some water.

'Now, Tweed,' Lucinda commanded with a smile. 'Who have you been hammering into the ground verbally? Tell all.' Her mood was playful.

'We've had a long and interesting chat with Larry. A very able man.'

'In many ways. Michael, believe it or not, is even

213

more capable. That is, before he had his attack of amnesia. I wonder what did cause that?'

'He had a nasty bump on the side of his head. The medical lot think that caused it. May have been hit on the head by someone.'

'That's sinister.'

'The whole thing is highly sinister, if that's the way it did happen.'

'You sound dubious.'

'At this stage of the investigation, Lucinda, I assume nothing. Except that everyone may be lying. And everyone is suspect.'

'So what is the motive?'

'Money and power.' Tweed had leaned forward.

'Don't think I get that,' she said after a pause. She reached for her coffee, sipped it, staring at Tweed. 'You're not going to enlighten me?'

'No, I'm not.' He leaned closer to her. 'We have now identified the last corpse. Number four. The man found by the side of the track on Dartmoor.'

'So who was he?'

'I'm not revealing that to anyone yet.'

'You think he might be the key to your riddle?' she enquired.

'Yes, he could be. I know a lot more now than I did when I visited Abbey Grange. When I saw the Reverend Stenhouse Darkfield ringing his bell nonstop in the church tower.'

'So you think that's significant?' Her expression was puzzled.

'At this stage everything—and anything—could be significant. Paula and I walked past a series of thatched cottages joined together. A hamlet, I suppose. What's it called?'

'Oh,' she said offhandedly, 'it's a nowhere place

214

with no name. You get that sort of thing on Dartmoor.'

Tweed finished his coffee, stood up. 'It's getting late. I imagine the plant has closed. I've never seen inside it.'

'I'll show you a view.' She took a mink coat off a hanger, put it on, caressed the fur. 'Bought at a knock-down price at a place in Bond Street going bankrupt. I'll come with you.'

Walking ahead of them along the corridor, she stopped suddenly. Using a key, she unlocked a wide panel in the wall, which slid back. She gestured to them to look beyond it.

They were looking down on a vast plant with wide aisles dividing long stacks of clean white shelves from each other. The lights were still on, no sign of staff, and the shelves were full of food products in brightly coloured containers. Cold air seeped into the corridor and Paula realized the whole plant was air-conditioned.

She stared down at an aisle, which had railway lines running down it, twenty feet below them. A stationary motorized engine was perched on the rails with a convoy of open white plastic trucks behind it. She pointed down to the strange train.

'What's that?'

'Larry's brilliant idea. Trucks laden with supplies drive to the back, a long way as you can see. Originally staff had to carry the supplies to the shelves. Now they load up the trollies and the engine carries them along the rails to where they're unloaded.' She closed the panel, locked it. 'We're not supposed to leave that open for long.'

'We'd better be going now,' Tweed suggested.

She turned round and came up to him so close he

215

caught a whiff of expensive perfume. Her voice was soft.

'Now tell me the identity of the fourth corpse. You know you can trust me.'

She moved even closer to him. Tweed stood his ground.

'Its identity is completely confidential.'

'Oh, well, I tried.' She turned towards her office. 'I've just realized I can't come down with you. I've forgotten to check the rear doors are locked.'

On the ground floor a uniformed guard opened the front door for them and said 'Good night.' It was chilly as they crossed the terrace and descended the steps, and Tweed used his remote to open the car doors. As Paula settled herself into the passenger seat he nipped round, jumped in behind the wheel, shut his door and inserted his key into the ignition.

21

Someone was tapping urgently on Paula's window. She looked out, saw Harry Butler's face, lowered the window. He thrust his head inside.

'I wouldn't turn that ignition key,' he told Tweed with a smile.

'Why not?'

'You left something behind.'

Bending down, Harry grasped hold of a small black metal box and perched it on the edge of Paula's window. Unfastening a catch, he raised the lid. A sprawl of wires jumped up, one red, one blue, one black. Paula peered inside. At the tip of

216

each wire was a small plug and below them a complex of curled wires. She shuddered.

'Looks just like a bomb.'

'It is a bomb,' Harry replied. 'Of enormous explosive power—enough not only to blow the car to smithereens but to take down half the wall of the building behind me. A highly sophisticated mechanism.' He grinned at Paula. 'Don't worry, I've removed the detonator. This little beauty had been cleverly inserted under the pedal Tweed would have pressed, even earlier, when he switched on.'

Paula wiped her damp hands on her jeans. Tweed leaned forward to see Harry clearly.

'How come you're down here?'

'I followed you. Someone has to take care of the both of you.'

'Tell me.'

Harry lowered the inert bomb to the ground. 'I saw your car parked all on its own in the open. Not a good idea. I was outside the gates when I heard a motorcycle coming down from London. It stopped a few hundred yards up the road, then turned and left. Nothing for a while. It was dark, so not easy to watch the car. Then the glare lights came on. I saw a shadow against the wall as someone vanished round the back. Didn't like the look of that.'

'Don't keep us in suspense,' urged Paula.

'I went to the speakphone, told the guard I was SIS. He opens the gates and I run down the drive. Show the guard my folder, tell him I'll wait outside to guard the car. He goes back in. Using a torch, I first crawl under the car, checking the underside of the chassis. Favourite place to plant a bomb. Nothing.'

'You were very thorough,' Tweed commented.

'Do let him go on,' Paula snapped.

'So next I use the torch to check the interior. Know a lot about cars. Saw something under the accelerator pedal that shouldn't be there. Used a jemmy to unlock the passenger door in seconds, crawled inside, found the bomb. Lucky I'm an explosives expert. Got out my metal clippers, used them to cut the wires—after taking a deep breath and praying. Question of knowing the correct sequence.'

'You guessed right, then,' Paula said.

'Guessing doesn't do the job, if you want to survive. It's a new French device. Recently one of Marler's informants gave him detailed photos of the bomb. I joined the boffins down in the basement while they analysed them. They found out how it worked. I was lucky.'

'*We* were lucky,' Tweed said. 'Lucky that you followed us. A feeble thanks for saving our lives.'

'All part of the job. Going back to Park Crescent? Then I'll follow you. First I'll dive into the back, tell you when to stop. My car's parked in a field just off the M3.'

'The killer seems to like this area,' Paula said thoughtfully as the gates were automatically opened and Tweed drove on to the motorway. 'That bullet through our window was fired not far from here.'

'That won't help us,' Tweed said as he stopped at Harry's request.

'I noticed,' Paula went on as they waited, 'that Lucinda felt it necessary to explain to us why she couldn't come down and leave at the same time. Whoever hired the assassin may well have known

218

about the bomb.'

'Same thought occurred to me,' he agreed.

*   *   *

The freighter *Oran* had now passed through the
Straits of Gibraltar and was steaming a hundred
and fifty miles off the coast of Portugal, heading
north. The weather was unseasonably warm in the
night, the sea unusually calm, gleaming like a vast
blue lake under the moonlight.

Abdul, a huge Arab, peered over the port side. A
cat's cradle was slung over the side containing two
Arabs. They had now painted out the name *Oran*.
With a bit of luck, Abdul thought, they'd have
painted in the new name before they sailed into the
rough sea of the Bay of Biscay.

High above the ship a different flag hung limply
from the pole. While in the Mediterranean it had
flown the Liberian flag. Now a different flag of
convenience had been hoisted, a Panamanian one.

Despite the fact that Abdul was taking the
freighter along little-used commercial sea lanes, he
still had lookouts posted on both port and
starboard sides. He began touring the vessel. On
the port side he stopped suddenly. One of the
lookouts was slumped against the hull, fast asleep.
His thin lips tightened.

He called out softly to two more Arabs, who ran
to him. He pointed to the sleeping lookout, gave
his orders in a cold voice. They obeyed
immediately, bent down, each taking hold of the
sleeping lookout's armpits, hauling him upright.

'Ali,' Abdul hissed in Arabic, 'you are a disgrace
to Allah. We do not need lazy slobs like

you aboard.'

He nodded to his two men. They hoisted Ali up higher so his shoulders were bent over the hull, over the sea. Abdul took out his curved knife, leaned forward, slashed the throat of Ali from ear to ear. 'No blood on the hull, please,' he said softly.

The two men reacted swiftly. They jerked the body, dripping blood, well clear of the hull, hurled it as far as they could into the sea. Abdul ordered them back to their posts. An experienced skipper, he knew the body would be carried away from the Portuguese coast, well out into an ice-cold Atlantic stream.

He checked his watch. He would reach his ultimate destination after dark, which was the plan. On time. He took out from under his long flowing galabaieh a sheet of paper. The instructions of his unknown employer were clear, passed to him by a middleman.

He should reach Angora port within ten days. By then the freighter would be loaded with the missiles to be launched from the long-range rockets already in their possession. The chosen target would be annihilated.

*   *   *

Tweed and Paula were approaching Park Crescent. Fairly close behind them followed Harry in his Peugeot, ready to roar forward in an emergency, his automatic weapon concealed under the overcoat on the seat beside him.

'Are we getting closer to the murderer?' Paula asked.

'I think it's possible we've already met the

savage.'

'So you've narrowed down the suspects?'

'No, not yet. Are you feeling fresh?'

'Very. I sense some other visit after we've been to the office.'

'Ivy Cottage, Heel Lane, Boxton, Berkshire. Off the road to Amersham.'

'Who on earth lives there?'

'Lived, unfortunately. Lee Greystoke. I think she may have found something important during her night-time visits to the Gantia plant. Being a woman, you're more likely to find where she's hidden it.'

'What is "it"?'

'I have no idea.'

'I can't wait. You do realize that it will be dark? Dark when we try to find this cottage. Dark when we get there. I can't imagine after at least three months the electricity's still on.'

'Any more objections?' Tweed said irritably. 'I can always get someone else to come with me. Are you tired? If so, I don't think you ought to come.'

'Losing your memory?' she snapped. 'A moment ago I told you I was feeling fresh. I do suggest we get Monica to fetch us refreshment from the all-night deli before we start out. We haven't eaten for hours. *You* haven't.'

'A good idea.' Tweed was calm now. 'I'd much sooner have you with me. Every day that passes the trail of the four-time murderer grows colder. Also, I have another sense that we need to move very fast.'

'I'll get out a map for a route to Berkshire—and I'll navigate.' She grinned at him. 'I do it better than you.'

'You certainly do.'

The whole team were inside his office when they walked in. Monica had closed the curtains over the dark outside. Harry immediately plunged into an account of the bomb. The effect on Marler was electric. He stood up, his expression unusually grim.

'That's it, then. You said, Harry, the bomb was a French design? Right. That means Charmian again.' He began pacing, much in the manner of Tweed. 'We've got to wipe out that guy fast. My guess is he's holed up somewhere in London. Harry must have been followed by him when the rat first saw Tweed leaving here.'

'Didn't realize I was being followed,' Harry said apologetically. 'Tons of traffic on the M3 until we were near Gantia.'

Marler wasn't listening.

'I'm going to talk to as many as I can of my ladies of the night. They are very observant, hear a lot. See you.'

Marler grabbed a long black leather sheath with 'Slazenger' printed on the side, slung it over his shoulder. Paula squeezed his arm for luck.

'I don't think what you've got inside that thing is sporty.'

'Armalite.'

Marler left, closing the door quietly. Paula raised her eyebrows as she stared at Tweed. 'I've never known him look so ferocious.'

'Neither have I. The hunter is now the hunted.'

* * *

Newman stood up, put on his lightweight overcoat,

left it unbuttoned so he could reach his .38 Smith & Wesson quickly. He was heading for the door when he spoke.

'I'm going after Marler. I have different informants from him.'

Peter Nield also headed for the door. He glanced round the office before he left.

'Marler will be heading for Soho. Like Harry, I know people in the East End. Someone will have noticed a Frenchman recently arrived. We'll get him tonight . . .'

'I'm not joining them,' Harry announced. 'I sense Tweed and Paula are going somewhere—she's been studying an Ordnance Survey map of Berkshire. I'll be right behind them. Paula, can you spare me a sandwich? I heard you sending Monica to the deli.'

'And I guessed you'd be coming along. I've ordered for three of us.'

*   *   *

Tweed was surprised at the weight of traffic at that late hour. Did it never stop? The endless crawl bumper to bumper? Only when they were beyond Beaconsfield did the weather change. Dark and drizzly in London, it was now a clear cloudless sky, the landscape crystal bright under the moon's glow, the atmosphere bitterly cold.

'It's so quiet now,' Paula commented. 'Incidentally, we're on the A355, so we'd better keep a close lookout. And it would help me if you slowed down.' She had her map open on her lap. She and Tweed were alert now after consuming the sandwiches from the deli. 'It's a turning off on the

223

right, Lucinda told you?'

'Yes. We've passed several with no names. Very helpful.'

He slowed as they came to another turn-off, a country lane with an evergreen forest on both sides. Paula tapped his arm. He slowed down to twenty miles an hour.

'This is it,' she said quickly. 'Heel Lane, Boxton.'

'Now all we have to do is to find Ivy Cottage,' he remarked. 'And Lucinda said it was isolated.'

'So keep crawling.'

The forest hemming them in on both sides was dense, and mist began to drift across the lane. Tweed grunted, concentrating on his headlights as they swung round curve after curve. Paula was gazing to her right. No sign of any habitation, no sign of life, no traffic. She glanced back down an exceptionally long stretch of straight road. Nothing.

'I think Harry missed the turning,' she warned. 'We're on our own.'

'I've got my Walther,' Tweed told her.

'And I've got my Browning, also my Beretta tucked down inside my boot—and this.' She produced from a sheath strapped to her right leg a knife. Tweed stared quickly at it and frowned.

'Where did that come from?'

'When I was down at the Surrey mansion training, the new chap in charge gave it to me. Made me practise using it against a leather dummy of a man. Wasn't satisfied until I'd rammed it in up to the hilt six times running.'

'He offered me one,' Tweed said. 'I refused it.'

'Attacked suddenly at close quarters, a knife can be the only answer.'

She had just spoken when they heard an oncoming motorcyle. It was moving, had its light full on in a blinding glare. Tweed flashed his lights but they had no effect. Paula had a glimpse of a rider clad in leather with a large helmet and enormous visor. Impossible to tell whether it was a man or a woman. Then it was gone.

She blinked several times to clear her vision. Then she was watching to her right past Tweed. He was still moving the car at a snail's pace. She gripped his arm.

'Stop! I think we've found it.'

'I didn't see anything,' he responded as he applied the brake.

'Then let's get out and look.'

He locked the door, followed her. A rickety wooden gate stood half open, leaning over. The path beyond, illuminated by Paula's torch, was narrow and hard mud spattered with a few pebbles. Ahead he saw she was right—there was an ancient thatched cottage with mullioned windows. It needed a coat of paint. Giant firs surrounded the cottage and it was quiet as the grave.

'This is it,' Paula whispered.

She was shining her torch on a grubby nameboard attached to the side of the house: IVY COTTAGE. Tweed peered over his glasses. The name board hadn't been attended to for ages.

'Damned silly place to put it,' he grumbled. 'Can't ever be seen from the road. Strikes me Lee didn't want anyone to find the place while she was here.'

Paula was standing still, one hand close to her ear. She had acute hearing. In the distance, coming closer, from the same direction they had driven,

225

she heard the sound of a motorcycle. Tweed now heard it too. It came closer, closer, then about a hundred yards from the cottage entrance it stopped. Tweed flapped a hand for her to turn off her torch, which she did. At the same time she gripped the butt of the Browning, hauled it out.

'It's the same motorcyclist that passed us,' she whispered.

The claustrophobic atmosphere of the cottage buried amid the walls of firs made her keep her voice down.

'How do you know that?' Tweed asked sceptically. 'Probably several people use motorbikes in this neck of the woods.'

'It had a souped-up engine which made a faint clicking noise. So did the machine that's come back.'

*   *   *

'It might be safer inside if we can get in,' Tweed suggested.

Paula turned round, lifted the rusty iron latch and realized the door had been slightly open as she pushed the heavy slab of old wood. Cautiously, she stepped inside on to a wooden plank floor. No luxury here. Tweed swiftly followed, closed the door almost shut, leaving it about a foot's width open. He didn't want the door to stick when they had to leave.

A musty smell greeted them as they walked over a pile of envelopes which had been pushed through the iron letterbox. Paula switched on her torch, shielding it with her hand. She warned Tweed not to switch on any lights yet.

226

Feeling her way round wooden chairs and tables, she went from window to window, closing the curtains, which needed a gentle tug. Then she called out to Tweed to find the light switch. To his surprise the lights came on, old workmen's lamps slung round the walls from hooks, the kind once used to warn motorists at night of obstacles.

They cast a red glow over the interior. When Tweed checked them he found a continuous cable attached to each of them. At the moment he had operated the switch he hard the sound of a portable generator purring softly.

'Lee was very clever,' he said. 'She realized she wouldn't be coming here for long periods, that the utilities would be cut off, so what does she do? She buys these old lamps and a portable generator, then fixes up cable linking the lamps and the generator. She must have been a technical wizard.'

'You've seen the state the place is in?'

Tweed had already observed that. The ground floor was one large room, a small kitchen let into an alcove. Old wooden cupboards standing against the walls had all their drawers pulled out, their contents spread on the floor. Tins and glass jars had been opened and emptied below the cooking area. Pushed against a side wall was a single bed, its mattress on the floor, slashed open.

'Ransacked, just like that houseboat detective's place,' Tweed remarked. 'Now, a woman lived here for short periods. So where would she hide something important?'

'You ask me that after someone wrecked the place?' Paula exclaimed indignantly.

'I'm assuming the ransacker didn't find what he—or she—was looking for. Meantime, I'm going

227

outside to make sure the lights don't show.'

He slipped quickly out of the front door, toured the cottage, watching his footing to avoid brambles. Lee had been clever. The curtains were thick, so the glow from the red lamps didn't show from the outside. Lee had been something else again. He wished he could have met her.

He arrived back at the front entrance, stumbled over the wooden ledge and sprawled into the room as the first bullet swept past him, shattering a mullion pane at the back of the cottage.

*   *   *

Tweed hugged the floor as more bullets came through the door opening above him. He already had the Walther in his hand, had now seen the muzzle flash. He began firing at where the assassin must be lying behind a tall fir. Already Paula was flat on her stomach beside him, after crawling along the floor. She also saw the muzzle flash, waited until Tweed had emptied his magazine, then she aimed and fired, first to the right, then the left, then back again to the right and the left of the tree. She had worked out that the gunman would move to one side or the other of the fir to continue his fusillade.

She was sliding in another magazine when she realized no more shots had been fired at the cottage. She waited. So did Tweed, thinking as she had done. Dead silence. No more shots.

They remained perfectly still alongside each other. A few minutes later they heard the sound of the motorcycle starting up, the souped-up whine of speed. It was travelling away from them, heading back down the lane for the road to Beaconsfield, or wherever.

'That was a close one,' Paula said as they stood up. 'I'm continuing my search.'

'I wish you luck.'

After a few minutes she arrived in front of a small fridge standing next to the kitchen, contents littering the floor. She opened the fridge, bent down, peered inside its emptiness. A truly foul odour of rotting food assailed her. She ignored it, then reached in with her bare hands and clawed at the back. The fridge colour was cream, but the rear struck her as lighter in colour.

Her persistent fingers removed a slim panel glued to the rear wall. Behind it was a cream-coloured envelope. She took it out, stood up, called out to Tweed.

'Could this be what you're looking for?'

Putting on latex gloves, he opened the flap and took out a sheet covered with computer figures. He looked at Paula and grinned.

'This is the key document which confirms the pattern for murder I've slowly built up in my mind. It confirms four hundred million pounds have been sent by electronic transmission from Bone in Angora to someone in Britain. The reference number's the same as the one on the sheets Keith Kent decyphered for me. This must be the printout of the transaction, sent by post or courier to whomever received the four hundred million.'

'Why?'

'To reassure whoever mastered the deal with Angora.'

'But whoever received this vast sum must have known they'd now got their hands on it,' Paula objected.

229

'The sender in Bone must have been anxious to be certain that was the case, so they followed it up with confirmation. This is what Lee, searching the executive offices down at Gantia, must have found. A clever lady. Frightened that the killer would try to get it back, she hid it here in this cottage—ready to hand to Drago when he came back from abroad.'

'So X, let's call the recipient of this fortune, found a way to become fabulously wealthy by supplying something of great value to Angora?'

'Yes,' Tweed said. 'But I sense it wasn't that simple. Before any of this happened I believe X had in some way rifled the Gantia till, so to speak, to the tune of four hundred million. Then he lost the whole lot—or she did. So to put it back in Gantia's reserves—before Drago discovered it was missing—X, in a desperate state—worked out this deal with Angora.'

'X had rifled the till of four hundred million, lost it, had to find a way of getting the same sum back to put it back in the till.'

'You've got it, Paula,' Tweed agreed.

'So you now know who the killer is?'

'No, I don't. Because I don't know who the reference number belongs to.'

There was a creak of wood under foot pressure near the front door. Paula had her Browning gripped in both hands as she took aim.

*   *   *

'Don't shoot the guard, although maybe I deserve it,' said the voice of Harry Butler.

He stood just inside the front door, both hands above his head, a small Uzi machine gun looped over his back. He had a downcast expression as he lowered his hands, walked up to them.

'What are you talking about?' Paula asked. 'Saying you deserve it.'

'I followed you from Park Crescent, keeping one car between us. Then, on the way to Beaconsfield, a car cut me off. I stopped just in time. By the time I drove on to the A355 I was well behind you, didn't see where you'd turned off. I was almost in Amersham when I turned back. I found Heel Lane. Just before I reached it a motorcyclist came out like a shell from a gun, raced back towards London.' He paused suddenly, staring past them. 'Hey, what's been going on? Those are bullet holes in the rear windows.'

Tweed tersely related their recent experience. Butler's reaction was to rush back to the front door, close it, then to grab a tall, heavy, overturned chair and jam it against the door. He came back.

'You know something? That motorcyclist thug must have followed me after he'd seen you leave Park Crescent. And I never spotted him in the dense traffic. Not doing very well, am I?'

'Stop it!' Paula hugged Harry. 'Remember you saved our lives on the M3 when you found that bomb. *I* nearly missed Heel Lane on the way out.'

'Strikes me,' Harry mused, 'Newman, Marler and Pete are wasting their time. Trawling Soho, the East End and wherever Pete is traipsing around looking for what's-his-name.'

'Charmian,' said Paula.

'First,' Harry explained, 'I heard a motorcyclist down on the M3 when this Frenchie placed a bomb in your car. Second, it was a motorcyclist who tried to gun you down here. Right? I thought so. This

231

hasn't been thought out. The assassin has been watching the office, probably hides his machine in the greenery across the main road beyond Park Crescent.'

'Sounds plausible,' Tweed agreed. 'Now Paula's found what I need, we'll get back there.'

'The others will never find this Frenchie,' Harry said as they left.

*   *   *

Marler was a walking machine. It was well after midnight and he was still prowling Soho. He'd accosted over a dozen of his lady informants, but had got nowhere. Charmian was either nowhere near Soho or had found a secret hideaway.

He walked into yet another sleazy 'club'. Hard to see inside through the clouds of smoke. Professional girls sat at cheap Formica-covered tables, pretending to sip at a drink of coloured water, arguing the price with a man.

A burly individual in shirtsleeves and braces grasped him by the arm. His expression was unpleasant, threatening.

'Cost you fifty nicker to come 'ere, mate.'

'I don't think so,' Marler said quietly, shoving his folder under the man's pockmarked nose. 'Any trouble from you and the hygiene inspectors will be coming.'

He walked on into the haze, spotted a girl with blonde hair who looked half intelligent. He sat down opposite her. She was checking him out, his clothes, his expression, before she spoke.

'You're not the fuzz. I can tell. You could be Special Branch is my guess. And you're not 'ere

232

for me.'

'You could be right. I'm looking for a man I can't describe. He's not been over here long and keeps to himself. He'll speak English, probably with a French accent. He does have a motorbike, probably a good one. Ring any bells?'

'Info costs money. I like you. Don't get me wrong. Info still costs money.'

Marler reached into his trouser pocket, brought out four fifty-pound notes, kept them in his hand. He'd extracted them from his wallet earlier. This was not the sort of area where you showed a wallet. She stubbed out the cigarette she was smoking in a tiny ashtray, lit another.

'The motorbike tells me something.' She looked at her empty hand. 'Haven't got any dosh yet.'

'Tell me, I'll decide if it's any good. If it's *very* good you get what I'm holding.'

'There's a Mrs Hogg. That's what she is, a hog for cash. I'd never stay there. So here's the address . . .'

*   *   *

After leaving Heel Lane at high speed, Charmian had made his way back to London. He wasn't happy. He'd botched the job a third time. No precedent for that—he always pulled off an assignment first time.

He moved fast on his Harley Davidson, keeping a sharp eye open for where a patrol car might be parked. To hell with speed limits. The gun he had used to try to kill Tweed the first time, a weapon with the numbers filed off, was now in a field he'd tossed it into.

233

Before starting out on this mission he had shaved off his curved moustache. His dark hair was concealed under a baseball cap. The telescopic ladder he had used to scale the wire fence at the Gantia plant was at the bottom of a pond miles away. The rifle he'd used to shoot at Tweed at Ivy Cottage was buried in the mud of a lake he'd passed. Charmian was a professional.

Eventually arriving in London, he had crawled through Soho, which he had earlier in the day reconnoitred. Feeling like a drink, he had entered several 'clubs', including the one patronized by Marler's bottle blonde. Here he had made his only mistake.

Approached by a woman Charmian had brushed her aside. His remark had not been complimentary: 'I can do much better than you elsewhere . . .'

Which was why the blonde girl had followed him, to see which establishment he had entered. Mrs Hogg's. Checking that no one was watching, he wheeled his machine into the alley at the back of her place, saw the fire escape running up past a first-floor room. With his gloved hands he disabled the machine, which tomorrow would end up in the Thames.

He walked back up the narrow side street, which led to the entrance. A board outside proclaimed, ROOMS TO LET—BY THE HOUR, OR THE DAY. A blatant invitation which Mrs Hogg kept there by passing the local policeman cash.

Beyond the entrance was a small reception area. Behind a wooden counter stood a fat woman with greedy eyes. She wore a cheap dress, waited for him to speak.

'I need the room for three days,' Charmian

began. 'On the first floor. One with a fire ladder—I fear the fire.'

'That's five hundred quid. Where's the girl?'

'No girl.' Charmian leaned over the counter. Mrs Hogg didn't like that. She stepped back, nervous now. 'I do not think anyone would pay this five hundred,' he said quietly.

'Three hundred,' she managed to snap. 'That's rock bottom. Don't think you can sneak in a girl up the fire escape. It's locked with a chain at the bottom.'

'I just need the sleep.' He already had his wallet out, placed three hundred pounds in fifty-pound notes on the counter. 'You stupid Brit woman,' he went on. 'I say I need the sleep.'

'You can always go elsewhere,' Mrs Hogg shouted, after grabbing hold of the money. 'Room 10. First floor. Up the stairs,' she sneered.

'You shut the stupid face.'

Holding the key she had given him, he walked up the middle of the stairs, which creaked. Room 10 was small, had a double bed—he guessed why—and a small toilet closet. He turned on the light, a forty-watt bulb, lifted the sheets and mattress off the bed, shook the mattress. No bugs. He made the bed up again quickly, switched off the light, went to the window.

He pulled back the curtains cautiously and stared down. There was a fire escape just outside his window. The alley below was a pool of darkness. As his night vision returned he saw his machine. He tried to lift the window. It was stuck. He took a deep breath, heaved with all his strength, jerked it up. That was how he would leave early in the morning. The payment for three days was to fool

Mrs Hogg into believing he'd be there longer.

He took off his cap, his leather jacket and trousers. Underneath was a pale-blue suit, which he kept on. He removed his boots, reached round his back to the knife tucked down inside a sheath behind his belt. It had a large blade with a keen edge on both sides. Placing it on the table beside the bed, he fell fast asleep, leaving the light on.

* * *

An unrecognizable Marler walked into the small hall where Mrs Hogg stood behind the counter, an old name board was propped up in full view: MRS DINA HOGG.

Marler had changed inside the toilet at the back of the 'club' where the blonde woman had given him the address. Having taken off his dark jacket, he turned it inside out, put it on. He was now clad in a light-blue jacket with yellow checks—very sporty. Next he rammed a cap on, hiding his hair. Taking out a pair of large square-rimmed glasses, he put them on, stared into the mirror over the basin. It was a different man who gazed back at him. He slung the dark sheath containing the Armalite close to his side. No one in the 'club' who had noticed it had thought it wise to ask any questions.

After lifting the bar across the exit door, he disappeared into the outside world. Within ten minutes he was walking inside the small hall where Mrs Hogg stood on guard.

'You on your own, too?' she rasped.

'Special Branch,' Marler hissed with a lisp. 'Have you a guest who speaks English with a

236

French accent?'

He hoped he had guessed correctly.

'What if I have?'

'You did hear me say Special Branch? I don't want to have to bring a team to turn this place over,' he warned, an air of menace in his tone.

'Yes . . . yes . . . I have,' she stuttered. 'Room 10. A corner room with a fire escape.'

'Don't make the mistake of phoning him while I'm upstairs.'

He didn't like the look of the ancient worn wooden stairs. He walked slowly, placing his feet as far as possible to either side. No creaks. Turning left along a narrow landing, he paused in front of Room 10. The end room, so it was the one with a fire escape and a window. Too dangerous to fiddle with the lock.

He walked back downstairs in the same way he had come up. Mrs Hogg's fat figure was shaking like a jelly. She was wiping her sweaty hands on her dress. Marler nodded, said only one thing before he went outside.

'More than your life is worth to phone him. A dangerous criminal . . .'

Outside he hurried back along the deserted side street, made his way back to the alley. He had a problem. He couldn't fire his Armalite. Mrs Hogg would hear the shot.

The alley was pitch black. He used a torch to check there were no drink cans lying about. Kicking one would wake up Charmian. He put a glove on his left hand, took out a picklock with his right. It was a big lock. They were always the easiest to open. Holding the lock with his gloved hand, he fiddled with the pick, had it open in seconds. His gloved hand held on to it so there was no risk of its clattering down into the alley.

He placed chain and lock on the floor, looked up. His eyes were now accustomed to the dark. He was surprised to see the room's window was wide open on a chilly night. Didn't like anything abnormal. He climbed the rusty iron steps two at a time, placing his feet carefully. The Armalite, ready for action, was gripped in both hands. He paused outside the open window screened by a curtain.

He was listening for any sound—snoring, heavy breathing of a man fast asleep, the creak of bed springs as the occupant quietly got up. Nothing. He would have to use the barrel of the rifle, preferably to bring it down across the bridge of the nose, alternatively across a kneecap.

He parted the curtain slightly, just enough to peer inside. A feeble bedside light was on, perched on a table. It gave him enough illumination to realize the bedroom was empty, the bed linen thrown on the floor. He stepped over the sill, crept to the tiny toilet room. Door open. Empty. The bird had flown.

He remembered his foot making a slight creak when he had been on the landing. Very slight but enough to alert Charmian. His reputation as a top professional was proving itself once more. Marler also checked the door leading into the hall and found it locked.

He returned to the window, peered out cautiously, ran down the staircase, slipping his Armalite back inside its sheath. He was whistling as he casually entered reception. Mrs Hogg was standing in the same position as earlier. Didn't the woman ever move?

238

'Your guest who was in Room 10 . . .' he began.

'He's gawn. 'Ad all his clothes on, bag over his shoulder, said he wanted a drink.'

'Thank you,' said Marler.

'He'll be back,' she called after him as he left for the street. 'Paid for his room for three nights.'

'No, he won't,' Marler said to himself grimly.

Which meant Charmian was still on the prowl, God knew where. It also meant he would try for the fourth time to assassinate Tweed. Marler just hoped he'd be there to prevent it.

22

Activity at Park Crescent in the middle of the night was frenetic. Paul and Tweed returned from Ivy Cottage to find the whole team assembled. Marler immediately told them about his abortive attempt to kill Charmian.

'He'll try again,' he concluded.

'Then,' said Newman, 'we have to make sure enough of us are with Tweed at all times.'

'No,' snapped Tweed. 'I have to operate alone or with Paula.'

'Then in that case,' Harry insisted, 'you change your car.'

'No,' Tweed snapped again. 'That would mean Charmian is dictating my way of life. I'm used to my car.'

'OK,' Harry persisted, 'I'm the smallest. I travel everywhere with you hunched up in the back. I'm going to do it whether you like it or not.'

'Don't forget,' Paula reminded her chief, 'Harry

saved us both from that bomb. You've got to listen to him.'

'Yes, you've got to listen to him,' growled Marler.

'You're going to,' added Nield.

'All right.' Tweed threw up his hands in exasperation. 'To keep you all happy I'll agree to that.'

'Even going home to your apartment,' Paula hammered. 'No more walking home till Charmian is in the morgue.'

'Next, I have to phone Lucinda,' Tweed decided. 'I want her to drive down to Abbey Grange to check out Michael.'

'Michael? Why?' asked Paula.

Without replying, he called Lucinda himself. He had her number in his head. A sleepy voice answered.

'Tweed here. Hope I didn't wake you.'

'You didn't. I can't sleep. Keep thinking about all those horrible murders. Wish I had something to do.'

'You have. In the morning I want you to drive down to Abbey Grange and check on Michael.'

'I can drive down now, get there early morning. He's still not said one word. I called Mrs Brogan. So if you hoped he'd talk to me . . .'

'No. I want you to watch him without his realizing what you're up to. Then let me know what your impressions are.'

'I'm on my way . . .'

'Hold on, we visited Ivy Cottage out at Boxton. Place had been ransacked. Same as in the houseboat where the detective, John Jackson, was found.'

'I'm on my way . . .' she repeated.

240

'You didn't tell her about the envelope I found in the cottage,' Paula commented.

'Didn't I?'

'And why are you sending Lucinda down to watch Michael?'

'Everybody except me is forgetting about him. I want to see how she reports the situation down there.'

'That's right.' She smiled ruefully. 'Go cryptic on me.'

'Now let's see if I can get any cooperation, even sense, out of the MoD.' Again he dialled the number himself on his old-fashioned phone. 'MoD? Tweed here, Deputy Director, SIS. I need to speak urgently to Commander David Wells. He's usually on night duty. My code? Stop wasting my time or you'll lose your job. *Just get Commander Wells.*'

'Who is speaking?' a cultured voice enquired after a long pause.

'Tweed. David, I need to know—'

'You didn't give the code.'

'Damn the code. You know my voice. Is this a secure line?'

'At this end, yes. Don't know about yours . . .'

'I want your searcher ships—and aircraft—to scan the route up north from Gibraltar for a freighter. Old job, tonnage fifteen to sixteen thousand tons. Single funnel. Name of vessel *Oran*. Flies Liberian flag.'

'This is confidential. We do have search ships out already—concentrating on the Straits of Dover and the Anglian coast. As regards the Med, the Americans have sent out searchers from their big base at Naples, concentrating on the eastern Med.

Happy now?' David's tone was becoming bored.

'Wrong damned area,' Tweed snapped. 'I've given you a very precise description. And the crew are all Arabs.'

'Really? Then it would automatically be stopped and searched by a corvette at the Dover Straits.'

'Supposing that isn't its destination?'

'There's a limit to the areas we can cover. And Naples would not appreciate suggestions from us.'

'Great collaboration. One more question. We know Angora has obtained a large delivery of long-range rocket launchers from North Korea, but no missiles. How much would the sort of missile they need cost?'

'I can't imagine why this interests you. One missile would cost about one million pounds.'

'One million pounds per missile?' Tweed repeated.

'Yes. That paranoid North Korean dictator, Kim, sent the launchers in an advance vessel, then followed it up with the missiles on another ship which promptly collided with an American destroyer in the Sea of Japan. Tokyo reported their divers found forty armed missiles aboard the sunken ship. Armed! They must be mad to send them armed. But Kim *is* mad.'

'So Angora's now desperately short of missiles, can't yet launch them against a big city target in Europe?'

'I would presume so.' Commander Wells paused. 'Tweed, you're not off your rocker, are you? The newspapers are full of reports that you're investigating a pretty ghastly murder case. I don't see any link between what you've been asking me and the mass murderer.'

'I do now.' Tweed controlled his desire to slam down the receiver. 'David, thank you for being so helpful.'

'Any time, old boy . . .'

'Just before you go, any chance of sending searchers out to check the waters off Portugal, Spain and France?'

'None at all. Fully stretched now.'

*   *   *

During their conversation Paula had brought over a notepad in case Tweed needed it. She heard the last part of the conversation, perched on the edge of his desk, her arms folded.

'I couldn't help hearing the bit about the link between the skeletons and this freighter, the *Oran*. I can't see any connection between the two elements.'

'Which is why I'm sitting here and your desk is over there.'

'I understand,' she said quietly.

She was sliding off his desk when he reached forward, grabbed her by the arm. 'I'm sorry. That was unfair of me, unforgivable.'

'You don't have to apologize.' She smiled warmly. 'We all know you're under great pressure. We're just surprised you haven't sworn at any of us.' She smiled again, returned to her desk, peered between the curtains after drawing them back a few inches. 'It's really dark outside,' she said as she sat down. 'Clouds blotting out the moon. Shouldn't someone check to make sure Charmian isn't waiting out there—as he did before Tweed and I drove out to Boxton?'

243

'I should have thought of that,' said Marler. 'I'm going out to have a shufti.' He saw Paula's expression. 'Arabic for take a look around.'

'I'll come with you,' piped up Harry.

The atmosphere of tension was demonstrated by the fact that Marler took out a Walther, slipped it under the raincoat he put on. Harry fitted a knuckleduster over the fingers of his right hand.

Despite street lamps outside it was pitch black in the shadows. Marler was the first to spot a figure crouched on the pavement on the far side of the main road. They separated, Marler approaching from the left, Harry from the right. The figure remained motionless. Close up he saw it was a tramp, his black overcoat old, rumpled and stained.

'What are you doing here?' Marler demanded.

'Been here quite a while,' Harry said, guessing.

'Got a fiver, sir?' the tramp asked. 'I haven't eaten for hours.'

Marler frowned. He was surprised at how well educated the tramp's voice was. What was going on?

'For a tramp you speak pretty well,' he said grimly. 'What's your name?'

'Ken.' A pause. 'Ken Millington. Or Lord Ken Millington at one time eons ago.'

The name triggered off a memory inside Marler's head, the recollection of one of the top-flight journalists Drew Franklin's lighter-weight articles on 'characters'.

He switched on his torch, shone it down on the tramp's face. About forty years old, his face was covered with bristles, his nose was long and sharply pointed. Obviously he hadn't shaved for days. His hands were clad in old woollen gloves with holes in them. His shoes were old, well worn, tied with string instead of laces.

'If you're a lord,' Harry said aggressively, 'why are you in the state you're in? Never seen a tramp with a voice like yours. Tell the truth before I beat you to a pulp. Who was it hired you to keep a watch on our building?'

'Hang on, Harry,' Marler said. 'Better explain yourself now before my friend gets to work on you.'

'There are others like me,' Millington explained. 'In my case I was bored silly by the life my wife wanted to lead. Parties every night. A load of idiots. Then my wife leaves me for a millionaire. I decided I wanted freedom, the freedom to live my own life. No responsibilities. So I walked out on my greedy family—after willing my assets to a charity. I like this life. It's freedom,' he repeated.

'For fifty pounds, maybe more, would you do a job for us?' Marler suggested.

'For fifty I'd jump over the moon. An honest job, you mean?' he asked suspiciously.

'My boss,' Marler continued, 'was almost murdered by a thug. Hired by a rival businessman. The thug speaks English with a French accent. Can't give you much of a description, but he's recently shaved off a dark moustache which curled round the ends of his mouth. He's French and dangerous. If you see anyone lurking round here, watching our building . . .'

'The insurance outfit in the Crescent?'

He was referring to the plate on the wall outside the entrance to SIS headquarters. It read GENERAL & CUMBRIA INSURANCE. It was the cover name for the SIS. Harry was still suspicious.

'How come you noticed that from over here?'

'I walk around an area before I settle for the night—to find the most comfortable perch. It was here with a cushion against the railings.'

'Here is your fifty,' interjected Marler impatiently. 'You see anyone suspicious lurking about, walk slowly over to the insurance building, press the bell, three long rings. The guard will let you in and call me.'

'This is too much money,' Millington protested. 'I'll take ten, then the rest if I can serve you.'

'Keep the lot . . .'

They explained to Tweed what had happened when they returned to the office. Tweed was more impressed than Marler had expected.

'That was a good idea. We need an element of luck to help us.'

'He sounded a fake to me,' Harry commented, disgruntled.

'There are such people,' Paula told him. 'They get fed up with *les richesses*, yearn for freedom to live their own lives. This Millington apparently said as much.'

'And Lucinda,' Tweed reflected, 'is now on her way driving down to Abbey Grange. I'll be interested in how she phrases her report.'

'I still don't get it,' Paula said sharply.

'We've been absorbed in so many other aspects,' Tweed explained, 'that we'd almost forgotten the existence of Michael. Yet it all started with him. "I witnessed murder." Assuming he *is* suffering from amnesia.'

'You don't believe the psychiatrists?' Paula mused.

'I don't believe a word anyone has told me. As to

your psychiatrists, in a biography of Winston Churchill I read he called them trick cyclists.'

'But could Michael keep up not saying a word all this time?' Paula persisted.

'Unlikely—but not impossible. And at the time of the murders he was allegedly somewhere in the States. Again, like the rest, no alibi. Plus the fact we're up against Armenian deviousness. Their way of life. Larry, Lucinda, Michael all had the same Armenian father, albeit an English mother.'

'Then we can cancel out Aubrey Greystoke,' Paula argued.

'No, we can't. He's been working with Armenians long enough to have picked up their way of thinking.'

*   *   *

The freighter was now sailing a hundred and fifty miles off the French coast. Poring over a chart, Abdul realized the importance of steering well clear of the projecting peninsula of Brittany and the island of Ushant. He changed course, now sailing further northwest.

It had been night but now, in the east, a mix of silver and pink glow was appearing. Dawn. Strictly against maritime law, Abdul was sailing without lights. Gazing ahead, he saw the small French fishing vessel. He gave the swift command to increase speed. That vessel could report the presence of his own ship when it returned to port.

The first warning the French crew aboard the fishing vessel had of the danger was when they saw the looming prow of the freighter almost above them. The prow smashed through the craft, cutting

247

it in two. The two sections of the hull began to sink at once. Abdul saw only one Frenchman dive overboard.

Grabbing his bullhorn, he turned, gave his order in Arabic to two of the men below. They dived over the port side, came up, shook their heads, saw the Frenchman swim towards the distant coast in the hope of finding another fishing vessel. One of the Arabs was a fast swimmer. He came up behind the Frenchman, hauled a large curved knife from his belt, whipped it through the air and sliced off the head of the fisherman.

On the bridge Abdul nodded in satisfaction. His two Arabs were now swimming back to the freighter, where a climbing net had been thrown over the side for them. Abdul saw a pool of gory blood colour the surface where the Frenchman had disappeared. A small wave swept over, dissolved the red pool. Back to normal.

Abdul had also observed that a strong current was carrying debris from the wrecked fishing boat out into the Atlantic. It would also remove the bodies and the decapitated head bobbing on the surface.

'Praise be to Allah,' he said aloud, bowing to the east. 'May he keep the sea calm on our return journey.'

*   *   *

'We're going to see Drago Volkanian,' Tweed told Paula.

'When?' She stood up, parted the curtains cautiously. 'It's only just dawn.'

'Now. Four ninety Jermyn Street is not far away.'

248

'But won't Drago be asleep? We won't be very welcome.'

'Like me, I don't think he needs much sleep and he's a very worried man. He knows something's going on but I'm sure he doesn't know what it is.'

'And you do?'

'Yes, it's going to be a race against time. There's a deadline, with the emphasis on dead.'

They both had their overcoats on when the phone rang. Monica answered, looked up at Tweed.

'You'll never believe who's downstairs wanting to see you.'

'I will if you tell me quickly.'

'Abel Gallagher, head of Special Branch,' she growled, mimicking Gallagher.

'Coats off,' Tweed ordered. 'Now ask him to come up.'

Tweed was studying a file behind his desk and Paula had returned to hers, when the door opened. The burly bulk of Gallagher stormed in. Tweed invited him to sit down.

'To what do I owe this honour?' he enquired sarcastically.

'We're worried about you. The government is worried about you. You're supposed to be investigating this string of skeleton murders. Details are splashed in headlines all over the press. The public are getting worried. So what do you do? You leave the country, friggin' go abroad. Your place is *here*!'

'Who says so?'

'*I* do.'

'And what about this alleged going abroad?'

'An agent of mine at Waterloo spotted you

boarding Eurostar. Next stop Paris—and God knows where. What the hell do you think you're playing at?'

'Finished ranting and raving, Abel?' Tweed asked quietly. 'First, my investigation has nothing to do with you. Second, your department has no authority over the SIS. Third, who in the government is losing his nerve?'

'The Home Secretary,' Gallagher announced triumphantly.

'Then I'll get the PM to have a few words with him, after telling him my information source. You.'

'I have to do my job,' Gallagher said plaintively.

'Then go and do it,' Tweed suggested unpleasantly. 'And leave me to do mine. The door is there.'

Gallagher left like a large dog with its tail between its legs.

'You handled that well,' Paula said as she got up and put on her overcoat. 'He collapsed when you mentioned the PM.'

'Jermyn Street next,' said Tweed.

They drove off in the early-morning light with Harry hunched up out of sight in the back, his Walther in his hand. Paula peered out as they headed for Jermyn Street.

'Millie's still there,' she reported.

'Millie?' asked Tweed.

'My nickname for Ken Millington. Gallagher probably has people following us. We know he's into a bookie for a twenty-thousand-pound debt. I suppose he's not a suspect? We are talking about four hundred million pounds gone missing.'

'It's now back in Gantia's huge reserves,' Tweed told her. 'I looked at that document you found in

250

Ivy Cottage. It's a photocopy of a message from Bone in Angora. AB200017 X is its reference. Same as on the document you found at Christine Barton's flat. I think Lee Greystoke was smart. Prowling inside Gantia's plant she found the original on some executive's desk and photocopied it, so the executive responsible wouldn't know she'd been in the place.'

'So who is the filthy murderer?'

'Still no idea. We have to link up the reference with the person . . .'

'We're still all at sea.'

'So is the *Oran*. Hence the deadline.'

*   *   *

Drago opened the front door himself—doubtless after checking the security mirror above their heads. The outsize Armenian was fully dressed in a grey business suit stretched across his immense shoulders. He was smiling warmly as he invited them to step inside. There was no sign of the brown-faced girl they had seen on their previous visit. They were ushered into the living room as Drago's rumbling voice talked.

'Sir, I like people who can get up early. They are the people who run the world while others sleep. Something to drink? Coffee? I thought so.'

The tallest cafetière Paula had ever seen occupied the small table close to where they were seated together with the most expensive Rosenthal china. Three cups and saucers and plates. White bread rolls of a kind Paula had never seen before. She bit into one. Fabulous. Drago had poured the coffee.

251

'Now, Miss Paula, and you, sir, how can I help you? A man after my own heart who never stops. The papers are devoted to this horrible case you are engaged on.'

Once again his personality seemed to fill the large room, so dynamic and forceful. Tweed helped himself to a bread roll, drank some coffee, taking his time. He suddenly looked at their host, held his gaze.

'I'm double-checking. How many people have keys to enter your armaments factory?'

'Larry, of course, then Lucinda, Michael and Greystoke. A key was also in the possession of poor Lee. I do miss her.'

'Why Greystoke?' Tweed wondered. 'He's an accountant.'

'Exactly. You are shrewd to ask. It would seem strange to you that Aubrey was included in the magic circle. Under my supervision modifications —very expensive—were made to the system. So estimates were requested. Aubrey checked the costs as the work proceeded. I am careful with money.'

'I gather,' Tweed went on quietly, as though it were of little importance, 'some kind of lever converts the machines from producing artillery shells to missiles.'

'That, sir, is correct. It's a coded lever.'

'Coded?'

'I designed it myself. A simple code, if you know what it is.' Drago raised a huge index finger, swept it up vertically, then swept it across at right angles, down vertically, and jerked it aside to the right. 'That, of course, isn't the code, but it shows you how it works.'

252

'Who knows the code?'

'The same people who have keys to the armaments plant. Lucinda, Larry, Greystoke and Michael.'

'And some time ago you decided you'd produce no more missiles, that the plant would only manufacture artillery shells.'

'Absolutely. A complete ban on missiles. For ever.'

'I see.' Tweed paused, took a while drinking the rest of his coffee before he continued. 'So it would perturb you to know that someone has operated the coded lever and has been producing missiles on a large scale recently?'

The effect this suggestion produced on Drago was dramatic. His whole personality changed. His normally benevolent face was transformed into a state of savage fury. His massive jaw clenched, his mouth tightened until the lips almost vanished, his bony structure became prominent, his eyes narrowed into vicious slits. Tweed waited. Eventually Drago found his voice, a ferocious rumble.

'How can you know that such an atrocity is being perpetrated?'

'From various sources of information picked up from different places. They lead to only one conclusion. Some forty missiles have been—or are being—produced.' Tweed fired another shot. 'And are you aware that for a certain period of time the sum of four hundred million pounds went missing from your reserves?'

'Four hundred million?'

Drago's expression had now become apoplectic. Paula decided they were now seeing the real

253

Drago, the man who had escaped from the inferno of Armenia, probably injuring or killing anyone who stood in his way. Tweed reached for the cafetière, refilled Paula's cup, his own, then offered to refill Drago's. The reaction was a brutal wave of his huge hand, refusing the offer. They waited, sipping their coffee.

It was obvious Drago was fighting for self-control. Gradually he settled back more peacefully into his large chair. He gazed at Tweed and rested a shaking hand on the arm of his chair before he could speak in a normal voice.

'You know which of the four is responsible for this act of treachery?'

'Not yet. My next visit may enlighten me.'

'Then I shall leave immediately for . . . the plant.'

'Dartmoor?'

'My destination is my affair.'

'Now.' Tweed leaned forward. 'I will tell you what you are going to do. You will stay here at Jermyn Street until you hear from me. Is that clearly understood?' he said grimly. 'There are factors —dangerous international factors—you know nothing about. Your intervention could ruin my investigation.' Tweed stood up abruptly, his tone still grim. 'I rely on you to do exactly as I have suggested. Do not stir from here. You don't know enough. I do. Thank you for your hospitality. I must keep moving. Time is not on our side.'

Paula had also stood up, was about to follow when Drago gently took hold of her arm. He whispered so only Paula caught what he said.

'You know, my dear, if Tweed was available I would hire him at a huge sum to take over control of Gantia.'

As they climbed into their car the invisible Harry called out quietly from the rear.

'No one came near the car while you were away. The desperate enthusiasts are just beginning to appear, hurrying on foot to their jobs.'

'Desperate enthusiasts?' queried Paula, puzzled.

'The ones with bosses who arrive at eight in the morning. To check up on their staff.'

'How on earth do you know that?' she wondered.

'Got a drinking pal who works in a big firm. He told me he does that. Said life has become a pressure cooker, that in a few years' time at this rate half of them will end up in a hospital or an asylum.'

'He's got a point,' said Paula as they drove along the deserted Mall. 'Quality's gone out of the window. Speed, speed, speed is all they think of.'

'And,' Harry concluded, 'some of them walk miles now the Tube and the trains are so bad.'

'Are we heading for that stockbroker's?' she asked. 'The one whose name Professor Saafeld found on a screwed-up ball of paper under the foot of the first skeleton we found on Dartmoor?'

'You are perceptive.'

'I'll navigate,' she said, an A to Z of London open on her lap. 'Haldon Street is a turning off Threadneedle Street.'

'Will they be open? It's very early,' Harry wondered.

'If they're not, we'll find a parking slot and wait.'

*   *   *

'It's that building on the right,' she warned as Tweed crawled down Haldon Street.

He'd have had to crawl in any case. Even at this early hour the traffic had become dense, moving at five miles per hour. Tweed stopped, signalled left as he saw a Buick backing out of a parking space. Behind him a driver who had decided it was his pressed his horn nonstop.

'Hysteria starts early,' Paula mused as Tweed slid inside the now vacant slot. The driver of the car behind shouted something foul and made a rude gesture with his finger as he drove past. Tweed ignored him as he alighted outside the building with double doors and a legend etched in a window: DORTON, KENWOOD & SMYTHE, STOCKBROKERS. A light was on behind the glass. Was probably on all day—Haldon Street was narrow, hemmed in by tall blocks. The sun would never penetrate down inside this backstreet canyon.

'Be as quick as we can,' he informed Harry before closing the door.

Paula was already pressing a large ancient bell. She had to wait, Tweed alongside her, until the left-hand door was opened, the hinges creaking. A small man stared at them as though they were the last people on earth he wanted to call.

'You investors?' he demanded in an effort at politeness.

'We are investors in information,' Tweed said with a pleasant smile, holding up his identity folder.

'SIS? You've come to the wrong place.'

'No, we haven't. Could I have your name?' He pointed to the etched names in the glass. 'There are several of you.'

'I'm Smythe, the only one left. I guess you'd better come in. Ladies first. Take a pew—you'll have to shift papers off chairs.'

Tweed couldn't place his voice. It wasn't Cockney, but it did have undertones of the way Harry spoke. At the same time it was well educated. Smythe was not the public's idea of an occupant of the Surrey stockbroker belt. He wore a shirt open at the neck, hadn't shaved, his dark trousers had a sharp crease, his black shoes were polished. An odd mixture of apparel.

Paula was seated at the large ebony table, having carefully removed a pile of papers, stacking them neatly on a sideboard. She had prepared a chair for Tweed. As he sat down Smythe lifted another pile off a chair, dumped it on the floor. 'Junk,' he said. Turning the chair round, he sat leaning forward against its back, his shrewd eyes gazing at them.

'You're Smythe,' Tweed began. 'What happened to Dorton?'

'Retired with a pile at the height of the boom. Went off to the Bahamas with a playgirl. He was shrewd in some ways, stupid in others. The playgirl has probably eaten her way through half his fortune already.'

'And Mr Kenwood?'

'Disappeared overnight about three to four months ago. Just walked. Not like him. Never heard a word since.'

'Could you describe Mr Kenwood? Height, weight, age—that sort of description?'

He listened while Smythe gave surprisingly precise data. It fitted in every detail the professor's description of the first skeleton

257

discovered on Dartmoor, just off the track. Tweed knew that at long last he had identified the fourth body.

'Could you give me some idea of his work and his clients?'

'Confidential.' Smythe grinned. 'Don't wave that folder at me. He dealt with some very big investors, was secretive about who they were. Which was proper. We all worked our own clientele.'

'When you say big, how big?'

'Well, he was the only one of us who plunged his clients into the dotcom debacle. I didn't phrase that well. He always warned them it could be another South Sea Bubble, but some of them insisted on diving in big.'

'Four hundred million pounds big?'

'My God!' Smythe threw up both hands. 'That really would be pushing it.' He lit a cigarette. 'There was one client who seemed to grow money who went into dotcom as though money grows on trees. Woody—that's what we called Kenwood —did let slip drinking with me in a pub that he hoped his biggest client didn't shoot himself.'

'So it was a man—not a woman?'

'Come to think of it, he said he hoped this client wouldn't put a gun to *their* head. So it could have been a woman. Yes, I suppose it could have been. Ken was a ladies' man. If a woman investor came to us I'd let him cope with her.'

'You must have a record of clients for the tax people,' Tweed suggested.

Smythe drank some more cold coffee from his still fairly full mug. After placing it on the edge of the table, he walked over near to Paula, pulled open a drawer, took out a small leather-bound

258

book and waved it.

'Details are all in here. Highly confidential.'

'We need to borrow that, Mr Smythe. This is a murder investigation.'

'Got a search warrant?' Smythe asked with a smirk, confident he'd scored a point.

'No, I haven't,' Tweed admitted.

'Then you don't go nosing into our—now my—clients' lives.'

He dropped the book back into the drawer, closed it and came back towards where Tweed was standing. As he did so Tweed glanced at Paula. She nodded. Tweed's elbow shifted, knocked the almost full mug of cold coffee on to the floor. The mug broke into pieces, liquid pooled across the floor.

'I'm so sorry.' Tweed took a plate off the table, bent down, began picking up pieces of broken china, collecting them on the plate. Smythe crouched down and also began collecting wreckage as Tweed apologized again.

Paula opened the drawer very quietly, grabbed the leather-bound book, slipped it into her shoulder bag and closed the drawer carefully. It was a trick they had used before on rare occasions to obtain much-needed evidence. She was checking her watch as the two men stood up and Smythe looked across at her.

'Now I'll need a mop to clean up this mess of coffee,' he grumbled.

'I'm so sorry,' Tweed repeated. 'I think this would be a good time for us to leave.'

'So do I,' snapped Smythe.

'We may now have the final key,' Paula said, a rare note of excitement in her voice, as they approached their car.

'If that notebook tells us who invested four hundred million in a dotcom that crashed, you're right,' Tweed agreed as they arrived at their parked car. '*If* it does,' he added.

23

Paula suggested taking over the wheel while Tweed looked at the record book. He agreed. As they settled themselves a voice from the back, Harry's, called out in a whisper.

'It's OK. No one came near the car.'

'You know where we are, Harry?' Tweed asked.

'Should do. One of my favourite pubs is at the end of this street. Why?'

'Because you're going to act as a courier to return this book to the place we've just visited. Just hand it in, answer no questions, get out of the area.'

Paula was driving west out of the City by a different route. By her side, Tweed had put on latex gloves before opening the book she'd dropped in his lap. No fingerprints. There was more traffic already, so there were plenty of stops, which gave Tweed the chance to examine the pages carefully.

The data was precise: client's name, date of purchase of shares, name of company invested in, price they were bought at, price when sold, profit—or loss—date of selling, the initials of which broker handled the transaction, commission earned by broker. He gave Paula some idea of its contents.

'It's a gold mine,' she exulted.

'Not yet. It's alphabetical under client's surname. I've tried V for Voles. Nothing. Now G for Greystoke. Nothing.' He riffled through all the pages, surprised at some well-known names who had used this broker. He started again at the beginning. By driving through the backstreets of Covent Garden she had made good progress when he grunted.

'Found something?' she asked eagerly.

He had reached X for client's name and there it was. An investment of £400 million, bought at £500 per share in a dotcom he remembered reading about, splashed in the papers because it epitomized the scale of the dotcom crash.

'The client's name is X,' he told her.

'One hell of a lot of use,' she commented.

'Wait. The initials of the broker who handled it are AJK. That has to be Jacko Kenwood, now a corpse. Four hundred million was invested in Orlando Xanadu.'

'Doesn't mean a thing to me.'

'I remember reading it. Floated at three hundred pounds a share, X shovelled in four hundred million at five hundred pounds a share. Orlando soared to a max of eight thousand pounds per share. X, like so many other optimists, did not sell. Orlando then nose-dived vertically to nothing. A nominal price of two pence a share, but it ceased trading.'

'So X lost the lot. A mere four hundred million. I couldn't imagine how such a gigantic sum could have gone down the drain.'

'Neither could I. There's a bit more data. Before X there's an interesting reference. It reads

261

AB200017 X.'

'That's the reference on the papers I found under a drawer in Christine's flat, and then later on the document photocopy I discovered behind Lee Greystoke's fridge at Ivy Cottage.'

'Exactly. So we have advanced. It ties the transaction to someone at Gantia. All this happened some time ago, but X would need time to find a way of recouping four hundred mil to put it back into the reserves.'

'Smythe must have other records of their transactions. I'm sure he must possess other documentation.'

'My thoughts too. Lend me your mobile.'

'You hate them but you're always borrowing mine.' She reached down in her shoulder bag while the traffic was stationary and gave it to him.

'Lucky I noticed his phone number on a letterhead.' He called the number. 'Mr Smythe? Tweed here. Sorry to bother you again but have you by chance had your premises ransacked at any time?'

'Yes, I bloody well have. Ages ago. Came in to find the place a complete wreck. Clients' files strewn all over the floor, cabinets jemmied open. Took me weeks to try and put everything together again. I didn't know enough about Kenwood's transactions to persist. Just jammed stuff back and left it at that.' His annoyed voice changed, became polite. 'Do you know something about this?'

'I'm afraid not. Thank you again for your cooperation.'

He disconnected while Smythe was still blathering and gave the phone back to Paula with a sigh. She looked at him.

262

'Well?'

'Like the other places we've visited, including Jackson's houseboat, Smythe's offices were ransacked. For X's documentation. And, thinking back, I fear the detective was tortured before he was killed.'

'Ugh!' Paula shuddered. 'So we still don't know who this monster X is.'

'But we do now know for certain it's all focused on Gantia, and Abbey Grange.'

*   *   *

Aboard the freighter, Abdul, who rarely slept, was on the bridge. His vessel was now well west of the island of Ushant. With triangular slim rods he was calculating distances. He also checked his watch. It was essential he reach his destination well after dark.

He began changing course. Soon the freighter was heading slowly northwest. Walking to the other end of the bridge, he looked down on the collection of Arabs who had no duties concerning the movement of the vessel. He shouted his instruction down in Arabic.

They had to lie down on their sleeping bags and get some rest. He wanted them fresh for the arduous task of loading up the freighter when it reached the destination known only to him.

Abdul checked his chart again. He checked the freighter's speed, estimated distances. The sea was rougher. He should get there well after dark, at about 2200 hours. The vessel was now on course, would soon pass distant Land's End, then proceed up the Bristol Channel off the northern coast of Devon.

24

'That tramp's still there,' Paula remarked as she swung into Park Crescent. 'I'd better take him some more food from the deli. And a container of hot tea.'

'No,' Tweed ordered. 'Get Monica to take him something. She's clever at moving around without anyone bothering to notice her.'

It had been raining heavily on their way back from the City but now it had diminished to a faint drizzle. The streets were clear of pedestrians. Tweed was out of the car the moment Paula switched off the engine, rushing up the steps, ringing the bell, dashing past George once the door was open, running up the stairs. Paula and Harry followed, marvelling at his new-found agility.

'I see everyone's here,' Tweed observed as he threw off his overcoat and sat behind his desk. 'None of you are to leave without my permission. Understood? Harry, Pete, I want our two Land Rovers checked to make sure they're in perfect working order—with full fuel tanks. Before the day's out they'll be driving over rough country.'

'They are,' Newman told him. 'I spent time today checking all transport. Why the Land Rovers?'

'I've told you that,' Tweed said abruptly. 'Because they're perfect vehicles for crossing difficult country.'

'Where?' Newman persisted.

'The West Country. Now leave me alone while I make a vital call. Two, in fact.'

Tweed was so absorbed he hadn't noticed Paula

approaching Monica, who was still on the phone arguing with Chief Superintendent Buchanan. For the fifth time she patiently said, 'Tweed is not available. He's on the second phone. And, no, I have no information as to how the investigation is proceeding.'

Paula had left, after scribbling a brief note: 'Gone to deli to feed tramp.'

Tweed dialled the number he had automatically memorized when he'd seen it on a letterhead in Smythe's office.

'Not again,' Smythe rasped when Tweed had given his name. 'I'm in the middle of a delicate transaction. Call another day, if you must.'

'Smythe, your partner, Kenwood, who went missing, is dead.'

'What! Where? When? How did he—'

'Had he any kind of physical disability?'

'Well . . . Yes. Years ago he broke his ankle skiing in the Dolomites. A multiple fracture. It was a complicated op.'

'So how did he come out of it? Specifically. How did he walk?'

'He limped. Some of his so-called pals nicknamed him Limpy. But I want to know is—'

'Call you back. Other phone's ringing.'

He'd looked round for Paula, assumed she'd gone to the loo. He made his announcement to everyone with a certain self-satisfaction.

'We've finally identified positively the fourth corpse. The one Paula and I found on Dartmoor. A stockbroker called Kenwood. That is also the final link I was missing from the pattern of catastrophic events I've been building in my mind. Harry, we are all on the move before it gets dark. I foresee a savage battle with ruthless opponents. We need to travel heavily armed.'

'Enough said.' Harry was on his feet, heading for the door. 'Can I put the weapons aboard the Land Rovers, providing I stay with them on guard? It'll be an arsenal.'

'That's what we may need. Yes, stay on guard at the back.'

'It would help,' Marler drawled, 'if we had just a few more details.'

'Later. Another phone call to make now.' He used the second line—Monica was still arguing with Buchanan on her line. Again he dialled a number from memory, the number of Abbey Grange. Lucinda answered.

'Tweed here.'

'Surprise, surprise! Checking up on me?' Her tone was sarcastic.

'You sound tense.'

'Long drive. A ton of traffic all the way down. A macho fool cut me off. I had to do an emergency stop. With a cement mixer on my tail. Driver stopped just in time.' Her voice softened. 'How can I help?'

'First, I did want to make sure you'd arrived safely. And how is Michael?'

'Behaving strangely. Apart from meals, he's locked in his room. I banged on the door, he let me in. On one of those sloping drawing boards he was copying diagrams from *Gray's Anatomy*, if you please. Gruesome.'

'Any other developments? Oh, I assume Michael hasn't spoken?'

'Not one word. Developments? Larry's on his way down here, should arrive soon. And, to top it all, Aubrey's coming by himself.'

'Greystoke? What on earth could he want down there? Is this usual?'

'Not really. He does come occasionally. I assumed they were holding a meeting. But Larry's secretary said she'd no news of any meeting when I spoke to her.'

'She called you—to say Larry was coming?'

A pause. 'No, she damned well didn't. I called her about an important delivery I'd forgotten to warn them about. Told her to stay all night if necessary until it arrived. She wasn't pleased—has a new boyfriend. I ordered her to stay. When I get back to town can we meet, have a chat over a drink? At my apartment, say?'

'Thank you. I'm sure we'll catch each other soon.'

He put the phone down and sat back, realizing he'd been sitting ramrod upright. He gazed round the room.

'That's odd. All four suspects will be at Abbey Grange this evening.'

'All four?' Newman queried.

'Larry Voles, Lucinda, Michael and the accountant, Aubrey Greystoke. Odd. Very odd.'

'Monica's still trapped, holding off Buchanan,' Nield remarked, nodding to where Monica was still battling on the phone.

'What on earth for?'

'Probably about this.' Newman waved the latest copy of the *Daily Nation*. 'Their star reporter, Drew Franklin, has really gone to town in his usual eccentric style.'

He handed Tweed the paper, folded open at the main page. The headline was disturbing, as it was meant to be.

FOURTH SKELETON KILLER MURDER
Police baffled

Discovery of two mauled skeletons on Dartmoor has been followed by a third skeleton on a houseboat at Wensford, off the M3 ... London now at risk ... Skeleton body of woman forensic accountant found at her flat in Fulham area ... Baffled police hand over case to Tweed, Deputy Director of SIS, and warned: Lock all windows and doors. Do not answer callers after dark. You could be Skeleton No. 5.

'Franklin should be shot,' Tweed exploded. 'He's causing panic everywhere. And he's muddled up the sequence of our finding the victims. Fulham came third.'

'Oh, that's deliberate,' Newman said cynically. 'Makes for a better story. All London will now be terrified. Drew knows a good story, even if it means twisting the facts.'

'Where's Paula?' Tweed said, suddenly aware he hadn't seen her for quite some time.

'She went out to the deli to get food for the tramp,' Monica told him. 'I couldn't go because I was fencing with Buchanan, who wanted to talk to you. He—'

'How long ago?' Tweed demanded, rising up from behind his desk.

'It must be quite a while ago now,' Monica reported, now worried herself. 'Well over three-quarters of an hour. Could be longer.'

'Get out on the streets and find her,' Tweed shouted with mounting anxiety. 'The lot of you. Now! I'll handle the phone.'

25

Earlier Paula had left the building on her way to the deli in the direction of Baker Street. She glanced round, saw no one except the inert figure of the tramp across the main road. The heavy rain had driven people indoors temporarily.

Her shoulder bag hung loosely as she turned the corner. Walking briskly, she had reached up to haul the shoulder bag's strap more securely up her shoulder as she reached a cul-de-sac on her left.

It happened so quickly she had no time to react. A hand had reached out, grabbed her left arm, hauled her off the main street. Her shoulder bag slipped off the shoulder and flopped on to the pavement. She caught a whiff of chloroform, jerked her head away from it, sucked in a deep breath. A cloth was pressed over her nose. The grip on her left arm was very strong.

Goddamn Browning was inside the shoulder bag somewhere on the pavement. A large thick white cloth enveloped her like a tent. Something hard struck her on the head, slid off the side. She was struggling to get out of the all-enveloping cloth, partially dazed by the blow to her head.

A rope was wrapped swiftly round the cloth several times. It pinioned her arms to her sides. Then it was wrapped round her legs and pulled tight. She was lifted up, thrown on to the back seat of a car through the already open door. A body fell on hers.

Hands felt under the cloth up her legs. She thought this was rape. The hands grabbed both of hers, forced them together. Plastic handcuffs closed over her wrists, clicked as they locked. Hands grasped her body, rolled her off the seat on to the floor. She lay still, hoping her attacker would believe the chloroform had worked. Hands reached her face. She opened her mouth to scream. A mistake. A cloth gag was forced between her lips, tied behind her neck. She couldn't call out now.

Finally, something that felt like a duvet was pressed down on her. She guessed this was to conceal her if anyone saw into the car. The weight of the man's body hauled itself off her. A car door slammed. In no time the car's engine started and the vehicle was moving. She sensed it turn towards Baker Street. Instead of futilely trying to struggle, she eased her head sideways, so she could breathe easily.

As the car picked up speed she realized how unfortunate was the timing. It was not yet rush hour. The driver could keep the car moving at a reasonable speed. She struggled with her locked wrists. The handcuffs held her tightly. She knew plastic handcuffs, a comparatively recent invention, were impossible to break, to ease her wrists free.

*   *   *

Half an hour later Newman returned to the office, holding something that made Tweed feel sick. Paula's shoulder bag.

'Where did you find it?' Tweed asked quietly.

'Nearby. Go out of the Crescent, turn left, then you pass on your left a quiet residential cul-de-sac. It was on the pavement close to the entrance to the main road.'

'Anyone see what happened?' Tweed asked in a voice that seemed too self-controlled.

'No. I checked at the houses close to the entrance. Got no answer from one. Crossed the road. An ancient lady opened the door. Said she'd earlier seen a blue car parked. Asked her the make. No idea. Knows nothing about cars.'

'And, of course, she didn't get a plate number?'

'No, she didn't. Paula's been kidnapped. Doesn't take a lot of imagination to guess who the kidnapper is.'

'Charmian,' said Marler, who had just come back.

'Oh, God,' said Tweed. 'What does he want?'

'You, probably,' Marler said grimly. 'Wait for the call.'

*   *   *

The evening before, Charmian had called M as arranged. He had not told his unknown employer about the Ivy Cottage fiasco. He was always careful to engender confidence, to avoid any mention of assassination attempts that failed.

'M speaking,' the man-woman voice had answered his call.

Charmian had given up trying to identify the gender of his employer. He assumed M spoke through a silk handkerchief wrapped round the receiver.

'M?' he queried.

'M for mosque. What is it?'

'What is it Tweed values more than his own success?'

'His close assistant, Paula Grey. Slim, jet-black

271

hair, five feet six or so in height. She—'

'I know now,' Charmian interrupted. 'I have seen her. I will report in a few days.'

So far his attempts to kill Tweed had misfired. The shot into his car from the field bordering the A303. His attempt to cause an accident when he'd driven the Volvo in front of him. The bomb at Gantia. His bombardment of Ivy Cottage. Time to change tactics.

Now he might have the answer. Kidnap this Paula Grey. He had spent miserable hours hidden in shrubberies not far from where the tramp was, keeping watch. It had rained but Charmian was wearing a heavy waterproof raincoat and a fisherman's hat.

Charmian had infinite patience. He could wait in one position, however uncomfortable, for his target to appear. Then, on the afternoon of the following day, she had appeared, walking alone. Throwing off the raincoat and hat, he had grasped the bin liner containing the thick sheet and had moved.

*   *   *

The atmosphere inside Tweed's office was almost unbearably tense as they waited for Charmian to call. Marler had no doubt the assassin *would* call. He had kidnapped Paula as bait to lure Tweed to his destruction.

Tweed himself outwardly seemed the most composed. He sat at his desk with his hands clasped. His expression, difficult to read, reminded Marler of a stone face. Earlier, despite the awful anxiety gnawing at him, Tweed had given his team their instructions.

272

'When it gets dark—or dusk—you all leave in the Land Rovers heading for the West Country. I've shown you the route on the map, the same one Paula and I followed when we visited Abbey Grange. Until you approach Exeter . . .'

He waited while Marler with Newman unfolded the map again and bent over it. Marler used a small steel pointer, tracing the route as he spoke.

'Down the M3 until we reach Junction 8. There we turn off along the A303, heading straight for the West Country.'

'You've got it,' Tweed told him. 'Near Exeter it gets complicated, but I'll navigate for you.'

If you're with us, if you're alive, Marler thought, but kept the thought to himself.

'I assume,' Tweed continued calmly, 'that the Land Rovers are now equipped with all the weapons we're likely to need.'

'You asked that before,' Harry told him.

'So I did, and the answer was yes.'

The phone rang. Everyone except Tweed stiffened. They all had a deep affection for Paula. Monica listened, handed the phone to Tweed.

'It's for you,' she said grimly.

'Who?'

'It's him. I'm sure of it.'

'Tweed speaking.'

'As you probably know by now, I have Paula.'

'Put her on the phone to say a few words. Then I know she's—'

'Shut the face and listen,' the voice hissed. It had a trace of French accent and was unnervingly menacing. 'You will come to get her yourself. In your normal car. If anyone is with you or near you she dies instantly. The barrel of my gun inserted in her mouth.'

'If she's harmed in any way I promise you a lingering death.'

'*Don't threaten me!*' the voice screamed. 'You will drive alone to the destination. Stonehenge. You know where that is?'

'Yes.'

'You will leave immediately in your own car. *Alone*. I see any of your team, she will die in seconds.' The voice became sarcastic. 'Do you not think you waste the time? Come on. You come in by main entrance.'

'It will be locked after dark. And at this time of year . . .'

'The gate will be unlocked. You waste the time . . .'

The connection was broken. Tweed gently handed the receiver back to Monica. He looked round at anxious faces.

'He's holding her at Stonehenge.'

'What?' exclaimed Marler.

'Yes, Stonehenge. Of all places. But it has an advantage. Along the route the rest of you have to follow, you pass Stonehenge . . .'

'We'll sort out the bastard for good,' growled Harry.

'You'll do nothing of the sort. Charmian was very clear I travel in my own car and alone. He sees anyone else and immediately kills Paula. You leave before me and you do not even look at Stonehenge as you pass it. Near Wylye just beyond the dual carriageway you wait in a lay-by. I will join you later.' He paused. 'I will sack anyone who disobeys my order.'

Monica was appalled. She had never heard

Tweed speak in such a way before. She jumped up quickly.

'A quick cup of tea before anyone leaves.'

She was out of the room as Marler leaped to his feet. He ran to Tweed's desk. His tone of voice was commanding.

'Give me Loriot's private number in Paris.'

Tweed, his mind on his recollection of Stonehenge and its layout, wrote down the number. Marler snatched the piece of paper, ran to Monica's empty desk, sat down and dialled the number. He hoped to God Loriot was in his office.

'Who is this, please?' Loriot enquired in French.

'Marler. You remember me?'

'My dear chap, of course I do. When are we going to have the pleasure . . . ?'

The chief of French counterespionage had reverted to speaking in perfect English. Marler cut off his greetings.

'Listen. This is a major emergency. I must know everything you know about Charmian, the assassin.'

'Cold-blooded hired killer. The best. We still have no description of him. He is like a fox.'

'Is he religious?' Marler asked quickly.

'He is a Catholic. A lapsed one. But we believe that although not a churchgoer he does attend confessional. We think he is in Britain.'

'Would he kill a priest if the money was right?'

'Oh, no!' Loriot sounded horror-struck. 'Not for all the gold in Fort Knox.'

'Thank you. I must go. Time is running out.'

'What was all that about?' asked Newman.

Marler ignored him. Slipping on his raincoat, he headed for the door, speaking to Tweed as he ran.

'I need fifteen minutes, Tweed. You wait until I

275

get back. He'll wait for you to arrive. It's you he wants.'

*   *   *

Once outside in the drizzle, Marler dived down the steps into the front area below ground, unchained the Harley Davidson, hauled it up the steps by sheer brute strength and was skidding out of the Crescent in no time.

He headed for a nearby theatrical costumier's that boasted it could dress an actor in any clothes required. He walked in with a bin liner in one hand, a sheaf of twenty-pound notes in the other.

He told the proprietor what he wanted and asked if he could have them in five minutes, including checking the fitting. The man knew his stock, knew where everything was. Marler stripped off his raincoat, tried on what he had ordered. Perfect fit.

He asked the price, threw twenty-pound notes on the counter. His purchases went inside the bin liner. Then he was out of the shop, stuffing the bin liner inside his pannier and on his way back to Park Crescent.

Arriving, he took out the bin liner and dumped the machine back into the area. Entering the building, he dashed through to the back, scribbled a note for Harry and attached it to the first Land Rover, then got behind the wheel of its twin.

*   *   *

Tweed had swallowed his last mouthful of tea when Harry ran into the office, waving a piece of paper and in an unusually agitated state. He stopped in front of Tweed's desk, catching his breath.

'Marler has driven off in one of the Land Rovers. The so-and-so left me this note.'

Tweed picked up the note Harry had dropped on his desk. It was clearly written in a great hurry but was still legible: 'Sorry, Harry. Am following up a tip. Marler.'

'Doesn't even say a tip about what,' Harry raged. 'And now we have only one Land Rover to take us all to Wylye . . .'

'Calm down,' Tweed said quietly, swiftly adjusting to the new situation. 'Harry, you will be driving. There'll still be plenty of room for Newman and Nield. You still have plenty of weapons in the Land Rover, don't you? Good. When you're passing Stonehenge everyone except yourself will crouch down and cover themselves with canvas. You can leave now? Then leave. Now!'

Monica spoke when the team had dashed out of the office, a puzzled expression on her face.

'I saw you take Paula's mobile before Marler rushed off. So what's the use of that with your team miles further on at Wylye? I've looked at the map.'

'You never know,' said Tweed as he slipped on his overcoat. 'One more thing. It's unlikely, but if Charmian phones and asks to speak to me you reply that I left for an unknown destination some time ago. Be vague.'

'Good luck,' Monica wished him with a tremble in her voice.

*   *   *

Tweed's mind was a tumble of different scenarios as he drove out of London on to the M3. He seemed to have missed rush hour by minutes although it was now dark. Was Paula still alive? He suppressed the flood of emotion that threatened to fill his brain. He had visited Stonehenge several years before and his excellent memory could visualize the extraordinary and vast prehistoric circle of megalithic stones, reputed once, ages ago, to have been a place of worship to strange gods.

Stones? They were immense blocks standing vertically, some at least eighty feet high. To keep out vandals a high wire fence had been erected round the whole area. They were located on a hill just beyond where two roads forked. The A344 to the right headed northwest while the A303 continued to the southwest.

The only entrance was off the A344, a heavy gate you paid to enter through. At this time of day after dark it would be closed—probably closed anyway at this time of the year. Yet Charmian had ordered him to use this entrance. He'd probably by now have broken the lock. If I use that way in, Tweed thought, he'll be waiting for me with a bullet.

Recalling some of this before racing out of Park Crescent, he had obtained from George, the guard, a strong pair of metal clippers. He was sure Charmian would, perched up on the hill, be watching for his arrival. So, he'd think Tweed had made a mistake when, reaching the fork, he continued a short distance along the A303.

He'd park a short distance beyond the fork. He also recalled that on this side a steep grassy slope climbed to the top where the megaliths were standing. Using the metal clippers, he would cut a hole in the fence, crawl through, slowly make his

278

way to the top.

He pulled in to a services on the M3, checked the working mechanism of his Walther, slid back the full magazine. He thought he would probably die as he appeared over the top of the hill, but he hoped he'd fire one deadly shot at Charmian at the same moment that the assassin fired to kill him.

Later, turning off the M3 at Junction 8, he saw a clear road ahead, pressed his foot down. His mind switched to the West Country. Earlier, at the office, he had phoned a friend who was a retired marine expert. Without giving too much detail, he had asked him to calculate the probable progress of the *Oran*. With details like the tonnage of the freighter, its probable speed, date and likely time of passing through the Straits of Gibraltar, the marine expert had given him his estimate of when it was likely to reach the West Country.

Sometime tonight had been the expert's rough forecast. What had given Tweed more confidence in this estimate was when he had heard from Lucinda that all the executives of Gantia were travelling to Abbey Grange.

Larry, Lucinda, Michael and Aubrey Greystoke. One of them, he was convinced, was the Skeleton Murderer. And the same person was behind the missile plot. They had needed £400 million to make up for their losses on the dotcom Orlando Xanadu, to replace the huge sum they had transferred from the reserves of Gantia, had *stolen*.

Tweed had included Michael among the suspects because he had never been completely convinced that he was suffering from amnesia. Professor Saafeld, now the top postmortem expert in the country, had once told Tweed what he thought of

279

the people Churchill once described as trick cyclists. 'I've known a lot of them. They're all nutcases. Why? Because they spend so much time dealing with unbalanced patients they end up like them. Nutcases.'

Absorbed by his swirl of thoughts, trying to blot out of his mind his terrible anxiety about Paula, Tweed was driving on autopilot. He was surprised when he saw the signpost to Andover off to his right. He was less than twenty miles from Stonehenge.

26

At Stonehenge the twenty or so megaliths reared up massively in the moonlight like sentries out of a horror film. Their huge bulk seemed to signal they would be there for ever. A few had fallen and lay on the scrubby hilltop like immense seats. A chill wind blew from the west.

Paula did not like the ominous silence that hung over this weird, menacing place. She was only thankful she had thrown her overcoat on before she'd dashed out of Park Crescent on her way to the deli. She still felt frozen with fear, with the cold.

On arrival, Charmian had parked his car behind a hedge a short distance up the A344. He had then carried Paula, wrists and legs bound, a gag across her mouth, to the entrance gate. One bullet from his 5-mm Glock had dealt with the lock. Picking her up again, he had found the perfect place to secure her.

After perching her on one of the fallen megaliths,

he had used more rope to fasten her to it. She was sitting up and her feet just reached the ground. He wanted Tweed to see her before he killed him with the first bullet. Then he would kill her.

From her perch she had a clear view of the road from London until Charmian, anxious to conceal her from passing motorists, pushed up a large rock and blocked her view. She knew that Tweed would come to rescue her and this was her greatest fear. Her captor dominated the whole area from the hilltop.

The wind, which had created an unnerving howl, died away and the awful silence closed in, broken only by the sound of a passing car or juggernaut. One large vehicle's engine made such a row she seized her chance, leaned with all her weight against the large rock. It fell off the megalith without making a sound as it thudded on the scrubby turf. Now she had a clear view of the road. Charmian, absorbed with his night glasses, checking each vehicle as it passed, did not notice the absence of the rock.

To prevent her body becoming as stiff as the megaliths, she frequently worked her legs, pinioned at the ankles, up and down. She worked her arms and her wrists as far as she could. She soon realized she could never get free. She was frightened, frustrated, cold. She wet the gag with saliva but again realized she could never get rid of it. She heard a vehicle approaching slowly, saw it was a Land Rover, the single driver impossible to see because he had the visor well down. It crawled past and proceeded along the A303. Moments later a juggernaut thundered past, blaring its horn nonstop as it continued along the A303. Why?

Charmian, confident she was helpless, never gave her a glance. Standing close to a giant megalith, he concentrated on gazing through his night glasses. Several more cars and trucks swept past, mostly along the A303, then another Land Rover appeared, moving much faster. Peering through his glasses Charmian saw a driver and no one else. The rear of the vehicle was covered with canvas, doubtless covering some product for delivery.

Time passed and Paula knew she was reaching screaming pitch. She forced her body to relax, took in slow deep breaths and overcame the threat of hysteria.

Charmian was dressed for the occasion. He wore a polo-necked sweater under his wool-lined windcheater. There was no glove on his right hand, which gripped the Glock handgun—a diabolical weapon which could blow a man's head off his shoulders. His head was protected by a woollen hat and occasionally he would drink water from a pocket flask. He never offered any to Paula, whom he regarded as no more than a key object of his assignment.

Paula gritted her teeth. In the distance, coming down the road from London, she had seen Tweed's car. She looked desperately around for something that would make a noise. Then she looked down to where her feet just touched the ground. A broken chunk of megalith was resting on the edge of a small slope.

Charmian jerked round as he caught movement out of the corner of his eye. He stared in sheer bewilderment. Coming up over the top of the slope from the direction of the A303 was a tall figure, walking slowly. It was the way the figure was clothed that shook the assassin. The figure was clad completely in black. A long black coat reached to its ankles. On its head was a wide-brimmed black hat. All round its neck was a white collar. In its left hand it held a cone-shaped vessel at the end of a thin chain. He was swinging it gently from left to right, then back again. Water dribbled from the vessel. Charmian was shocked. A priest.

He knew a little about Stonehenge. Several years before, he got off a train in Salisbury. His assignment: to assassinate an ex-prime minister. Immediately he'd entered the town he knew he was in danger. Someone had spread the news of his intention. The place was crawling with police—on foot, in slow-moving cars. He had slipped into the nearest pub to escape detection. There he had met a farmer who had told him about Stonehenge, its origin long ago as a place of ancient worship. He had offered to drive Charmian to show him Stonehenge since it was on his way home.

Charmian had accepted with relief, seeing his way of escaping safely from Salisbury. One man on foot would be suspicious. Two men in a car would mean nothing. On a lonely road close to Stonehenge Charmian had expressed a wish to relieve himself. The moment the car stopped he strangled the driver, threw the body into a deep pond and used the car to drive to Newhaven. Here he had caught the ferry to France.

All this came back to him as he stared, bewildered, at the distant figure walking slowly, swinging his vessel, spreading water. He must be consecrating the ground for some strange reason. Paula also was gazing at the figure, which in some way seemed familiar.

Tweed's car arrived and Charmian jerked his attention away from the priest. To his surprise, instead of taking the left-hand fork up the A344, the vehicle cruised slowly along the A303. He heard it stop. He raised his Glock, aimed it at the crest of the slope.

*   *   *

Tweed climbed out of his car, suppressing a mixture of terror and fury. Silhouetted against the moonlight, he had seen the forlorn figure of Paula, on the fallen megalith. At least she was alive. He puzzled briefly over the parked Land Rover ahead, its hazard lights flashing. He began climbing the slope, head well down, leaning forward, Walther in his right hand. He knew reaching the crest would be crisis time. He would have only one chance, if he had any chance at all.

*   *   *

Paula guessed Tweed was on his way up. Her nerves were screaming. She took a deep breath of the cold air, suppressed her fear. She had to guess the correct timing. Her face froze with determination. She stretched her right leg down as far as it would go. The rope round her waist dug deeply into her, tied to the fallen megalith. She counted, trying to imagine how many steps it would take Tweed to reach the crest.

Charmian stood very still against the giant megalith. Both hands gripped the Glock. He swivelled it back and forth over a small arc. He was trying to estimate where Tweed would appear. The silence over Stonehenge seemed even heavier. No traffic for the moment.

Paula's right foot touched the rock chunk resting above the small slope. She took another deep breath. It happened so quickly it appeared to have been synchronized. Paula kicked the rock chunk. It rolled forward down the small slope, stopped. The sound distracted Charmian for barely a second. His head jerked round, jerked back. Tweed had leaped up the last few feet of the crest, was standing on it. He pressed the trigger. At the same moment the 'priest' had produced an Armalite from under his black habit, aimed it, seen the assassin's face in the cross-hairs, fired the explosive bullet. At the very same moment, a millisecond before the assassin could fire his Glock, Tweed's bullet slammed into his stomach as the Armalite's bullet hit the bridge of his nose, shattering his head, spraying the megalith with blood and flesh and bone and brains. His headless body sank to the ground. Marler, still holding his Armalite, tore off the long black coat, threw the hat down. Paula opened her mouth to speak and nothing emerged as she sagged, still conscious but exhausted with tension.

*　　　*　　　*

Tweed ran forward to Paula but Marler had already reached her. With a pocket knife he cut the ropes binding her to the fallen megalith, cut the ropes round her wrists, cut those round her ankles. She slid off the stone, tried to stand up, began to fall. Tweed grabbed her round the waist. She buried her head against his chest, trying to speak in a choking voice, then Marler removed the gag.

285

'God! I was so worried about you . . . so worried I felt I was . . . going insane.'

'Sound sane enough to me,' Marler said briskly. 'Like some water . . . ?'

'Oh, yes, please,' she begged hoarsely.

Marler unscrewed the cap from a flask he'd extracted from a pocket. He held it away from her as she reached for it, his voice stern.

'Listen to me. You take a few sips, then pause. Then a few more sips. Another pause. You can drink more soon.'

She nodded to show she had understood, grasped the flask, forced herself to ration herself to a few sips. The water trickled down a throat that felt parched. She coughed, waited, took a few more sips. They went down without her coughing. She waited. Then she gradually drank normally. Life seemed to return to every part of her body.

'Thank you,' she said in her usual voice, handing back the flask. 'I damned well needed that.'

Standing still, she bent her legs gently several times and soon they felt they would support her. She walked back and forth, Tweed on one side, Marler on the other, talking.

'The way you walked, Marler, seemed familiar, but I never guessed it could be you.'

'Why the fancy dress?' Tweed asked, introducing an element of humour deliberately.

'I phoned Paris. Loriot told me Charmian was a Catholic. Not a churchgoer but attended confessionals. I gambled he wouldn't shoot a priest. It came off. Now we clear up, get rid of the evidence.'

'How?' asked Tweed.

'Come with me.' Marler looked at Paula, decided

she needed something to occupy her mind, however gruesome. He pulled a large white cloth from inside his overcoat and handed it to her. 'Think you could clean the mess off that megalith? If it drops on to the body so much the better.'

His psychology was good. Recovered from shock, Paula welcomed a task to busy herself with. She gave the corpse only a brief glance as she stepped over it and used the cloth to wipe the side of the megalith. She knew this hideous creature was going to kill her after he had murdered Tweed.

Tweed followed Marler a short distance along the top to where he stopped, pointing downwards. A large metal grille with slim steel bars covered a square hole in the ground. A lock was closed at one end. Marler bent down, took out the lockpick he always carried. He was wearing gloves as he gripped the lock with one hand, to prevent it slipping down between the bars. He opened it with his lockpick.

'A drain,' he explained. 'Must piss down with rain up here and gullies channel it to this drain.'

'It rains cats and dogs,' Tweed agreed. 'What's the plan?'

Marler didn't reply at once. Grasping a large stone, he dropped it down the drain after lifting the cover, which was hinged. They listened. After what seemed an hour they heard a distant splash.

'Deep enough. Now I'll get the body.'

He picked up the large black coat he had thrown off. Earlier he had removed the costumier's labels. Carrying it to where Paula was working, he found she had cleaned the side of the megalith clear of Charmian's remains. She looked calm as Marler took the filthy cloth off her, dropped it on the headless body streaming with blood at the neck. He lifted it and she slipped the black coat under it, following his orders. He wrapped the coat round the body, with plenty of cloth round the neck. Then he lifted it round the waist and carried it to the drain, followed by Paula.

'What's that?' she asked, staring at the square cavity.

'A drain,' Marler replied. 'Probably leads to a sewer.'

'A perfect resting place for it,' she said.

Lifting it vertically, careful to keep the whole body wrapped in the black coat, he dropped it. They waited. Again it seemed to take forever before they heard a distant splash. It was a long way down. Marler collected the black hat, crammed inside it the chain and vessel which had dribbled water and dropped them into the black hole. He stood up.

'That's it.'

Tweed had moved to the other end, used gloved hands to lift the heavy drain cover. He swung it on its hinges back into its original position. Marler fixed the large lock, clicked it closed, stood up.

He gazed round the forest of giant stones, checking to make sure nothing had been overlooked. He turned to Tweed.

'There'll be blood on the ground at the base of the megalith, but it'll soon turn brown.'

'More likely washed away by heavy rain. Now, we must head fast to Wylye, where the others will be waiting. You ride with Marler, Paula. I'll park my car near Wylye and transfer to a Land Rover. We must keep moving. A grim night lies ahead of us.'

27

Tweed led the way along the A303 to Wylye while Paula rode in the front passenger seat with Marler. Glancing at her, Marler saw she was having trouble keeping her eyes open. He pulled in to a lay-by. After taking off his overcoat, he folded it and told her to get into the back seat, where he arranged the coat as a makeshift pillow.

'Stretch out, head on pillow, and sleep,' he ordered.

'Thank you,' she said with a smile.

She was fast asleep before he started driving again. Back at Stonehenge the sky had been clear, the moon had shone. Now the weather was changing. A fleet of dark clouds cruising in from the west blotted out the moon. Marler wondered whether these conditions would suit Tweed's plan, whatever that was. He had said he'd explain the next move when they reached the rest of the team.

Ahead of them, Tweed slowed up as he approached the Wylye area. He turned in to a lay-by as he saw a parked Land Rover. Empty. No sign of anyone. Cautiously, he climbed out, the Walther in his hand.

'Don't shoot your friends,' a familiar voice called out. The voice of Harry.

He appeared at Tweed's side, holding a small Uzi machine pistol. He was followed by Newman and Pete Nield. Tweed stared—they were all carrying weapons. What on earth had happened?

'We decided to be very careful while we waited for you,' Newman explained. 'A couple of patrol cars full of police came out of a side road. We saw them behind us just in time to race here and park the Land Rover without lights. They didn't see the vehicle, just headed towards Exeter with their blasted sirens wailing, lights flashing.'

'What's going on?' asked Tweed half to himself.

At that moment Marler arrived with his Land Rover. Paula had woken up, sensing Marler had slowed down. Tweed explained what Newman had told him. Paula was bleary-eyed but became alert as she listened.

'So what's all this about?' she enquired.

Tweed was about to reply when Paula's mobile in his pocket began buzzing. Swearing under his breath, he put it to his ear and spoke quietly.

'Who is this?'

'This,' a voice thundered, 'is Chief Superintendent Buchanan. Where are you? I got this mobile number from Monica. Told her you were in trouble . . .'

'You *what*?'

'Only way I could get her to give me this number. So where are you?' he repeated aggressively.

'You sound rattled, Roy. Why?'

'Haven't you read the splashy headlines in the newspapers? They imply the police aren't doing their job about the skeleton murders. That we're baffled. *Baffled*, for heaven's sake. And that you are in charge of the investigation and haven't got anywhere. I've decided to take over.'

'You can't do that.' Tweed's voice hardened. 'I was given complete charge of the investigation —because you're up to your neck in anti-terrorist manoeuvres.'

'Where the hell are you now?' Buchanan raved.

'On the verge of discovering the identity of the fourth body found on Dartmoor,' Tweed lied, furious.

'I've read your reports on progress—if you can call it that—so far. On the basis of your data I've sent a team to arrest Michael on suspicion of murder.'

'Cancel the instruction immediately. Withdraw the teams *now*. You're doing a marvellous job of messing everything up. And since when did you take major decisions on the basis of press reports? You're making an arrest to cover your backside. I am ordering you to get out of the way of my investigation.'

'I do have the Home Secretary's backing.'

'He gave the order to arrest Michael? Did he?'

'Well, he left the decision to me, so—'

'Buchanan.' Tweed's tone was grim. 'If you do not withdraw the order to arrest Michael, to recall your teams, I shall at once phone the PM.'

There was a long pause. Buchanan knew Tweed could always gain the PM's support in an emergency. Paula, standing with her hands in the pockets of her windcheater, was watching Tweed's expression with delight. In a battle with the establishment she thought she knew who would win.

'Are you still there, for God's sake?' Tweed shouted.

'Yes. You don't have to be so tough. All right, I will now radio the teams, tell them the order to arrest Michael is cancelled, that they must return to base. Be it on your head.'

'This investigation has *always* been on my head. Have I your word? I need a direct unequivocal reply.'

291

'All right,' replied Buchanan. 'I've told you I'll cancel the whole operation immediately. I only hope you know what you're doing.'

'At least one of us does . . .'

He hit the 'end' button on the mobile. The whole team were gathered round him as he explained tersely what had happened. As he concluded Paula tentatively made her comment.

'Supposing Buchanan is right about Michael?'

'That's what we'll eventually find out, probably later tonight.' He then gave them a brief report on the Stonehenge terror, the end of Charmian. Harry frowned, stared at Paula, worried.

'When did you last eat, Paula?'

'Frankly, I'm starving, but I'll survive.'

'Might be able to help,' said Harry. He disappeared to where the second Land Rover was parked. He returned with Monica's insulated enamel food carrier, opened it, produced packets of wrapped sandwiches, a small bag of fruit and a bottle of water. 'Which Rover are you travelling in?'

'She'll travel with me,' Tweed ordered. 'We'll be in the back so I can think.'

'I'll drive,' Marler told him.

'Then I'll drive the other one,' Harry announced, 'with Pete and Newman as my passengers.'

'We'll wait here a few minutes,' Tweed said, taking the food carrier from Harry, then escorting Paula to the vehicle.

'Thought he was in a rush,' Marler remarked.

On the back seat of the Land Rover Paula was devouring one sandwich after another as though she hadn't eaten for days. Tweed checked his watch.

'We'll give them ten minutes,' he decided.

'Who?' Paula enquired as she started on the fruit after a long drink from the bottle of water.

'You'll see, if they come.'

A few minutes later they saw the approaching police cars. Two cars tore past in the direction of the M3. Tweed smiled grimly.

'Buchanan has obeyed my request. He's recalled that team he was sending to Abbey Grange. Now we can get started. Marler, you take us in the lead with Harry following behind us. I'll navigate—it gets tricky near Exeter. We are aiming for the A30, then we turn off left along the A382 down to Moretonhampstead—which is where we turn right again along the road which eventually lands us outside Abbey Grange.'

'Then we're not going to Post Lacey?' Paula asked.

'No. This first lap is so I can check Abbey Grange. See who's there. Also to look at the place Lucinda called Nowhere Village. It's on the second lap, later, that we may well need Harry's heavy armoury.'

'That line of old thatched cottages all joined together?' she suggested.

'That's the place.' He again checked his watch. 'Now all of you. Move!'

Marler kept up a good speed, especially driving along the frequent dual carriageways with Harry keeping a sensible distance behind him. Traffic was light and the night was pitch black as a heavy overcast of clouds drifted above them.

'I know what I was going to ask you,' Paula said, suppressing a yawn. 'You seem to think all Armenians are devious. Why?'

'*Some*,' he corrected her. 'It's understandable recalling their history, which few people do. In the middle of the Great War, about 1915 to 1916, the Turks, who hate Armenians, launched a terrible massacre campaign. A form of genocide. They slaughtered over one million Armenians. Those who survived did so by becoming very devious. It was the only way to stay alive. The world has forgotten that horror.'

He looked at Paula. It was obvious she was having trouble keeping her eyes open. He folded his overcoat into a pillow once more, laid it on the seat between them, told her to curl up and go to sleep. He had heard Marler remarking to Harry in the lay-by how he had done the same thing.

She fell into a deep sleep immediately. She was woken only by a nightmare. She dreamed that the giant megaliths were marching on her, were about to stamp her to death. She blinked, sat up, gazed out of the window. Unlike their earlier trip, the vast bulk of Dartmoor, like a threatening menace, was no longer white with snow. Its immense bulk was black and looming up on her left.

'Where are we?' she asked.

'We're way beyond Exeter, on the A30, just about to turn left down the road to Moretonhampstead. Then it won't be long before we're on the road to Abbey Grange. I've told Marler to park about a hundred yards this side of the mansion. Then we can arrive unexpectedly.'

'That could be difficult,' she commented.

'No, it won't. We'll see the huge bulk of Hooked Nose Tor now it's moonlight. That tor is close to the east side of the mansion.'

'So you see, Paula,' Marler joked, 'we've been

plotting while you were in the land of Nod.'

They soon arrived at the ancient town of Moretonhampstead. Paula gazed out. The streets were deserted at that hour, the shops all closed. There were lights in residential houses.

'It's attractive,' she said. 'A lot of character. Looks as though it's been here for ages.'

'It has,' Tweed told her as they took the road for Abbey Grange.

They were soon well clear of the town and Dartmoor closed in on both sides. Even in the moonlight it looked forbidding and bleak. She stared ahead as Marler slowed down, parked. The silhouette of Hooked Nose Tor stood out sharply in the moon's glow. The strange similarity to a man's head had a sinister look seen in profile. Harry's Land Rover parked a dozen yards behind them. Tweed got out, ran back.

'You all stay here until you see me again. You can get out to stretch yourselves, but walk away from Abbey Grange.'

He ran back and Paula was waiting for him in the silent road by the high wall round the mansion. Marler peered out to speak softly.

'You want me to stay here to keep an eye on the vehicle? Good. See you sometime . . .'

28

'It's very quiet,' said Paula as they approached the double-gate entrance. 'No one about. A bit creepy.'

'It's Dartmoor,' Tweed replied as he opened the left-hand gate leading to the path round the end of the mansion to the terrace.

They had reached the end of the path when Lucinda appeared on the terrace. She was very smartly dressed in a pair of white slacks with razor-edge creases and a thick woollen white polo-necked jumper.

'Well,' she called out, smiling, 'the great detective is back again. Come to find another murder?'

'I hope not. Where is everyone?'

She ticked them off on her fingers. 'Michael is floating about somewhere on the moor; Larry has arrived, not sure where he is; and the superior Aubrey is probably inside having a drink—not his first, I'm sure.'

She hugged them both and Paula noticed that her long blonde hair was perfectly brushed, a golden cascade. As they reached the French windows leading inside, Mrs Brogan appeared with her normal disapproving expression.

'More of 'em,' she grumbled. 'So how many am I supposed to cook for? No advance warning, of course.'

'We shan't be eating,' Tweed assured her. 'I'm going for a stroll by myself.' He gazed along the terrace, beyond it. 'Is there a path up Hooked Nose Tor?'

'Two paths,' snapped Mrs Brogan. 'One up, one down. Don't advise you to go up there.' Wearing an apron, she raised one meaty arm, pointed at the tor. 'Paths are narrow. You go up there, slip off the top, then you falls 'undreds of feet, end up as spiked meat at the bottom.'

'Thank you for the warning,' Tweed said with a smile. 'I have done a little mountaineering in the past.'

'Do you want the bathroom, Paula?' asked Lucinda. 'Top of the stairs, then third door on your left.'

'I could do with a quick shower,' Paula admitted.

'Don't hurry,' Tweed urged her. 'I'm not sure how long it'll take to scale this fellow.'

He descended the steps from the terrace. The windows facing the moor were a blaze of lights. He kept his gaze away from them to preserve his night vision, then took out his torch. He reached the base of the giant, had the choice of two paths, chose the one on the left, which looked less steep.

He held the torch in his left hand so the right was free to feel his way along the steep rock surface. The path was narrow and curved continuously round the massive rock. He had a motive he had not mentioned for his climb. He guessed the view from the top would be panoramic, well above the roof of the mansion and with a clear sight of the church tower, the church—and the Nowhere Village beyond, as Lucinda had nicknamed it.

Looking up, he saw above his path a wide ledge which, he guessed, was the second path leading downwards. There was a light breeze blowing from the west and the air was refreshing. Not relying on the moonlight, he beamed his torch on the path. On his right the granite wall rose steeply. He was very high up now. Glancing down, he saw far below at ground level large pointed rocks. Hence Mrs Brogan's remark about 'spiked meat'.

Leaning back against the rock, he took out his monocular and focused it on the church tower. There was a light on behind a Norman arched window. Curious, at this hour. He glanced down again. The killing height he had reached did not worry him. Affected by any trip on the sea, Tweed had never been bothered by vertigo.

The huge hooked nose of the tor was only a few feet ahead of him. He focused the monocular on the church. No lights. He then switched his focus to Nowhere Village, then to the road in front of the line of cottages. Large black oil marks, two lines, well apart and recent. He frowned.

He was vaguely aware of a white shape behind him as a strong hand rammed into his back, unbalancing him, swaying him to the brink of the precipice. He forced himself to lurch forward, his right hand clutching for something to hold on to. His gloved hand grasped the lower part of the projecting nose as he felt dizzy. He leaned his body against the wall of the tor, his hand still grasping the nose. He felt helpless, disarmed. The Walther was tucked into a hip holster on his left side. No way could he reach for it with his right hand, which was the only chance of getting his balance back and not falling off the ledge.

He concentrated on repeating the letters of the alphabet from A to Z. The pain from the blow against his back was subsiding. His legs, which had felt like marshmallow, were stiffening. He determined to test his legs, standing first on the right one and bending the left at the knee. Then he reversed the process. They were holding firm.

He found himself reluctant to release his grip on the nose. 'I can't stay up here all night,' he said aloud. Clenching his jaw, he took his right away from the support, began to take short steps along the path winding its way round the tor. The steps became longer, but only by a few inches. The dizziness had cleared, he felt more normal. He rounded a corner. The path split into two sections, one continuing upwards—presumably to the summit—the other section descending. He chose to go down.

Descending was surprisingly tricky. His calf muscles ached with the strain. He still kept his body leaning against the tor's wall to help maintain balance. He didn't look down once. Not a good idea at this stage of his ordeal. Just concentrate on not making a single mistake.

It was a surprise when he arrived at ground level. He sat on a large flat stone to take stock. He was glad now he had made the attempt. From high up he'd glimpsed a faint light in Nowhere Village. He'd also seen the light in the bell tower, which struck him as odd. Time to get moving again.

*   *   *

He was walking below the terrace towards the steps when Larry appeared, as though he had just walked up the track. Tweed stared. Larry was dressed in a smart white suit: white jacket, white trousers, white shirt, white tie and white hand-made shoes.

'Tweed, of all people,' Larry greeted him with his usual warm smile. 'You can join our party,' he went on as they mounted the steps side by side. 'You will be most welcome. I'll have someone intelligent to talk to instead of being bored to death by Aubrey.'

At the open French windows Lucinda appeared, a glass of champagne in one hand.

'Tweed is going to join our party,' Larry called out buoyantly.

'That's great . . .' Lucinda began.

'I'm afraid not,' Tweed said firmly. 'I have

another appointment.'

'Did you do it?' Lucinda wanted to know.

'Do what?' Larry asked as Lucinda handed him a champagne glass she had grasped from a tray on a table just inside.

'Climb Hook Nose Tor, of course,' Lucinda said gaily, addressing Tweed.

'Yes, I just about managed it,' Tweed replied.

'What!' Larry sounded appalled. 'Climbing that thing in *daylight* is bloody dangerous. At night it could have been suicide.'

'I managed,' Tweed repeated.

Paula appeared, holding a champagne glass, which Tweed noticed was nearly full. For appearance's sake she had just been sipping it. She was sparkling, her eyes fully alert, then she saw Tweed clearly. Her expression changed. Placing her glass on the table she jumped on to the terrace.

'Your right coat sleeve is covered in rock dust.'

She began using her hand to brush it off after putting a glove on. Her head was shielding Tweed from Lucinda and he frowned at her, warning her not to ask any questions. Larry leaped athletically into the living room, then turned round.

'Do join the party,' he said cheerily. 'Be a sport. Excuse me. Must go upstairs and freshen up.'

'Lovely idea,' Lucinda purred. 'You can sit next to me with Paula on my other side.'

'Please thank Larry for the invitation,' Tweed replied, 'but as I told him I do have another appointment. May I ask, what is the party celebrating?'

'Come along the terrace for a moment,' Lucinda suggested, taking him by the arm. 'You, too, Paula,' she called over her shoulder. She lowered her

300

voice. 'It's called a White Party. Hence we're all dressed the way we are. Every now and again Larry has this irritating idea of holding a party for all the chief executives to reward them for their dedicated service. His words, not mine. Larry insists it has a theme, so this is the White Party. Last time it was the New Orleans Party, which was hell. I had to mug up how they dress in the Quarter, as they call it over there.'

'Where's everyone else?' Tweed enquired casually.

They heard slow footsteps coming up on to the terrace from the moor. It was Michael, clad in what looked like a white dinner suit, except he wore his normal shoes. Lucinda called out, 'Where have you been?' Then she swore softly. 'I still make the mistake occasionally, saying something to him and forgetting he still hasn't spoken one word. That awful amnesia.'

Tweed was watching Michael. He was walking in the stiff-legged manner, back erect, which was the only way Tweed and Paula had seen him walk, leaving the psychiatrist's clinic in London to get into Tweed's car, on the moor later. He looked along the terrace and Paula saw the same blank glazed look. He showed no sign of recognizing anyone as he proceeded into the mansion. Tweed lit one of his rare cigarettes, gave one to Lucinda when she asked for one and lit it for her.

'I just wonder,' he remarked in an offhand manner, 'how Michael knows what clothes to put on.'

'Well you might,' Lucinda responded. 'I lay out all his clothes on the second bed in his room. Otherwise I'm sure he'd be totally confused.'

301

'Before we leave, have I missed anyone?' he enquired.

'The most glorious sight of all,' she said, dripping with sarcasm. She grabbed his arm again. 'Come inside, this you must see . . .'

Entering the spacious living room, they saw the large table laid for dinner. Four places. Bowls of white roses—which had to be silk, Paula thought. Sprawled in an armchair, a bottle of Scotch on the small table by his side, was Aubrey Greystoke.

He wore a white naval officer's uniform, complete with a white peaked cap as worn in the tropics. The cuffs of his sleeves were embroidered in gold. Paula put her hand to her mouth to avoid bursting out laughing. He looked quite ridiculous.

'You're supposed to be drinking white champagne,' Lucinda snapped. 'Larry will be furious when he sees the Scotch.'

'Just emptied . . . bottle of champagne, my dear. See, there's the dead 'un. Surely I'm entitled to a chaser? I thought this was a party.' He suddenly became aware of Tweed and Paula, jumped agilely to his feet. In doing so his elbow knocked the empty champagne glass off the table. Before it could reach the floor his hand caught it in midair. He put it back on the table.

Nothing wrong with your reflexes, however much you've imbibed, Paula thought.

'I say!' Aubrey greeted them. 'What fun! You two joining the revelries. Great! I'll just go and warn Mrs Brogan. Two more for dinner.' He grinned. 'The old trout will love me but she is just a servant.'

He made it sound as though he were referring to a peasant. He was stopped by Tweed.

'Thank you, Greystoke, but we can't stay. Have to

302

get on elsewhere.'

'Bad show, but still, you do have your responsibilities. Next time, maybe.'

Lucinda hugged them both again after Tweed had assured her they had transport. They descended the steps with the distant sound of Lucinda arguing with Mrs Brogan. Paula waited until they had turned the corner and were walking up the path to the gate by the side of the mansion.

'Now, what happened? When I first saw you on the terrace your face was as white as their bloody party. Did something happen on the tor? Why all that rock dust on your sleeve? I need to know. I'm worried.'

'It was an episode of great importance. From very high up I could see a faint light in the bell tower—and another one in that row of cottages. We're going to take a look now at both places before we leave for the main event.'

'That doesn't explain your lack of colour. You're concealing something.'

'Well,' Tweed told her as they reached the gate, 'there was also an attempt to murder me. Someone came up behind me high up and shoved me in the back. It would have been rather a lethal drop.'

'Oh, my God! You should never have climbed up there.'

'Yes, I should. It gave me final confirmation where to look for the Skeleton Killer.'

'I don't get it.'

'Just before someone tried to push me down so I'd end up like spiked meat, to quote Mrs Brogan's graphic phrase, I caught a flash of white behind me. Couldn't see who it was but when I get down to the ground what do I find? Four people all dressed in

303

white. Larry, Lucinda, Aubrey and Michael. One of them is the Skeleton Killer.'

* * *

A shadowy figure appeared close to the far side of the wall as they walked into the road. From the shape, the way it held itself, Tweed identified it at once.

'Keeping guard over us, Harry?'

'Thought I'd keep one eye open,' replied Harry as he walked up to them. 'Anything exciting happen in there?'

'Nothing I didn't expect,' Tweed said quickly before Paula was able to say anything. 'We're on our way to a row of cottages just down the road. Might need your toolkit to get inside.'

'Back in a minute . . .'

They walked past the bell tower, which had a light on inside, then past the church, which was in total darkness. Paula felt inside the shoulder bag Marler had brought all the way from the cul-de-sac where she had been kidnapped, gripped the butt of her Browning.

'Something about this area which makes me nervous,' she said.

'And so often your instincts are right,' Tweed remarked.

Arriving at the dark row of cottages—no glimmer of light from behind the closed blinds this time—Tweed cautiously led the way round the back. He listened. He shone the light beam of his torch on a heavy closed door. Two large Banham locks were fitted to it, one above the other. He tried the handle, pulled. It wouldn't move.

'Think this is my job,' said Harry's voice behind them. He was carrying a toolbox, which he placed on the ground, opened the lid, brought out a large collection of keys. 'A bit of peace and quiet, please.'

Peace and quiet? The silence of the moor was already getting on Paula's nerves. Newman appeared, squeezed Paula's arm, nearly made her jump out of her skin. Tweed put a finger to his lips.

The third key Harry tried opened both locks. He grunted with satisfaction, stood back and gestured.

'Open sesame. Might be an idea to go in armed,' he whispered.

Tweed already had his Walther in his hand as he slowly turned the handle. The door swung inward, noiselessly. Well-oiled hinges. He smelled an aroma of well-maintained machinery as he walked a few paces inside, listened, then switched on his torch full beam.

The cottages were hollow, one running into another for quite a distance. They were mostly occupied by an endless conveyor belt of complex machinery. In the middle ran a long tube of metal with runners to speed up whatever they carried. Newman had walked, using his own torch, to the end on their left, then round the beginning of the conveyor belt and continued towards the far end of the machine.

Tweed followed him with Paula and Harry behind, and stopped at the point where the conveyor belt started. His torch focused on a metal device at head height, a combination of small metal levers turned at different angles. He recalled Drago's description with hand gestures demonstrating how the armaments plant was converted from producing artillery shells to missiles.

'Come quietly along here,' Newman's distant voice suggested, 'and watch your footing.'

His voice echoed eerily inside the strange plant. Tweed looked back at the door. Either Paula or Newman, maybe Harry, had closed it. In crocodile formation behind one another, torches aimed at the floor, they walked quite a distance before they reached Newman. He held up a hand to stop them.

'No further. You're not going to like this, Tweed.'

Newman's torch swung away from the conveyor belt to a heavy cradle protected with rubber, standing about four feet high and positioned against the wall. Resting on it, glowing silver in the light from Newman's torch, was a long, slim, metallic object the shape of a very thin sausage.

'A missile?' Tweed said quietly.

'Exactly. And it's armed for instant detonation when the tip hits its target.'

'Oh, my God!' Paula said to herself, her stomach compressing.

'Why?' asked Tweed.

'Think I know what happened. They've produced heaven knows how many missiles. And recently —hence the faint smell of shaved steel. That happens during its early passage along the belt. Did you notice an alcove leading to the belt a few yards back? You did. That's where they attach the tip of powerful explosive. They either had enough when this one arrived, or it wasn't passed as approved. So some maniac lifted it off the belt, placed it on the cradle and left it there without removing the explosive tip.'

'Maybe we'd better get out of here,' Harry suggested.

'You're all getting out, except me,' Newman told

them. 'At the time of the Afghanistan war the MoD showed me a film about missiles, after I'd signed the Official Secrets Act again. Then I wrote that article for the *Daily Nation*, explaining why the war was necessary.'

'I remember it,' Tweed said. 'So why are you staying?'

'Have to,' Newman replied easily. 'I know how to disarm this thing. Criminally careless of them to leave it armed. If any vandals get in here and fool with this thing they could blow this place, and the road outside, to smithereens. Any cars passing would become scrap metal. I do know how to do it. So, all of you, push off and don't stop until you reach the church.'

'I don't like you doing this,' Paula protested.

'Shut up and shove off now,' Newman snapped, deliberately rude to get them out.

Harry led the way, followed by Paula and Tweed. Before he closed the door Tweed called out to Newman.

'Watch it. We're off . . .'

*   *   *

At Tweed's insistence, they walked rapidly back along the road. Arriving outside the bell tower, Tweed sent Harry back to the rest of the team with orders for them to stay where they were until he arrived. Harry asked whether he should tell them what was going on. Tweed told him to keep his mouth buttoned up.

'We'll go in here and explore,' Tweed said after Harry had gone.

He pushed open the heavy door of the bell tower,

307

peered inside. He walked in with Paula and stared round, looking for the Reverend Stenhouse Darkfield. No sign of anyone. He frowned, checked the corners. No one.

The rope that operated the huge bell high above them was still. It hung limply, showed no evidence of recent movement. Tweed stared up at it.

As they left and returned to the road, Paula gripped his arm. From the direction of the armaments plant they heard a steady humming sound of machinery moving. It was quite loud and then it stopped.

'What was that?' Paula asked, scared.

'My guess is it was good news. Newman's disarmed the missile. Afterwards, he set the machinery moving to see what happened. I think that was a good sign. Now for the church. Maybe the vicar's inside.'

'Without a light?'

'I'll go in first,' Tweed said firmly.

He pushed open one of the double doors, paused, listened. Not a sound. His expression was grim as he felt around for the switch to turn on lights. The interior was suddenly flooded with light. He walked forward, step by step. Ignoring his order, Paula followed, then froze in mid-stride.

On the altar, facing them, the Reverend Darkfield was staring at them. At least his severed head was. Placed where they had once found the head of a calf. Tweed went closer. Blood dripped over the edge of the altar. The eyes were open —someone had inserted matchsticks to keep them that way.

29

Paula ran out of the church. She thought she was going to throw up. Reaching inside her shoulder bag for a handkerchief, her hand touched her water bottle. She grabbed it, tore off the cap, inserted the neck in her mouth and gurgled as she was swallowing. The water quenched the queasiness in her stomach. She recapped the bottle, shoved it in her bag and began walking back and forth across the road, taking in deep breaths of cold air. Tweed's hand was gripping her arm.

'Why?' she eventually asked, standing on the far side of the road, as far away as possible from the church.

'I had wondered,' Tweed said. 'I heard the bell clanging when I phoned Lucinda. You've just heard the noise the armaments plant makes when it's operating. Someone paid the vicar to ring the bell nonstop to mask the humming sound when the plant was working.'

'But why kill him?'

'The last witness left alive who might have let slip what was happening.'

'How the hell did they get rid of the body, then?'

'Coming back up the path beside Abbey Grange, I noticed the marks of a heavy single wheel. My guess is the killer used a wheelbarrow to transport the body on to the moor, then dumped body and barrow into one of those deep slimy marshes Dartmoor is notorious for.'

'It could have been the cult,' she said, her voice trembling.

'Forget the cult. That's a story spread by the killer to mislead us.'

'What's happening?' Newman's voice called out. 'I removed the lethal tip from the missile, found a strongroom lined with steel and put it in there. Probably built for that purpose. Is something wrong?'

'Go inside the flaming church and you'll find out,' snapped Paula, still not her normal self.

Newman, clearly surprised by her attitude, glanced at her, then turned round and walked inside the church. He was inside longer than Tweed would have expected. When he came out he was holding his .38 Smith & Wesson in his hand. He walked up to Paula.

'I see now why you're upset. It's quite horrible. I've been checking every corner of the church in case the fiend who did that was still there. The place is deserted.'

'Probably has been for some time,' Tweed commented.

'Why was there a light in the bell tower,' Paula asked, 'but no light in the church?'

'The killer is cunning,' Tweed surmised. 'In case anyone did come along—as we did—they would explore the bell tower first, find the Reverend Darkfield wasn't there, and walk away. Since the church had no lights they wouldn't think of going inside it.'

'But you did,' Paula said.

'Yes, but I had certain data. Drago Volkanian told me he was in favour of conservation. This was proved by the supermarket depot on the M3. It looks more like Wisley Gardens than a plant. The linked-up cottages intrigued me. Eventually I wondered if they housed his so-secret armaments plant. He'd have had to get permission from the local council for planning. The idea of making that plant look like a typical Devonian row of thatched cottages would have appealed to them. But they wouldn't want noise, not industrial noise. So someone persuaded the Reverend Darkfield to ring the bell when it was operating. The killer simply paid him larger sums while the production line was secretly turned over to making missiles.'

'A feasible theory,' Newman agreed.

'Even more feasible when I noticed the oil tracks from large vehicles of very recent movement. And more are there now. Paula, you remember when Buchanan's assistant, Warden, drove us ostensibly to Abbey Grange, then lost his way and took us all the way across to the coast of North Devon by mistake? I let him continue when I noticed oil from large vehicles was marking the route we followed. You remember that?'

'Yes, I do.'

'And later we drove along a promenade-like road with the sea on our left? I got Warden to stop just past Harmer's Head cliffs and we explored a deep gulch in the rock wall. Inside we discovered something curious hidden away—a long railed landing stage with wheels to make it easy to move. Where else did we see something very similar?'

'My Lord! I've got it. On that island in the Med—where beyond the edge of the landing platform the *Oran* had used there was a very similar landing stage under the water.'

'So you know our next objective?'

'To drive the same route Warden took us by mistake. Because that could be the landing point

311

for the *Oran* on its way here from Angora to collect the missiles needed for the long-range rockets obtained from that madman, Kim, of North Korea.'

'And Drago's armaments plant here has very recently produced a large number of the missiles they need.'

'To fire at which target?' Newman asked.

'I can only guess. Paris, London, Berlin?' He checked his watch. 'Now we must head fast for Harmer's Head, hoping we're in time . . .'

As they hurried back to where the Land Rovers were parked a question struck Paula. She asked it as they hustled along.

'You said "our next objective", as though there will be then a final one. What is that?'

'To return to Abbey Grange so I can attempt to identify who is what the newspapers, in their lurid way, have called the Skeleton Killer.'

30

Tweed, with Paula and Newman, ran quietly back to where the two Land Rovers were parked with the rest of the team.

'This is the plan,' he told them. 'We will now drive with me in the lead to the coast of North Devon. We drive a short distance past the row of cottages, then we turn right on to a rough wide track across the moor.'

'Who drives which vehicle?' asked Harry.

'I was coming to that. I will drive the first Land Rover with Paula by my side and Marler in the back. Harry, you drive the second one behind me.

Newman and Nield will be your passengers. It will be a rocky ride over rough territory and I'll be moving as fast as I dare. All clear?'

'There's going to be a firefight?' Harry suggested.

'Maybe. If so it will be a murderous one. Depends on the situation when we arrive at Harmer's Head.'

He jumped in behind the wheel of the Land Rover as Paula joined him, and Marler dived into the back seat. Marler was carrying his Armalite. He'd brought it with him concealed under his overcoat from Stonehenge.

Tweed crawled past Abbey Grange, the bell tower and the church with its hideous altarpiece. He pressed his foot down as soon as they were beyond the cottages. He turned his headlights on full beam. On the road ahead were clear oil marks of trucks with a wide span.

'Their maintenance is lousy,' he commented. 'Fortunately, we can follow them.'

At the point where, near a side road, the marks disappeared he swung the Land Rover along the track Warden had mistakenly driven along. It had been another piece of luck. The marks continued along the side road, which was little more than a wide lane bordered on both sides with gorse hedge.

In his rear-view mirror he saw Harry's vehicle close behind him, but not so close that it couldn't pull up if Tweed suddenly stopped. Tweed lowered his window and cold air flooded into the vehicle. Although now feeling very fresh, Paula welcomed its stimulus. She glanced at Tweed, whose expression was very grim.

'You're hoping the *Oran* will be there, collecting that huge collection of missiles?'

313

'Yes. Again, we need luck. At Park Crescent I phoned a marine expert, gave him enough data to make a calculation. If he got it right, tonight is when those missiles go on board. Again, we need a lot of luck.'

'You said we're heading for Harmer's Head. That isn't where we found the landing stage.'

'No, but it gives us the best viewing point where we can look down and see what—if anything—is happening.'

'So what do we do then?'

'I have no idea. I'll decide when we get there.'

*   *   *

Earlier the freighter had arrived off the North Devon shore. Abdul had first signalled the agreed code—four flashes, followed by three, followed by the final four. The skipper then waited tensely on the bridge, staring at the mighty cliffs above the landing point.

It was a relief when the same signal, the same sequence of flashes, was repeated from the coast. It was safe for him to steer his vessel into the difficult landing point. He steered through ninety degrees, heading for the shore.

He then went down to the stern end of the bridge, looked down at his men crowded on deck. He shouted his orders. To encourage them he threatened to cut off their heads if they messed up.

All of his men were on deck with the exception of those needed to attend to the engine room below decks.

There was a small group waiting ashore with the large trucks carrying the missile cargo. They were the loaders, the men who had carried the missiles from the Dartmoor plant to their trucks.

One man, the commander, spoke perfect English with a hint of an American twang. With an expertly created fake passport he passed as coming from the Lebanon. He had taken a military engineering course at a certain institution in Maryland. At the Dartmoor plant he had specified the materials needed to convert the conveyor belt from artillery-shell production to the system creating missiles.

When the cargo had been loaded the empty trucks would be driven a short distance along the coast road. At this point the drivers would push them over the edge into the sea. Along this section of the coast Abdul had charts which showed that the sea plunged immediately into deep water. No trace of their operation would be left behind. They would then board the freighter.

*   *   *

Tweed had reached the fork in the wide track. Warden had taken the left fork, which eventually landed them on the coast road. This time Tweed had taken the right fork where a signpost pointed to Harmer's Head.

Proceeding along this road, he had driven slowly. A careful examination of Ordnance Survey maps in his London home had shown him a minor track leading off to the left—to Harmer's Head.

He crawled, anxious not to miss the turning. Paula frowned, looked at him. His expression was one of extreme concentration. She began to worry.

'Do you know where we are? We've passed the road Warden turned on to a little way back.'

315

'I know. Now I'm looking for what will be a narrow lane turning off to our left. Doubt if we'll get a comforting signpost. We are really in the wilderness.'

'I thought we'd been there for some time. Bleak stretches of scrubby moorland, a few rocks here and there, wind-blown gorse. I don't think anyone lives up here.'

'Who would want to?'

'Mind if I smoke a cigarette?' Marler called out from the back. 'This is like the end of the world.'

'Go ahead,' Tweed answered automatically. 'I've got a window open.'

Paula heard faint mechanical noises, twisted round to see what was causing them. Marler, an as yet unlit cigarette in his mouth, was checking the mechanism of his weapon. Seeing her watching, he plunged a hand into a pocket, brought out an object Paula recognized. Marler grinned.

'An explosive bullet. Same type as blew Charmian's head into pulp at Stonehenge.'

'Messy pulp,' she reminded him. 'I was the one who cleaned up the side of the megalith.'

'And,' Marler said seriously, 'you were given that job to take your mind off the appalling experience you'd been through.'

'Well it worked,' she said, staring back at him. 'Because he was such a beastly creature it didn't worry me at all getting rid of what was left of him . . . Stop! Turn left,' she shouted as she gazed through the windscreen.

'I've seen it,' Tweed assured her. 'And there's a signpost. To Harmer's Head.'

He signalled left to warn Harry behind him, then turned slowly into a narrow lane with a wall of

316

beaten-down gorse on both sides. There was barely room for the Land Rover to squeak through. He just hoped the lane didn't narrow any more before they reached their objective.

Paula switched on the radio after turning the volume down. A weather forecast was just beginning. A major storm was coming in from the southwest. Gales up to 80 m.p.h. The wind was already beating at the windscreen but so far no rain. As he turned yet another corner Tweed saw a slight rise ahead. He crawled over the top, braked. They had reached the summit. Harmer's Head, guardian of this point for over a hundred years, was less than fifty yards away.

It was massive, as large and high as four detached houses merged together, the biggest chunk of granite Paula had ever seen. Observed from below, when they had looked up from the coast road, she'd had no idea of its immensity. It was roughly square in shape with one fairly flat side facing them. No sign of the sea yet. Harmer blotted out the view. Tweed crawled forward over barren turf, parked behind the rock. Harry followed his example, parking alongside.

*   *   *

Marler dived out first, followed swiftly by Paula, while Tweed switched off the engine. The moon was still out, not yet masked by the armada of low black clouds sweeping in over the sea. Marler peered round one side of Harmer while Paula did the same thing from the other distant side as she was joined by Tweed.

Harry was hauling out heavy bags containing his

317

armoury with the help of Pete Nield. They staggered under the weight to the shelter of the rock. Paula was amazed by what she saw far below, using her monocular glass.

Even from that distance the freighter looked huge. It was moored fairly close to the platform projecting a short way out from the road. A landing stage, railed, with wheels, connected it to the freighter from the mainland. Already the freighter was rising and falling as waves swept in from the sea.

'It's not the right ship,' she gasped. 'The *Oran* had the Liberian flag flying, this one has the flag of Panama. And it's *not* the *Oran*—it's the *Constantine*!'

'So the skipper is cunning,' Tweed commented, staring down through binoculars. 'The skipper *has* been cunning, changing the flag in the Atlantic and putting men over the side to paint out the original name and substitute *Constantine*, the name of a city in Algeria, up in the Atlas Mountains.'

'But—' she began.

'Don't argue,' he chided. 'Observe. The freighter we saw leaving the Ile des Oiseaux outside Marseilles had a large square dent in its port bow. So has the vessel down there. Must have hit a harbour wall somewhere. It *is* the same freighter.'

'And it's going to put to sea soon,' she said. 'Look at the funnel.'

She was right. Black smoke was floating out of the top, then was caught by the wind and described black convolutions as it was blown all over the place. She looked along the rock wall, saw Marler gesturing for them to come quickly.

They ran towards him, under cover of Harmer.

318

Behind them Harry had hooked the strap of a bag over his shoulder, followed by Nield, who was similarly encumbered. Both hurried to join Marler.

'A view straight down here,' Marler told them. 'A lot of activity. The crew are all Arabs, wearing headdresses. Loads of crates on deck. I think they've finished unloading. One crate's burst open, spilling missiles on the desk. Armed missiles. A careless lot, some of these Arabs.'

He handed his binoculars to Paula. Tweed was staring down through his own pair. Harry dumped his cargo, took out a grenade, shook his head.

'Don't know how we're going to get at that lot. They're too far away. What's that colossal boulder down there?'

'Toppling Rock,' Tweed told him. 'A huge thing. They say if you lean against it the rock wobbles but never leaves its perch.'

'Really?' Harry was fascinated. 'Must have a go . . .'

He was off before Tweed could stop him, warn him no movement must be seen from the freighter. But Harry was smart. He crawled down a gully on his hands and knees, moving almost as fast as a rabbit. Paula, fascinated, watched him. Shielded by the rock, he stood up when he reached it, heaved his whole weight against its side. It began to move seaward. Paula's hand flew to her throat as it shifted a foot. Harry's expression was a picture. A look of disbelief mingled with fear. He jerked his body away from it. Then Toppling Rock settled back on the perch it had occupied for heaven knew how long.

Paula wanted to burst into laughter. She rubbed a hand across her mouth to stop that happening.

Tweed was still staring down through his binoculars. Marler, concealed close to Harmer, was scanning every single foot of the freighter through the telescopic sight of his Armalite.

'All this weaponry and it's useless,' Harry called out in his frustration. 'Why the hell didn't I think to bring rocket launchers? They'd have reached the target.'

'You did all you could,' Paula said, squeezing his arm.

'There has to be a way,' Tweed persisted.

'Tell me then,' said Newman.

The storm clouds were very close but so far not a drop of rain had fallen. Their gloom didn't help the morale of the team. Tweed watched the landing gangway moving up and down with the swell of the increasingly turbulent sway.

Marler's Armalite was suddenly very still. He stared hard at the telescopic sight. Had his eyes deceived him? No, they hadn't. He checked again, adjusted the focus slightly.

*   *   *

Aboard the freighter Abdul had slipped inside the chart room. He was checking the devious route he must take to reach the small port in Angora where he would take his cargo. They were well organized at the other end of his voyage.

Trucks would be waiting at the port. The missiles would be transferred to the trucks. The *Constantine* would dock after dark. The transfer to the trucks would be completed well before dawn came.

It had even been arranged that the trucks would leave one by one, with large gaps between their

320

departure—as opposed to a convoy of trucks. This was vital. An American satellite passed over Angora regularly, photographing the whole area. The sight of a lone truck driving out into the desert would mean nothing to the American analysts of the pictures taken.

The trucks transporting the missiles from the port had been sprayed with a sticky substance, then sprayed again with sand. Seen from the air they would merge with the desert.

Abdul emerged from the chart room, was annoyed to see drivers onshore lazily clambering up into the cabs. He wanted to be well away from the coast before the storm broke. He shouted, using the foulest language.

'Tell the truck drivers to move faster. They must dump the vehicles into the sea a short distance along the road. Then they must run back here and immediately board the ship. If they delay departure I will have their heads.'

*   *   *

Marler was still checking through his telescopic sight. He had already inserted the explosive bullet. Now he was certain. An Arab on the deck was again carrying an obviously heavy container painted yellow. He would move it a few yards, then pause for breath. Marler checked once more. No doubt about it.

Painted in large warning letters in English was one word running round the surface of the whole container: INFLAMMABLE. The Arab, taking a rest from his labours, had planted the container down close to the crate which had burst open, spilling

321

missiles across the deck. Armed missiles, as must be those in many other crates on deck.

Other Arabs were slowly carrying a crate to a platform, which was obviously a lift descending into the hold. Presumably the hold was already crammed with similar crates.

'I think the truck drivers are about to move their vehicles. Doubtless to dump them into the sea a bit further up the coast road,' Tweed said bleakly.

'Do you want everything down there eliminated?' Marler asked Tweed. 'By which I mean missiles, the trucks, the freighter and all those Arabs?'

'Wipe the lot off the face of the earth,' Tweed said, his voice very cold.

Leaning against the side of the rock to give him perfect balance, Marler aimed his rifle. He had the cross-hairs fixed on the container when the Arab who had carried it bent down to lift it again. Marler, steady as the rock he was supported by, pressed the trigger. The team were gathered behind him, staring down.

The container exploded, blew up in a burst of spreading flame, reaching the exposed missiles. The Arab vanished in the huge flames that enveloped everything within reach. They had heard a muffled detonation. The spilt missiles exploded with a thunderous roar, detonating another dozen crates packed with missiles.

The world went mad. The massive shockwave blasted out with titanic force against the cliff. Perched by Harmer's bulk, they felt the ground tremble beneath their feet. Tweed began to hope they were far enough away.

Toppling Rock broke free from its pedestal, rolled down at ever-increasing speed. Arriving at a ridge, it bounced off into midair, fell vertically, landed with its great weight on the foredeck of the freighter. It crashed through the deck, vanished at the same moment the prow of the *Constantine* split off and dived down into the deep water out of sight. Already the large number of crates stacked with missiles below deck were exploding, lifting what remained of the deck skywards.

Another far more deafening roar, which seemed like the end of the world, blasted against the cliff below them. Immense slabs of rock plunged down, smothering what remained of the trucks on the coast road. The clouds in the night sky were illuminated in a monster red glow, which reminded Tweed of what he had read in Dante's *Inferno*. The middle and stern of the freighter heeled over towards starboard, exposing the lower part of the hull, now only a huge hole through which sea water was flooding.

The landing stage, which had linked it to the shore, curiously enough, appeared to have survived as it rocketed skyward, then broke into pieces and dived under the boiling sea. Outsized waves rolled in, over the sinking freighter, crashing on to the coast road littered with rock and remnants of the trucks. Receding, the waves carried back into the sea every trace of trucks and pieces of mangled bodies. Seconds earlier the single funnel had torn itself free, elevating like a rocket, flying out over the sea before it plunged down and disappeared. Every sign of the freighter had now gone, the wreckage sinking into its watery grave. Another huge slab of cliff below them had broken loose, slamming down on to the coast road, where it burst and all the pieces bounced off the edge, ending up out of sight in the water.

There was no sign of life, of survivors anywhere. Marler's single bullet, shrewdly aimed at the target he knew would act as a horrific detonator, had destroyed everything, everyone.

'Wipe the lot off the face of the earth,' Tweed had ordered. But he had never dreamed that his command would be carried out with such devastating completion.

31

Tweed ordered everyone to return to their Land Rovers but not to drive off until he did so himself. He had studied their expressions, had not been surprised to see several showing a state of shock. Few people had ever seen such total and terrible destruction.

Harry, the tough Cockney, seemed least affected. Without a word he returned from his vehicle to Tweed's. He was carrying the large insulated container, which he put down on the scrubby grass.

'Time for a spot of nourishment and coffee,' he said like a delivery boy.

'Thank you, Harry,' Paula said hoarsely. 'You're an angel.'

'There's some people who'd dispute your opinion,' he told her with a grin.

Paula opened the container, poured coffee from a flask, surprised to find it was still piping hot. Handing a cup to Tweed, she gratefully sipped from her own. Then she divided up the sandwiches, putting them on plates, handing Tweed a napkin.

'Seems a bit silly,' she began, 'bothering with napkins after what—'

'We don't want crumbs all over the floor,' he interjected in a normal voice.

'Won't the local police start making enquiries when they see the coast road? I used my binoculars briefly before we left Harmer's Head. It's pitted with holes and chunks of it are in the sea.'

'Fortunately, it'll be the local lot,' he replied. 'And all the evidence has disappeared. They'll assume that after all these years the cliffs became unstable and collapsed.'

'So now we have one more job to do. Any idea who the Skeleton Killer is?'

'It's someone who, some while ago, thought they saw their chance to become immensely rich. So they cleverly siphoned off four hundred million pounds from the reserves, then not so cleverly bought a huge number of dotcom shares. They ended up without a penny—and a desperate need to cover up what they'd done. The shell company they'd used to pretend that's where it had gone was fiddled in the accounts as a four-hundred-million-pound purchase in a highly profitable company. Remember Enron in the States. They removed huge debts into weird-sounding outfits and called them profits. When the dotcom company Orlando Xanadu crashed it led inevitably to a terrible chain of events.'

'How do you mean?'

'Anyone who might discover that vast sum was missing had to be eliminated. First, Lee Greystoke, who was poking around in the accounts department, sent, I'm sure, by Drago. Then, also sent by Drago, who was a long way off abroad, he employed Christine Barton, forensic accountant, to look into things. So she had to go.'

'Sounds so horribly cold-blooded.'

'It was. The next stage in the ghastly hunt was to murder the detective, John Jackson, in his houseboat. Christine's sister, Anne Barton, had become worried about her long absence. She employed the detective. The murderer found out somehow, so he was slaughtered.'

'One thing led to another.'

'Exactly. Finally, the broker, Kenwood, knew too much. He had secretly handled the disastrous investment in the dotcom. So he had to be exterminated. He was the fourth name on the list. "Ken" wasn't a first name—it was short for "Kenwood".'

'So what sort of person are we looking for?'

'Someone consumed by greed. Someone with a good planning brain. Someone who is a sadist—hence the mutilation of the bodies.'

'I can't think any of the four at Abbey Grange fits your description,' she said.

'You won't yet,' Tweed warned. 'Years ago, when I was at the Yard, I solved three major murder cases. I was getting an overblown reputation as brilliant. One reason why I joined the SIS. But I never dismissed as a suspect anyone who appeared normal, ordinary. Another detective, who was forced to hand over the third case to me, claimed that a certain person was not a suspect. He was too normal and ordinary. It turned out he was the murderer.' He switched on the engine. 'Now we'll get moving. Don't like the look of that storm coming.'

He was worried that they would be caught in the

narrow winding lane leading off the main road. The lane could become a river.

Harry's Land Rover followed them as Tweed, headlights on full beam, honking as they approached each corner, drove as fast as he dared. They were on the main road when the storm broke in full fury. Lightning flashed, thunder rolled, rain came down in torrents. They kept moving as the rain flowed down ditches on either side.

'You know,' Paula mused, 'we're going to arrive very late, or very early in the morning. The party will have ended and they'll all be in bed.'

'No, they won't. I'm sure Larry's the type who likes a party to go on and on. If necessary until dawn.'

'Fingers crossed.'

They were approaching the road to Moretonhampstead—and Abbey Grange—when the storm suddenly stopped, or moved away. As they passed the fake row of cottages, the church and the bell tower, Paula gazed the other way.

'Shouldn't we have called the local police about the head on the altar?' she suggested.

'I did think of it at the time and decided to wait. With the problem of the freighter I didn't want local police holding us up. Nor do I want that happening now. I'll call after our visit to Abbey Grange.'

*   *   *

Tweed and Paula drove quietly past the mansion's wall and parked where the Land Rovers had parked earlier. Harry's vehicle pulled up behind them. Before alighting, Tweed turned to speak

327

to Marler.

'I'm leaving you here. Only Paula and I are calling. More would not create the atmosphere I need.'

'Don't like it,' Marler protested. 'The number of attempts which have been made on your life.'

'I appreciate your concern. But I'm issuing you with an order. You did more than enough at Harmer's Head. So you wait here.'

Getting out with Paula, he gave the same instruction to the others, who had jumped out to join them. He met with the same protests, gave them the same firm order. Then with Paula he walked back towards the entrance. Paula tugged at his arm.

'I could have sworn I saw a police car parked further back.'

'You did. Can't imagine who it is, don't care. Can't be anything to do with the awful altarpiece. Lights still on in the bell tower, none in the church. Here we are.'

Walking down the path round the end of the mansion, they saw, the moment they turned the corner, a blaze of lights in all the downstairs windows facing the moor. There was also the sound of music. Sade's 'Smooth Operator'.

'Apt,' Tweed said grimly. 'That's what we're looking for. The smooth operator.'

They climbed the steps on to the terrace and the French windows opened, flooding out light. Lucinda was now wearing a long white dress. In her hand she held a champagne glass, which was almost empty. She raised the glass, drank what was left, holding the door as she swayed slightly.

'Tiddly,' Paula whispered.

'Welcome back, both of you. Party's just . . . warming up. We are making a night of it. Come on in, you two sleuths.'

She gave Tweed a long passionate hug when he reached her, her body pressed into his. She's well away, Paula thought, as Lucinda turned to hug her, then took their outer clothes and dumped them on the back of a sofa.

Tweed was smiling as he walked into the living room, scanning the place swiftly. Various coloured balloons hung from the rafters; a large white cake sat in the middle of the table, as yet uncut. Aubrey was sprawled on a couch, his shirt half out of his trousers. He was no longer wearing his absurd naval cap and held a glass of Scotch tilted at a perilous angle. He grinned foolishly at Tweed, raised his glass.

Larry, smiling warmly, was still seated at one end of the table. At the other end sat Michael, stiff as a poker, his glazed expression staring into space. He didn't appear to notice the new arrivals. All four suspects were present.

'Take it.'

Lucinda, managing to hold a silver tray straight, offered Tweed a glass of champagne. He grasped it as Paula sat down at an empty chair at the table, facing everybody. Tweed joined her. Lucinda gave her a glass, then walked to the far side and sat in an armchair.

Tweed raised his glass, still smiling. 'To three of the guests.' He paused. 'The fourth is a mass murderer of at least five people. Cheers!' he continued in the same casual voice, then sipped from his glass.

Paula was taken aback. She had never known

Tweed open up a conversation so casually, so brutally. As he sipped, Tweed looked again all round the room. Aubrey was the first to react. He sat up erect with surprising agility.

'What the hell was that? A joke? If so, a very bad one.'

'No joke,' Tweed continued amiably. 'The killer is greedy and a sadist who ravages the dead bodies of the victims.'

'I do like your sense of humour,' Larry responded. 'It's really original. Cheers!'

'I think he meant it,' Aubrey protested, then swallowed a large tot of his Scotch. Reaching for a bottle, he refilled his glass, drank some more. His bulging eyes were glaring at Tweed.

'Yes, Aubrey,' Tweed continued genially, 'I meant every word. It seems to bother you.'

'Well, you're a guest at our White Party and you go and—'

'Aubrey,' Larry interrupted, smiling, 'you don't know Tweed, so you take him seriously. A great mistake when we're about to cut the cake. A large piece for you?' he asked, addressing his offer to Tweed.

'Yes, please. A very large piece, if I may.'

'And the same for you, Paula, I'm sure,' Larry suggested as he stood up, picked up a knife and started slicing the cake. 'It was baked and decorated by Mrs Brogan, who may be a rough lady at times but is also a genius in the kitchen.'

He passed a plate of cake to Paula, then another one to Tweed. Lucinda sat up, used a hand to draw her dress over her exposed leg.

'What about me, Larry? I love cake. This looks simply divine.'

'Coming up, darling,' Larry assured her, wielding the knife expertly, cutting an exceptionally large piece, handing it to her on a plate. He cut a further slice as Aubrey leaned forward.

'That's for me, I hope. I could eat the lot.'

'What about Michael?' Paula asked.

Larry shook his head. 'Doesn't like cake. He's just eaten a monster piece of salmon with mashed potatoes. Doubt if he can move now. Here you are, Aubrey, don't stuff it in your mouth.'

'My table manners are impeccable. I often lunch at the Savoy grill. The head waiter knows me, keeps my special table. Is Tweed staying long?'

'Just as long as it takes to complete my murder investigation,' Tweed replied with another smile.

'I deeply resent your extraordinary implications about . . .' Aubrey had his mouth full of cake and spluttered, and half his mouthful ended up on the table.

'Tut, tut,' Larry admonished. 'If you act like that at the Savoy you'll find your table's no longer available,' he said with a grin.

'So how is your investigation proceeding?' asked Lucinda, lying back in her chair, her eyelashes fluttering as she gazed at Tweed.

'I think I'm nearly there,' he replied, his expression thoughtful as again he scanned the room. 'After all, it started here near Abbey Grange when Paula and I discovered the skeleton by the track down the moor behind me.'

Paula was suddenly aware of a vague tall figure standing outside on the terrace, masked by the net curtains. One French window was slightly open. She spread her large napkin over her lap, checked all the guests, then slipped her Browning out of her shoulder bag slung from her chair back, concealed the weapon under the napkin. She became nervous. Who could be standing so still on the terrace?

'Why should that prove—' Aubrey began.

At that moment Lucinda shifted position. Aubrey stared at her like a hypnotized man. He didn't complete what he'd started to say.

'It proves,' Tweed rambled on amiably, 'that whoever killed the stockbroker had to act quickly, so risked committing the horror not far from the mansion here. Which I find suggestive.'

'Stockbroker, did you say?' enquired Larry, putting down the slice of cake he'd been about to eat. 'Which stockbroker would that be?'

'A man called Kenwood of Haldon Street, the broker who dealt with the investment of four hundred million pounds stolen from the reserves of Gantia, transferred to a shell company, which had gone broke. This huge sum was brought back by electronic transmission. Without the horror which followed, it was an amusing exercise,' Tweed said genially, then sipped his champagne.

Paula at last caught on to Tweed's strange behaviour. Instead of grilling the suspects in his normal way, he was exploiting the surreal atmosphere of the silly party, throwing his listeners off balance.

'This enormous sum,' he went on, 'was then invested in a dotcom company, Orlando Xanadu, during the manic boom not too long ago. It eventually crashed, the fate of most dotcoms, so the stolen four hundred million was lost for ever. So far so bad. What came afterwards was a number of truly dreadful murders.'

'How do you know all this?' Aubrey burst out. 'Sounds like a fairy story.'

'Really?'

Paula was aware that the party mood had evaporated. Instead, an atmosphere of tension was invading the room. Larry was no longer smiling, his expression like carved stone. Lucinda, normally still when seated, was restless, shifting cushions as though seeking a comfortable position. Aubrey had become uneasy and kept crossing and recrossing his legs. Only Michael, sitting motionless at the head of the table to her right, was the same. His eyes were blank and glazed.

A French window behind them burst open. Drago Volkanian stormed in. The huge man wore a dinner suit, which stretched across his chest, straining at the button that fastened his jacket. Everyone looked startled, except Tweed. He had hoped his verbal references about missiles to the billionaire would eventually bring him to Abbey Grange.

'How bloody fascinating,' Drago thundered. 'While I am abroad someone dips their huge hand into the till, steals a fortune. I have been on the terrace awhile, have heard what Tweed has said so far. I return to treachery—and ghastly murder.'

Larry had stood up respectfully the moment his employer had appeared. Aubrey had clambered to his feet. Only Lucinda remained seated, one hand pushing back a lock of hair from her face.

'Welcome back, Drago,' she greeted him.

'Some welcome,' he snapped at her.

He walked with large strides round Tweed's side of the long table. He sat down with difficulty in an armchair close to Michael. Paula thought the whole chair would split open when he attempted to stand up. Drago's mood had dramatically changed. Clasping his huge hands in his lap, he spoke calmly.

'I think, Mr Tweed, it would be helpful if you continued with what Aubrey called your fairy tale.'

'Thank you,' agreed Tweed. 'And I think it important you do hear the rest. The thief who had created a black hole in the finances—although I think Drago is wealthy enough for it not to affect the company's finances—thought the existence of the shell company would cover the loss for a while. But Lee Greystoke, who I gather had a good brain, was asked by Drago from abroad to check the balance sheets.' He looked at Drago, who nodded. 'So Lee was a menace and was murdered quickly, her body mutilated with the knife which had cut her throat. Not a great loss, Aubrey, considering your harem . . .'

'You're saying *I* killed her?' Aubrey protested, jumping to his feet.

'So far, I'm only saying you wouldn't be heartbroken by her murder.'

'I protest at your hideous—' Aubrey began to shout.

'Sit down,' Drago ordered quietly, 'and stay seated.'

'Lee's body was dropped into a mine shaft,' Tweed went on as Aubrey slumped down in his chair. 'Very close to Abbey Grange,' Tweed explained, 'because, like the broker, Kenwood, it would have been too dangerous to transport the body elsewhere.'

'Sounds horribly plausible,' commented Lucinda, who was smoking a cigarette she'd inserted in her black holder.

'Oddly enough,' Tweed went on, 'the murderer discovered that Christine Barton, a forensic accountant, again probably hired by Drago ...' —he paused and Drago again nodded—'was examining all the accounts papers. Murder her inside her own flat in London was the obvious answer, then hide the body in her fridge.

'The murderer must have wondered when it was going to end,' Tweed remarked. 'Next—this is a guess—after slaughtering Christine the murderer checks items in that flat, finds a report and a receipt for a fee paid from a private detective, Jackson, with his address on a houseboat at Wensford. So Jackson has to be murdered—and mutilated for pleasure. This murderer revels in slashing up dead bodies, gets a kick out of this appalling activity.'

'Quite gruesome,' Lucinda commented, pulling a face.

'I agree with you,' responded Tweed. 'What struck me was it had to be somebody connected with Abbey Grange, also working at Gantia. Otherwise, how would they know about Christine —and Lee? Don't you agree, Aubrey?'

'Why ask me?' Aubrey spluttered, whisky dribbling down his shirt front.

It was at this moment that Michael, who presumably had taken in none of Tweed's deductions, stood up to leave the room. He walked, stiff-legged, towards the stairs leading to his bedroom.

At the foot of the stairs he paused, his right hand touching the carved man's head decorating the top of the lowest pillar. As he began walking slowly upstairs Paula noticed that neither of his shoelaces was tied. Trailing on the floor, they threatened to trip him up. She opened her mouth, then closed it, realizing he wouldn't even hear her.

Michael reached the last steps before the landing. His right foot tangled with the loose laces, he lost his balance, tumbled head over heels all the way down, smashing the back of his head against the carved figure.

Nearly everyone jumped up. Drago attempted to, but couldn't extricate himself from the chair, and so swore to himself.

Lucinda reached the prone Michael first, checked his pulse. She turned round to face the others.

'He's alive. Pulse ticking over normally.'

Behind her Michael was clambering to his feet as Lucinda ran to the phone. Paula was the first to notice that his glazed eyes and blank look had gone. He stared round the room. He was now walking normally. Because he had been silent for so long, it was a shock when he spoke, articulating the words clearly and bitterly.

'*I witnessed murder.*'

'What?' gasped Aubrey.

Michael said one more word. 'There.' His arm was raised, his index finger pointed.

32

Everyone froze for several moments. Except for Michael, who walked slowly forward, his accusing finger pointing. The person he was pointing at also froze, but only briefly. Lucinda put down the phone she hadn't used.

She stared at the finger pointed at her like a gun, shrugged, went to her armchair, sat down, moved a cushion concealing her handbag, opened it and slipped her hand inside.

'He's crazy,' she said. 'First it's amnesia when he bumped his head falling down the stairs the first time. Now he's gone right over the edge.'

'I saw you,' Michael said, his voice clear and balanced. 'I'd come back early from the office. I parked my car on the verge just outside Post Lacey. I always walk up from there. Which is why you didn't hear me coming . . .'

'You're quite mad . . .'

'No, you are. I walked up the track in the moonlight. I saw you grabbing Lee from behind, holding her hair, then you used a knife to cut her throat, turned it round and used it again. I was stunned. You were cutting pieces of her flesh off and dropping them into a bag. Then you dragged what was left of Lee and dropped her down a mine shaft.'

'You must see a doctor,' she said and lit a cigarette.

'You were startled when you saw me,' he went on. 'You grabbed my arm and we walked up to the house. You were talking nonstop, something about Lee had attacked you. You hustled me into the house and I couldn't decide what was true. You took me up the stairs. Near the top you said you'd twisted your ankle. Then you were in front of me, on the step above. You turned, used both hands to give me a great shove. I went all the way down those damned stairs, just as I did a moment ago. Hit my head on the bottom pillar and everything went blank.'

'We're home and dry,' said Tweed, still seated. 'We need only one witness to one murder. Michael is the witness.'

Lucinda jumped up. Her right hand held the knife she had extracted from her handbag. She rushed forward towards Michael. Everyone was taken by surprise. Everyone except Paula.

'Without one witness,' Lucinda screamed in a voice hardly sane, 'without one witness,' she yelled again, 'you can do nothing.'

She held the large knife up high, ready to plunge it into Michael. Paula was already close to her, the Browning she had snatched from under her napkin held in both hands. She called out a warning.

'Drop the knife, Lucinda, or I'll shoot you dead.'

Lucinda swung round. Her expression shocked Paula, almost froze her. Her eyes were slits. The eyes behind the slits were full of evil and hatred. Her mouth was twisted into a ferocious animal-like grimace. She didn't look human any more.

She rushed towards Paula. Again the knife was held high for a downward strike. Automatically, Paula noticed it had two edges. One a fine razor edge, the other side serrated. It had brown stains on it.

'I'll shoot,' Paula shouted at her.

It didn't stop Lucinda. She moved forward with astonishing speed. The handle of the knife was tightly gripped in both hands. She took a deep breath, psyching herself up to plunge it deep into her opponent's body.

'You've always got in the way,' she screamed, spittle dripping from her mouth.

Paula fired once. The bullet slammed into Lucinda's chest. Blood spurted. Amazingly, it

338

didn't stop Lucinda's oncoming rush. Paula fired again, then again. An expression of surprise, disbelief, crossed Lucinda's face. Then she fell forward, smashed her head against the floor, lying very still.

Tweed checked her carotid artery, looked up at Paula, shook his head. Someone had rushed in from the terrace. Tweed stared. It was Chief Superintendent Buchanan, dressed in a suit. Tweed had earlier jumped up from his seat, holding his Walther. He'd not dared to use the weapon because Paula had been in the way. Buchanan's manner was authoritative as he strode forward.

'It's still your case, Tweed, so regard me as backup. I saw and heard everything that happened. Mr Drago Volkanian was most cooperative when I signalled to him to ignore me outside on the terrace.'

'I've killed a woman,' Paula said quietly. 'Killed a woman.'

She was in a state. The climax of so much exertion recently, so much horror, had finally exhausted her stamina. Tweed put his arm round her, used his left hand to take the Browning by the end of the muzzle and drop it into an evidence bag.

'I'll have to stand trial,' Paula said in the same quiet voice.

'Nonsense,' said Buchanan with deliberate abruptness. 'You fired in self-defence. The room is full of witnesses who will agree that forcefully, including myself. There will never be a trial,' he predicted. 'Maybe a statement from you later. That will be it.'

'We should call an ambulance,' Tweed suggested.

'Already coming.' Buchanan waved a small

339

mobile phone.

Tweed looked at Drago Volkanian. The billionaire had made no attempt to rise from his chair. Possibly for the first time in his life he looked stunned. After getting Paula comfortable in a chair, avoiding the one Lucinda had sat in, he went over to Drago. 'Are you all right?'

'So she, Lucinda, was responsible for the frightful murders?'

'No doubt about it. These days women do kill. Read the newspapers. It's the age of equality,' Tweed said ironically.

Epilogue

Three weeks later, the team were assembled in the Park Crescent office. They were there to welcome back Paula, now seated at her desk and looking her normal eager self. Buchanan had visited them briefly, refusing Tweed's offer to sit down.

Instead, he made straight for Paula's desk, his face wreathed in a smile. She looked up at him warily.

'It's all over,' he told her. 'You've made your statement, a copy of which was sent with other witnesses' accounts to the public prosecutor. They all came back to me with a blunt note. "Why have you sent this junk to me? It's clear as crystal there is no case to answer. Don't waste my time again."'

'Thank you for coming over to tell me,' she replied in a normal voice. 'The odd thing is, I did rather like Lucinda. She was so alive.'

'None of her foully-treated victims are alive,' he reminded her. 'Must go now.'

'I found something last night in a jacket pocket,' Marler reported. 'Sorry, but everything was a bit of a rush. Before we dumped Charmian's body down that drain at Stonehenge I'd searched him quickly, found a wallet and tucked it away.'

'Anything interesting?' asked Tweed.

'An expertly produced fake passport in an English name, plenty of British money.' He paused. 'And a temporary certificate allowing him to fly light aircraft over here.'

'That plane I saw!' Paula exclaimed. 'First following us on our visit with Michael navigating us to Abbey Grange. Then later as we drove up the A303, had to stop because of the Gantia truck stolen and blocking the way. So the bullet through our window which just missed us . . .'

'Obviously fired by Charmian,' Marler drawled. 'Not his finest performance, fortunately.'

'Too close for comfort,' Tweed remarked.

Newman was waving the day's copy of the *Daily Nation* he had been reading.

'I don't think any of you heard the latest news. Last night four American B52 bombers flew over Angora and wiped out their long-range rocket installation in the desert.'

'Better late than never,' Tweed observed caustically. 'Three weeks since we destroyed that freighter and its deadly cargo. If it had survived it would have arrived at a port in Angora, the missiles would have been rushed to that installation and launched.'

'One favour I have to repay,' Marler said. 'What's Loriot's private number?'

From memory Tweed scribbled the number of the French counterespionage chief. He wondered what Marler was up to as he passed him the sheet of paper.

'Is that Loriot?' Marler asked after making the call.

'*Oui*. And that is Marler. I recognize the distinctive voice.'

Loriot prided himself on his command of English.

'Just calling,' Marler said, 'to tell you not to worry any more about Charmian. He's been dealt with over here. Cheers!'

In his Paris office Loriot chuckled and turned to

his assistant, Marianne.

'Spread the word. Charmian no longer exists. You know what Marler said? "He has been dealt with." I do love British understatement.'

CHIVERS LARGE PRINT
–direct–

If you have enjoyed this Large Print book and would like to build up your own collection of Large Print books, please contact

Chivers Large Print Direct

Chivers Large Print Direct offers you a full service:

• Prompt mail order service

• Easy-to-read type

• The very best authors

• Special low prices

For further details either call Customer Services on (01225) 336552 or write to us at Chivers Large Print Direct, **FREEPOST**, Bath BA1 3ZZ

Telephone Orders: **FREEPHONE** 08081 72 74 75